# Edwin: High King of Britain

# EDWIN

# High King of Britain

## The Northumbrian Thrones 1

*Edoardo Albert*

LION FICTION

Published by Lion Fiction
an imprint of
**Lion Hudson plc**
Wilkinson House, Jordan Hill Road,
Oxford OX2 8DR, England
www.lionhudson.com/fiction

ISBN 978 1 78264 033 2
e-ISBN 978 1 78264 061 5

First edition 2014

**Acknowledgments**
Extract p. 92: From *The Exeter Book Riddles* by Kevin Crossley-Holland (London: Enitharmon Press, 2008). Used by permission of Enitharmon Press.

A catalogue record for this book is available from the British Library

Printed and bound in the UK, February 2014, LH26

# *Contents*

# Acknowledgments

Despite what it says on the cover, no book is written alone and this one is no exception. I would like to thank Tony Collins and Alison Hull at Lion Fiction for giving me the chance to tell Edwin's story, and that of the men next on the Northumbrian throne in the forthcoming volumes, and Jessica Tinker and Rachel Ashley-Pain, my editors, for improving the book immensely.

Paul Gething of the Bamburgh Research Project taught me most of what I know about the Anglo-Saxons, and he was the reason for us going up to Northumberland in the first place. I still remember the jaw-dropping impact of turning up the coast road from Seahouses and seeing the brooding bulk of Bamburgh Castle, squatting on its extrusion of the Great Whin Sill, commanding land, and sea, and sky.

That Bernard Cornwell and Justin Hill read my book was satisfaction enough; their comments were more than I could have hoped for. My parents-in-law, David and Margaret Whitbread, have helped in more ways than they realise. Harriet, my wife, and my sons, Theo, Matthew and Isaac, have cheerfully endured the penury of having a writer as husband and father – I owe them more than is possible to say.

This book is dedicated to my mother and father, an Italian and a Sri Lankan, who made new lives in a cold northern land. Little did they suspect that their son would end up writing about it.

# The Kingdoms of Britain, c. 625

DAL RIATA
GODODDIN
Lindisfarne
Ad Gefrin
Bamburgh
BERNICIA
Monkwearmouth
RHEGED
NORTHUMBRIA
Jarrow
DEIRA
Isle of Man
York
ELMET
Isle of Anglesey
LINDSEY
GWYNEDD
Tamworth
Crowland
MERCIA
MIDDLE
ANGLIA
EAST
ANGLIA
POWYS
MAGONSÆTE
Oundle
DYFED
HWICCE
Rendlesham
Gloucester
ESSEX
Cirencester
London
Bath
Rochester
Canterbury
WESSEX
Winchester
KENT
Glastonbury
SUSSEX
DUMNONIA

MERCIA  Kingdom ruled
by the Anglo-Saxons

POWYS  Kingdom ruled
by the Britons

Sea, swamp, or salt marsh

# Dramatis Personae

## Northumbrian royal families

**Edwin** King of Deira and Bernicia. King of Northumbria. High King of Britain.

**Ælla** Edwin's father. King of Deira.

**Osfrith** Edwin's eldest son.

**Eadfrith** Edwin's younger son by his first wife.

**Cwenburg** Edwin's first wife. Daughter of King Cearl of Mercia.

**Æthelburh** Second wife to Edwin. Daughter of Æthelbert, King of Kent.

**Eanflæd** Daughter to Edwin and Æthelburh.

**Ethelhun** Son to Edwin and Æthelburh. Twin to Ethelthryd.

**Ethelthryd** Daughter to Edwin and Æthelburh. Twin to Ethelhun.

**Wuscfrea** Youngest son to Edwin and Æthelburh.

**Æthelfrith** King of Bernicia and Deira. First king to unite Northumbria.

**Oswald** Son of Æthelfrith.

## People of Northumbria

**Forthred** Friend and thegn to Edwin.

**Guthlaf** Warmaster to Edwin.

**Wældhelm** Weaponsmith to Edwin.

**Nia** Wife to Wældhelm.

**Acca** Scop to Edwin.

**Coifi** Chief pagan priest to Edwin.

**Bassus** Thegn to Edwin.

**Cenhelm** Thegn to Edwin.

**Hunlaf** Warmaster to Æthelfrith.

**Dæglaf** Retainer of Æthelfrith.

## Kingdom of the East Angles

**Rædwald** King of the East Angles. Probably the man buried in the main Sutton Hoo mound.

**Ymma** Queen of the East Angles.

**Rægenhere** Son of Rædwald and Ymma.

**Eorpwald** Son of Rædwald. King following Rædwald's death.

## Kingdom of Mercia

**Cearl** King of Mercia.

**Penda** Warmaster to Cearl.

**Beocca** Door warden to Cearl.

## Kingdom of the West Saxons (Wessex)

**Cwichelm** King of the West Saxons.

**Eumer** Messenger of Cwichelm.

## Kingdom of Gwynedd

**Cadfan** King of Gwynedd.

**Cadwallon** Son of Cadfan. King of Gwynedd.

**Briant**. Abbess. Daughter of Cadfan. Sister to Cadwallon.

## Kingdom of Kent

**Æthelbert** King of Kent. First Christian king of an Anglo-Saxon kingdom.

**Eadbald** King of Kent after Æthelbert. Brother to Æthelburh.

**Paulinus** Christian missionary from Italy.

**James** Christian missionary from Italy.

**Oslac** Wagon master.

# *Glossary*

**Angles** One of the three main peoples that migrated to Britain in the fifth to seventh centuries from the Jutland peninsula. The Angles settled in the east and north.

**Bernicia** Anglian kingdom centred on Bamburgh. With Deira, one of the two constituent kingdoms of Northumbria.

**Britons** Original inhabitants of Britain. Ruling families, and possibly much of the populace, displaced by incoming Anglo-Saxons between fifth and seventh centuries.

**Deira** Anglian kingdom, centred on York. With Bernicia, one of the two constituent kingdoms of Northumbria.

**Freya** Anglo-Saxon goddess, known for her beauty.

*Hwæt* The traditional way to begin a recitation or song. Can be translated as *listen, hear this*.

**Hel** The underworld of the Anglo-Saxons. A place of grey shadows rather than torment.

**Jutes** According to Bede, one of the three main immigrant peoples originally from the Jutland peninsula. The Jutes settled in Kent and the Isle of Wight.

**Loki** Thunor's brother.

**Saxons** One of the three peoples that migrated to Britain in the fifth to seventh centuries; they came from the North Sea plain around the River Weser. The Saxons mainly settled along the Thames Valley and to its south and west.

**Scop** A bard and poet – the keeper of the collective memory of his people.

**Seax** A short sword/long knife, worn by all Anglo-Saxons (indeed, it gave the Saxons their name).

**Spear** The mark of a free Anglo-Saxon. Slaves were not allowed to carry weapons.

**Thegn** A nobleman – that is, a warrior.

**Thunor** Battle god of the Anglo-Saxons.

**Tufa** Imperial standard of Edwin.

**Wayland** God of smiths and smithwork.

**Witan** The leading men of a kingdom, called to council, particularly to accept a new king.

**Woden** Chief god of the pagan Anglo-Saxons.

**Wyrd** Key Anglo-Saxon concept. Can be translated as *fate* or *destiny*.

## How do you pronounce Æ?

In old English, Æ (or "ash" to give it its name) represented a vowel that sounded like a cross between "a" and "e". Try saying it like the "a" in "cat".

# PART 1

# *Exile*

# Chapter 1

"The king is going to kill you."

Edwin, senses trained by years of wandering exile, had heard the quiet approach to his room, but when he saw Forthred push open the door he laid his sword down.

"I take it you are not referring to my brother-in-law?" Edwin saw the expression on Forthred's face. "I thought not. You would not have crept to my room to announce that Æthelfrith wants me dead. So, which king wants to kill me now? It is a long list he joins."

Forthred pushed the door shut. "Rædwald. Our host," he said.

Edwin nodded slowly. "I thought it must be. How did you hear?"

Forthred smiled. "You know what they call me – Forthred Falls Over? These people think I have no head for drink, falling from the bench after one or two horns have gone round the hall and sleeping until morning. But the things I have heard whispered after the scops have lain down their lyres have kept us alive through these years of exile – and saved me many a thick head in the morning!"

"Would that I could do the same, but Rædwald would have no truck with a man who could not match him in the cups. Now, tell me what you heard."

Dropping his voice even though his master, by reason of his royal status, had a room to himself, Forthred whispered the news.

"Think on the new man we saw tonight at feast. He is a thegn and he took King Rædwald's time through the daylight hours with only the king's counsellors for company."

Edwin nodded. "I saw him arrive with a wagon lain with gifts, but I heard him speak – he is no Northumbrian. Are you sure Æthelfrith sends him?"

"I thought the same, lord. A Mercian by sound and look, bringing gifts from Cearl to lay at the feet of the High King. Surely there would be no danger there for us. But in our time here, I have become… close to one of the queen's women, and she told me that though the visitor be Mercian, he comes from Æthelfrith."

"But Æthelfrith has sent twice before asking Rædwald for my head. Why should this third occasion be different?"

"Gold – gold most finely wrought from the emperor's court in Byzantium – in chests full. Jewels, garnets, rubies to make a king's eyes weep. Is that reason enough?"

"For what you describe, I would be tempted to hand myself over to Æthelfrith if I could claim my own blood money." Edwin smiled grimly. "Kingship comes dear bought and is more dearly kept; no wonder Rædwald is tempted by such a treasure. But Æthelfrith has offered him treasure before. Is this so much more?"

"This evening, after I took my second drink from the horn and fell to the floor, as is expected of me, I made sure to stagger closer to where Æthelfrith's man sat, at the high table with the king." Forthred shook his head. "I could not hear clearly what they said, but I looked, lord, and to my eyes Rædwald seemed wary of this man. He comes, I thought, with hard words as well as rich gifts."

"Æthelfrith wants dominion over all the kingdoms of this land," said Edwin. "To that end he needs allies, and he must secure his own claim on the kingship of Northumbria. What better way than to suborn Rædwald with threats and sweeten him with blandishments? I am in Rædwald's power, to give over to Æthelfrith or not as he sees fit. But Forthred, what proof have you that Rædwald this time has taken the bait and bowed to the bit?"

"My lady brought me the news. The queen, Ymma, heard it from the king's own mouth this night, and her women are astir with the tidings, for the queen is angry that so mighty and powerful a king as Rædwald should act thus, bowing to the threats of another Angle. The queen says that her husband is the proper king of the Angles of this land. Ymma fears too what will befall should he act against the laws of the hearth and give over a guest to an enemy. But the king will not be gainsaid. He will have his treasure and hand you over."

Edwin nodded. "Thank you, friend. May the gods favour you with long life and a place at their table."

Forthred grimaced. "I have already lived longer than I expected. Come, lord, we know the worst; there is no time to wait. Rædwald will send for you in the morning. I have horses waiting, the moon is nearly full and there is light to ride; we will be far away by the time the sun rises." Forthred slid one of the heavy gold torcs from his arm. "This will buy us passage on a boat to the land of the Scyldings, and there we will be beyond the reach of Æthelfrith or Rædwald."

But Edwin did not stand. "Old friend, I thank you for your vigilance and the news you bring. But I cannot leave. King Rædwald and I have pledged allegiance and friendship to each other. If I leave tonight, without word or farewell, then it is I that break oath." Edwin laughed bitterly. "I have little enough treasure left to me after these many years of exile; I will not squander what is most valuable to me: my word."

"But lord, it is Rædwald that betrays honour and friendship in agreeing to kill you for Æthelfrith."

"I would rather Rædwald killed me than Æthelfrith, the betrayer, the liar." Edwin stood up and faced Forthred, the exiled king standing half a hand taller than his retainer. "How many years have we spent together, far from our homes and our land?"

"Too many, my lord."

Edwin took up the pouch that hung from his belt. "Hold out your hand." He poured into Forthred's palm a number of smooth, round stones. Each stone was different, in either colour or texture.

Forthred looked at his lord. "Most kings carry jewels in their belt. Why do you carry stones?"

"Count them," said Edwin.

"One, two… twelve." Forthred held up his hand. "There are twelve stones."

"One for each year of my exile. A stone collected in each kingdom we have fetched up in." Edwin held out his hand and Forthred returned the stones.

"This one," Edwin held up a rough grey stone, "is from the kingdom of Mercia, where I had friendship with King Cearl and he gave me his daughter to marry. My sons are with me still, but Cwenburg has gone to her fathers. This stone," a pebble of mottled greys and browns, "is from the kingdom of Wessex, where I had little welcome and less goodwill – we had to flee from there lest Cwichelm turn me over to Æthelfrith. And this stone," a glittering black oval, "is from Gwynedd, the kingdom of the Britons, where Cadfan treated me as a son and I was happy to stay there as a son, until the man I thought my brother in blood, Cadwallon, betrayed me to Æthelfrith." Finally, Edwin showed Forthred a dull, rusty red stone. "And this stone is from here, the kingdom of the East Angles." Edwin held the stone up between two fingers, but even in the torchlight it remained a dull, ominous red. "A bloodstone." Edwin looked at Forthred. "I will not run. My wyrd is written in these stones. My exile ends here, in blood, and I care not now whether it be my own or another's."

"Lord, maybe you do not care if you live or die, but I do. I gave my oath to your father to protect you, with arm and sword and heart's blood, and that is what I have done through our years of exile. I will not let you die through the guile of a betrayer."

Edwin shook his head. "But is Rædwald a betrayer?" He held up his hand as Forthred made to protest. "I know what you heard and what you have been told, but Rædwald has treated me well through our time here. Twice before Æthelfrith sent embassies asking for my head, and Rædwald sent them away. I owe him thanks and honour for that. Until I hear from his own mouth that he has left the path of honour and agreed to turn me over to Æthelfrith, I cannot flee – not in the night, like a slave absconding from his master! Then I would be the one dishonoured and that I will not endure."

Forthred stared at his king. "Do you think Æthelfrith cares for honour or the laws of hospitality? This is the man who stole your crown, who killed your brother at the feast where he married your sister. You know what the Britons call him in their tongue? Flesaur – the Twister. He twists everything he touches, bending all to his will. Already he has put the Irish to the sword, he has destroyed the armies of the Britons. The Mercians have sworn fealty to him, and the West Saxons too. Only this people, the Angles of King Rædwald, and in the south the Jutes of Æthelbert of Kent do not bend the knee to him. Æthelfrith is like a dog with a flea – he will not stop scratching for it, even if he tears open his own flesh. You are that flea, lord. Æthelfrith cannot stop scratching until he finds you. When will you learn that?"

Edwin looked up at Forthred, but instead of anger there was only tiredness in his eyes. "Æthelfrith would kill you for such an insult," he said. "My father and brother would have done the same. But I have need of time and space to think. Go."

"I will go, lord, but… but I have one more thing to say." Forthred looked questioningly at Edwin, knowing that he was pushing at the edges of what Edwin would accept, but he went on. "You may be ready to die, but your sons are not, and neither am I. We want to live."

Edwin gave no answer, but watched as Forthred made the courtesy, striking his forearm to his chest, and left, his footsteps receding over the rustling carpet of rushes Rædwald's slaves laid each morning. The taper spat and burned smokily. Edwin stared at it, remembering, with a freshness that always startled him, his wife Cwenburg dousing the taper as she looked to him to join her in their bed. Cwenburg had died seven years ago of the shaking fever, but still the memory of her would strike him keenly when his mind was distracted and uncertain. As far as he knew, the gods had no place in their halls for women who had died of sickness, not even if they were queens in exile. But so keen was the strike of her memory that it was hard not to believe that she was watching over him from the shadows.

However, ghosts withered if they were not tied to a place. Edwin had moved so much over the years since Cwenburg's death that he feared eventually she would not be able to find him any more. Then she would be left to wander into the twilight and be lost. So the occasions when he saw her again each became more precious than the last.

As quickly as it came, the memory left him, and Edwin could not stay in the smoky room any longer. He stepped out into the king's hall and stood listening. The meagre light of the few tapers that still burned flickered on the walls, and shadows moved over the hangings dangling from the ceiling. A breath of air made its way between the high pillars that supported the roof, and touched Edwin's cheek. He looked around for movement, but there was none. The benches and tables for the evening's meal had been pushed back against the walls. The king's men, those who were unmarried, mostly lay upon the benches, their breath a melding of snores and whispers that formed the constant night noise in any king's hall throughout the land. A restless dog whimpered in its sleep, kicking in a dream, then settled. The lingering smell of wood smoke mingled with the last scent of charred pork and the sour-sweet tang of spilled mead and the malt undertow of beer.

It was all so familiar to Edwin – he had seen and smelled and heard the same in every hall he had stayed in over his years of exile. Even when he had gone among the Britons, staying with Cadfan the King of Gwynedd, the sights and sounds and smells of the king's hall had been much the same, although there was one difference: the smoke the king's priests sent up as part of their rituals and prayers. That had been thick in Cadfan's hall, a cloying, lingering taste in the back of his throat and upon his clothes. The priests of the Angles and the Saxons and the Jutes used no such incense in the halls of their kings, but they prayed to different gods.

The air in the hall was too rank, too suffused with the smell of men and food and dogs. Edwin headed towards the hall's great door and the clean night air.

The door was barred. Edwin poked the man slumped against it with his foot and he jolted awake, hand dropping to his sword belt, but then pausing when his eyes focused on Edwin.

"Warden, open the door. I have need of air."

The warden clambered to his feet and levered the bar back, its weight made as nothing by pivots upon the back of the door.

"Your man, he needs air after a single horn." The warden pushed the door open enough for a man to slide through the gap. Edwin did not move. The warden sighed and pushed the door open further. Still Edwin did not move. The warden shrugged, grabbed the heavy wood and walked it all the way round so that it stood fully open, in a manner appropriate for a king's exit.

Edwin walked through the door. He might be a king in exile, but he was still a king, and honour was his due.

The warden took up his station by the open door. "Will you be long, lord?"

Edwin looked at him. The warden straightened. Alone among the men in the hall he wore a sword at his belt, as befitted his station as door warden. Torchlight, guttering weakly from the hall, glittered on his belt and buckles – gold inlaid with garnets, Edwin noted, of the finest workmanship. Rædwald was an open-handed king, giving great gifts to those who served him.

"The night is not old, warden. You have scarce begun your duties. See that the door is open for me when I return."

The warden appeared to sigh, but he had the wit to ensure that he made no sound. Edwin walked out into the night.

He continued walking down the gentle hill towards the foreshore. Rædwald's hall lay in sight of the sea, on one of the mounds that rose from the sea marshes and swamps that made the land of the East Angles a liminal place, neither land nor water, but shifting and solid beneath the feet and under the eye. Edwin followed the sound of the waves lapping on the beach, and soon he saw lines of white, lit by moonlight, as the waves drew in and curled onto the sand. The wind carried the salt tang of the sea, and for a while he retreated into memory, recalling how his father had taught him to rig a boat and sail it across the breeze. But he shook himself back into the present with a shiver. A cold finger from the frost giants of the north came over the water and ran across his face, a first hint of the winter to come. Edwin heard and felt the scrape of sand against his feet and stopped. The king's hall was but a promise of light, a glow beyond the hilltop behind him. His head rocked back and Edwin looked up at the stars.

He wondered, and wandered, among them. There was the Bear, stalking north, and the Bear Cub, creeping away in fear from the terrible still point in the sky. Edwin remembered his fear as a child when he heard a scop singing of the day when the Bear finally caught the North Star after its long, patient stalk. Then the Bear ate the star, and the sky fell, as a tent falls when its pole is removed. But the Bear had not moved in Edwin's life, and his years had provided more urgent fears than the sky falling in.

The Milky Way, the long cape that Woden had thrown across the sky as he tried to climb the World Tree to reach the North Star, glowed from horizon to horizon. The scops said that wyrd toppled Woden as he reached up to grasp the star, bringing him down, down, down through the air, and his fall was so great that he had made the hole into which the sea flowed around the island of Britain. Edwin sometimes wondered why Woden had used a cape for climbing and not a rope, when everyone knew that wool, though generally strong, could sometimes tear through. But the gods were silent on the reasons for their actions.

The sea hissed on the sand. The sound drew him. What Forthred had said was true; they could embark on a boat, take sail across the sea to the cousins of his people, the Scyldings, the Geats and the Frisians, and be assured of the welcome due an exiled king bringing a small but battle-hardened retinue of warriors with him. Any king would welcome the addition of Edwin, his sons and his retainers to his own forces, and once he had fled across the sea there would be no further reason for Æthelfrith to pursue him. And should his service go well, it would be rewarded with gold, and land, and power. Although his kingdom had been stolen from him in these islands, he could win another overseas, as his own forefathers had done when they left the land of their birth on the windswept peninsula of Angeln and taken the whale road to Britain. Edwin smiled. The land his forefathers had settled was no less windswept than the one they had left. He could allow those winds to carry him back to his ancestral home; he could return across the sea and leave these islands behind.

Edwin stared out over the incoming wave. If Rædwald handed him over to Æthelfrith, alive or as a corpse, his sons would be part of the gift. It was too dangerous to leave them alive, with an obligation to wreak blood vengeance. But if he went over the sea, his sons would live. He might live to see his grandchildren.

The wave hissed over the sand as it withdrew. Edwin shook his head. He might live to lose the strength of his arm, the wind from his lungs and the wit from his head, like those old warriors who did not stray far from the warmth of the fire, but grabbed any young man passing to regale them with tales of battles long ago fought and enemies years dead. It did not do for a king to grow old. Edwin smiled bleakly. Just as well then that kings did not grow old.

The sound came to him over the sigh of water on sand and wind through trees. A hiss, the sound of sand being displaced and sliding downwards. The sound of movement. Edwin's hand went immediately to his waist, but his sword was not there. No man might carry a sword in Rædwald's hall, save the king himself and the door warden. Edwin slid his seax from its sheath, taking care that the long knife – as much a part of a man as his tongue – made no sound as he drew it. Crouching, so that he would not be silhouetted against the white of the breaking waves behind him, Edwin listened. It made sense, if Rædwald had decided to hand him over to Æthelfrith, that the king should send one of his men to kill him now, in the silence and the dark, away from his sons and followers. There would be knives ready for Osfrith and Eadfrith, waiting upon the return of the assassin. Then their blood would flow, his line would be extinguished, and Æthelfrith could rule untrammelled.

But he was not going to die, not here, not now. Edwin slowed his breathing, bringing his suddenly racing heart back under control. With the sound of his own blood no longer blocking his ears, he concentrated all his attention into hearing. And smell.

He caught it then – a hint of the close, throat clutching smoke that had filled the halls of Cadfan of Gwynedd. For a moment Edwin wondered why a killer should smell of incense, but the thought was driven out by the rustle of marram grass. There. The killer had moved south, to make sure he could not be seen against the fires of the king's hall. He had circled round and was approaching along the line of the dunes. Keeping watch, Edwin crouched low and felt with his hand. The ground to his right was hard-packed thick sand. He could move across it without setting off any sand slips. Holding the seax between his teeth, arms and legs wide to spread his weight, Edwin inched to his right. A glance showed a darker shadow – a valley between the sand hills that would provide cover. Edwin slid towards it, eyes scanning for any movement. He had been outside for many minutes and his eyes were night bright, seeing by starlight.

A pebble, half buried in the sand, shifted beneath his foot and then scuttled down the sand hill, its passage as loud in the silence as an oath. Edwin froze. Even in the open it was hard to see a man at night if he kept absolutely still. But it was too much to hope the assassin had not heard the sound. Noise, however, gave only an approximate location. Sight was needed for murder. Edwin knew he needed to be first to see his opponent if he was to have any chance of killing a man armed and ready.

There. A shadow, darker than the rest, between the dunes. Did it move? He watched, eyes narrowed, but his other senses spread wide lest he be taken unawares through his own concentration.

Yes, it moved. It was coming towards him. Edwin took the seax in his hand, covering it with his other arm in case it should catch the glitter of a star and throw it to the man who stalked him. His breathing was low, not even a whisper, his head as clear as the sky and his heart calm. This was the peace before killing, the peace his father had taught him.

The killer came slowly, steadily onwards, and as he approached, Edwin saw that he was cloaked and hooded. No sign of his face could be seen under the cowl. Edwin knew the fighting styles of Rædwald's thegns well. If he could see the face, he would know how to fight him. The man was closer now, within fifty yards, but there was something strange about his approach. He walked without concealment, taking the broad path between the dunes while letting his feet crunch over the sand. This was the approach of an executioner, not an assassin.

Surely none of Rædwald's men were such fools as to approach him thus, without stealth, if they meant to kill him?

A diversion? Edwin sent his other senses questing, in the air and through the ground, but he could discern no other approach.

The man was closer now and though he still could not see his face, Edwin saw that he was not carrying a sword, nor a shield. The starlight made no glitter on the pole the man dug into the sand as he walked and, unless he had blacked out the head, that meant he carried a staff, not a spear. Edwin's brow creased. It was not unknown for an assassin to bludgeon a man to death, but a staff was as likely to break on a head as to break a head. Nor did the man have the build of someone who habitually used a cudgel, for he appeared tall but lean, rather than having the bulk of bone and muscle and blood required of a man who wielded his strength as his main weapon.

The man was near now, but set on a course that would take him across the shadows in which Edwin hid. At his closest, he would come within five feet. Edwin fingered the seax, keeping his wrist loose. A knife held in a tight wrist could too easily be jarred out of the hand if it struck armour or bone. He could slip out of the shadows and slide the seax into the man's armpit, where even if the blade missed the heart the man would die from blood loss within minutes.

Edwin waited, still, poised. The assassin closed. Ten feet. Nine. Eight.

The assassin stopped.

Beneath the cowl, the head turned.

Edwin tensed, ready to spring.

The man reached up and lifted the cowl from his head. He turned his face towards Edwin, but although it was uncovered, the night still concealed his features.

"My lord."

Edwin stood, sliding up from his crouch as smoothly as a cat. The seax glittered in the starlight.

"What do you want of me?"

"I know well why you stand outside the king's hall through the dark of the night." The man's voice was deep and strong, with the resonance of a scop, but his words carried a strange accent, unlike any Edwin had heard before.

"Who are you?"

"I know why you stand vigil by the sea through the darkest watches of the night, alone and troubled in mind, my lord. I know the evil that threatens you, the betrayer who will hand you over to your enemies, and I ask you this: what reward would you give the man who can save you from evil? What would you do for the man who persuades King Rædwald to remain in his honour and not hand you over to your enemies?" As the man spoke, his voice grew lower, quieter, but Edwin could still hear it clearly, for all other sound had faded from the world. "What reward would you give that man?"

Edwin – a tall man – looked up into the face of his questioner. "For such a deliverance, I would give whatever was in my power to give."

The dark man grasped his staff, planting it more firmly in the ground, but he made no move to approach closer.

"And what if that man prophesied, and prophesied in truth, that you would become king, putting down your enemies in their pride? And that you would ascend to a greater power than any of your fathers, a greater power than any king in these islands has wielded since the days of the emperors?"

Edwin could not tear his gaze from the shadowed eyes of the cloaked man. Who was he? Was he a god?

"If such things came to pass, I would give more generously than any king – gold, and jewels, and horses."

The stranger inclined his head. "And if this man unknown to you, who spoke in truth revealing the paths of the future and the glory that awaits, also brought guidance for life and salvation, knowledge unrevealed to your fathers and forefathers, would you follow his counsel and obey his advice?"

Edwin fell silent. The stranger waited for his answer.

"If such a man exists, who by his counsel can deliver me from my enemies and raise me to the throne, then assuredly I would follow his advice and wait upon his counsel."

The cloaked man bowed his head. His lips moved, and Edwin heard the murmur of words in a language unknown to him. Then he raised his head and stepped towards the king. Placing his hand upon Edwin's head, he said, "Remember this. Remember well this sign I place upon your head. When you receive this sign again, remember our conversation and remember your promise."

The cloaked man stepped back and raised his cowl to cover his head.

"Who are you?" asked Edwin. "Are you a god?"

The man, his face now lost again in shadow, turned away.

"Remember the sign," he said, and walked into the shadows.

Not daring to move, Edwin watched as the stranger merged into the night. Woden, the All-Father, wore a hood when he wandered the world. Edwin shivered. It was late summer and the night was not cold, but he shivered, in awe and fear and, most dreadful of all, in hope.

# Chapter 2

"My lord, my king, my – may the gods forgive me – husband, I do not believe I can bear the dishonour of being known as a queen who feasts a guest one day and then hands him over to his enemy the next." Ymma, queen of the East Angles, mother of the princes Rægenhere and Eorpwald, sat upon a stool brushing her hair. Rædwald, king of the East Angles, watched her in silence. The tapers in the royal bedroom burned evenly, their flames rising straight, for the tapestries that hung from the walls stopped the night breezes doing more than raising a whisper.

The queen ran the finely toothed bone comb through her golden hair. Rædwald watched, as he always watched when Ymma brushed her hair, for never had he seen gold more flowing, although he had won in battle gold from the kings and emperors of lands far, far away.

After adjusting the polished metal that reflected her image, Ymma continued with her brushing, running the tines through her hair from the scalp all the way down to her waist. Rædwald's eyes devoured the sight, for only he among men saw the queen with her hair unbound, falling freely as far as her hips, a golden train finer than any he could give her. His concubines, the pick of the women taken in battle and raid, were all dark, black of hair and dark of eye, but his wife was golden.

"So, tell me again, how has Æthelfrith's man persuaded you to surrender honour and renown, and to give up your friend and guest to the Twister?" The queen did not turn to look at him, for in adjusting the metal she had brought her husband into view.

Rædwald ran his finger and thumb over his moustache and brought them together on his chin. He knew Ymma could see him, and his face grew hot under her gaze. He fiddled some more with his moustache. He did not know how to answer. For the answer, in truth, was fear. And although the fear was wrapped in gold and buttered with jewels, nevertheless it lay at the marrow and in the blood of his decision.

"Well?"

The king scratched the underside of his chin. He coughed, a weak sound even to his own ears.

Ymma stopped brushing. She sat waiting, her back turned to him, the white skin of her right shoulder revealed as her shift slid down her arm.

"It's…" The king's voice dried into silence.

The queen waited.

Rædwald stood up and moved out of the view of the mirror. "There are some decisions a king has to make…" His voice trailed away.

"Gold." He tried again, weakly. "Æthelfrith's messenger promised me three boats full of gold, and four white horses."

Ymma turned around. "What did he promise you before?"

"The first time, he offered only one boat and no horses. The second time he sent to me for Edwin, he said he would pay two boats and two horses. I knew he would offer more if I said no."

"So, your honour and name, which you would not give up for two boats of gold and two horses, you happily give up for three boats and four horses. I see they are worth one boat and two horses. Not very much for the glory of a king."

Rædwald shook his head to clear the fog that was filling his mind. It had all been so clear when he had made the decision. Now Ymma was complicating it all.

"You do not understand. It is not about the treasure…"

"Is it fear then, my lord? Do you fear him? There would be no shame in being afraid of so great and mighty a warrior as Æthelfrith." The comb hissed through the golden waves of Ymma's hair, the same sound the sickle makes at harvest time shearing through the stalks of wheat.

"No! No… I do not fear Æthelfrith. But I am wary of him, Ymma. While I have been forced to spend the past three seasons dealing with

Æthelbert of Kent – successfully – so that we are now allied in blood and friendship, Æthelfrith has been busy. He has the North Angles and Middle Angles under his lordship. The Hwicce and the West Saxons are with him too. I cannot simply ride out against him."

The comb stopped.

"Why not?"

"Why not? Why not? It would be suicide, woman, suicide."

"Not if he didn't know you were coming."

Rædwald made to answer, then stopped. "What do you mean?"

The queen resumed her patient brushing. "I have heard the stories you men tell in the hall; how Æthelfrith has won so many battles through taking his enemies by surprise that they call him 'Twister' and 'Dodger'. Would Æthelfrith win if he were taken by surprise, before he had the chance to call the North Angles and Middle Angles, the Hwicce and the West Saxons to his aid?"

"And how am I supposed to take Æthelfrith by surprise, woman?"

"Follow his messenger." Ymma stopped brushing her hair and turned to face the king. "Gather your thegns, and as soon as you hear where Æthelfrith is, ride after him with all your men and attack. He will only just have heard that you have refused his messenger; he will be thinking what to do, whether to offer more or gather all his men and ride against you, but he will not have them together. The summer is almost over. The men return to the land to gather in the harvest, and only Æthelfrith's own thegns will be with him. Fall on him, kill him, and then it will be Rædwald who will be king of the Middle Angles and South Angles, and Edwin will rule the Angles of Northumbria, but at your sufferance. You will be the greatest king in the land; you will be High King."

Rædwald shook his head. He knew the plan would not work – it was mad, Æthelfrith too dangerous – but he could not think of any precise detail where it fell down. In the end he said weakly, "Æthelbert might have something to say about me being the High King."

Ymma laughed. "He can say what he wants; you will be the king of all the Anglian kingdoms, and overlord of the Saxons. He can have the Jutish lands and his new god."

"Don't mock Æthelbert's new god, Ymma. He is powerful. That's why I had the priests of this god bless me when I was in Canterbury; that's why I have had an altar to him set up in our temple and one of Æthelbert's priests to sacrifice upon it."

The queen shrugged, and Rædwald couldn't help notice the way her shift slipped further from her shoulder. "Sacrifice to him, too, then. If you have this new god aiding you, as well as the old gods, then surely you will kill Æthelfrith, for he only has the old gods helping him."

Rædwald smiled at the thought. "True," he mused.

"Not that you need the extra help," said Ymma, "for everyone says you are a greater warrior than Æthelfrith."

"Who says that?"

"Ask any scop who comes with songs and news and tales of lands far and near – ask them who the greatest warrior in Britain is, and you will hear them answer: Rædwald of the East Angles."

"But I have heard scops sing of Æthelfrith as the greatest warrior in the land."

"The craftiest warrior, the most cunning, maybe, but not the greatest fighter. No man alive has an arm to match yours, my lord, nor valour so great." Ymma twisted a strand of hair through her fingers. "Shall I tell you why I want you to fight and kill Æthelfrith, lord?" She looked up at him through her eyelashes. "It is because whenever I hear a scop singing of the power of Æthelfrith, and his majesty, I feel sick, sick to my stomach, that the glory and honour that should be yours, the mightiest, the bravest, the strongest of the kings of the English, is given to him, a liar, a betrayer, a… a twister." Ymma now looked her husband straight in the eye, with no artifice or wile. "Will you not keep your word, lord; save your sworn friend Edwin from his enemy and then together ride out against Æthelfrith and slay him?"

Rædwald felt the blood pounding at his temple. His vision blurred for an instant and he felt himself sway, but then his sight cleared and he saw his wife waiting upon his response, the answer of the king.

"I will," he said.

# Chapter 3

"Here, come ride beside me." Rædwald gestured Edwin forward. "What do you see?"

Edwin paced his horse so that it walked a head behind the king's mount. He scanned the flat land, broken by watercourses and rivers winding between trees and rush-lined banks from west to east, heading towards the great broad mouth of the Humber. To the east, land and water met, mingled and became the impenetrable marshes that surrounded most of the kingdom of Lindsey. It was a barren land, devoid of farms, with only the meanest folk scratching a living from eel fishing. The spires of smoke from their fires, used to dry the caught eels, rose up into the sky out of the marshes. From the banks of irises and reeds, Edwin glimpsed the occasional flash of movement as the marsh people kept watch on the passing riders, their faces and eyes as blank as the dark water of their homes. Water flats, sheet silver grey under the clouds, interspersed the fading green of the summer rushes and reeds. Come the winter, the land would turn as dull and brown as the marshes, and the water folk, if the ice came, would be driven inland to dig for roots and tubers that they might live.

"I see marsh and rivers and sky, my lord, but no sign of our enemy," said Edwin.

Rædwald laughed, delightedly slapping his horse on the neck. The horse, accustomed to the heavy hand of its rider, did not break step.

"You look all around, searching for Æthelfrith, but I am looking in front of my horse's nose! There," Rædwald pointed ahead, "what do you see there?"

Stretching ahead of them, heading north, was the only straight line to be seen: the road. It cut across river and marsh and flat, barely deviating from the straight path north to York. It was broad enough for four horses to ride abreast. It curved downward from its centre, as smoothly as a gentle hill; the hooves of the horses thudded upon the hard stones of the road.

"The Emperor's Road." Edwin nodded. "Of course."

"It's only by this old road that we are able to move fast enough to catch up with Æthelfrith." Rædwald turned round to look at the column of riding men: there were sixty of them, the thegns of his household riding behind the wolf pennant of the Wuffingas, the royal clan of the East Angles, and Edwin's few men, distinguished by the wild boar crests on their helmets.

It was a mighty army.

Spotting his son, Rædwald called him to the front.

Rægenhere trotted his horse up along the flank of the army, his blond hair, fair like his mother's, glowing as brightly as the gold of his arm rings and the buckles on his cape. He took the place on the right hand of his father.

"I wanted to show this to you as well as Edwin." Rædwald pointed at the road. "The Emperor's Road. Learn it well, for when Æthelfrith is dead and Edwin is king of Northumbria, it is upon this road that our armies and Edwin's must travel if we are to bend the other kingdoms to our will."

"I prefer to travel by boat," said Edwin.

Rædwald glanced at Edwin's stiff, upright posture. "So I see."

Edwin snorted with laughter. "I am not usually uncomfortable on a horse, but my own beast went lame and I am unused to this animal as yet. A boat allows you to carry more away after a battle – more gold, more horses, more slaves."

"You take your boats, I will take my horses. At least I don't have to wait for the wind."

"If the wind fails, we row."

"And do all the work, like a slave." Rædwald glanced at Edwin, but the Northumbrian stared straight ahead. Rædwald looked to his son and winked. Rægenhere stifled a laugh. He knew well this mood in his father – before battle, a terrible joy filled Rædwald. He might do anything in such a humour, from gifting a thegn the wealth of a king to insulting a warrior so vilely that he could satisfy honour only by calling the king to the duelling cloak. But this was also the time to ask the king a favour, and there was one Rægenhere was minded to ask.

"Father," he began, and a voice that had not yet completely broken screeched into falsetto before settling back into a man's register. "Father, will you give me leave to lead my men into battle?"

Rædwald looked searchingly at his son. The boy was almost a man, but in size and skill of arms he already exceeded most of the men. The thegns loved him, for his generosity, for his laughter and for the childhood that had been lived among them. They would fight, and die, for Rægenhere when the time came and Rædwald himself went to his forefathers.

From his place on the king's left, Edwin looked over at father and son. He remembered his own first experience of battle as a confusion of noise, fear, rage and a sudden terrible clarity as a warrior in the melee after the shieldwall had broken closed on him, and he had realized that in an instant he would live or die. The warrior had raised his arms for a killing, crushing blow with the axe, but his leading foot slipped upon a broken shield and he stumbled. Edwin had reacted without thought, the sword thrust the product of years of training. The man looked at him, his eyes wide, and Edwin stared back, both hands on the hilt of his sword as he pushed it. The warrior shook as the sword sucked the man's soul into its iron, every muscle going into a spasm as the life left his body. Edwin remembered nothing else clearly, but that man, the first warrior he had killed, remained as vivid in his memory as Cwenburg, and he feared that his ghost would endure longer than hers, for his ghost lived in Edwin's sword.

Rædwald punched his son on the shoulder, a blow that would have unhorsed a poorer rider than Rægenhere. Edwin was relieved not to be on the receiving end of such affection himself, for he would surely have been sent sprawling.

"Yes, my boy, yes. You are grown now, a man, and it is time you led other men into battle. Our scouts tell us he only has thirty men with him, so we will split into three groups and surround him. You will lead the centre."

Rægenhere beamed in delight at the news, a smile that made him look again the boy he had only just left behind.

"I will command on the left and Edwin will take the right." Rædwald looked to Edwin to make sure that he had grasped the significance of the orders. Edwin briefly nodded to indicate he understood. In the shieldwall, a warrior protected the man to his left. That made the right side of the shieldwall the point of greatest danger, for if the end man fell, it could lead to the shieldwall collapsing in confusion. Rædwald had charged Edwin with protecting the right flank. The left, where Rædwald had stationed himself, was where he intended to break Æthelfrith's line. The centre, protected by either flank, simply had to hold. It was the simplest job in battle, and as such well suited to a first command.

"I will give you Eadbald, Garwulf, Brid, Heca, Torhthelm and ten others. Good men, all of them, but you are their master." Rædwald took his helmet from where it rested upon the high pommel of his saddle and held it up. It was a magnificent helmet, with engraved cheekguards and trailing mail to protect the neck. "Here, as this is your first battle, I will give you my helmet, son. It has brought me much fortune. May it do the same for you." And he passed it to his son.

Rægenhere took it in trembling hands, his eyes shining. This was a gift only a king could give. Few men even in a rich kingdom could afford more than a simple helmet, for the skills to make one lay beyond that of the ordinary smith.

"Go on, try it," said Rædwald.

The young man placed the helmet on his head, its cheekguards hiding the fluff of his downy beard and the mail trailing over his shoulders.

Rædwald turned in his saddle.

"What do you say, my thegns? Is he not a true king's son?"

The column of men put up a cheer, while those in the vanguard drew their swords and flourished them.

Even from behind the helmet, the brilliance of Rægenhere's smile was enough to brighten a dull autumn morning.

But while Rægenhere dropped back among the men to accept their back-slapping, shoulder-punching good wishes, Edwin looked ahead, scanning the horizon. His sight was sharp and long, and he saw, where the road mounted high upon a causeway through the silver stream of a shallow river, a glitter and shimmer of movement.

They had caught Æthelfrith.

# Chapter 4

"Quick."

The man pushed the boy up upon the horse before stopping to cast a quick appraising glance at the approaching group of riders. He waved to one of the battle-hardened warriors who waited, sharpening swords and knives upon whetstones or chanting prayers to the gods. "Dæglaf, go with him."

"But Father, I am not afraid. I want to stay with you. I want to fight." The boy was fighting back tears, but he was losing the battle.

"I know you are not scared, and if I didn't have a more important task for you there's no man alive I would rather have beside me in the shieldwall. But you must take word to your mother and brothers." The man slapped the horse's rump, but the boy, well trained in horsemanship, reined the animal back.

"I can take word to them when we have won, Father."

Æthelfrith, king of Northumbria, looked again at the approaching riders. He only had thirty men with him. The riders, a mighty army, numbered over fifty. He could afford no weak spots in his shieldwall, nor could he spare the men necessary to guard his son during battle. There was no more time for talk.

He looked up at his son and the bleak hardness that had won him battles the length and breadth of the country overlay his eyes.

"Oswald, you are twelve; you are too young to fight a man's battle."

The boy's face crumpled and he lost, decisively, the battle against crying he had been waging. Turning the horse's head he urged the animal on, over the causeway and up the Emperor's Road, to the north.

Æthelfrith grabbed the bridle of Dæglaf's horse. "Get him safe," he said to his warrior. "Get him home. Do not turn back."

The old warrior nodded. "I will look after him, lord." Dæglaf had spent many hours playing with and training the boy as he grew towards manhood and he loved Oswald as his own. "May the gods protect you."

"They always do." Æthelfrith grinned up at the warrior, who did him homage before urging his horse after Oswald. Æthelfrith turned towards the approaching riders and the smile dropped from his face. "It's the fates who worry me."

Æthelfrith took a deep breath, dipped briefly into the memory of his many victories, and strode forward among his men, a fierce smile upon his face. The men of his household, battle tested though they were, could count as well as their king – they knew they were at a disadvantage and no man raised a murmur at Æthelfrith sending his son away. But now, seeing the battle grin on Æthelfrith's face, they grew bolder. The Twister had extricated them from tighter situations than this before.

Æthelfrith scanned the watching, watchful faces. He knew each one as well as a brother. They had fought with him up and down the country, defeating every army that stood against them and reaping such plunder that one boat had sunk beneath its load as it laboured up the River Ouse. They waited for him to speak, but as they waited some eyes flicked towards the riders and he could see them count off the spears and compare them against their own numbers.

"Are you scared?" Æthelfrith paused, looking from face to face. "Well, I'm not. Yes, there are more of them, but I know you, I know you better than your own mothers, and each one of you is worth two or three of them."

One of the men, Hunlaf the warmaster, stepped forward. The riders were stopping and getting ready to dismount. Horses were for riding to war, but battle was fought on foot.

"We should cross the causeway," Hunlaf said, "and meet them on the other side. Then only a few will be able to cross at a time, and we can kill them as they come."

Æthelfrith held up his hand. "A good plan, my friend, but unwise." He turned so that he could see the dismounting riders.

"See how they stumble, the confusion in their ranks?" And it was true. Rædwald's men were milling around in some disarray as they attempted to sort out who was to remain behind guarding the horses and who was to advance. Raising his voice, so that it carried over the flat distance between the two armies, Æthelfrith said, "They are frightened of us! I smell their fear." He turned back to his men. "If we retreat, they will think we fear them. Fight here, and they know we fear nothing and no one."

"We can be outflanked," said Hunlaf doubtfully.

"Only if we remain still and wait for them. But we will do what they do not expect – we will attack them!" Æthelfrith saw the men's faces brighten. Action was always preferable to the long gnawing nerves of waiting. "I have seen Rædwald fight. He has no skill, no subtlety, but he is brave and strong. So we attack him. Kill Rædwald, and the rest will flee."

"How do we know who to attack?" asked Hunlaf.

"Look for his helmet. It is the finest I have ever seen, and I will enjoy wearing it myself before this day is out."

"You'll have to wash the blood out first," said Hunlaf.

The men laughed, clashing their swords on shields and armour, and Æthelfrith joined in. "There is a river right here. We shall make it run red with the blood of our enemies!"

"Right, I'm going to have a drink first!" said Hunlaf, and amid general laughter the men went to the bank and drank their fill. Æthelfrith watched them with pride. He turned his eyes further north and saw the horses of Oswald and Dæglaf making their way north along the Emperor's Road. However the battle went – and there was a chill in his blood that gainsaid the confidence with which he spoke – Æthelfrith knew that they had sufficient head start to get away from any pursuers. Satisfied, he turned to look at the disposition of Rædwald's men. So he did not see Oswald and Dæglaf halt and take up position by a copse of trees, watching and waiting for the battle to begin.

# Chapter 5

Edwin was worried. He had formed his men, some twenty of them, into a tight shieldwall. To his left, Rægenhere fussed about the men in the centre, organizing them and pushing the end men more tightly into line. Beyond him, Rædwald waited for his son to finish his preparations. Two hundred yards away, by the causeway over the River Idle, Æthelfrith and his men stood in loose formation. Their horses had been taken over the river and picketed there, without even a single man to guard them. Edwin knew those men of old. He knew them to be skilled and brutal warriors, and though they were outnumbered, Edwin looked measuringly at the men lined up beside him and found them wanting. His own few retainers, men like Forthred, he knew could hold their own against the Northumbrians, for they were kin, but the East Angles were a more mixed bunch.

Rædwald's plan was to use the three shieldwalls as three sides of a fence, and the river as the fourth, closing the fence tighter and tighter until Æthelfrith's shieldwall was overwhelmed by the greater number and weight of the East Angles. But looking at the disposition of Æthelfrith's men, Edwin feared that he was not going to fight in the way Rædwald wanted him to fight. However, he had no choice but to follow Rædwald's plan – if nothing else, their numbers should tell in the end, for by his count the East Angles outnumbered the Northumbrians two to one.

Rægenhere was still not ready. Edwin inspected the ground between the two armies for any hidden gullies or traps, but the plants here were trodden flat by the confluence of all tracks, animal as well as human, onto the causeway. The river itself, as far as Edwin could see, was running cleanly past the causeway.

From across the intervening ground, Edwin began to hear taunts and chants. One warrior, as big and burly a man as he had seen, strode forward until he was within a hundred yards of Rædwald's men.

"Is there any man there brave enough to fight me?" He beat his fist against his armour. "I am Hunlaf. If no man is brave enough to fight me on his own, I will fight two together. Come on!"

Edwin looked along his line. Some of the younger men, stupid with the pride of youth, shifted restlessly. One began to step forward.

"Forthred." He had placed his most trusted man on the left of his shieldwall, and Forthred, nearer the young man, hauled him back and spoke quietly but viciously into his ear until he nodded in assent.

Hunlaf looked along the still battle lines facing him and spat. Then he loosened his trousers and urinated.

"Now I piss on the ground. After the battle I will piss on your bodies."

The Northumbrians cheered and shouted.

Edwin looked along the line. Rædwald dropped his hand.

"Now," he said.

The three lines began to advance. Hunlaf, in a sudden hurry, scurried back to his men, trying to fix his trousers as he went. The younger men among the East Angles shouted taunts in their turn, but Edwin saved his breath. He pushed his shoulder against the man to his left, trying to stop his line drifting apart from Rægenhere in the centre.

"Keep left," he shouted, but the camber of the ground, falling away from the road, drew his men away. On the far left he could see Rædwald was finding it difficult to keep his line tight against Rægenhere's men as well. Only the centre moved easily, for it had the road to advance upon. Rægenhere and his men were ahead of the two wings, although the plan called for Rædwald and Edwin to advance faster and seal in the Northumbrians.

"Hurry!" Edwin tried to move the men into a shambling run, but the wall began to break apart and he had to slow them down to remake the line. From the left he heard war cries, shouts and out-and-out screams. It sounded as if the battle had begun there. He tried to crane his neck, to peer past the line of his own men's out-thrust shields to see what was happening in the centre, but his vision was blocked. And then the battle came to him, and he stopped thinking about anything else.

\*

Æthelfrith watched the slow approach of the three lines of shields. He saw how easily gaps opened between the shieldwalls, how they drifted apart as the land sloped, and he knew what he had to do.

Passing along his own shield line, he gave out his orders to men who were so excited they barely heard him.

"Ulfric, Sigelac," he said to the men on the flanks of his line, "take ten men and harry the left and right shieldwalls. Keep them busy, keep them occupied, keep them away from the centre." He looked into Sigelac's eyes, saw them distant and unfocused in the pre-battle haze, and slapped some attention into him. "Do you understand? Harry and delay."

Sigelac, his gaze dragged away from the oncoming men, nodded. "Harry and delay."

Æthelfrith turned to Hunlaf. "You're with me, Hunlaf." He nodded towards the centre. "Rædwald's there – I'd know his helmet anywhere. We take the rest of the men and break the centre. When Rædwald is dead, the rest of them will crumble and we can finish them off."

Hunlaf, his mind already retreating into the red haze of battle fury, grunted his answer. For himself, Æthelfrith wondered what gift the gods had given him that, even in the midst of the fight, his mind did not cloud over as most men's did, but instead became as clear and calm as a winter's morning. It did not matter. The gods gave gifts to whom they wished, and wyrd weaved it all into itself.

Æthelfrith looked up and down his line. The East Angles were within fifty yards. He always believed in letting the enemy do the work of closing the gap – his men would do the work of killing.

He raised his sword and pointed it at Rædwald's advancing men.

"Whoever brings me Rædwald's head keeps Rædwald's treasure!"

he yelled, and his men cheered, gold lust vying with battle lust in their blood.

Æthelfrith smiled. Rædwald thought he had trapped the Twister. He was about to learn there was nothing as dangerous as a Twister, trapped.

Æthelfrith brought the sword down. His men began to move forward, trotting first, slowly increasing their speed with the practised ease of experienced warriors, so that they would meet the oncoming line when they had reached their maximum speed. Most battles were won when, after many minutes of heart-bursting effort as the two shieldwalls pushed against each other, the strength of a single man failed, the shieldwall was breached, and the suddenly vulnerable warriors on either side were peeled off. It was little more than a contest of brawn, weight and endurance. Æthelfrith did not fight like that. His men attacked in a looser formation, every warrior trusted to find a weak point in the enemy shieldwall and pierce it.

Æthelfrith's teeth bared – he was smiling, the death's head smile that had been the last sight of so many men. He could see Rædwald up ahead, at the centre of the line, his shieldwall jostling as the startled men tried to peer over their shields at attackers who were advancing in no way known to them. He glanced sideways at Hunlaf and saw the man had fixed Rædwald in his sight too. The warmaster's stride lengthened. He held his shield out in front as a battering ram, its heavy central iron boss painted the dull red of dried blood. With the men on either side protecting him, Hunlaf smashed into the centre of Rædwald's shieldwall like a bull charging a fence.

Æthelfrith jumped over the men sprawling on the ground and brought his sword up in a short killing arc under the chin of a man who a moment before had been trying desperately to free his shield from the wall so that he could protect himself. Blood bursting from the wound, the man fell back, crashing into his fellows behind him, the violent spasms of his dying body wreaking further havoc in Rædwald's defences.

Behind him, Æthelfrith could hear Hunlaf peeling away the other side of the shieldwall, the clang of sword on metal giving way to the dull, cleaver thud of blade slicing and piercing flesh. Overlying everything were the shouts and screams of the dying and the killers, uniting in the war hymn that called the gods down from the skies and Woden's eyes, the ravens, for their feast. Æthelfrith slid his sword in under the guard of the next man, and saw his eyes widen as the blade buried itself in his guts.

A shout. Above all the screams and cries, a yell of triumph, the sound of gold lust and battle lust, and Æthelfrith saw a hand held high bearing a richly worked helmet, with cheekguards and trailing mail.

"Rædwald is dead!" Hunlaf exulted.

Æthelfrith looked for the body and saw it sprawled on the ground before his warmaster. But there was something wrong about what he saw: a fresh face, barely bearded, and hair of the fairest gold, though now blood smeared. He looked up at Hunlaf shouting his triumph, and suddenly a raw dread filled the Twister's stomach.

"That's not Rædwald," he said.

\*

Edwin heard the howl above the shouts and screams, above the cries of men dying and calling on their mothers and their gods, above the clang of metal on metal and the thud of metal on flesh. He heard the howl rise above all the sounds of battle, and for a moment the fighting ceased. It was a sound that the earth might make if it were giving birth, or the stars if they fell. It was such a noise that the handful of Northumbrians who were harrying Edwin's line quailed and fell back from their feints and thrusts with long swords and longer spears, and the East Angles turned as one to stare to their left.

From his position on the far right of the battle, Edwin looked across and saw that the centre line of the East Angles had broken down completely, falling into the confused melee of small fights that meant it was all but over. Among the fights, Edwin saw a Northumbrian wielding a helmet and shouting a triumph and, with a sudden lurch, he knew all too well from whom he had taken that helmet.

But that was not where the howl had come from, although there too, in the centre, it seemed that all stopped at the dreadful sound. No, the howl of anguish came from Rædwald's flank, and from that flank Edwin saw a single figure break from the centre of the shieldwall and, still making that unearthly, tortured cry, hurl itself into the melee of men struggling in the centre.

It was Rædwald. Edwin saw that from the man's armour, and he fell upon the Northumbrians like a charging boar, a man suddenly mad with grief, and his men followed him, their king's rage and grief filling them with the lust for blood vengeance and his howl giving them the strength to exact it.

Near at hand, Edwin saw the handful of Northumbrians who had been occupying his forces quail as they too realized that the current of battle had shifted and the fatesingers had changed their song. Now was the time to act.

"Attack!" Edwin lowered his shield as a ram, and led his men in a stumbling but still coherent charge. The Northumbrians, assailed from both sides, broke. Some tried to run, to make it back to the causeway and the picketed horses, but the East Angles pursued them, flicking out swords to cut hamstrings and bring the men crashing down upon the ground.

In the centre, only Æthelfrith remained. Hunlaf was down, his bowels spilling, the biggest man in the Northumbrian army cradling them as he cried his way into death and called for his mother.

The Twister twisted. He was surrounded. The East Angles made a rough circle about him and Rædwald stepped into the circle.

"You killed my son," he said.

Æthelfrith flourished a courtesy. "It was an accident; I meant to kill you." From the sides of his vision, he could see the ravens had already arrived to feast and to carry the spirits of the dead warriors to Woden's halls. He would be there soon. But still twisting, he felt for the right words, and found them. "If you hadn't given your son your helmet, he would still be alive, Rædwald. He died because of you." Æthelfrith was trying to provoke mad, blind rage in Rædwald. He succeeded.

The king of the East Angles brought his sword down and Æthelfrith met it, but such was the strength of the blow that half the Twister's shield sheered off. Æthelfrith went to thrust his own sword into Rædwald's stomach, but the king brought his shield down on top of the stroke and drove the sword into the ground at his feet, then charged the boss into Æthelfrith's extended arm, breaking the bone. A second stroke with the sword, to Æthelfrith's unprotected left, and the sheer weight of the blow broke his collar bone.

Æthelfrith stumbled. On his knees he looked up at Rædwald. In a mind that was rapidly dimming, he felt a supreme annoyance that he was going to die at the hands of a warrior who had none of his cunning – brute, raw strength had won the day for Rædwald.

"Make it quick," Æthelfrith said.

Rædwald looked down at the man swaying on his knees on the blood-soaked earth.

"No," he said.

*

Dæglaf grabbed the kicking and shouting boy as he tried to mount his horse and ride back to his father. He held him tight as he thrashed and cried, and he made sure that he could not see as, across the river, his father took a long time dying.

*

"Edwin!" Rædwald, his face smeared with Æthelfrith's blood, looked around the watching men. "Where are you? Edwin!"

Edwin, the exiled king of Northumbria, stepped forward warily. There was a madness in the king, the madness of grief and vengeance, and such a fury could take many forms.

Rædwald, seeing Edwin, ran to him, grabbed him and dragged him between the bodies and the men who sat in mute weariness.

"Look." Rædwald pointed to one of the bodies. "I have bought you your kingdom back, Edwin, and the price was my son." Rædwald pushed Edwin down so that his knees went to the ground.

"Your kingdom cost me my son. You kneel to me, Edwin. You kneel to me, now and forever. Do you understand?"

And Edwin, king of Northumbria, knelt by the side of the River Idle on the blood-soiled earth, before Rædwald, king of the East Angles and High King of Britain.

# PART 2

# *Throne*

# Chapter 1

"The king is dead!"

The cry went forth, wailing over the calls of the gulls, reaching up and up to the castle on the rock. Forthred, the first man down to the boat that had pulled up on the thin strip of sand beneath the castle rock, was the first man back up the winding rock-carved stairs. He found Edwin in the great hall, sitting in the judgement chair, delivering justice to the queue of petitioners before him.

Forthred pushed past the gaggle of arguing men and women, earning himself a few stern looks, muttered curses and a dig in the ribs in the process.

"My lord."

Edwin barely looked up. He sat leaning towards an old woman, cowled and shawled, who spoke no English but only the tongue of the Britons. However, Edwin knew the language well and Forthred, although he felt the news bursting within him, held back as the king did the crone the courtesy of bending his ear and mind to her complaints and arguments. She pointed a wavering finger at the mass of waiting, arguing petitioners, and Edwin waved a man forward, a minor thegn by the look of him, although Forthred did not recognize him. The king listened as they both spoke, arguing with each other, until finally he stopped them. Edwin looked up, for the whispers were now passing around the hall, silencing arguments and displacing conversation. He glanced at Forthred, who made to step forward with his news, but Edwin stayed him again with an upraised hand.

The hubbub in the hall had now died down enough for Forthred to hear what the king said to the plaintiffs. Edwin spoke, first in English and then in the language of the Britons, so that his meaning was clear to both plaintiffs.

"You set your word, each against the other. Answer now, tell me you speak the truth, and I will render judgement as I see fit."

The thegn, his face florid with outraged honour and, Forthred suspected, too much rich food, launched into a diatribe against the old woman for dragging him before the king when he had been one of the king's most trusted and valued men who had helped him subjugate the land and keep the peasants in check.

"Which king?"

The thegn came to a stuttering stop. "I – I beg your pardon, lord?"

Edwin looked mildly at the man. "I do not know you, and I have been king of Bernicia these past two years. So, I ask again: which king did you render all this service to?"

The man's nose went even redder and his eyes shifted uneasily.

"The, ah, the last king, lord, but that doesn't mean I don't serve you as faithfully. It's just that I've been busy on my land and my wife has been ill and…"

Edwin held up his hand and the thegn's voice trailed away. "Many of Æthelfrith's retainers have served me well, but they have generally made themselves known to me. Now, woman, tell me your truth." And the king spoke a few words in the language of the Britons. The crone brightened and began to speak, the words fluid and musical and far too quick for Forthred to follow.

Edwin nodded as the crone spoke, looking over at the thegn as the old woman made her argument with jabbing finger and jabbering tongue. The thegn's grasp of the language of the Britons appeared to be little better than Forthred's, for he had to look to his companions for a translation of the crone's case.

"Very good." Edwin sat back on the judgement chair and gestured the crone to take her place beside the thegn. He looked at the petitioners, the old woman gabbling soundlessly through her toothless lips, the thegn red and sweaty with embarrassment.

"Pay the old woman her weregild," Edwin said, staring at the thegn, "and do not think that being of the same blood as my forefathers trumps the ancient customs and laws."

The old thegn stared at the king, his face becoming even redder with anger. But when he did speak, it was not to argue but to ask a question.

"Have you heard the news, lord?"

Edwin's eyes narrowed as he looked sharply at the thegn.

"What news?"

The thegn sniffed. "The king is dead." He sniffed again. "All kings die." And he turned and made to stalk from the hall.

But Edwin rose from the judgement seat and where the thegn's face was red, Edwin's was as pale as death.

"Stop."

Forthred, seeing the bitter flare of his master's anger, stepped forward, but Edwin stopped him with a gesture. The thegn stopped, his back still turned to the king. The crone licked her lips, eyes flicking from her master to her king and back again as she strove to understand what was being said in an alien tongue. The people in the hall – petitioners, servants, slaves, thegns – fell into a watching, waiting silence. Even the news that had fluttered around the hall minutes before was hushed.

The thegn turned back to his king. The blood had drained from his face, but his lips were set firm and his eyes were steady as he faced Edwin.

"You upheld the ancient customs and laws for this lying old woman. Will you spurn them now because I angered you?"

The hall waited in silence, and even the dogs, sensing the tension, were still.

"My lord."

The voice was quiet, but in the quiet it carried. Edwin looked to his left and the eyes of everyone else in the hall turned to Forthred.

"My lord, King Rædwald is dead."

And around the hall, everyone let out their breath. Edwin's face did not change – no colour came to his cheeks or blood to his lips – but his jaw tightened.

For a minute the king made no answer and in the hall there was no sound. Then Edwin turned to the day's remaining petitioners.

"Go," he said. He looked around the hall. "Everyone, go." He turned his gaze upon the thegn. The old warrior held his gaze for a moment and then bowed, the red flush dying from his face. He was going to live. "Go," said Edwin. "But insult me again and I will put you to death."

The people drained out of the hall, gossiping and talking as they went. Forthred remained, standing quietly by the judgement seat, and when the hall was empty Edwin turned to him.

"When did he die?"

"Two days past."

"You are sure? The news has come most quickly."

"The winds were fair and the ship sailed fast. Its master, I think, hoped to be rewarded for bringing the news to you first."

"Did you?"

"Yes, lord."

Edwin stared into the hall without seeing its wooden columns, high roof or the hangings that trembled upon the walls as they attempted to seal it from the cold winds that blew in over the grey sea.

"How did he die? Was it in battle?"

"No, lord. He died after falling from his horse."

Edwin gave a snort of grim laughter.

"His horse?"

"Yes, lord. It was a gift: a stallion fresh come from the king of the Franks, a white horse, magnificent and headstrong."

"My father told me to be wary of gifts from the Franks, for they give with the right hand and take with the left." Edwin shook his head. "A fall." He lapsed into silence, his gaze focused on the intermediate, indeterminate space between near and far. "So Rædwald the warrior goes down, a shade, to Hel, while Æthelfrith, the man he defeated, feasts at the table of the All-Father." Edwin looked to Forthred. "That does not seem right."

Forthred shrugged. "Even the gods are subject to wyrd. At the Last Battle the All-Father, Thunor – they will all fall."

"But at least they will be there, fighting the frost giants, with Æthelfrith at their side. Rædwald's ghost, a gibbering lost thing, will not even remember the strength and rage with which it cut down Æthelfrith. Only a shade will remain, a shadow that fades as the sun fails and darkness takes everything."

"The fate singers weave wyrd and we, men and gods, must endure."

Edwin nodded slowly, then stood. "I have been in this hall too long today and the reek sits heavy in my chest. Come with me. There is more I must learn."

The door warden bowed as the king and his chief retainer left the hall. The gaggle of unheard petitioners, spotting Edwin, made to follow, but the door warden gestured for them to wait.

"The king will hear you from the judgement seat, not –" he looked to where Edwin and Forthred were headed – "the toilet seat." The petitioners laughed and settled back to their waiting.

But Edwin and Forthred did not cross to the north tower with its garderobe jutting out over the rock beneath. Instead, they climbed the battlements and stood upon the thick timber-topped wall that looked out over the sea and the ship moored beneath.

The wind, cutting and clear, whipped over the waves. Edwin faced into it and breathed its coldness in.

"There is no one to hear us here, Forthred." Edwin looked out over the ridged grey water to the wave-breaking islands that rose, long and low, a mile and more from the shore. "With Rædwald dead, where lies the power in the land?"

Forthred looked at the profile of the man he had served as exile and king, and he made the courtesy, his clenched fist and forearm sounding out dully as they struck the muscles of his chest.

"With you, lord."

The wind blew harder and Edwin shivered, but it was not from a cold to which he was inured that he shook.

"He made me bow to him. He forced me to my knees in front of his men, in front of mine, and made me do homage." Edwin turned to Forthred, and his eyes were as grey and cold as the sea. "He bought me my kingdom and defeated my enemy, but he ground my knees into the blood-soaked mud and forced the homage I would have willingly given. But he is dead now, and no other man will make me kneel."

"But I will kneel to you, lord," said Forthred, and he went down on one knee before Edwin.

"Get up, get up." Edwin hauled Forthred back to his feet. "We have endured too much together for you to kneel to me, old friend. But tell me, who do you think will take rule of the East Angles after Rædwald?"

"Most probably Eorpwald, Rædwald's son."

"Do the thegns wish him for king?"

"He is young and not the warrior his father was, but unless a thegn can rally the rest to him, Eorpwald will be king."

"So he needs support. I will give it, at a price." Edwin turned his back to the sea and looked over the high walls of his castle to the west, seeing the well-tended fields that fell away from the castle rock to the woods and the rising, bare-backed hills beyond.

"This was Æthelfrith's land. When I came here after the battle, Æthelfrith's thegns could have held the castle long against us, but they pledged themselves to me and they have been true to their word. But still, though it be the strongest castle in the land, I have no love for it. Bamburgh. A hundred kings could come against it and they would fall before its walls. But still I do not love it. It is time we went back south, Forthred, to our own old lands. Will Eorpwald come if we summon him to York?"

"There is a man on the ship who can tell us, lord. He seeks audience with you."

"Who is he?"

"Wældhelm, the smith."

"Rædwald's smith?"

"Yes, lord."

"Why has he come?"

"He brings his wives and children; I saw them on the ship. If he brings them over sea, he must be seeking a new lord."

Edwin peered down over the battlements to where the ship lay, pulled up onto the narrow stretch of sand beneath the castle rock.

The sailors were setting up their tents alongside and a group of children were playing chase with each other and the waves. Standing apart from them, looking up at the castle, was a man who even from this height looked big among the others.

"Bring him to me."

Forthred made to leave, then stopped. "Where will we find you?"

"Bring him to the hall."

# Chapter 2

Edwin sat upon the judgement seat. The petitioners stood outside, for he had told the door warden to await Forthred and the man he brought before allowing the squabbling, arguing mass of men, women, children and dogs inside. In the corners of the hall, slaves and servants cleared and cleaned, readying the long tables for the short midday meal. From outside, mingling with the sound of the arguing petitioners, came the thud of wood on wood and, more occasionally, the ringing of metal on metal as his men practised their arms under the watchful eye of his warmaster, Guthlaf.

The door warden pushed open the carved and painted oak door and stood to the side as Forthred entered, followed by a man a full head taller and with a chest and shoulders to match his height. But as they approached, Edwin saw that the big man dragged his right leg in the characteristic sidelong pull of a man who has been hamstrung.

Forthred made the courtesy, then turned to introduce the man he led.

"Wældhelm the smith, lord."

Edwin inclined his head and turned his gaze upon the smith. The man bore, in many small scars and burns, the marks of smithship upon his hands and arms, and he smelled of the craft too. Smoke had darkened his flesh and yellowed it, like a preserved fish. The smith looked at the king through narrowed eyes. But Edwin realized this was not a sign of suspicion, but the result of many years spent staring into the white heart of fire.

The smith made the courtesy. "Rædwald, king, is dead. I seek a new king."

"I already have a smith," said Edwin. "Why should I take you?"

"You do not have a smith like me." Wældhelm turned and gestured to the door warden. "Bring it forward." Turning back to

Edwin, the smith said, "I cannot carry a sword in your presence, so I asked the door warden to guard my gift. Look on that and then tell me you already have a smith."

The door warden brought forward a sword, scabbarded in rough leather. Wældhelm stepped towards him, but the door warden did not give up the weapon. He looked at Edwin questioningly. The stranger was a giant of a man; to hand him a sword when there were so few to guard the king seemed foolish.

"I will take it," said Forthred smoothly. He grasped the weapon. The hilt was plain, neither jewelled nor engraved, but their practised eyes told them it was well made. Forthred looked at the smith, his hand poised.

"Shall I?"

"Yes," said Wældhelm.

Forthred drew the sword.

The king gasped. Forthred gasped. Even the door warden – who had seen more swords than anybody else – gasped.

The sword was three feet long, double edged and pointed, with a fuller running three-quarters of its length. But what drew the exclamations were the patterns of light and dark metal that ran the length of the blade, like sand ridges upon a beach.

Wældhelm laughed, even his narrowed eyes opening out in pleasure at the reaction to his work.

"Test it, lord; try it. Believe me, you will never have held a sword like this. It will cut through a good shield with one strike."

Forthred looked at Edwin, saw the way the king's eyes had locked upon the blade, and he handed the sword, hilt first, to the king. Edwin held the sword up, turning it this way and that, letting the light play upon its pattern, and holding it out straight in front to feel its balance.

"It will hold its edge through a battle and be as keen at the end, when all your enemies lie dead about your feet and the ravens have come for their souls, as it was at the beginning when the young men were calling insults and the old men were running whetstones down their blades."

"Get a shield." Edwin pointed the door warden to an old leather-bound lime-wood shield. While the warden fetched it, Edwin swung the sword through the air in the careful, prescribed strokes that his father and his sword master had taught him as a boy. He could hear the sword hiss as it cut the wind, a sound as unmistakeable as a wave upon sand.

The warden strapped the shield to his forearm and made to hold it up, but Wældhelm stepped forward. "Not if you want to keep your arm," he said. "Hold it between your hands."

The door warden looked to Edwin, who nodded his assent. Holding the edges of the shield, his hands wide apart, the door warden steadied himself, rooting his feet against the coming blow. But when the strike came, he hardly felt it. For the sword cut through the shield as if it were new leather. The incredulous laughter of Edwin and Forthred filled the great hall. And the smith smiled.

"Nor will it break." He held out his hand.

Edwin handed the sword to Wældhelm. The smith took it and paused for a moment, the only man there with a drawn sword in his hand. In the sudden silence, Forthred felt for his seax and the door warden went for the hilt of his own sword, but Edwin made no move towards the blade that hung from his waist. Wældhelm looked around the three watching men.

"Shall I?"

"Yes," said Edwin.

"Lord," said Wældhelm, and he pushed the tip of the sword into the gap between two flagstones and began to bend the blade. Accompanied by gasps and muttered oaths, the smith bent the hilt further and further and further, the effort causing drops of sweat to break on his skin, until the pommel touched the very floor and the straight sword had become an arch.

"Watch now," Wældhelm grunted through gritted teeth, and he pulled the point clear. The blade sprang back, shivering to the true, and Wældhelm gave the sword to the marvelling hands of king and thegn and door warden.

"I have never seen a sword bend like that before," said Forthred in wonder, as he, Edwin and the door warden passed the weapon to each other.

"No sword of mine has ever broken, not in battle, not in duel, not in practice."

Edwin held the sword out straight in front of him, feeling it as light in his hand as the wooden practice sword he had wielded as a boy.

"I will smith for you now," said Wældhelm, "and make you swords such as this."

Edwin looked over at the giant smith.

"Yes." He passed the sword back to Forthred, who held it up to the light and slowly turned it before his wondering sight. "You are not oath bound to Rædwald's son?"

"My oath was to Rædwald alone. He takes it with him into the ground."

Edwin slipped off one of the heavy gold armlets from his upper arm. He held it out, and the smith stepped forward. Both men took hold of the thick gold ring.

"I give you this gift, and more gifts too I will give, so long as you honestly serve me."

"I take this gift and pledge my service to you." Wældhelm took the ring and placed it on his own arm, although his muscles were so thick that the armlet would not go past his forearm.

From the door there came a rustle of argument, and Edwin looked over to see that a gaggle of petitioners had taken advantage of the door warden's absence to enter the great hall. He sighed and made his way towards the judgement seat.

"Forthred will find lodgings for you and your family," he said to the smith as he waited for the petitioners to sort themselves out. "But tell me, how did you become lame?"

"My father cut my hamstring when I was a boy in sacrifice to Wayland, that he might gain the knowledge to make a sword such as this."

"And did he?"

"No. But I did."

Edwin laughed. "The gods give gifts to whom they will. But I will give you many gifts for a sword such as the one you brought me."

As he moved towards the judgement seat, a thought occurred to Edwin and he stopped. He turned back to Wældhelm. "How did you know to find me here, at Bamburgh? I could have been at York, Yeavering, Goodmanham, Leeds – I have many houses."

"Wayland told me where to find you," said the smith.

Edwin felt upon his flesh the creep that told of being watched, unseen. He nodded and, leaving Wældhelm, took his place upon the judgement seat. The petitioners were arranging themselves into groups, but before the first came forward, Edwin motioned to Forthred. "Call my thegns, counsellors and priests here this evening. We must feast Rædwald's spirit, even though it lingers among the shadows, and I will have need of counsel."

The king watched Forthred lead the huge smith from the great hall. With Rædwald dead and his master smith seeking a new master in Edwin, the opportunity had come to take the overlordship of the kingdoms of this island. Hence the feast. Edwin had a proposal to make to his thegns and counsellors and priests.

# Chapter 3

"*Hwæt!*"

The scop's voice, modulated by many years of making itself heard over the tumult of a feast, rang out across the hubbub of sound. The conversations, stories, boasts and arguments died away as the men seated at the long tables that ran the length of the hall looked up from their neighbours to see the scop standing, waiting, in front of the royal table that ran crosswise across the top of the great hall.

The scop began to strum his lyre, the six strings ringing out through the space, and the few voices still speaking fell silent until the only sounds were the servants clearing up food, the dogs squabbling over scraps and the scop singing history.

Raising his voice into the half-chant, half-song of a story, the scop began to tell again the tale of the Battle of the River Idle, where Æthelfrith had fallen at the hands of Rædwald, and although all the men present knew the story well, yet they fell silent, listening with appreciation as the scop wound new rhymes and rhythms into his telling, mixing the normal poetic patterns with more complex bursts of sound that drew appreciative thumps upon the long tables. The description of how Æthelfrith the Twister fell and his drawn-out death brought gasps of sympathy and anger, for the scop brought to life the grief and revenge wrath of Rædwald and the disgrace of a great warrior such as Æthelfrith reduced to begging for his own death.

With a final series of rousing, rhythmical strums upon the lyre, the scop slammed the song to a close and stood smiling as the men in the hall shouted their appreciation and drummed the bone handles of their knives upon the wooden tables.

The king sat up straight upon the bench. To his right, Forthred propped his head upon his hand and closed his eyes. Edwin smiled and moved the cup, half full of sweet and very strong mead, out of reach. After all their years of exile, Forthred was enjoying the licence now to feast and drink without thought of care.

Waving the scop over, Edwin took a jewelled pin, albeit a small one, from his cloak and handed it to him.

"A good telling, Acca."

"You think so? What about the lines where I made 'Rædwald' rhyme with 'ball'? You don't think that pushed it too far towards half-rhymes and lost the balance between the assonance and the rhyming scheme?"

Edwin thought on the matter, while the scop looked on anxiously. "You may be right about that…"

"I knew it, I knew it," said Acca, hitting a fist into his palm in annoyance. "I knew it was wrong even as I sang the words. But what about the way I held the lyre back through Æthelfrith's death, playing single strings rather than strumming? I've heard scops sing it strong, beating out the rhythm, but I thought by making it quiet and plaintive it would bring out the pity of his ending. Do you think that worked?"

"I would say…" Edwin paused, Acca leaned forward apprehensively, and Forthred's head, propped upon his hand, slipped off and hit the table. "Yes," finished Edwin. He signalled a servant to bring cold water for Forthred. "Now, pass the lyre round and let the men sing while you rest your voice, Acca. You have done well. But when next the lyre is passed to you, sing a story of one of my victories."

"Oh, of course, lord; it's just that the Battle of the River Idle has such a pathetic conclusion, it never fails to draw tears and cheers."

"Whereas my victory over Lindsey simply ends with the king of Lindsey pledging allegiance to me. Nothing pathetic or heart-rending there."

"No, my lord."

Edwin leaned towards the scop. "Make something up then," he said. "Sing a song that will make the men cry and cheer and gasp about me."

"But these men, they were all with you when you defeated Lindsey," said the scop. "How can I change what happened?"

Dropping his voice further, Edwin explained. "You don't change anything, Acca. You tell it as it was, and the men will remember."

Acca smiled. "Of course, my lord. Our memories are in our songs."

Edwin nodded. "Precisely. Ensure my men remember well, Acca, and you will be well rewarded."

The scop bowed and withdrew, already trying out under his breath variations on the old poetic patterns.

Forthred, head lying upon the table, moaned in uneasy dream. Edwin pointed a servant carrying a bowl of water towards Forthred and moved out of the way. The servant poured the water over Forthred's spluttering, oath-uttering head, to roars of approval from the men sat at tables below.

While Forthred was still shaking his wet hair and glowering at the laughter raining down upon him from the men, Edwin leaned over and, placing his hand on his damp shoulder, said, "I want you awake and alert, Forthred."

"Can't take your drink, Forthred?" Swaying in front of the high table, a cup in each hand, one of the young men stared blearily up. "I challenge you – I will drink two cups for each one of yours!"

Forthred, who could sober up almost instantaneously when necessary, pushed himself to his feet, to the cheers of the hall.

"You'd need to, Bosa, to fill the empty space under your hair!"

The men cheered and Bosa, not yet too drunk to realize he had been beaten in a contest of wit, drew further cheers himself by draining, one after the other, the two cups he was holding and then staggering unsteadily but just about successfully back to his seat in the hall.

As the men settled down to the drinking and talking and singing that could linger long into the night, and the servants replaced torches and refilled cups, Edwin called his chief thegns and counsellors around him.

"Rædwald is dead. His son, his surviving son, is not the warrior

Rædwald was and he will need my support to keep his crown. The price of that support will be Eorpwald recognizing me as his overlord. The Mercians have no strong king, for Cearl, my father-in-law, is old now and few men make their way to his household. The West Saxons and the East Saxons may fight for lordship of the Saxons between themselves – we shall treat with whomsoever is triumphant. Of the kingdoms of the Britons we need take little account – our forefathers drove them from this land and they remain weak and divided, lesser men than us. That leaves Kent."

Edwin looked around his assembled men. These were the men he had campaigned with; a few had gone with him into exile and returned, after Æthelfrith's death, to reclaim their rightful place at the king's side. Others had served Æthelfrith once, but they served him now, and faithfully. With these men he had conquered the marsh-hidden kingdom of Lindsey, loading his warband upon shallow-bottomed boats and poling them across rivers and swamps until they came, unawares and unexpected, upon King Cædbæd and his meagre band of retainers. The king, choosing discretion, opted to sue for vassalage and Edwin had gladly accepted, taking as gift many slaves, an extraordinary amount of gold and silver, and more preserved eels than their noses could endure through a long, hot and weary journey home.

Guthlaf the warmaster spoke. "Kent is strong, but not as strong as us. However, should Kent make alliance with the East Angles, or the Saxons of West or East, it would match us."

Edwin looked around his counsellors. By their assents they said they agreed with the words of the warmaster.

"Although they are Britons, we should not forget Gwynedd either," said Forthred. "Their king, Cadwallon, is a bold warrior and he has put new fire into their cold hearts."

"No, I know Cadwallon of old," said Edwin. "We can forget him."

Forthred looked steadily at Edwin. "Are you sure, my lord?"

"Yes," said Edwin. "There is nothing to fear from Cadwallon. When I was at his father's court, he was ever the lesser between us. He will not rise against me."

"Very well," said Forthred. "Then that leaves Kent."

"Yes," said Edwin. He looked around his men. "It is time I took another wife."

# Chapter 4

"You know how I persuaded the queen that we should travel by land to her new kingdom, to learn more of this strange country, rather than travelling more swiftly by boat?" Paulinus – an Italian, a priest, a missionary and a stranger in a strange land – turned to his companion. James was a fellow Italian, a deacon and another shivering visitor to a place where it seemed summer never came. A red nose emerged from the cloak that James held over his head and shoulders in an attempt to deflect the wind blowing from the north, over the sheet silver meres that paced east alongside the North Road.

"Dess, I remember you explaining dhat to King Eadbald," said James in a voice remarkably clear of reproach, although stuffed full of catarrh.

"I think I may have made a mistake."

The wagon was stuck. That in itself was not so unusual, as the Great North Road had decayed in many places to stretches of rubble-strewn ruts, which the wagoners had to relay or haul past before the procession of vehicles, horses and men could get moving again. But this time the wagoners were standing around in a talking, head-scratching group that gave no indication of digging, laying or any other activity. Paulinus tried to see into the wagon ahead, where Queen Æthelburh travelled with her maids, but the rear flaps were closed against the wind. Of course, that was no guarantee that the queen was within the carriage – Æthelburh was as skilled on a horse as most men and just as likely to be riding alongside the bridal procession on her milk-white mare as jolting along in her wagon. Besides, she had told Paulinus during one of their camps, she found the odour of the plodding oxen that pulled the wagons too ripe – she preferred the warm smell of horseflesh. However, her horse was standing patiently by her wagon, so the queen was most likely within. This was proved a moment later when Paulinus saw her head rise up over the top of the wagon – Æthelburh was standing on the driver's bench.

"What is wrong?" she called out to the wagoners.

The group fractured and one of the wagoners came back to the queen's wagon. "There's a river ahead, my lady, and we are not sure if we can ford it."

"Send a man through it on horseback. If he can ford it, then so can we." As the wagoner scurried back towards the ford, the queen saw Paulinus watching her, and a smile flashed across her face. "You wanted to see more of my country, father," she said. "It seems that God has heard your prayer."

"No," said Paulinus, wagging his finger, "you must not take the Lord's name in vain – it is one of the great commandments. Surely I have taught you this?"

"Of course you have, father," the queen laughed, quite irrepressible in her good humour, and Paulinus reminded himself that she was little more than a girl still, although also a queen of some fifteen years. "Although you are not the only one to have taught me," she added, her eyes flashing with the mischief of a hinted secret. "But please, come and talk with me. I have heard enough gossip from my women as to what sort of man my husband will be."

Paulinus scrambled down from the wagon, while James wrapped his cloak more tightly around his body, seeking refuge from the wind.

"*In principio creavit Deus caelum et terram…*"

Slowing to a stop, Paulinus looked up in wonder as the opening words of the Bible flowed out into the cool, clear air, sung in the chanting mode that he remembered all too clearly from his childhood and youth in Italy, but had not hoped to hear in this barbarian land.

"*…terra autem erat inanis et vacua et tenebrae super faciem abyssi et spiritus Dei ferebatur super aquas…*"

The voice was high, clear and pure, and indubitably female. Paulinus stared in wonder at the queen as she looked into the distance, chanting in the Roman style.

"*...dixitque Deus fiat lux et facta est lux.*"

But as Æthelburh drew to the end of the third verse, and the first act of creation, her gaze dropped to the watching, slack-jawed priest, and laughter overcame her.

"H-how do you know...?" began Paulinus.

"Latin? My mother taught me." Æthelburh beamed down at the priest.

"No, no, I meant, how did you learn the Roman way of singing?"

Æthelburh laughed again. "Brother James has been teaching me, and what with this journey taking so long, I have had much time to practise, have I not, James?" The queen cast a sparkling glance at the deacon, who blushed to the roots of his tonsured hair. Paulinus looked at James, and the deacon blushed even redder. But Æthelburh saw his reproof.

"Don't scold Brother James, father, and don't worry that any occasion of scandal might arise from it, for we were at all times accompanied by my maids – who are learning the Roman way of singing too by the way, so that I might sing the Office with them. As we are going into a pagan land, we must needs allow them to hear the beauty of our faith, father, for it was the song of the monks in Canterbury, at St Peter's, that first pierced my soul when I was a child."

Brother James gave a quick, grateful smile to the queen, entirely missed by Paulinus, and withdrew into the safety of his hood. The priest, nonplussed, scratched his nose and searched for inspiration on the horizon. Which was why he was the first to see the glint and flicker of light striking polished metal.

"My lady, you're higher and your eyes are young and sharp. What do you see over there?"

The queen looked, then stood up, shading her eyes.

"Oslac!" she called and the thegn in charge of the men guarding the bridal party came trotting over on his skewbald pony. "There," she pointed. "I think we may be in trouble."

The time it had taken Oslac to reach her had brought the glints closer and now Paulinus could see what was sparking the light: men on horseback, the sun catching their armour, their helmets and most of all their upraised spears.

"How many?" Paulinus shouted to James, for the younger man had the sharpest eyes of anyone in the bridal party. Throwing back his hood, James stood and, lips moving silently, began counting. While he did so, Oslac screamed at the wagoners to draw the wagons close together, and called his men to form up in line, ready for battle.

Paulinus looked up at James. "Well?"

The deacon, his face suddenly drained of its blush, looked down. "Too many," he said.

Æthelburh looked down at Paulinus, and her face, which before had been so clear, was now grim. "Your curiosity may be about to cost us all our lives, father." Before an open-mouthed Paulinus could frame an answer, the queen had gathered her ladies into her wagon while the wagoners urged the labouring teams of oxen closer.

The priest watched the riders approach. Their horses were bigger than the ones he had seen employed before in Britain, and there was a strangeness to the warriors that he found hard to identify, although as they came closer he saw that rather than the blond and brown hair worn by most of the Angles and Saxons he had seen, these men were mostly dark, their white skins made all the paler by their black hair. They were now close enough for him to count too, but there was no need. A glance was enough to see the truth of what James had said: there were too many of them. This was no raiding party, but a full-scale warband out for plunder, conquest and slaves. Paulinus thought ruefully of the gifts Eadbald had laden upon them to ensure Edwin's support for his kingship. Such riches were the stuff of a war party's dreams. As for him and his brother deacon, there was little chance of survival at the hands of pagans – the best they could hope for was to be sold as slaves.

Brother James touched him on the arm.

"Today we will be with the Lord in paradise," he said simply.

"If we are, then our mission will have failed and the queen will be dead or in bondage. And I will have to answer for her death to God." Paulinus shivered with dread. And although he tried to pray, the words stuttered on his tongue and in his mouth, for he could not tear his eyes from the display of barbarian savagery he was witnessing. The advancing riders, trotting across the rough pastureland that lay west of the road, were coming towards them two abreast, and each man carried a spear in his right hand, tip afire in the slanting sunlight, while his shield was held on his left. These shields were different from those Paulinus had seen in this savage land, for the Angles and the Saxons and the men of Kent favoured round shields, painted in rude, flowing patterns, with a central protruding iron boss that could be used as a weapon in the heaving, sweating scrum of a shieldwall. But the riders had curved rectangular shields, more like the devices he knew from his homeland, and while they too were painted, the devices he saw were not all strange, for some seemed like rough representations of the Chi Rho, the first two letters of Christ superimposed upon each other, and others suggested attempts by the unlettered or the uncouth to write Greek letters, such as alpha and omega.

Æthelburh, looking from her wagon, saw the shields too and a sudden, swift surmise filled her.

"Pray!" she shouted to the two watching Italians, and when she saw that they could not understand the English word amid the hubbub, she shouted, "*Ora!*" before turning to her own women and leading them in chanting psalms.

Paulinus shook himself out of his trance.

"Pray, Brother James; pray as hard as you have ever prayed, that this day the red crown of martyrdom is not placed on our heads."

Brother James fell to his knees, and his voice, an incongruously beautiful baritone in the desperate circumstances, became the foundation upon which the higher voices of the women built towers of prayer, reaching up to the sky. The riders, rather than advancing upon the bridal party, abruptly began to peel apart, forming a line that now ran parallel to the road and, once all the riders were in line, the horsemen stopped and turned their beasts to face the wagons. The sun, riding low into the west, shadowed the riders' faces, but now it was clear just how gravely the bridal party was outmanned.

And there the riders waited.

Oslac strode out from the wagons into the neutral ground between the two groups.

From the riders, a single horseman walked his beast forward. Even to Paulinus's untutored eyes, it was clear this man was the leader of the riders, for he wore a helmet richly patterned in gold, with a scarlet crest riding over its crown in the manner of soldiers of the emperors of old, and his shield was patterned in gold too.

Oslac waited, his hand resting upon his sword hilt but not drawing it, his shield relaxed but ready by his side.

The horseman drew his animal to a halt some ten feet from Oslac. The two men kept silence, and from the watching parties the only sound was the chant of the psalms from among the wagons. Watching, Paulinus saw the horseman's eyes flick towards the wagons and there seemed to be surprise and recognition in his expression. But then the rider focused again on Oslac.

"Who are you to cross the ancestral lands of my people without my leave?" asked the rider. And although Paulinus understood the words, they were uttered with a strange, singing accent that he had never heard before.

"Who are you to stop us, sent by Eadbald, king of Kent?" demanded Oslac.

"You are a long way from Kent, friend. I have a mind to see what it is that you carry in those wagons."

"There will be fewer of you to see what we carry then."

"Fewer, perhaps, but enough I think." The rider gestured and his men walked their horses forward a few steps.

Oslac licked his lips. He was a thegn, a warrior, and he had lived with death through most of his life. He was not afraid of dying, but he feared breaking the oath he had sworn to deliver Æthelburh to her new husband. For none of the gods, be they the old gods of his forefathers or the new god of his king, looked kindly on oathbreakers. His best, his only, chance was to try to persuade this man not to attack.

"You may attack, you may even win, but to do so would earn the blood enmity not only of Kent, but of Edwin of Northumbria."

"You are going to Edwin?" The rider swung off his horse and advanced on Oslac. "Do you know what he is?"

"He is king of Northumbria, the most powerful lord in the land," said Oslac.

"He is an oathbreaker and a liar!" The man removed his helmet and Paulinus saw that his hair was black, as black as a raven's wing, but his skin was as white as the neck of a swan. "Anything you take to him I will take from you!"

"Would you take his wife?" The voice of Queen Æthelburh rang out, sweet and pure, and despite the protests of her maids Æthelburh stood up in her wagon so that all might see her.

The man stopped and stared at her.

"You are his wife?"

"His betrothed. Promised and affianced. Would you have me break my word, and my brother, King Eadbald, break his?" The sun, low in the west, lit the face of the queen, and the strands of hair that escaped from beneath her shawl to fly about her face in the wind shone gold in the light. Behind her back, visible only to her women, Æthelburh's hands twisted upon each other, but her face was serene.

"I would have you find a truer husband than Edwin."

"Who are you to traduce the name of my betrothed?"

"I am Cadwallon, king of Gwynedd, native son of this land and scourge of those who have taken it from me and my people!"

At his words, the queen's glance flicked again to the markings on the shields of the men of Gwynedd, and she looked over to Paulinus and James. There was a chance, a tiny chance, if she could appeal to a part of Cadwallon that he would not expect to be importuned by men from Kent.

"*Ora!*" she hissed.

Paulinus nodded to James, who was still upon his knees, and together they began to chant the psalms of the day.

Cadwallon stiffened as the sound carried across to him over the rough grass. He turned to stare at where the chant came from, and saw there the two men, one upon his knees and the other standing, hands upraised in prayer.

"What is this?" Cadwallon turned back to the queen and pointed at the priests.

"Surely you know," said Æthelburh, and with her hand hidden behind her back she gestured for her women to join the prayer.

Cadwallon stared at the priests, wide mouthed, and then jerked visibly when the women's voices joined the chant, rising above the Italians and inflecting it with the accents of a land at the edge of the world.

Oslac, seeing the man's distraction, began to inch his sword from its sheath.

The queen herself joined the prayer, chanting the ancient words of comfort and protection.

> *"De profundis clamavi ad te Domine*
> *Domine exaudi vocem meam fiant aures tuae*
> *intendentes in vocem deprecationis meae…"*

And over the rough green pastureland and the silver meres, up and down the rutted tracks of the Great North Road, spreading into the great silence of an empty land, the chant flowed, as strange and new as a baby's first cry and yet as familiar as the return of spring.

Listening, tears ran down Cadwallon's face, and as the psalm reached its end he raised his own strong voice in unison.

> *"Quia apud Dominum misericordia et copiosa apud*
> *eum redemptio.*
> *Et ipse redimet Israel ex omnibus iniquitatibus eius."*

The chant fell back into the great silence, a silence made more profound by the intake of breath, in wonder and awe, of all the men listening.

Cadwallon stepped closer to the queen, out of reach of Oslac. Conscious of Cadwallon's watching men, Oslac took his hand away from his sword, but he began to manoeuvre himself closer to the king of Gwynedd.

"You are Christian?" Cadwallon asked in Latin, looking up at Æthelburh as she stood upon the wagon, her robes and headscarf brilliant blue in the sunlight.

"Yes," said the queen in the same language, striving to keep her voice from quavering in fear and desperate hope. "I am Christian."

"But the Angles and Saxons are pagans. Whence comes your faith?"

"From God," said Æthelburh. "But I learned the tidings of happiness from my mother. She is of the Franks."

"Then why go you, a Christian woman, into the hands of pagans and idolaters?"

"My brother, King Eadbald of Kent, had Edwin agree as part of the marriage settlement that I and my people should be able to practise our religion without hindrance. Besides," and here Æthelburh bent slightly towards Cadwallon and lowered her voice as if sharing a confidence, "I take with me these Christian priests, who have come to us all the way from Rome, in the hope and prayer that my new husband may come to know the truth and abandon the worship of stones and wood and vain things."

"No!" Cadwallon stepped towards her, so taking Æthelburh by surprise that she all but flinched. "No, you must not take these people the truth! The Lord says that we are not to cast pearls before swine. These people are pigs, and worse than pigs, the despoilers of this land, murderers, thieves, rapists, who came as guests and stole everything from their hosts. Give them the gift of truth? Never! Let them sup their fill of the damnation that is their due; let them die and go down to hell where the worm feeds and the fire burns, and they shall know something of the suffering my people, the people of this land, have endured at their hands. Let them die true death and not know hope. They are not worthy of the hope you bring."

As he spoke, Cadwallon shifted back and forth in his agitation, not noticing the slow, stealthy approach of Oslac. Nor did the queen see Oslac come closer, so compelling was the king of Gwynedd in his rage.

For his part, Oslac had understood little of what passed between Cadwallon and Æthelburh, for much of it had been in Latin. He knew only that he was trusted to bring his queen safely to her new husband, and to that end he had given his oath to Eadbald, his lord.

With all attention still upon the king, Oslac moved within range. Cadwallon stared up at the queen, who shook her head before his fury, but then – too late – she saw what Oslac intended. In one single fluid motion the thegn drew his sword and thrust, aiming for the small of Cadwallon's back, where a blade will kill most surely although not most quickly.

The king of Gwynedd would have died there, beside the North Road on the marches of the kingdom of Lindsey, if Oslac's foot had not slipped upon the wet grass, pitching him forwards and sending his thrust off centre, and if Cadwallon himself, reacting to the alarm he saw on Æthelburh's face, had not begun to turn, presenting a narrower target than the full expanse of his back. As it was, the blade slid along his flank, scoring the chain mail into his flesh but not piercing it, and Oslac, stumbling, heard the iron hiss of a knife drawn as he fell forwards, trying to pull his sword back for another blow. But he was wide open now, unprotected on his flank, and Cadwallon's knife slid into his neck, and he fell. And as Oslac lay upon the ground, his sight darkening, he saw Cadwallon put his sword to the queen's breast and he knew, with his last thought, that he had failed in his oath and no god would accept him into his hall.

"Stop!" Cadwallon raised his voice in a mighty shout, bringing the sudden pouring of men forwards to a sudden halt. His sword did not waver from where he held it, the point steady before the heart of the queen. From behind Æthelburh there came the frightened whispers of her maids, but everyone else on the field, a field that teetered on the brink of becoming a battlefield, was silent, watchful, still. The men of Kent, charged with bringing their queen to her new husband, stood ready to attack. The warriors of Gwynedd, ready to protect their king, were poised to charge. And poised between them, suspended upon a thread, was the life of the queen.

"I did not want Oslac to attack…" began Æthelburh, but Cadwallon pushed the point of his sword against her flesh, so that she felt it prick through the cloth and touch her skin, and she fell silent.

"I should have known better than to hear one of your people – ever you lie, when you seem most fair. You are no Christian! No Christian would enter into parlay with an enemy and then try to stab him in the back…"

"I am a Christian, baptized," said Æthelburh, clinging to the one commonality between her and the man poised to kill her.

"Then why did you have your man try to kill me?"

"It was not at my command that he did so."

"If not yours, whose?"

"I – I do not know. P-perhaps a devil put the intention into his heart."

"It was the devil's work, but done at your bidding, queen, as Adam sinned through Eve."

"No, no, I had no part of it. He acted on his own."

"A warrior act without orders from his lord? I think not."

"Oslac was a free man, a thegn charged with bringing me safely to my new husband. He took an oath to protect me."

Cadwallon glanced at the dead man lying on the ground, his glassy eyes staring up at them as if he was following their exchange from the shadows.

"He failed." Looking back to Æthelburh, Cadwallon smiled. "And he has left in my hands the betrothed of my enemy. The Lord God avenges himself upon oathbreakers, and this day he is avenged."

Æthelburh fell silent. Although the queen's face was calm, there was no concealing her tension from a man schooled by combat to read physical language.

"It would be a sweet revenge, a most meet revenge, if I should deny Edwin his beautiful bride. Or maybe I should send him his bride in such a condition that he will not have her?"

A tremble began to spread through Æthelburh's body, starting out from her centre until her hands and fingers shook and she had to take hold of her right arm with her left hand to prevent herself losing control and being disgraced in front of her enemy. For a moment, she closed her eyes and began to pray, the words moving her lips although no sound emerged from her mouth.

"Wait. What are you saying? Witch, do not try to place a spell upon me!"

Startled, Æthelburh opened her eyes. "I was praying," she said.

At her words, Cadwallon stepped back, and some of the fury drained from his eyes. "You were praying," he said. "You are in truth a Christian." He shook his head as if to clear the blood rage, and when he looked at the queen again his eyes were clearer. He pointed to where Oslac lay.

"Since he is dead, you must have charge of your people. Very well, I give to you this choice: we can fight, in which case your husband will never know his wife, and your men and your servants will die here. Or I will take the treasure and the gifts you are taking to that dog of a husband, but I will let you live to know your husband, and I will take your people as slaves. What say you?"

"Why would you let me live, to serve my husband and to give him further reason to hate you?" Æthelburh asked.

"Because I want him to hate me! Because I want Edwin to know that I had his betrothed at my mercy, and spared her. Because I want you to ask him why he betrayed the people of Gwynedd, people who had sheltered him in his exile. Because I would not kill you and have your blood stain my soul when I come before the great and terrible judge." Cadwallon shook his head. "It is stained enough already, my lady, and though I have many monks on the Holy Island of my country praying for me day and night, I fear for my soul. So I will spare you and take only what is mine, if you will tell your men to stand aside."

Æthelburh looked at the surrounding warriors. Cadwallon's men outnumbered her own men by two to one. They were poised, drawn up in battle line, ready to advance, and while her own men were ready too, they were hampered by the wagons and carts that they had not had time to adequately draw together. There was little chance of victory. But if Cadwallon chose to fight, he would lose many men as well, and that gave her hope. For sure his warband was on its way elsewhere and it could not continue if half its members lay dead or injured upon this field.

"I will not have my people taken as slaves," said Æthelburh.

Cadwallon shook his head. "Do not force my hand, lady. I have said I will spare you – that is enough."

"I cannot let you take them."

"Then you will all die."

Æthelburh nodded. She took a deep breath. "Very well. Begin with me." And she stepped forward so that the point of Cadwallon's sword touched her breast.

"No!"

Paulinus, who had been struggling to understand what was being said in the uncouth tongue of these islands, looked around, startled, to see James off his knees and running towards the queen. He hurried after him, shaking off a restraining hand and warning voices telling him to stand still.

Cadwallon saw James running towards him and turned his sword to meet him. From his waiting men there came a warning growl, but Cadwallon waved his hand for them to hold their position, and he raised his sword so that it pointed at James's heart. The deacon came to a stop.

"Me...be slave," James said in faltering English. "No kill queen."

Cadwallon replied in fluent Latin. "Were you the one chanting the psalm?"

"Yes," said James.

"We both were," added Paulinus, joining him.

"You are priests?"

Paulinus looked down ruefully at his travel-stained clothing. Outside the sacrifice of Mass, it was difficult to tell that he was not as other men.

"Yes," he said.

"I'm a deacon," added James.

"You go among thieves and oathbreakers." Cadwallon lowered his sword. "But for your sake, and for the sake of the faith we share, I will let you go and I will take no slaves though you offer yourself in ransom for these others. They are pagans, brother, and not worthy of you." He turned back to Æthelburh. "Your bravery and beauty is beyond all that the dog Edwin deserves. I would urge you to return to your father's land and leave the dog to lick up his vomit, but I know you to be too honourable to abjure your vows. Very well, go to him, but tell Edwin he will die at my hands."

Æthelburh looked steadily into the eyes of Cadwallon. "Why do you hate my husband so?"

"Why do I hate Edwin? Ha, why do I despise the deceiver, the treacherous, the snake nurtured at our breast who turns to bite us? Do you not know that he sought shelter with my father during his exile, when all hands were turned against him, and my father willingly took him into our family and adopted him as a foster son alongside me. Edwin was the elder, and I admired him, lady; I loved him as a brother in blood as well as by oath, and he remained with us for long years. Never did he receive anything but kindness from my people, though he came from an enemy race and his people did mine great hurt in that time. Yet he shared our table, fought alongside us, sang with us, and all along he nurtured behind his fair-seeming face the intentions of the devil."

"But what did he do to you?"

"He broke his oath, lady, and worse." Cadwallon stared at the queen for a long time as if weighing up what more he should say. Then moving closer he said, "This is for your ears alone. When he was a guest in my father's house, Edwin raped my sister and got her with child."

Æthelburh blanched. "I – I do not know what to say."

"Ask your husband," said Cadwallon.

"I beg your pardon?"

"Ask your husband," said Cadwallon. "Before you join him in the marriage bed, ask him what he did to Briant, daughter of Cadfan and sister to Cadwallon. Ask him!"

"Yes," said Æthelburh, "Yes, I will ask him."

"Good. Then at least you may know what manner of man you marry and mayhap there will still be time for you to return to your brother. Now I must take your treasure." Cadwallon waved towards the waiting, watching men. "Tell them to stand back, to keep their hands from their swords and their mouths closed, and we might end this day with no more blood shed than this fool's." Cadwallon indicated Oslac's corpse.

"May we bury him?" asked Æthelburh.

"Do whatever you want with him. Just stand your men down."

Æthelburh called some of her retainers to her, and they dragged Oslac's body to the east side of the road, while the rest of the men, and her women, gathered in a worried, watching body as the raiding men of Gwynedd scoured the wagons and carts, turning out jars, opening pots, unrolling cloth; stripping the bridal party of anything of value as efficiently as a swarm of rats, but rather less tidily.

While Cadwallon's men continued to sack the wagons and carts, Æthelburh ordered her retainers to dig a grave for Oslac.

"Will you bury him, father?" she asked Paulinus.

"Was he a Christian?" The Italian looked, rather dubiously, at the dead man.

"He was of my brother's people, the men of Kent, and by my brother's and our father's choice they are a Christian people. Bury him so."

"Very well, my lady." Paulinus paused. "My lady?"

"Yes?"

"I sinned by asking that we come this way, by land, so that I could learn more of this strange country. This man paid for my curiosity with his life."

Æthelburh looked bleakly at him and her face suddenly looked much older than her years. "He did."

"I am sorry and I will do penance for my sin."

"Start your penance by sending his soul to God, father. Oslac died trying to protect me."

So by the side of the road, on the marches of the kingdom of Lindsey, as the men of Gwynedd laughed and joked over their spoils and the men of Kent watched in glowering silence, the words of requiem flowed outwards, and the first man to receive a Christian burial north of the Wash and east of the Pennines since the coming of the Anglo-Saxons was received into the earth.

# Chapter 5

"You did what?"

Edwin rose from his throne – the intricately carved and painted wooden throne that his men carried from one royal demesne to another on the never-ending royal circuit around the kingdom – and advanced on Paulinus. The priest, although as tall as the king, felt his soul quail before the grim man approaching him, his arms wrapped in glistening torcs of gold, a wolf pelt wrapped about his neck with shoulder clasps of blood-red garnets, and belt and buckles of rich if savage workmanship. A thought flickered through Paulinus's mind, of Pope Leo I facing down Attila the Hun and, armed only with faith, forcing the barbarian chief to withdraw from Italy.

Edwin stopped in front of the priest. "What were you thinking?"

"I-I wanted to learn something of this strange land," Paulinus stuttered.

"Your curiosity cost me dear. King Eadbald sent many, many gifts with his sister, and they are taken."

"Yes, yes, I am sorry. At least your bride is here."

Edwin paused in his questioning. "Yes." He shook his head and turned his back on the priest. "I had thought to learn more from you of this new belief that has come to us from over the sea." He gestured to the fire pit in the centre of the hall and a man, a strange creature draped in a raven-feather cloak, rose from where he squatted and came to the king's side. "This is Coifi, my priest, my caster of runes and traveller to the high halls of the gods. If you had been worthy, I would have asked you to face him, to place your magic against his that I might see which belief is the stronger. But you had not even the wit to bring me my queen over the sea; I do not put men up against boys."

Coifi shook his bone rattle before the priest's face; it made a noise like dice tumbling in a cup. Paulinus did not flinch, but he could not stop a flicker of alarm passing over his face, nor the look of quick triumph that flashed over Coifi's, and he cursed himself for his weakness.

"Go to the queen," Edwin said, "if she still cleaves to you who brought her into such peril, and tell her that her husband will tolerate no further delay. We marry today, or she returns to her brother. Tell her she has until the sun sets to decide."

Paulinus made to speak, but there was nothing he could say for the moment. He bowed and withdrew, pausing at the door of the hall to look curiously at the man by the king's side, whispering to him. He had read Tacitus's description of the religion of the German tribes in the days of the emperors, and these people were descendants of those tribes.

For his part, Coifi stared as frankly at the departing Italian, noting how his skin was bark brown rather than the clay white of his people or the silver-birch pale of the Britons, and the tall and stately way in which he walked, very different from the scuttling gait of the priests of the gods in this land. But then Coifi had heard tell that the priests of this new god did not look for the falling out of patterns in the casting of bones or the way blood, spilled in sacrifice, might pull aside for an instant the veil of the future and allow the devotees of the gods to prophesy victory or defeat, and thus win favour and riches with kings. Not needing to keep constant watch for what wyrd might be saying, no wonder the stranger walked in such a calm manner. Coifi, catching the fall of a burning log in the fire pit from the corner of his eye and spinning upon it, wished he could. He stared into the embers, looking for something there, and wishing that this time the gods would tell him clearly the answers to his king's questions. For the king had need of counsel, and although Coifi was by no means his only counsellor, he knew that to the man who gave the king the best advice great gifts would be given: rich presents, and honour, and wealth…

"Coifi?"

Caught up in his priestly reverie and the attempt to read the fall of logs in the fire pit, the priest had forgotten that he was talking to the king. He jerked, shook himself and pulled upright.

"Yes?"

Edwin laughed. "I thought you could prophesy. Couldn't you tell I wanted to speak to you?"

"I – there was something in the fire."

The king's eyes narrowed. "What?"

"I – I don't know," Coifi admitted. "It was almost clear. I could almost see, when you called."

"So the fault was mine?"

"Yes – no! No, of course not, lord." Coifi made a shambling obeisance and snatched a glance at the watching priest. Paulinus, still smarting from his own encounter with Edwin, could not help sharing a rueful smile with the man before hurrying from the hall on his own task.

"Good, I am glad. If the fault was mine, then no doubt the gods would look unfavourably upon me as I decide what to do about Cadwallon. As it is, I require you to cast the runes and read the auguries on him, that I might better know the workings of wyrd, and to bring me the answers this evening, when I meet my counsellors."

"Yes, my lord, I will unpick the weavings of wyrd for you and lay them at your feet."

Edwin looked at Coifi. "Yes, you do that."

\*

"My lady, if you will not tell me why you are reluctant to marry the king, I cannot help you." Paulinus looked around at the gathered women. "Would it be better if we were to speak in private?"

Æthelburh shook her head, although her eyes sparked with amusement. "On the day of my wedding, I do not think it would be a good idea for me to be alone with a man, even one who is a priest, father."

"Ah. Of course. Quite right. Yes." Paulinus blushed, his blush deepening when he saw the queen smile at his reaction.

"As to my hesitation, do not worry, father. I know my duty and I will marry. Besides, for such an old man, Edwin is... quite handsome, don't you think?"

Paulinus blushed again. He knew that Æthelburh enjoyed teasing him, but he was as incapable of sparing his blushes as he was of losing his accent.

"Father?"

"Pardon? Oh, yes, handsome. Yes. No. I don't know."

"My maids tell me he is forty! Can he really be that old?"

"Forty. Yes, he is forty. That is right. Quite old."

"But if he is that old, will he be able to... you know?" The young queen looked innocently at the old priest, who blushed puce, his blush burning all the hotter as he heard the queen's women giggling among themselves.

"I-I am sure he will do his duty," said Paulinus.

Æthelburh stiffened and the maids fell silent. "Do you think I will be a 'duty' for him?"

"No, no," said Paulinus, wondering why the Lord, in the shape of Bishop Justus, had seen fit to appoint him as spiritual guide to a young woman as high spirited as the queen. "No man could find you a 'duty', my lady."

"No man?" asked the queen, staring at him innocently again.

Under his breath, Paulinus cursed himself as he felt his face burn with embarrassment once more. He had to change the topic of conversation before he was rendered incapable of speech.

"You have not told me the reason for your reluctance to marry the king."

The half-smile disappeared from Æthelburh's lips. "I – I cannot speak of this, father." She looked around the room and the maids all busied themselves in their sewing and preparations, striving to give the appearance of a complete lack of interest.

Paulinus nodded. "Maybe... maybe if we walked and saw the preparations for your wedding feast, that would allow your maids to continue their work in peace?"

"Yes, yes, father." Æthelburh gave swift instructions on what she expected done to her dress by the time she returned, then accompanied the priest towards the great hall. But before they arrived she grasped Paulinus's arm.

"Is he there?" she asked.

"I will go to see," said the priest. The queen waited, and when he turned back to signal the all clear he saw that she was jiggling from one foot to another like a nervous child.

The two of them walked up and down the hall, inspecting the long tables, the rich hangings upon the walls, the fresh-cut straw strewn upon the floor. The servants and slaves were busy about their work, sometimes all but bumping into the queen or the priest in their rush.

"Well, child, can you speak now?" asked Paulinus.

Æthelburh shook her head. "I promised," she said. "But… I gave no promise on taking advice. Father, if someone told you something dreadful about somebody else, would you believe them?"

"It would depend on who told me, and upon the person whom they were telling me about."

"But if you knew little of either?"

"Then I would not make up my mind until I knew more."

Æthelburh nodded to herself. "Yes. Yes, thank you, father." She looked up, her indecision now gone, and smiled. "I must make myself ready for my husband," she said.

# Chapter 6

The wedding feast was sumptuous, made more so to undo the disgrace of there being no gifts that Kent had to give to Northumbria, beyond the bride herself. But the assembled thegns, seeing the girl standing beside the tall, grim figure of their lord, agreed that that gift was great indeed. For his part, Edwin smiled briefly when the queen's veil was drawn aside and he looked upon her face, but apart from that he barely looked at her. Throughout the feast the king had a distracted and distant air, as if his thoughts and heart were very far away. As for the queen, with her head covered and for much of the feast her face veiled, it was well nigh impossible for an observer to tell how she viewed her nuptials.

The food was lavish, with the centrepiece, placed upon the king's table, being roasted cranes that had first been plucked and skinned, and then, after cooking, refeathered to appear like living birds for the feast. The food renders of many royal demesnes had been called upon to fill the bellies of the king's guests – his thegns, his warband, his bards and priests – and despite their great numbers, they all ate and drank so well that the king's cooks had barely any work to do until lunch the next day.

The queen, however, ate sparingly and the king glowered down the hall at the assembly, drinking far more than he ate. But Edwin was one of those men on whom drink had little effect, try how he might, and to take his thoughts from the humiliations Cadwallon had heaped upon him, he slapped his hand down upon the table.

"Acca! Give us a song."

The scop sprang up from where he had been sitting. In preparation for the king's call, he had been avoiding the rich, fatty food, for it sat upon his liver and impaired his voice, but drinking liberally of the rare, rich red wine that had been brought from the land of the

Franks for the feast, for its velvet touch soothed the throat and made it easier to sing.

Taking his lyre, Acca turned a practised eye upon the rowdy assemblage, with the tables still thick with food and the drinking horns being drained in contests and companionship, and decided against anything too long or too sad. The elegies, the laments, the tales of battles lost in magnificent defeat when thegns sold lives dearly around their fallen lord, were for late in the evening, when drink made men maudlin. Now it was time for something rousing – he glanced at the newly wed couple – something rude.

Acca strummed the lyre, stamping his foot in accompaniment.

"*Hwæt!*" he called. The hall didn't exactly grow silent, but the noise, the talking, boasting and arguing, lulled, and for this early in the feast it was as much as he could hope for.

"Riddle me this!" This call drew an increasing circle of silence around the scop. There was nothing the king's retainers loved more than to argue and discuss and chew over a good new riddle. And Acca had a new riddle, perfect for a wedding feast, to tease them with tonight.

"I'm a strange creature, for I satisfy women, a service to the neighbours! No one suffers at my hands except for my slayer. I grow very tall, erect in a bed," and here Acca glanced coyly in the direction of the newly weds, to the accompaniment of raucous cheers from the men in the hall.

"I'm hairy underneath." Laughter erupted, and Acca strummed the lyre at double time, milking the merriment. "From time to time a good-looking girl, the doughty daughter of some churl, dares to hold me, grips my russet skin, robs me of my head and puts me in the pantry!"

Catcalls rang out and Acca, with his back to the high table as he played with his audience, did not see the blush deepening to crimson upon the queen's face, nor the darkening mien of his king.

"At once that girl with plaited hair who has confined me remembers our meeting and her eye moistens."

"Enough!"

Acca, disorientated, spun around. He had reached the climax of the riddle and the audience was baying for the answer. He had been ready to tease and taunt them for as long as they could bear, when the shout, like a whip, cracked over his shoulder. Edwin stood glowering at the high table, his face pale with anger, and his queen sat blushing furiously beside him.

The laughter and crude jokes that had filled the hall a moment before were abruptly cut off. Acca gulped, his glance skittering from Edwin to Æthelburh and back again, and he gabbled.

"It was an onion, lord, an onion. I meant no offence."

Edwin made to speak, then stopped. The riddle's answer was being passed in whispers around the hall, accompanied by suppressed guffaws and occasional groans.

"An onion?" asked Edwin, caught up, despite himself, in the solution.

"Yes, yes," said Acca. "Onions grow tall in a vegetable bed, with their hairy roots beneath, and they make their killer cry. Just an onion, lord."

"I see, I see." Edwin slowly sat down, and Acca felt the life draining out of his legs as relief overwhelmed him. "Carry on," said Edwin. "Give us a story now."

"My lord." Acca felt the room spinning around him. The wine was more potent than he had realized, and with the shock he had just received, he knew he needed some time to recover. "My lord, may I, may…" Acca felt his gorge rising and, clutching his hand over his mouth, he ran pell mell from the hall, accompanied by a round of good-natured jeers.

Edwin looked around the hall.

"Is there anyone else here who can give us a tale? A new story, one that we have not heard before."

The thegns and warriors looked to their neighbours, but none stood up. They all knew the old stories, most of them by heart, although Acca always managed to introduce some fresh element to each telling. But a new story? None of them had any to tell.

"No?" Edwin looked over to the table down one side of the

hall. "Men of Kent, have you no tales to tell us from your land? Something to divert our attention."

At the invitation, the men who had accompanied the queen north began to whisper among themselves, seeking to nominate a storyteller. But before they could do so a figure slowly rose, and all eyes went to him.

"I have a story to tell," said Paulinus.

The king looked around the hall, but there were no other volunteers. New stories were rare in the hall, and the thegns and warriors all looked curiously at the stranger to see what story he brought. Even the servants and slaves, bustling around the feast, forbore eavesdropping on conversations to hear what Paulinus had to say.

"Very well. Tell us a story," said Edwin.

Paulinus licked his lips and looked nervously around the hall. Although he was used to saying Mass, and preaching, this was different. But then he saw that the queen was looking at him, and she smiled and nodded, and the priest was encouraged.

"There was once a wedding feast, very like this one, but it happened far away in a land where the sun is so hot it burns the skin of the people dark. But something terrible happened at that wedding, which of course would never happen here: they ran out of wine!" Paulinus paused and looked around the hall. All attention was fixed on him. They had never heard anything like this before.

"One of the guests at the wedding was a woman named Mary, and when she realized that the hosts had run out of wine, what do you think she did? Did she denounce the groom and his family as misers and hoarders? Did she leave, vowing never to come back?" Paulinus swivelled around, including everyone in the story. The hall had grown still and all but silent. Even the servants and slaves were listening.

"No! This woman, Mary, went to her son and told him, 'They have no wine.' Now her son, Jesus, was no ordinary man, but nobody apart from his mother knew that yet. It was a secret." Paulinus whispered the word, but the hall had become so quiet that everyone heard him.

"So Jesus told her, 'Woman, what has this to do with me? My hour has not yet come.' But Mary, she knew her son, and she went to the servants and said to them, 'Do whatever he tells you.' Now, the people in this part of the world kept huge stone jars for filling with water, jars so big I could empty all the cups here in the hall into one jar and it still would not be full. There were six of those jars nearby, six of them mind, and Jesus told the servants, 'Fill the jars with water.'" Paulinus spotted one of the slaves quietly refilling a cup, and pointed. "A servant like him. So, of course, the servants filled up the six stone jars, though they must have been wondering why they were being asked to fill jars up with water when the wedding had run out of wine. When the servants had filled the jars right up to the brim, Jesus told them to fill a cup and to take it to the master of the banquet. The master of the banquet was a worried man. He had run out of wine. The guests were calling for more to drink and he had nothing left with which to fill their cups. What would you do if that happened here?"

"Cut off the steward's head!"

"Feed him to the dogs."

"Feed him to the Britons!" This last retort drew laughter from around the hall, and taking advantage of it Paulinus held up his hand and waited until silence returned.

"The servant took a cup filled with water from the jar to the master of the banquet, who was thinking about running away at this point, and gave him to drink. Now, the master of the banquet did not know where the drink had come from, so he tasted it and it was wine." Paulinus paused and looked around the hall. All faces were turned towards him.

"The water, ordinary plain water, had been turned into wine. And not just any wine. No. The master of the banquet, thinking that this new wine must be from some secret store the bridegroom had, drew the bridegroom aside and whispered to him, 'Everyone serves the best wine first, and then brings out the cheap wine when the guests have had too much to drink, but you have saved the best wine until last.'" Paulinus straightened up. He looked around the hall and heard the silence and the soft drawing in of air. The silence continued. And continued.

"Well? What happened then?" Coifi was standing at the high table, his hands on the wood, leaning towards the silent priest with eyes as agog as a child hearing the tales of his ancestors for the first time.

"Yes, what happens?"

"Tell us!"

Paulinus licked his lips, his mind a sudden blank. There wasn't anything more to the story, was there? But then the next lines of Scripture came back to him and he knew what to say.

"That was just the first of the signs that my Lord Jesus did; there were many more wonders that he performed, wonders more marvellous than anything you have heard, and I will, if the king permits, tell you of these wonders in the days and weeks and months after the wonderful wedding we are here celebrating." Paulinus picked up his cup from the table and raised it to the king and queen. "You have saved the best wine for last, my lord," he said, whereupon he drained the cup and, as he had seen others do in this barbarous land, returned it upside down to the table and resumed his place at table, to the cheers of the men of Kent and table thumping from the Northumbrians.

At his words, Æthelburh blushed. Paulinus could not help feeling a small thrill of justification at the sight, after the mortifications the queen had inflicted upon him earlier. She dipped her gaze before stealing a glance at her husband. But while the rest of the hall cheered Paulinus's words, Edwin's face was distant and withdrawn, pale with memory, and just as suddenly the blush left Æthelburh's face.

"Did I miss something?" Acca, restored, returned and ready, looked around questioningly at the roaring crowd of men in the hall. Only Coifi did not cheer, but sat darkly beneath his raven-feather cloak, a spectre at the feast. His lips moved silently, and beneath the table, under the noise of the hall, a bone rattle clacked.

The king waved Acca to him. "The priest told us a new story, Acca. Now tell us one of the old tales. I have the matter of Cadwallon to discuss and settle with my counsellors."

While Acca took his place in the centre of the hall, Paulinus returned to the table given over to the men of Kent. James greeted him there with a broad smile and proffered a cup of wine, which Paulinus gladly took. Spreading the gospel was, he decided as he drained the cup and held it out for a refill, thirsty work.

James nodded surreptitiously towards the high table. "The feathery one does not seem happy with your words. Do not turn around, but when you can, look. He is speaking quiet words under his breath, laying a curse on you, perhaps."

Naturally, Paulinus turned around. He saw Coifi staring at him through hooded eyes, lips moving and arm quivering, and, slowly and deliberately, Paulinus cast a blessing over him, his own hand with finger outstretched moving to zenith, nadir, west then east as he inscribed the figure of the cross between them and over the pagan. At the gesture, Coifi blanched and the hands that were hidden beneath the table rose up and moved in counter motion, lips muttering a charm.

Edwin's fist came crashing down on the table.

"Stop!"

The hall, which had been settling into a new tale from Acca, careered into silence. The king glared at the priests of both old religion and new.

"I will not have magic done in this hall."

Coifi pointed his bone rattle at Paulinus. "He started it, my lord."

Paulinus, a picture of outraged innocence, rose to his feet, stuttering his denial.

"I care not who started what. That is enough. Enough."

Paulinus sat down slowly, conversation resumed and Acca restarted his story.

Edwin turned to Coifi. "I have a task for you: read the signs and find what wyrd holds for Cadwallon of Gwynedd – will the gods aid me against him?"

The priest bobbed an answer, his eyes skittering around the hall for the signs that might fall now, anywhere, from anything or anyone, and scurried to the fire pit where he squatted, swaying slightly, his face lit by the flames.

Æthelburh watched him go, then turned to her new husband.

"I know I am young, and you are a great king and wise, but may I ask of you a question?"

Edwin, surprised, looked at his wife, then nodded. "You may."

"I thought you commanded that no magic be done in this hall?"

"I did."

"But isn't he" – she pointed to where Coifi squatted, shaking himself and passing his bone rattle over the flames – "doing magic in this hall?"

The king made to answer, then stopped. He looked at Coifi, who chose that moment to rise up like a raven, with outstretched arms before the fire, then back to Æthelburh, who was staring at him with all the wide-eyed innocence of her few years.

"As you said, you are very young."

Æthelburh nodded. "Yes, very."

"There are some things you will only understand when you are older."

"I am sure."

"Yes."

"How much older?"

Edwin chewed his upper lip. "It is not a matter of time, but understanding."

Æthelburh inclined her head. "You will help me understand, my lord?"

"Of course. Yes." Edwin gestured to two young men to come over. "You must meet my sons."

Æthelburh's face paled. She looked up at the two young men who came to stand in front of the king and his new, young queen, and saw them look down at her with guarded, unfriendly eyes.

"Osfrith." Edwin indicated the taller and older of the pair. "And Eadfrith. My sons with my first wife."

The princes made the courtesy, but in such a way that it was impossible to tell whether it was directed to their father or his bride.

"They were hunting when I met your brother Eadbald and arranged the marriage contract."

Æthelburh smiled weakly at the two young men. They were both, she judged, older than her. The princes gazed down at her without expression.

"Forthred." The king called his friend and chief counsellor over from the end of the table to which his relatively lowly birth consigned him. Then he turned to Æthelburh. She was, he saw, looking suddenly pale and ill.

"Are you not well? Do you wish to go without and take the air?" he asked.

"N-no. I will be all right." Æthelburh managed a weak smile, but her mind was churning. Had her brother known that Edwin already had two grown sons from a previous wife? He must have known – the births and deaths of the sons of kings were a subject of greater interest in the royal households than even the outcomes of battles.

"I would ask my sons to tell you something of our ways now, but I have need of them and their counsel. You could... listen to Acca's tale." Edwin waved his hand towards the scop, who was in full flow, holding all the hall and most of the high table in thrall. "We have much to decide."

"May I listen?"

Edwin looked at his wife with some surprise. "We speak of war. This is not women's work."

"Of course not. But it is the task of a queen. In Kent, my mother always joined in the councils before King Æthelbert, for that was the custom among the Franks from whom she came to marry my father."

Edwin ran his fingers through his beard. "You say it is the custom of the Franks?"

"Yes, my lord." Æthelburh primly lowered her eyes as she answered.

Edwin turned to his sons. "What say you?"

Osfrith shook his head. "Our mother never took part in war councils." He did not look at Æthelburh as he replied. The younger brother, Eadfrith, for his part gazed down at her with frank interest and, Æthelburh thought, some sympathy.

Edwin nodded. "True, true. But she was Mercian, and times change. The Franks are powerful and rich, and they claim the inheritance of the emperors of old." Edwin turned back to his young wife. "Yes. We will follow this new way. Join with us, listen. After all," and here he turned back to his sons, "she has seen and talked with our enemy most recently. Let us hear what she has to say."

Edwin gestured his men to gather and waved Coifi away from the fire. However, the priest, lost amid the flames, took a while to realize he was being summoned. It took a thump on his shoulder and a thumb jerked towards the waiting king from a grinning warrior to jerk Coifi from his reverie and send him scampering through the mead hall.

The king, still standing, looked down at the approaching priest. "From my difficulty in attracting your attention, I take it you have seen the paths of wyrd?"

Coifi made no answer with his mouth, but he shook his rattles under the eyes of the king, his eyes rolling back to reveal their whites. Spittle drooled down into his beard.

Æthelburh, seeing Eadfrith staring at the display with a half-smile on his lips, whispered to him, "Is he mad?"

Eadfrith covered his surprise at being thus addressed and whispered back, "Watch this." Then, with no one but the queen aware of what he was doing, he slipped an armband from his wrist and flipped it towards the writhing priest. With scarcely a break in his contortions, a thin hand darted out and snatched the gold from the air, thrusting it into the dark safety beneath Coifi's cloak. Edwin threw a glance towards his younger son, who smiled back innocently. Then Eadfrith leaned towards Æthelburh and whispered, "If Coifi is mad, it is the gold madness that afflicts him."

Edwin reached out, suddenly, swiftly, like a striking snake, and grabbed Coifi's arm. The priest, as suddenly, stopped his writhings and stared up at the king.

"What net has wyrd cast for us, Coifi?" asked Edwin. "Is the time ripe to attack Cadwallon?"

"Oh, ripe, ripe as barley in autumn, as apple on tree, ripe, ripe," said the priest, and Æthelburh saw the tension drain from her husband. But before it could drain completely, Coifi shuddered convulsively, almost breaking Edwin's hold on him, then stared white eyed into the distance and, rigid with foreboding, announced, "But beware, beware, the leap of salmon and raven's call, the plots of women and" – Coifi's eyes focused sharply on the king – "new gods who have no power in these lands."

Æthelburh stifled a gasp. Edwin looked hard at his priest, drawing him in closer. Under the king's scrutiny, Coifi's eyes rolled again and he went limp. Edwin let him slide to the floor.

"Well, the old gods appear to be in our favour," said Edwin. "We will not this time ask the priest of the new god to divine his god's favour." He stepped over Coifi's prone body – Æthelburh realized, from the way nobody in the hall paid the slightest attention to his collapse, that it was not an unusual event – and returned to the high table, gathering his thegns, sons, councillors and wife around him.

From their place down the mead hall, Paulinus and James kept a weather eye on the proceedings at the high table, but there was little to see beyond men speaking animatedly, and besides, they found themselves being distracted by the story Acca was telling. In this tale, the great hammer of Thunor, the god of thunder, was stolen by giants. Thunor, with his brother Loki, travelled to the land of the giants to win it back, but to gain entrance to the giants' court, Thunor had to pretend to be the beautiful and much desired goddess, Freya. The men loved this story, particularly the part when the giant lifted Thunor's veil and made to kiss him, thinking he was Freya, and they pounded the table in appreciation.

The Italians looked at each other. James shrugged. "Well, I suppose it is not as bad as Jupiter turning into a swan to ravish a maiden."

The king stood from the table, and his chief men and thegns stood with him. They had made their decision.

The hall fell silent. Edwin spoke.

"The king of Gwynedd has done us great harm. He sought to dishonour my friend and ally, King Eadbald of Kent, by stealing the rich gifts he sent with his sister." Edwin paused. "My wife." Even as he uttered the words, they sounded strange in his throat and he could not bring himself to look at Æthelburh. The queen, although her eyes were demurely downcast, felt the lack of weight that came with his regard, and wondered at it, for she was young and knew herself to be beautiful.

"We will not endure such an insult," Edwin continued. "And though Cadwallon and I be brothers, sworn, bonded in blood, this night I abjure our brotherhood and swear before you and before all the gods that I will take his lands from him, take his riches from him and cast him from his halls into the night! What say you?"

The men cheered, rising from their seats and pounding the tables with their fists.

The king looked out into his men, the men who would ride with him against Cadwallon, and his eyes blazed with a cold fire. Whispers spread like ripples as the men speculated over the treasures they might gain, for rumour had it that the kingdom of Gwynedd still had many treasures from the days of the emperors.

"Patience, men, have patience," said Edwin. "We will depart soon, and there will be rich gifts for all. But before we depart, I have some business of my own to attend to." The king turned to Æthelburh. The men erupted into raucous cheers, with not a few choice or crude comments thrown into the general hubbub.

Æthelburh stood up. The veil that had covered her face was now thrown back, and glints of her golden hair glittered beneath the rich cloth of her kerchief. She followed her husband as he walked from the hall but, watching from their places, Paulinus and James saw that Edwin never once looked back at his bride. For her part, Æthelburh walked stiffly, striving not to hear the ribald advice of the king's now very drunk men.

Paulinus turned to his countryman. "We should pray for her, James."

And so, while the rest of the hall dissolved into a drink-induced stupor, one corner was filled with the quiet murmur of prayer.

\*

Edwin closed the door of his chamber. It was the one room in the hall that offered privacy, for apart from the king everyone else lived communal lives, with screens and hangings over alcoves the only other form of seclusion. He turned to Æthelburh. She was standing, quite still, in the centre of the room, her eyes downcast, but in the sudden quiet, here behind the thick wooden door, he was struck by her youth. He himself was forty years old now. Some of his hair was turning white, and scars of battle and the leathering of sun and wind had worn his skin. Sometimes Edwin felt weary, a bone-heavy, heart-heavy weariness. The spirits of the men he had killed sat heavily in his memory, for while he had forgotten the faces of most of them, their blood was on him and it could not be washed off. He was old now, and unlike the young men took no pleasure in battle glory, nor did he boast of deeds done and men slain. But looking at Æthelburh properly for the first time, he saw a lightness of heart and spirit that went beyond her youth. But still she did not raise her gaze to her husband.

"Well?" Edwin asked eventually. "Will you not look at your husband?"

Æthelburh shook her head. "I – I cannot," she said.

"Why not?"

"I… I am a virgin, my lord. My maids told me what I must do, but I am not sure I can."

A smile twitched at Edwin's lips. "If it were so difficult, this middle-earth would be an empty place." He placed a finger under her chin and gently lifted her head, so that she looked him in the face. Meeting his eyes, Æthelburh blushed, but she did not lower her head.

"My… my lord, there is one other thing."

Edwin nodded. "Yes?" It was as well he was no longer young – in his youth he could not have been so patient. But there was something about this young girl, one moment so vibrant and engaged, the next demure and chaste, that reached into the cold ashes of his heart.

"I could not speak of it in council, for it concerns your honour."

Edwin: High King of Britain

A frown creased Edwin's face. This was not the sort of matter he had expected to be raised on his wedding night, but he nodded for Æthelburh to continue.

"My lord, when the king of Gwynedd, Cadwallon, stopped and cruelly robbed us on our journey here, killing Oslac, my captain, he told me that he hated you for…" Æthelburh hesitated, then plunged on with her explanation: "…for what he said you did to his sister."

Edwin's hand dropped from Æthelburh's face. "What did he say I did to his sister?"

"He – he said you raped her and got her with child."

"Did he say this publicly, or to you alone?"

"To me alone, lord."

Edwin bent down towards his new wife, his eyes searching. "Have you spoken of this?"

"No, my lord," said Æthelburh.

"To anyone?" Edwin gripped Æthelburh's arm. "Think. Not to your maids, your guards?"

"No, I haven't."

"Your priest?"

"No, my lord, not even him."

Edwin bent closer, looking deeply into Æthelburh's eyes before nodding and releasing her arm. "Good. Speak of this to no one." The king half turned away, lost in thought. Æthelburh waited, but when he made no further effort to speak, she could not but ask.

"Is it true, my lord?"

Edwin looked up, and his face showed that he had been dragged from some deep well of memory.

"Is what true?"

"Gwynedd's accusation, my lord."

A veil came down across the king's face. Looking at him, it was if Æthelburh looked into the face of a dead man, so waxy and stiff were his features.

"I said you are not to speak of this."

"My lord…"

102

"No!" More softly, "No." Æthelburh's face fell and her head dropped, but Edwin pushed a strand of hair that had fallen from beneath her kerchief aside. "Do not doubt me, wife."

Æthelburh looked up, and her smile was as sudden as it was dazzling. "I do not doubt you, husband."

Later, when Æthelburh lay sleeping beside him, her arm draped over his chest, Edwin stared up into darkness and tried to see again, in memory, the face of Cwenburg. But the more he reached for her, the further her memory slipped away until he could not even remember the sound of her voice or the smell of her skin. And then, alone, in the silence of the night, Edwin wept.

# Chapter 7

"Anglesey!" The ship's master pointed through the sea spray to the wave-flecked island ahead.

Edwin rose from where he had been sheltering against the rain and wind. Behind him, in the centre of the boat, the horses shifted nervously, unsettled by the motion and the spray that occasionally burst over the side of the ship. The men given the task of quietening the horses through the sea voyage from the Isle of Man had had a difficult job, and on one occasion a horse had come near to panicking and throwing the rest of the beasts into disorder. But the men had worked hard, even the warriors who had thought to rest during the sea passage, and now Anglesey was within sight.

To the east, the mountains of Gwynedd cloaked themselves in cloud, with only the occasional tear in the mist revealing their lowering faces. Even now, after so many years, Edwin shivered at the sight. His ancestors came from the flat lands that lay east of the North Sea, and they had sailed far up the rivers that scored the low-lying eastern half of this new country to make kingdoms and homes for themselves. He was a man at home in a boat, or on land that stretched to distant horizons, where an enemy could be seen from afar and the weather's turn from even further. The mountains, these unforgiving teeth of rock and scree that gnawed the west of the country and ran down its spine, were different. In them the day could turn from summer to winter in the time it took to spark a fire and huddle against the storm. Upon them were the wraith-haunted tombs of old, tombs that were already old during the days of the emperors, and their cold presence had terrified the soul of a young man, little more than a boy, learning the ways of warriors beneath their unblinking stare.

Edwin remembered one rain-soaked day – all his memories of his time in Gwynedd were steeped in water, be it mist or rain – riding

into the mountains with Cadfan, king of Gwynedd, his retinue of
warriors and a single, excited boy, chattering to Edwin as they rode
behind. Edwin, the elder, tried to ignore the boy's talk, for he wanted
to listen to what the men were saying, but the boy insisted on asking
him who he thought would win in contests between the various
warriors, until finally Edwin had told him to shut up, emphasizing
the point with a slap to the back of the head. But the blow caught
the side of the boy's head and knocked him from his horse.

Cadwallon had lain, slightly stunned, beside his horse, his shock
turning to shame as the men began to laugh and he had seen his own
father shake his head.

"Go back," said Cadfan to his son. "I cannot have with me
someone unable to remain on his horse."

"But, Father..." Cadwallon began, but the king of Gwynedd
held up his hand and the boy fell silent. It did not do to contradict
a king, even if he was your father.

"You, go with him," Cadfan said to Edwin.

"I don't need..." Cadwallon tried, but again Cadfan cut him off.

It was a silent pair of boys, one just old enough to ride, the
other pushing manhood, who headed back to camp. They threaded
between the peaks, the mountains as quiet as they were, but while
the boys refused to look at each other, they each individually felt the
hills looking down upon them. And then the fog came.

"We must stop," Edwin said. He was the first to speak, but being
the elder he had charge of the young prince and heir to Gwynedd.

"You stop, I go on," said Cadwallon.

"No, we must stop." Edwin grabbed the bridle of Cadwallon's
horse and forced it to a halt. In the shelter of an overhanging rock,
the boys made a cheerless camp, their horses acting as dripping
screens against the damp, the boys themselves too proud to take any
warmth from each other, and slowly feeling the heat leeching from
their bodies into the rock.

And, slowly, Edwin became conscious of the rock taking more
from him than heat. A dreadful lassitude came over him as he
thought of how fine it would be to rest here, against the stone, and

move no more. By the silence and stillness of Cadwallon, Edwin knew that the boy too heard the whispers and was settling into the shadow world. There they would have stayed too if the fog had not parted for an instant, allowing them to see that the stone they rested against was one of the door pillars to a barrow of the dead, and the dead were calling.

The boys ran, not caring that they left their horses behind, and their pride. Soon the fog began to tear and thin, but they still heard the deadly cold voices bidding them return to take their ease in the halls of the dead. It was only when they stood beneath the sun, on green grass, that the boys stopped running. The horses, sensible beasts, swiftly followed and set to quiet cropping while their riders inexplicably rolled on the grass, laughing with shared relief.

Standing beside the steersman, Edwin shook himself out of memory as the clouds closed around the mountains of his youth. He had not expected to return to them. He touched the steersman's arm and pointed.

"Steer us west, around the island."

The helmsman dug the steering oar into the dark water, the wind tugged the square sail, making wood creak and rope snap, and the boat skimmed over the waves, running parallel to the shore. Edwin checked behind and saw that the boats commanded by Forthred, Osfrith and Eadfrith were matching their course to his. Satisfied, he stood upon one of the war chests that lined the bottom of the boat, providing seats for the men when they were needed for rowing and places to stow the weapons of war and later the plunder that the weapons reaped, and looked to larboard, over the dark water to the fertile island beyond. Anglesey was the bowl the rest of Gwynedd supped from, its well-watered fields and rich soil providing the wheat and barley that allowed the people of the rest of the kingdom to scrape through times of dearth to the few occasions of plenty. Without Anglesey Gwynedd would starve – forcing Cadwallon either to come to battle with exhausted, hungry men, or to flee. This strategy was the fruit of Edwin's knowledge of Gwynedd, knowledge reaped through his growing years at the court of King Cadfan. As he looked at the waves gurgling up the yellow beaches that surrounded much of the island Edwin smiled without mirth at the weavings of wyrd. The sisters of fate had spun a bitter childhood for him when Æthelfrith had killed his father and taken his birth kingdom, Deira, from him, but the time in exile in Gwynedd meant that he knew where the weakness of Cadwallon's otherwise impregnable mountain realm lay.

"There is another, smaller, island west of Anglesey, separated by narrow channels from its parent. The Britons call it Ynys Gybi." Edwin pointed ahead and the helmsman peered through the spume thrown up by their skudding progress across the choppy waves. "Steer around it and follow the coast south-east. We will come then to a narrow sand mouth, where our ships can be beached."

The helmsman, a man of few words like all his breed, nodded his understanding. Edwin looked along the length of the boat. It was a large craft, over 80 feet long, with sufficient space for plunder and the slaves he expected to take in this war. Most of the horses they had brought with them were being carried in Forthred's ship. His own vessel, being the first to land, was thick with warriors. It was easy to tell which of the men were experienced and which new: the old hands sat wherever they could find somewhere dry and out of the wind, sleeping, while the young men, hungry for glory, stared over the sides of the ship, alternating boasting and thoughtful silences. As the vanguard, Edwin mostly carried experienced men with him, but it was always good to blood a few youngsters with the old hands. His sons, Osfrith and Eadfrith, brought with them higher proportions of young men, but that was to the good. They would be blooded together, and the new-born warriors welded to each other and to his sons, forming the next generation of kings.

At least, that was the intention. Edwin thought of the king lists that Acca loved to recite, genealogies going all the way back to Woden or Thunor or one of the other, lesser, gods. In the lists, king followed king in dizzying, bloody procession. As strength and fortune failed one, another would rise up, all according to the weavings of fate. Before they set sail, Edwin had sacrificed to the fate singers, the pale sisters, while Coifi shook his bone rattles and his new wife and her priests looked on in what he took to be horror. A white heifer, sheep, a white goat, all slaughtered and their blood thrown upon the ground in the sacred grove where Coifi gathered his power. But Edwin knew that the fate weavers wove what they would, unmoved by sacrifice or tears, a warrior's bravery or a child's plea. Despite Coifi's assurances, he doubted that the fate weavers' favour could be bought with the blood of animals. He knew that there were some among his people and his ancestors who sought favour by giving greater gifts, be they richer treasures or human blood, but he had seen such sacrifices rejected as often as they were accepted. No, the fate weavers wove wyrd as they would and neither men nor gods might change that pattern; mortal or immortal, they could only endure.

As the small flotilla of ships sailed around Ynys Gybi, Edwin called upon some of the younger men, who had the sharpest eyes, to keep watch on the land. With the sun risen, it was inevitable that sooner or later someone would see the boats and raise the alarm, but now they were on the final stretch, he hoped his boats, driven by a freshening west wind, would outpace any messengers. The only way the Britons might get word to his destination before he arrived was by horseback, and any riders should be clearly visible to his lookouts.

Rounding the final headland, Edwin saw the remembered beach open between the two headlands that concealed and protected it. There were a number of boats drawn up upon the sand, but they were of the meaner sort, the vessels of poor fishermen rather than the long-prowed warboats of kings. For a moment he felt a stab of disappointment – he had hoped to catch Cadwallon unprepared and unawares. But he must be elsewhere in Gwynedd. No matter, the plan was to take Anglesey – Cadwallon's presence would have been an unlooked for favour from the fates.

Pointing to where he wanted the boat to land, Edwin kicked the leg of the nearest sleeping man, who jerked awake and looked up at his king.

"Paddles," said Edwin quietly, and the man, an old and experienced warrior, nodded and went about waking and making ready the rest of the men. The helmsman dug the steering oar into the water and the ship began to turn, the westerly wind helping more than hindering as the boat headed north, driving into the southern underbelly of Anglesey island. As Edwin kept watch, the men unshipped the paddles that lay along the bottom of the boat. There were oars lying there as well, vital if the wind should fail and the ship be becalmed, but the paddles were more effective at driving a boat up upon a beach – and they made much more useful weapons should they have to push out from the beach while under attack.

The boat rode over the swells that rose higher and sharper as they approached land, the men poised to begin paddling, and then, as they started cutting through the white-tops, the helmsman gave the signal. As one, twenty paddles bit into the sea and the boat leapt forward, through the creamy swirls until the prow scraped onto sand, at which the men gave the final convulsive heave, those in the front using their paddles as poles upon the wet sand, and they thrust the boat up upon the strand. The vessel strained, but before the boards had a chance to settle into their own unsupported weight, the men were out of the boat and, swords in hand, sweeping outwards to check for sentries.

In short succession the boats commanded by Forthred, Osfrith and Eadfrith pulled up on the beach. Men unloaded the horses, whispering commands and gentling the beasts. There were not enough animals for everyone to ride, but Edwin's plan did not call for everyone to ride.

"Well met," said the king, as Forthred hurried to him, leading a pair of fine horses. Osfrith and Eadfrith rode behind, with some ten men astride beasts and the rest jogging over the sand.

"An easy journey," said Forthred, handing the king his horse and swinging up upon his own. "Let us hope the land proves as kind."

Edwin mounted his horse. "It is a rich land, old friend, and a kindly one. It will treat us well."

Forthred slammed his forearm against his chest, a broad smile upon his face. "It is good to go to war with you again, lord."

"If I am right, there will be little war but much plunder – Cadwallon is not here." Edwin pointed at the complex of buildings that overlooked the bay. "That is Aberffraw, Cadwallon's demesne in Anglesey. But he is not there."

Forthred squinted at the buildings. "How do you know?"

"When the king and his retinue are there, Aberffraw seethes like an ant hill, with servants and slaves, and local people coming for the king's justice. Now, see, it is quiet."

It was true. Only a single thin trail of smoke ascended from the buildings, but Forthred still frowned, for Cadwallon's house on Anglesey was unlike the high wooden halls favoured by the kings of the Angles, the Saxons and the Jutes. Instead, it was built of brick and covered in grey slate, so that it looked more like a cut quarry turned upside down than a dwelling place for men.

Edwin, seeing his expression, explained. "It is built after the style of the emperors of old. Indeed, some among the Britons still call themselves Romans, and bridle should you name them wrong. Cadfan told me Aberffraw was built for a Roman when the emperors still ruled."

Forthred nodded. "It is old then."

"And weak. Its walls are bare, like cloth too long used, and a man with an axe may break the gates in five minutes if he be given the time. But there will be little defence. When the king is not there, only a few servants and slaves remain. They will not fight. Take Osfrith and Eadfrith, and take Aberffraw. When you have reived it, burn it."

"And you, lord?"

"I have another, richer, destination in mind. A short ride inland, there is a monastery…"

Forthred's eyes gleamed with gold lust at the very word – some of the most valuable reives they had had in the past had been when they fell unsuspected upon one of the monasteries of the Britons, rich with gold and men soon to be slaves, poor in swords.

"...but this is a monastery for women."

If anything, Forthred's eyes gleamed even brighter.

Edwin shook his head. "No, old friend, not these women, for they are the daughters of kings. The women of the Britons value their purity above all things and many choose – and are allowed – to enter a monastery rather than marry. But as the daughters of kings, their monastery will be rich and their ransoms richer – as long as we keep them undefiled. Therefore, I go with few men, and we ride, for we must be fast." Edwin leaned closer to Forthred and lowered his voice. "See to my sons, Forthred. Osfrith commands, but if he should falter or fail, you must take charge. I leave a man with a fast horse behind – send for me if need arises or Cadwallon is seen."

"Osfrith is a good boy, and generous. The men follow him willingly."

"He has not been properly tested. Tell me truly when I return how he fights, whether with wit or wisdom."

Forthred made the courtesy and fell back, while Edwin spurred his horse to his sons to give them their final orders. Then, as the sons of the king and Forthred, on horseback, led a gaggle of warriors on foot towards Aberffraw, Edwin gathered his mounted men around him.

"We go to a monastery of women."

Edwin scanned the watching faces and saw many ribald grins and narrowed eyes.

"If any of you try to take a woman, I will cut your throat and leave your body to be eaten by the pigs of the Britons."

The faces, which had been flushed and expectant, suddenly glazed.

"You will have riches from these women, but this is a treasure that must remain unspoiled for it to be reaped. These women are virgins, the daughters of kings – kings who will pay rich ransoms for the return of their daughters, but only if you keep your hands clean and your trousers on."

Some blood returned to the watching faces, for the gold lust was as fierce as the woman lust. Edwin was a generous king, who gave rich gifts freely – indeed, the men clustered around him bore witness to his generosity in the belts and buckles and torcs and armbands that they wore – but all kings, even the greatest, needed gold and searched for it as greedily as a new born searching for its mother's breast. Riches were most often torn from the bodies of the dead, in the shape of their armour and trappings and weapons, or earned with the bodies of the vanquished as they were sold as slaves, but now the watching men grinned, and their smiles grew vulpine as they slowly realized the true worth of the plan their king sketched out for them. Oh, he was a crafty one, this one; a worthy successor to Æthelfrith the Flesaur, and he would make them rich.

Edwin led the group of riders up out of the beach area. To their left, Aberffraw, the demesne of the kings of Gwynedd, was beginning to burn as the assault led by Forthred and his sons swept aside the few defenders. It was going so well that Edwin saw no need to stop, but rode inland at the head of his small troop, following the footpaths that cut between the long strip fields, ridged and furrowed into parallel rows by generations of ploughmen and their teams of oxen. There were men, and some women and children, in the fields, weeding and scaring away birds, but they fell back when they saw the armed men riding towards them. Those who could do so fled for the relative safety of the copses and marshes that interspersed the fields; those who saw the riders too late to find safety strove to make themselves as inconspicuous as possible. On another occasion Edwin might have sent some men to round up a few peasants to be taken on board the ships, but on this day he had other priorities. As he and his men were on horseback, there was no way the peasants could send a warning faster than they would arrive and, being peasants, they would have no more idea where to send to find their king, Cadwallon, than they would to find their gods.

"God," Edwin corrected himself under his breath. Most of the Britons worshipped one god, of course, not many. As the horse waded across a shallow ford under the shadow of a wooden cross, he recalled that the Britons did seem to know where to find their god, be it beneath his sign, or in the strange meal that they shared in their churches, where they even ate their god.

Edwin shook his head. He had never understood that. Surely gods consumed the offerings and sacrifices of men, not the other way round?

But that could wait for another day. Waving his men to a halt, he rode towards a watching peasant who had mistaken stillness for invisibility. The man, seeing Edwin ride towards him, made to run, then realizing the futility of flight he shrugged and waited.

Edwin drew his horse to a halt. "Where lies the monastery of kings' daughters?" he asked, using the language of the Britons.

The peasant shaded his eyes as he looked up at the horseman. "There be no monastery of kings' daughters here," he said.

Steel rasped, and in an instant the peasant went slightly cross-eyed as he tried to focus on the blade touching his chest.

"I speak your tongue, peasant," said Edwin. "Do you not think I know your land? Where is the monastery of kings' daughters?"

"I were about to say, while there be no monastery of kings' daughters in these parts, there is a nunnery nearby." Edwin lowered his sword and the peasant tugged his hair in acknowledgement.

"Whereaways?"

"Yonder," said the peasant, pointing north and further inland. "See thou the woods, shaped as a whale breaking the waves? The nunnery be yonder."

Edwin urged his horse back to the waiting men, and the peasant stood watching, leaning on his staff as they rode away. Once the riders were safely out of sight, many of those who had hidden ran up to him.

"What did the Saxon want?" they asked.

The peasant shrugged. "King stuff," he said, and went back to his hoeing.

The peasant spoke truly. As they rounded the wood, the nunnery came into view: a collection of low buildings clustered around a central, higher one, with a roof that reached, impressively, as high as a tall tree. Almost as soon as the riders saw the nunnery, the nunnery saw them, for a bell began to toll urgently, and they saw a frantic boiling of human activity that resolved itself into watchful stillness as they came closer.

Edwin held his hand up and drew his horse to a stop. The men behind him did the same.

"Shields," he said, drawing his own round shield over the left side of his body. His helmet in place – the king alone wore a full face helmet, its cheek guards and face-covering intricately carved and with a flaming red boar's hair tuft set upon its crest – Edwin signalled for the men to advance at a walk. Every man came on with sword drawn, eyes scanning for danger, but no one moved among the scattered buildings. As they drew closer to the nunnery, Edwin felt the same sense of oppressive heaviness that always attached to the brick buildings of the Britons. The Angles and the Saxons and the men of Kent built in wood, raising great halls as tall as trees, but the Britons still attempted to follow the ways of the emperors, although their structures had none of the desolate grandeur of the Romans. Edwin had seen the ruins of many towns, he had walked among their remains, and it seemed to his wondering eyes that giants must have built them and lived in them. But such was not the case with this nunnery: it was human scale, and most of the buildings were rude affairs of wood and wattle. Only the church, at the centre of the huddle of buildings, was made of brick, and closer inspection revealed that even the church was brick only in part: the mortared walls reached only to head height and then, as if someone had run out of bricks and resorted to more readily available material, the rest of the building's height was provided by wattle and daub added on top of the low round of bricks.

Edwin held his hand up and the men stopped. The only sound was the shifting of their horses; even the nunnery's animals, cooped in rough enclosures and pens to the north of the buildings, held a watchful, waiting silence. Edwin could feel the weight of eyes upon them, hidden gazes staring fearfully from behind screens and over doors, but he could see no one. Where would they be? He scanned the buildings and then alighted on the obvious choice. They would be in the church, praying to their god for deliverance. Moving his horse forward at a steady walk, still scanning to left and right, Edwin rode towards the church, his men, their armour clinking, riding behind. The church's wooden door was closed.

Then from the left the twang of a bow string and the hiss of an arrow, its fletching cutting the air. Edwin caught the flight at the edge of sight and shifted his shield upwards just in time. The arrow glanced off the limewood. Even as it was looping slowly back down to the ground, the men nearest to its source had leapt from their horses and run to the small outhouse, shields covering their approach, and battering open the door they dragged out the archer. He was a boy, dark haired, dark eyed and pale with the surety that he was about to die. Edwin saw that the bow he had fired was a child's weapon, the sort of thing he had used himself when he was eight and went hunting duck.

"Shall I kill him, lord?" The warrior held his seax to the boy's throat – being a child there was no glory in his death, so the warrior was going to use the knife rather than the sword to draw the life from the boy.

"Was he alone?" Edwin looked towards the outhouse.

The other men emerged from it, signing the all clear.

"Lord?" asked the warrior.

"No! Do not kill him. He is a stupid, brave boy." The voice rang clear from the direction of the church and the Northumbrians turned to see a woman standing at its now open door. She wore a long, dark habit, tied around the waist with a leather belt, and a veil covered her hair. "As brave a boy as you were."

The king held his hand up – a sign that his men should wait and hold their positions – then he rode towards the church.

"Briant."

"Edwin."

Neither moved. Behind Briant, women, all wearing the same style of clothes as her, were peeping fearfully from the church. Edwin's men, although they remained on watchful alert, exchanged meaningful glances as they looked at the women.

"Are any of Cadwallon's warriors here or on the island?" Edwin asked, using the language of the Britons. "Speak quickly and speak truly."

Briant hesitated and was about to turn to look at her women when Edwin urged his horse closer. "Answer truly!"

Briant straightened and looked Edwin in the face. "Here there are none; the men here present are servants and labourers."

"On the island?"

"I have had no news of Cadwallon and his men these past two months, not since the Feast of Pentecost."

From behind, Edwin heard his men murmur as those who spoke the tongue of the Britons translated what had been said to the others. He held up his hand for silence.

"There is no one here to oppose us?" Edwin switched to the language of his own men.

Briant paused. She looked past Edwin at the waiting group of heavily armed men. And then, speaking Edwin's tongue as fluently as he did, she answered. "If you take or harm any of my sisters, God will cut you down in your pride and your women will weep for you and your sons will not know their fathers. This I promise, by the blood of he who saves us, though we die."

The clink of mail and the hiss of metal told Edwin, without having to look around, that the curse had disturbed his men.

"In my experience the gods are not so reliable. But let us say your god will do as you threaten – I and my men have sailed far and ridden long; we will not leave empty handed. I will sell you your sisters' lives and freedom if you will buy them from me."

Briant stared long and hard at Edwin before answering. "I – I will buy them."

"You choose well. Come, show me your price and I will see how many lives it buys."

"What of Uwain?"

"Who?"

Briant pointed past Edwin. "The boy who shot an arrow at you. He is only a child. Will you let him live?"

"If you have the treasure to buy his life, I will sell it to you, and the others. Now, where is the blood price to be found?"

"Our treasures are in our church," said Briant. "But it is a holy place and no pagan may enter."

"I will enter, or if not I alone, then all of my men and me together. Which is it to be?"

In answer Briant stood aside from the door.

Edwin turned to his men. "Wait and watch – there is no threat within, but I am uneasy. I feel in my bones that someone is coming." Then, dismounting, he strode into the church and Briant followed Edwin.

The nuns clustered like frightened children in the sanctuary at the far end of the building. Their wide eyes peeped through the gaps in the brightly painted rood screen that separated the high altar – in reality a rude and roughly worked block of stone – from the nave. Lined up in front of the nuns were a group of poorly armed men wielding spears and clubs and cudgels, but with little more than leather jerkins for protection and no shields. Although they outnumbered his men, a glance told Edwin that they were not warriors, and however brave they might be they offered no defence against his escort. He swiftly took in the rest of the church, its walls painted with scenes from the holy book of the Britons, and the three high small openings in the walls that allowed light in from without. To help with illumination, rush tapers burned smokily along the walls, and smoke gathered in the thatch, moving like mist over marsh. There was no sign of any trap.

Edwin spoke to Briant out of the side of his mouth without turning his head, so that those watching from outside would not realize he was conversing.

"Is she here?"

Briant answered in like fashion.

"Yes. There, second from left."

"I see her. She takes after you."

"I see you in her."

117

"What is she like?"

"She is a good daughter and a good sister. God willing, she will be mother to this community when I am dead."

"May that be long. For now, I must take something to give to my men, or they will not be restrained. What do you have?"

"The holy vessels and holy book, but they cannot be profaned. I – I have the jewels my father gave the sisters when I came here. Will that suffice?"

"They will need to be rich jewels indeed, Briant, for there are women here that would bring high prices."

"If you try to take any of my sisters, you will have to kill me first, Edwin."

"Do you think I would be talking to you now if I wanted to do that? Bring me what you have; be quick now."

Briant hurried down the nave of the church, her long robes rustling over the rushes that lay on the hard-packed earth floor, and spoke quickly to one of the nuns. But as she did so, Edwin heard swift movement behind. He turned to see one of his men scurry to the church.

"Riders approaching," he said to Edwin.

"How many?"

"Only four."

"Hide the horses, have the men take cover in the church. We will provide a surprise of our own for our surprise guests."

His orders delivered, Edwin strode after Briant, causing frantic whisperings from the watching nuns and the futile waving of spears and cudgels by the old men and young boys who were attempting to guard them.

"Briant, my pagans are going to have to profane your holy place, but with your help no blood need be spilled here."

The nun hurried back to Edwin. "What…" she began, but Edwin interrupted her.

"Four riders approaching. Do you know who they are?"

The nun gave a panicked glance past Edwin and saw some of his men already taking up position in the church.

"No. Yes. Maybe. Please," she clutched Edwin's arm, "if I or our child mean anything to you, do not kill them."

"Who are they?"

"I – I… my brother said he would come back to Inys Môn this season; most likely these are his heralds, telling his coming."

"Call them into the church and my men can take and disarm them. Or we can fight and kill them outside. Which is it to be?"

"You will not harm them?"

"We will try not to kill them. I can give no more assurance. But without your assistance they will certainly die, and probably one or two of my own men. And then the others will be the harder to check when it comes to dealing with your women."

Briant nodded. "I will call them."

Edwin made to turn away, but she grasped his arm. "If you kill them, the disgrace will fall on me."

Edwin nodded. "I understand, Briant." He took her hand from his arm. "Now go, stand in the door of your church and welcome them in."

As the nun made her way to the entrance, Edwin arrayed his men and gave them their orders. Those nearest the door were to use their shields, with their heavy metal bosses, to knock the newcomers from their feet, while the others were to wait with swords drawn and rope ready, to step in if the fight grew too fierce or to bind the prisoners should it go well.

For himself, Edwin took his place nearest the door, in the little recessed cell that stood beside it, providing shelter for the man who guarded the entrance to the church. It also ensured that he was close enough to hear what Briant said to the men.

A quick glance told him that all was ready, then Edwin eased himself backwards into the shadows and waited.

The horses drew up outside the church. Briant stood, in shadow but visible, in the doorway.

"Where is everyone, Briant?" a cheerful voice asked.

"We are within," said Briant. Edwin could hear the strain in her voice, although Briant strove to keep it light.

"I did not know this was a feast day. We will join you." And past Briant, his cloak flung back and his head bare, strode Cadwallon, king of Gwynedd.

The struggle was brief but violent. At the end of it, two of Cadwallon's three bodyguards lay bleeding out their lives into the rush-strewn floor of the church, as did one of Edwin's men; the third bodyguard was held, unconscious, dangling between two panting Northumbrians, and Cadwallon struggled upon the ground, held by three men who were using their shields to grind him into the floor. Edwin glanced up and saw the collection of old men and boys who lined the sanctuary girding themselves to attack in protection of their king – they would die, but with so many of his own men occupied, it could get messy. Stepping smartly around the men struggling on the floor, Edwin drew his sword and pushed the point into the hollow at the base of Cadwallon's neck.

"Take one step forward and your king dies!" Edwin roared over the shouts and confusion in the church.

Cadwallon, suddenly, terribly, conscious of who had caught him unawares, fell still. The old men and boys, muttering, shaking their cudgels and spears, shuffled back to the sanctuary where the nuns whispered and prayed.

"Get him up," Edwin said to his men, and they pulled Cadwallon to his feet, his arm twisted behind his back.

Briant pushed her way forward. "You promised you would not hurt him," she said.

Cadwallon started, and the knife held against his throat pricked blood. But it was surprise rather than escape that had prompted his movement.

"Why didn't you warn me?" he asked. "Why did you betray me?"

Briant shook her head. "You were lost, brother; there were men waiting outside and within and there was no escape. But Edwin promised that he would not kill you." Briant turned to the king of Northumbria, who was staring at Cadwallon. "You promised," Briant repeated.

"I did not know that we would land so big a fish," Edwin said quietly. "A royal fish no less. Ha!" He clapped his hands together, but the sound died away into the rushes of the floor and the thatch of the roof.

"You gave your word that you would let live whoever I called into this church," Briant said. "Would you have it known that Edwin, king of Northumbria, is faithless? Do you want men to say that Edwin gives his word only to break it? For know this, if you should hurt my brother now, I will spend all the years remaining to me on pilgrimage through these islands, proclaiming the news to whoever will hear me that Edwin is a faithless king."

Edwin turned to Briant. "You would have to be able to travel round these islands first to do that."

Briant nodded, as if her suspicions were being confirmed as they spoke. "Only death will stop me telling of such faithlessness. Kill me then, and have done with it – only kill me before you kill my brother, that my own part in his death be hidden from my eyes." And as she spoke she pushed herself forward, so that the point of Edwin's sword rested upon her breast.

"Briant, no," called Cadwallon, but Edwin had already lowered his sword. The king stared levelly at the nun, and his face had become a mask.

"You think I would kill you?"

"You viper, you've done worse to her before," shouted Cadwallon, beginning to struggle against the men holding him. But almost without looking, Edwin slammed the pommel of his sword back into Cadwallon's head, and the king of Gwynedd slumped into a state of semi-consciousness.

"Well?" said Edwin.

"Should you kill my brother here now, after I have brought him to you on your assurance of his safety, then I would be the greatest of traitors and my infamy known to all: you would have killed me, Edwin, more surely than with any sword. Is that what you desire?"

Slowly, Edwin shook his head. "No, that is not what I desire, Briant. My wish was to see you and my daughter, and that I have done. I gave you my word once that I would not speak, ever, of what passed between us, and I have kept that promise through all these years. You should know I am no oathbreaker." Edwin turned to his men. "Wake him," he said. And while they slapped the king of Gwynedd into consciousness, Edwin stepped closer to Briant and spoke to her softly. "Does my daughter ever ask after her father?"

Briant whispered in return. "She believes her father to be dead, and her mother too – and that she was raised by the sisters here, their favourite child."

Edwin nodded. "It is for the best." He took one final look at the nuns gathered upon the sanctuary. "The second from the left?"

"Yes, that is her."

"Lord."

Edwin turned to see Cadwallon groaning back to consciousness. "I will keep my word, Briant, but your brother has a debt to pay to me now, and I will extract it, although he lives." Edwin strode over to Cadwallon. The king of Gwynedd hung limply between the men holding him, his eyes glazed. Edwin swept the bowl from the font and threw the water into Cadwallon's face, jerking him back into awareness.

"You stole from me my bride's price. Now you will pay me in return."

Cadwallon spat, and the blood-specked spittle dripped down Edwin's chest, but the king of Northumbria made no move to wipe it off.

"Go ahead, kill me. My God will take me to his holy place, and he will cast you into the fire forever, serpent that we nurtured at our bosom."

"Oh, I am not going to kill you, old friend and brother. I owe you your life at least, this time, for did you not spare mine once, many years ago?"

"Yes, and I curse the day I did so."

"But do you remember how you left me that day you spared my life?" Edwin stared at Cadwallon. "I see you do. It was small mercy to leave a man unarmed and naked, tied in a boat cast upon the sea. More execution by other means than mercy, it seems to me. But it was not my wyrd to die then, brother, and the gods carried my boat to shore and I lived, and survived, and grew strong, and now I am here, in your land that I claim for my own. I will take from you recompense for what you took from my wife, her bride price, the great treasure of the men of Kent, that I will have. But you will live, brother; live on in the knowledge that you owe your life to me."

The king of Northumbria glanced at his men. "Strip the king of his weapons, his treasures and his clothes. There is more on him than in a dozen churches."

Cadwallon began to struggle, but another blow to the head sent him reeling to the ground, and then the men fell on him like the ravens that picked flesh from battle corpses. The armlets, the great gold torc that marked Cadwallon as king, the gold buckles and jewel-studded pin that held his cloak were tossed into a growing pile upon the floor, onto which followed the mail jerkin and padded jack that Cadwallon was wearing. Edwin picked up the mail; the links were among the smallest he had ever seen, and the oiled metal flowed over his fingers like water.

Cadwallon's men were also stripped of their goods, the two dead men being left naked upon the floor, while the one still living was herded from the church and hog tied over the back of his horse – he was young and strong, and would fetch a good price.

"Wake him," said Edwin, and the last of the water from the baptismal font was poured over Cadwallon. Edwin's men hauled the king of Gwynedd to his feet. He stood naked in the church, his arms tied behind his back, but still there was an air of majesty to him.

"Take him," said Edwin, "and cast him into a boat upon the sea. Let us see if your god saves you as my gods saved me."

"I will kill you," said Cadwallon. "This I swear. One day you will see me cutting your sons from you, leaving them dead upon the ground, and only then will I come for you."

"You will have to live first," said Edwin.

"Oh, I will live. My God will save me."

"We shall see – but I have kept my word." Edwin gestured to his men. "Take him."

"Wait!" Cadwallon shouted, and even the Northumbrians paused in carrying out their orders. Cadwallon turned to Briant and very deliberately spat upon the ground in front of her. "You are no sister of mine."

"Take him!" said Edwin, and his men jerked Cadwallon out of the church. The king, alone in the church, turned to Briant. "You saved him," he said quietly, but she did not hear.

"Go," said Briant. "Please go, and do not come back."

Edwin nodded. "I would that this had not happened, Briant. But I will keep my word. Your brother will be set upon the sea in the straits between Anglesey and Gwynedd; unless your god turns his face from him and his boat founders, it should be no great matter for him to come to shore."

Briant turned away.

"Farewell," said Edwin, but she did not reply.

Returning to the ships, Edwin found Forthred, Osfrith and Eadfrith loading the vessels.

"How went the day?" he asked Forthred.

Forthred waved a disgusted hand at the meagre store of plunder they had raised from Aberffraw. Behind him smoke rose into the sky as the buildings burned and the assembled crows and ravens squabbled over the flesh spoils.

"At least we did not lose any men," said Forthred. "It would have stuck in my throat to lose anyone for so little." He turned to look at his lord, and his eyes narrowed as he saw the tightness around Edwin's eyes. "What happened at the monastery?"

"We caught a fish, the biggest fish, but then we put it back in the water."

Forthred gasped. "Cadwallon?"

Edwin could contain his amusement no longer. "He walked straight into us," he laughed, "and we took him and stripped him. There," he pointed to where his men were laying out the extraordinarily rich treasure they had taken from Cadwallon, to the gasps and cheers of the others.

Forthred grasped his master's forearm, his fingers tight on the gold band around his wrist. "You took Cadwallon?"

Edwin laughed again. "We did, and you are holding one of his bands now. Here," Edwin took it off, "take it." And he handed the beautifully wrought gold band to Forthred. But his old retainer did not even put the band on, so astonished was he at the news.

"What did you do with Cadwallon's body, lord?"

"Oh, he is not dead. We cast him, naked, upon the sea."

"Lord, that was not wise. If he should live, he will seek revenge most bitterly."

Edwin laughed. "Even if the sea finds him too bitter a food to swallow, Cadwallon's power is ended. His people will not follow a king brought so low."

Forthred grimaced. "It may be so, but for my part I would that you had killed him. For it seems to me that his people love him greatly and hate us the more, and will follow him if he lives."

Edwin clapped a hand on Forthred's back. "He said his god would save him. I saw how the tides raced in the straits where we set him upon the waters – if his god saves him from that, then we should think on taking this god for our own! Do not fret, old friend. Wyrd brought Cadwallon low and delivered him into my hands; he will not rise again."

Forthred shrugged. "I hope so. The fate singers weave as they will and sometimes the weft rises after it falls – it did for us!"

"Cadwallon will not recover from this. Come, let us go. We have done all that we came here to do, and more."

It was only as he stood in the belly of his boat, its prow turned away from Anglesey, that Edwin realized he had not asked the name of his daughter.

# Chapter 8

"I'm scared."

Edwin smoothed a strand of sweat-stained hair from Æthelburh's forehead. For a moment, there was relief from the juddering contractions that seemed to be tearing apart the body of his young wife. Exhausted, Æthelburh fell back upon the bed while her women fussed around, burning incense, heating water and keeping up a constant background of low chants that to Edwin's ears sounded like spells but were, according to the women, prayers to their god.

"I have sent word for a midwife to be brought to you," said Edwin. "Your women do not seem best versed in matters of childbirth."

"Will you stay with me?" asked Æthelburh.

"No! No, it would not be right to do so. This is women's work, as war is men's. Would you follow me onto a battlefield?"

Æthelburh smiled an exhausted smile. "I wou..." And then the word was drawn out of her in a long, shuddering scream.

Edwin, alarmed despite himself, grabbed one of Æthelburh's maids. "Where is the midwife? Go find her, now." It had been so many years since Cwenburg had given birth to Osfrith and Eadfrith that he had forgotten the pain of it. As Æthelburh's body slowly stopped trembling, he looked down and saw that she had drawn blood from where she grasped his arm, such was the convulsive strength of her grip.

The pain passed and Æthelburh returned to herself, a fresh sheen of sweat coating her face. Outside, although it was March, a chill wind blew over the North Sea and down the grey cloud-mirroring waters of the River Derwent.

"If I die, will you allow Paulinus to baptize the child?" Æthelburh looked up at Edwin and her eyes were suddenly urgent with petition – the same clarity that Edwin had seen in the eyes of men before battle, when the fates whispered a warning of mortality. At the sight, fear drove long, cold fingers deep into the bowels of the king, but he strove, with the practice of his years leading men to their deaths, to hide that fear.

"You will not die, wife. Here, I give you this pledge against death and the weavings of the fate singers: the child will be yours to raise in your religion come what may, whether you live or whether you… you do not."

Æthelburh smiled, and Edwin caught himself trying to impress her face upon his memory, in surety against wyrd taking her from him, and he railed against his own fear while keeping his expression calm.

"Move aside, move aside, give the poor child some air!"

Edwin, king of Northumbria, found himself being pushed aside by a bustling old woman with a blue apron round her waist and her hair tied back by a red cloth. The old woman started ordering Æthelburh's flustered maids around, ticking them off for not having enough water, demanding the swaddling cloths and telling others to steep the roots and stems she produced from her apron in boiling water, so their steam might fill the room. She took not the slightest bit of notice of Edwin, so in the end he was forced to take hold of her wrist.

"You will see that she and the baby are well," he asked.

"Ach, I've birthed more babbies than you've brought men down into the dust – I'll see her well." The old midwife smiled broadly at Æthelburh. "She's a fine healthy lass, good hips too; she'll have the babby out in no time when it's ready." Turning back to Edwin the midwife said, "Now, get yourself forth. This is women's work, and no place for a man."

Edwin tried to say farewell to Æthelburh, but another contraction juddered through her body, and the women drew around the birthing bed, screening her from his view, so he withdrew from the room.

Gesturing a servant over, Edwin asked, "Where is the queen's priest, Paulinus?"

"Lord, he and the other Kentish men are in the building you gave them to worship their god."

Edwin nodded an acknowledgement, but before he could head towards the building the servant spoke again. "Lord, your thegn, Forthred, wishes to speak with you. An ambassador from Cwichelm, the king of the West Saxons, has arrived and desires audience."

"Tell Forthred to come to the Kentish priests' building."

As the servant ran off to find Forthred, the king left the hall and headed across the beaten-down earth of the compound towards the small timber building that he had allocated to Paulinus and James and their band of believers. Since his marriage to Æthelburh a year ago, the king had often asked the Italian to sit near him at feasts, that he might learn more of the religion his wife professed and, just as much, to hear tales of the lands over the sea, in particular of the country of the Franks across the narrow sea and, further south, the land of the emperors of old. Much fine jewellery and rich cloth came from the country of the Franks into Northumbria, and in return traders sent south furs, the great hunting deerhounds that were bred in Northumbria, or the fine horses that grew fat and tall on the lush northern grass, beasts fit for a king. The horses of the Franks and the other peoples across the narrow sea were small, shaggy beasts, unlike the tall, sleek-limbed animals of Britain. A merchant could take a single pair of horses, best of all a breeding mare, by boat across the narrow sea, and return with three boats full of the richest cloths, foods, jewellery and weapons, so highly valued were the horses from Britain.

As he made his way across the compound, marked out by a stockade of pointed logs driven into the ground, Edwin checked the moorings on the river. Yes, there was a new boat there, a coastal craft by its upflung hull and short mast, which must have arrived early in the morning. That was no doubt how the messenger from Cwichelm of the West Saxons had arrived. He could leave his servants to deal with the ambassador for the moment – he had other more urgent matters to attend to.

Approaching the building Paulinus used, which was set apart from the stables and warehouses and workshops that studded the royal compound, in the same way a smithy was removed from other wooden buildings lest sparks from the forge set fire upon the roofs,

Edwin heard voices raised in song, carrying clean lines of melody out through the windows. The shutters of the building had been thrown wide and the song emerged cleanly, a joyful, clear music, at variance with the doleful dirges he had heard Paulinus and James chanting for the last month or more. It was a sound unlike any he had known before, as calm as a mist-covered sea but filled with the warmth of summer crops ripening beneath a gentle sun and overlaid with the joy of a husband taking his newborn son in his arms for the first time.

As he came closer, the door of the building was flung wide and Paulinus, James and the men of Kent who had stayed to serve the queen processed out, chanting and singing, with James swinging a thurible from which grey ribbons of sweet, throat-clutching smoke swirled. Paulinus carried a tall wooden cross. The men were smiling, joyful, as they sang, and that joy carried over into their voices. In line, they processed around the compound, drawing stares and whispers and the odd shout from the servants and warriors who emerged from hall or stable or weapons' field to see what was going on.

Seeing that they were not going to stop on their own, Edwin put himself in the way of the procession. Paulinus gestured for James and the others to continue, while he stopped to speak to the king.

"What is going on?" asked Edwin. "Why are you so happy?"

"Surely I told you – ah, but you have been distracted these last few days. Today is the greatest feast of the year, the fulcrum upon which all our hopes sit and from which our joy rises: today is the day of resurrection, when our Lord rose from the dead, renewed, past all expectation, past all fear, and put down the evil lord of this world and was placed, by God his Father, upon a throne higher than all thrones, dominations or powers. Today is Easter day and death is defeated and the gates of hell thrown wide. Today the children of God in Christ Jesus enter into life eternal, beyond the walls of this world. What else would I be on this day but happy?" And the thin, severe, aquiline face of the Italian broke into a smile as pure as that of a child.

"I wish you joy in your day, and maybe we will speak of what this means later, but for now, call upon this god of yours who defeated death, that he may guard my wife, now in labour, against evil magics and the workings of the fates, so she may be delivered and my child born safely."

Paulinus, looking into the grim face of the king, saw there something he had not seen before: fear. The worry that comes of laying the destiny of one you love in the hands of blind fates and capricious gods. The priest grasped the king's arm.

"The queen will not die – she will live, and the child too. God would not allow it otherwise, that this most blessed day be marred by that which he came to destroy: death."

"I hope you speak truly. But in my experience, what the gods will or will not allow is not so clear. They build up and destroy as they will, and all that is left to men is endurance unto the end."

"My God – and there is only one god; these others you speak of are lesser spirits, demons most likely – my God is not capricious. He is gracious and kind, and repays honesty with abundance and the good man and true ruler with long life. You will see. We will send unceasing prayer to heaven this day, until the child and the queen are delivered."

Edwin nodded. "Thank you." Hearing footsteps approaching, Edwin glanced round to see Forthred hurrying towards him. "I have to go – there is business I needs must attend to."

"We will pray, and the queen and the child will live," Paulinus called after Edwin, as the king headed towards the great hall with his advisor whispering urgently into his ear. Then, assembling the procession, and with James leading them in chant, they returned to the small building that Paulinus had consecrated into a church, to pray and sing through all the remaining hours of the queen's labour.

"What is the urgency of this matter?" Edwin asked Forthred, as his thegn led him towards the hall.

"A messenger, an ambassador, has arrived from Cwichelm of the West Saxons," said Forthred. "From the gifts he brings, and the hints he gave me, it seems that he has come to pledge Cwichelm's allegiance to you, and to give honour to Northumbria."

"Why this change? Thus far Wessex has refused to acknowledge me as lord and cleaves to its claim of sovereignty beyond the headwaters of the great southern river."

"The messenger, his name is Eumer, says only that he brings gifts and words from Cwichelm that are for the king's ears alone. He willingly gave up his weapons upon arrival here, so I believe him to be in earnest."

Edwin pointed towards the boat moored at the jetty. "Is that how they came?"

"Yes, lord."

"Have you asked after their route?"

"No, lord. Should I have?"

"It would take us, what – ten days, two weeks? – to march our men to the land of the West Saxons. One week if all were mounted. It would be interesting to know how long it took for them to sail here, and what was their route. I would guess they came down the Thames, then sailed along the coast, before rowing up the Derwent to here. But on the other hand, do you think that boat would be seaworthy in this season?"

Both men inspected the forty foot, shallow-bottomed vessel.

"If the messenger – you say his name is Eumer? – sailed up the coast in that through this season, then his message must be urgent indeed." Edwin smiled grimly. "I find that the more urgent the message from a king, the better it is to make the messenger wait. Where are my sons, Forthred?"

The thegn laughed. "Where do you think they are?"

"The practice grounds?"

"Where else?"

"Let us go and call them. They should attend this meeting and hear what news Eumer brings of Cwichelm and the West Saxons, and the kingdoms of the south."

The two men headed past the great hall to the far side of the compound. The storehouses that wared the king's share of the local crops and animals were still relatively full, as the royal party had only arrived at the vill on the River Derwent two weeks past. They would remain until the queen was delivered and purified and ready to travel again. Past the warehouses, they came to an area where the earth was packed hard and studded with the booths of the armourers, grinding wheels sparking, sharpening weapons, while the men of Edwin's household practised their fighting skills under the watchful eyes of the older, more experienced thegns, and Edwin's warmaster, Guthlaf.

Upon the war ground, the men stood facing each other in two lines, each armed with shields and old, blunt practice swords. Osfrith stood in the centre of one group, Eadfrith commanded the other.

"What are you teaching them, Guthlaf?" asked Edwin.

The old warrior grunted, his concentration elsewhere. "The wedge and the forceps."

"Who is the wedge and who the forceps?" asked Edwin, since the lines were both still straight.

Guthlaf turned and grinned at his king. "I told the boys to make their own minds up – that way neither knows what the other will do."

Edwin smiled. "As in battle. Good, Guthlaf. Give the signal."

The old warmaster raised his sword. Both lines waited, eager and expectant, and Edwin could see that his sons had seen his presence – they would strive the harder for victory before him.

Guthlaf brought down his sword.

Osfrith immediately put himself at the apex of the wedge, the flank men pushing in behind to give the formation added strength and depth, and they began to advance, shields locked and swords drumming shield rims as the men yelled their battle cries. Facing the advance, Eadfrith dressed his line, gradually pulling the centre back little by little, so that the advancing wedge would be caught and enveloped upon all sides, rather than striking a single section of the line. Guthlaf, Edwin and Forthred watched with practised, critical eyes – timing was everything in such manoeuvres. Move too early and it gave the attackers sufficient time to change their line of attack, so they could hit the vulnerable place where the defending line curved in. Move too late and the line would be too straight and brittle, and the charging wedge would break it.

Leading the attack, Osfrith began to pick up the pace, moving from a fast walk into a trot, all the time beating the rhythm on his shield rim. His men, shields still locked – although the experienced watching eyes saw the beginnings of a gap on the near flank, where some of the younger men were growing too eager and advancing too quickly – pushed him onwards, the men behind adding their weight to the charge, though they would be blind to the first impact.

Edwin himself had led this charge in battle, and looking at his elder son rehearse it now, he remembered the sensation of simultaneously charging and being carried along, as if he were a swimmer riding a breaking wave towards a threatening, rock-strewn shore. The point man, alone of all the charging warriors, could see clearly the waiting line. It was up to him to shift the point of impact to left or right, to hit the shieldwall where it looked weakest. He remembered the battle cry rising up and out and through him, as if he spoke with the voice of all his men. He remembered the awful bright clarity that came on the back of the battle fear, as time slowed and he became the death dealer, splitting men's souls from their bodies, opening their bodies to the ravens and the crows.

It was a high-risk tactic. Should the enemy time its movement correctly, the wedge would be enveloped and the flank men exposed to a far greater threat than men standing firmly side to side in the shieldwall.

"He's leaving it too late." Forthred pointed at Eadfrith's line, which still stood perpendicular to Osfrith's advancing wedge, which had just upped its pace from trot to slow run.

"We will see," said Guthlaf. "That boy is a sly one – methinks he has some trick to play yet."

Edwin said nothing. Osfrith was the elder, and a faithful, dutiful son, but Eadfrith with his laughter and his recklessness brought a lightness of heart to his father that Edwin strove to conceal.

Osfrith and his men gave their battle cry, a guttural growl of mixed syllables, and, with the distance between the two forces now down to only twenty feet, they began to charge.

Edwin held his breath. Forthred was right. Eadfrith had left it too late to pull the centre of his line back.

But Eadfrith did the opposite. He stepped out of his line, as did another man some twenty yards to his left, and they both, as one, bent and lifted.

The timing was perfect. Osfrith, leading and with the best view, managed to vault the rope, but the men following caught the rope on their knees and like forest trees toppling in a storm went down one after another.

Guthlaf laughed. "What did I say? That boy is a wily one." Forthred joined the warmaster in laughter, but Edwin kept his face expressionless. In the matter of his sons, it did not do to show favour to one over the other, but Eadfrith's resourcefulness had nevertheless impressed him.

However, despite the charge falling over itself onto the earth, the practice battle was not over yet. Osfrith, isolated and humiliated but enraged because of that, charged into the opposition line on his own and began laying around wildly with this blunt sword, his rage clearing a space around him. But sheer weight of arms would bring down his battle fury in a short enough time. Still, Edwin could not help but be impressed with the way Osfrith stood up to the press of men around him. Battle madness – the special gift of Woden – could sometimes lead a single man to change the course of a battle, although in Edwin's experience it more generally led to a glorious pile of corpses around a single dead body and the rest of the battle going on unchanged, unless the battle-mad warrior managed to get to the enemy leader.

But he had seen enough. This was the sort of exchange, where men were humiliated and struggling up from the ground, which could breed the type of rancour that produced fights, duels and knives slid across sleeping throats in the night.

"End it," Edwin told Guthlaf.

Forthred, hearing the order, grinned at the king and put his fingers in his ears.

The warmaster stepped forward and, swelling like a displaying cockerel, bellowed, "Enough."

Despite the fingers, Forthred winced. One of the key attributes of a warmaster was to possess a voice loud enough to be heard over the screams and shouts of a battlefield. Guthlaf possessed such a voice.

The battling factions – Eadfrith's men having moved forward to deal with the floor-bound mass of their attackers – slowly came to a heaving, sweat- and in some cases blood-stained halt. Osfrith stood panting and all but spent among a circle of wary enemies, most of whom bore some mark of his battle fury. Eadfrith meanwhile, hardly even breathing hard, was smiling so broadly that his teeth glinted in the pale March light.

"Osfrith, Eadfrith, to me," Edwin called. Then, stepping forward, he passed quickly through the men, passing out short words of praise to those he had seen fight well.

His inspection over and with his sons by his side, Edwin said to Guthlaf, in a voice that all could hear, "When you are finished with them, bring all into the hall. We have an ambassador arrived from the king of the West Saxons, and we must feast him."

The men cheered their approval, but Edwin had not finished yet. He held up his hand for silence.

"And more reason to feast, my wife Æthelburh labours to bring forth my new child."

The start of a louder cheer went up, only for it to be choked off by an unearthly, drawn-out scream that spoke of a world of pain undreamed of by even these battle-hardened men.

The sons of Edwin, standing behind him, heard the sound too. Osfrith's face, already stiff with the humiliation of his battle loss, hardened further, but Eadfrith looked alarmed.

"How much longer, father?"

Edwin shook his head. "I do not know. I hope not long." Shaking himself out of the shock the scream had produced, Edwin told Guthlaf to carry on, then led Forthred and his sons towards the hall.

Osfrith ran up to his father's side. "Guthlaf did not say they could use tricks like that – I thought we were practising the wedge formation."

Edwin glanced at his son, flushed with self-justification. He was a fierce warrior, and a brave one, whom men would follow, but they might find themselves following Osfrith to destruction if he did not better learn the ruses of war.

"Tricks are part of war, Osfrith. Learn to watch for them."

From his place on Edwin's other side, Eadfrith gave his brother a broad grin, then stuck out his tongue.

Osfrith made to jump at him, but Forthred, following and watchful, grabbed the young man and soothed his anger with quiet words, while an exasperated Edwin turned on his younger son.

"Eadfrith!" Edwin could see the young man was trying to look sorry, but a smile kept breaking past his attempts to control it. There were times when he still looked like the boy who had played pranks on his father, lifting Edwin from the gloom that had settled over him after Cwenburg's death, and the king found it hard not to smile in return. But Edwin knew all too well how often battles had been lost and kingdoms destroyed through the rivalry of contending sons; he had no intention that this should happen with his own.

"Enough."

Eadfrith struggled his face under control. Edwin half turned so he could see both his sons. "Do you not see this is why I pit you against each other in training? You each have much to learn from the other. Osfrith, you fight like Rædwald, all bravery and strength, but you must learn to watch and wait for your enemy's devices to be revealed before attacking; Eadfrith, cunning and trickery will serve you well, but even the most well-thought-out plan can be overturned by the battle fury of a single man – learn to respect that, and devise some stratagem to cut down such a warrior before he can turn the fight against you. Do you understand?"

The two young men – one eagerly, the other grudgingly – gave their assent.

"Now, being young you no doubt think the greater part of kingship is war. But I, being old and king for many years, tell you this is false. The greater part of kingship is talk, and we go to do that now. Dress yourselves and join me and let this messenger from the West Saxons see the wealth and splendour of the Northumbrians with his own eyes."

# Chapter 9

Edwin and Forthred found the ambassador from the king of the West Saxons waiting for them in the great hall. Seeing them approach, flanked by the door warden and Edwin's bodyguard, the ambassador sprang to his feet, and as Edwin came closer he slammed his forearm against his chest in honour of the king, then bowed his head.

"Eumer, thegn to Cwichelm, king of the West Saxons, honours Edwin, lord of Deira and Bernicia, master of Northumbria!"

Edwin surveyed this messenger. Eumer was a short, powerfully built man, with a broad brow and pale blue eyes. His clothes were travel stained, but he wore a golden torc of the finest workmanship around his neck, and his cloak was pinned with a gold brooch inlaid with garnets that sparkled blood fire in the light of the hall's torches. By his appearance, Eumer was no ordinary thegn, but a man gifted with the richest of a king's gifts, and thus bound into the closest service to his lord.

"Well met, Eumer of the West Saxons. Edwin, king, greets you and gives greetings to his brother king, Cwichelm." Edwin gestured to Forthred. "Make ready a feast for our guest, for I see that you have travelled far to find me. After you have taken your fill of food and drink, we will speak."

Eumer stepped forward without invitation, and immediately Edwin's bodyguards closed in front of him, hands upon the hilts of their swords, although they did not draw their weapons. The West Saxon raised his hands slowly and carefully, to show that they were empty, before speaking.

"Lord and king, my message is urgent."

Edwin surveyed the shorter man. "Do you intend to start upon your return to Cwichelm this day?"

"Um, no, lord and king."

"Then your message will keep until food has been eaten, toasts made and gifts given."

Eumer made to begin an answer, thought better of it and bowed before smoothly returning to his place.

Edwin looked around for Forthred, but his friend and counsellor had gone to order the servants to start preparing the welcome feast. There was something about this messenger from the West Saxons that he did not like, but he could see that he was weaponless – the door warden had even taken his seax from him. Edwin frowned. They would have to give Eumer a seax to eat. Forthred was no fool, however; the knife would be blunt and short, adequate for spearing meat from the steaming broth, but hardly able to do any more damage than that.

As the servants and slaves scurried around placing cups on the long tables and feeding the fire, the men, somewhat bruised from the earlier encounter, slowly drifted into the hall. Guthlaf, looking pleased with how the session had gone, came over to Edwin.

"What does he want?" he asked, staring over the king's shoulder to the waiting messenger.

"I have not asked him yet. First, we eat and drink, then we talk."

Guthlaf grinned. "A wetted wit talks the more freely."

"Indeed." Edwin glanced around, then lowered his voice, bending closer towards his warmaster. "Do you think Osfrith will ever learn to see when a trap is being sprung upon him?"

Guthlaf looked doubtful. "With your son, if I may speak plain…" He looked at the king, who signalled his assent. "With Osfrith, what he shows is what he is: he is prickly, proud and brave. The men respect him, for they know he will never let them down, and I can think of no one better suited to marshalling the shieldwall. But he has no cunning or craft. He is like a wild boar: to be feared when enraged, to be avoided when he charges, and ripe to be gutted when his target skips aside."

Edwin nodded. "It is much as I thought. He is alike to Rædwald, my sanctuary and succourer of old, and that is no bad likeness of itself, as Rædwald, through his battle fury feared by all, became the most powerful king in these islands." Then Edwin shook his head. "But things are not now as they were then. Men's tongues have grown cunning and their word worthless – lies kill as many as the sword. In such a world I fear for Osfrith."

"As long as he retains the counsel and love of his brother, he will be well. The men respect Osfrith, but they love Eadfrith: he is still their little mascot, but grown now and with the wit of Loki about him. He is never going to miss an enemy's tricks – more likely the enemy will not see his tricks!"

"I know, but more to the point my sons know it too. How can I ensure that they remain brothers and allies after I am dead, when there is so much about them to turn them into rivals and enemies?"

"You could give one of them Deira and the other Bernicia?"

"And have one of them supplant the other, as Æthelfrith did my father?"

Guthlaf shook his head. "May wyrd weave many years yet for you, lord. Then the question may not need answering."

Edwin looked grimly at his warmaster. "Do you know any old kings?"

Guthlaf pursed his lips in thought. "I do not."

"Neither do I. Only Cearl of Mercia is older. Forty years ride upon my shoulders, and my hair feels winter's touch."

"But you are still young enough to sire a child," said Guthlaf with a grin.

Edwin started. In the press of the day's business, he had all but forgotten his wife's labour. "Guthlaf, send for word – how goes the queen?"

"No need, father."

Edwin turned around to see Eadfrith approaching, clad in the finery of the son of the king of Northumbria. His cloak was the rich red of Frankish wine, the garnets that inlaid the brooch and buckles were as red as fresh blood, and his tunic was bright woad blue.

"I sent a servant to inquire: Æthelburh still labours, but the midwife says there is no reason to fear; the child is not breach and Æthelburh is young and strong."

Edwin nodded. He looked around. "Where is Osfrith?"

"Still dressing. Being the elder and slower, it takes him longer."

Edwin kept his face impassive, although he felt a smile tickle the corner of his mouth. Eadfrith needed no encouragement from his father when it came to teasing his elder brother.

"We will wait for him at table. Time for a song. Acca!" Edwin looked around. "Where is Acca?"

"He is not here, father. I saw him earlier today, whispering. He told me the vapours and mists rising from the river had robbed him of his voice."

"No doubt he prescribed many cups of wine as a restorative?"

"I believe he is sleeping off the effects."

Edwin grimaced. There were times when the temptation to cast Acca into exile became almost overwhelming, but then he would sing a song of such mastery and eloquence that he redeemed himself. Still, if the scop was not available, many others could be called upon to provide some entertainment through the feast.

"Coifi, give us a riddle while we wait for the food."

The priest, squatting by the fire, his cloak of raven feathers hanging dully over his shoulders, looked around at the call, his head moving sharply and his eyes black bright, like a bird's.

"A riddle, Coifi," repeated Edwin, "as Acca sleeps in the arms of the daughters of Ægir."

Coifi hissed, and the men nearest him unwittingly drew away. "I saw in the fire, in the flames, that you would call on me, lord, to answer for that drink-addled fool." He shook his bone rattle, and it too hissed. The men around him inched along the benches away from the priest, leaving him in a circle of space.

Edwin inclined his head. "As you foresaw my scop's indisposition and my calling on you, you no doubt have a riddle prepared for us."

Coifi shook his rattle again, weaving it through the air in intricate patterns that drew the eye, as its sound called the ear. Not for him the shout of "*Hwæt!*" Slowly, amid the hubbub of preparation, the waiting, hungry men fell into the closest approximation to silence that was possible.

At that moment Osfrith entered the hall. Eadfrith, noticing him, elbowed his father. "See," he said.

It was true: Osfrith was dressed magnificently, with gold and silver chains and belts accentuating the weld yellow of his tunic and the red madder of his cloak. And by virtue of being the eldest son, he wore a circlet of worked wound gold around his head.

"He certainly looks like a king," commented Eadfrith as his brother made his way over to them. Edwin chose to ignore the undertow of criticism in Eadfrith's voice, and he welcomed Osfrith to the table.

"Have I missed anything?" Osfrith asked, reaching for a cup of beer.

"The king of the West Saxons wants you to marry his daughter," said Eadfrith.

Osfrith spluttered beer over the table. "What?"

"No," said Edwin, glaring at his younger son. "But Coifi is about to spin us a riddle."

"Oh, his riddles are excellent," said Osfrith. "Much better than Acca's."

"I wager I answer Coifi's riddle before you," Eadfrith suddenly cut in. Before Edwin could stop the rivalry, Osfrith spat on his hand and thrust it across to his brother. "Two white mares."

"Done!" said Eadfrith.

"Coifi!" yelled Osfrith, his voice cutting through across the hall. "Start the riddle again. My brother and I have two white mares riding on which of us can solve the riddle first."

Coifi shook out his raven cloak and the old dry feathers rustled like dead leaves. The priest held out his hand and waited until someone put a cup of beer in it. With the added interest of two white mares – a huge fortune – riding on the riddle, the hall fell into almost complete silence. Edwin, though, saw the messenger from the West Saxons look with hooded eyes between his sons and he knew that the man had noted their rivalry.

Coifi drank the beer in one long, throat-bobbing draw, to the cheers of the men in the hall. He was about to hold out the cup for a refill when Osfrith called, "Get on, Coifi."

The priest fixed the prince with his black eye. "I drink for the god," he said.

"So do I," muttered Eadfrith. Edwin fixed his face straight, but felt his lip twitch.

Coifi solemnly drained another cup of beer, drinking more reflectively this time, but still without pause or apparent breath. The men cheered again, but Coifi silenced them, turning on the spot, his bone rattle hissing. The priest looked around the hall, daring any man to speak.

"As I looked upon the weavings of wyrd in the fire, in the smoke, in words heard and in the patterns of shadow and light, the god spoke, and told me this riddle." Coifi spread his arms out and with his raven cloak looked more than ever like a great, dark bird. "Let anyone here who thinks he can see the mind of the gods unweave my words and tell their meaning."

Coifi drew himself up. The men in the hall looked on in silence – even the slaves stopped their preparations for the feast.

"What good man is so learned and so clever that he can say who drives me forth on my way?" Coifi's head snapped from one side to the other with the sharp, percussive movements of a carrion bird.

"When I rise up strong, at times furious, I thunder mightily and again with havoc I sweep over the land, burn the great hall, ravage the buildings." Eyes so wide they showed white, Coifi stared around and the men, watching, hushed, could see the bare bones of the hall, ravaged and brought down, by war perhaps or a party of raiders.

"Smoke mounts on high dark over the rooftops. Clamour is everywhere, sudden death among men." Whispers spread around the hall as men gave their guess and others nodded in agreement. At the high table, Osfrith looked smug.

"When I shake the forest, the trees proud in their fruit, I fell the boles. With my roof of water, by the powers above I am driven far and wide on my avenging path." Faces that were confident suddenly looked puzzled, while others pinched tighter in concentration, realizing that the riddle contest was still open.

"I bear on my back what once covered the forms of the earth-dwellers, their body and soul together in the waters."

Coifi fell silent. He turned in the accustomed and expected way of the riddle game, right around the listening, silent men, seemingly looking each in turn in the eye before coming to a halt, looking at the high table and the watching, breathless brothers.

"Say what covers me or what I am called who bear this burden."

Silence filled the hall. Edwin, sitting between the brothers, glanced from one to the other. Each had his brow furrowed; their lips moved as they muttered and discarded answers.

Then Eadfrith spoke out. "As you are the eldest, Osfrith, you should answer first."

Osfrith, his face pale, rose to his feet as was required. He licked his lips. His mind had gone completely blank. He could not even think of any wrong answers. He shook his head.

"I – I do not know," he said. "I will give you the horses tomorrow, brother." Osfrith slumped back upon his chair and Eadfrith, smirking, began to raise his cup to him.

"So, what is the answer, Eadfrith?" Edwin looked blandly at his younger son. "I take it you know?"

Eadfrith swallowed. "Er, give me a moment…"

Osfrith, suddenly raised from gloom, glared across at his younger brother. "Stand up and tell us then if you know," he said.

Eadfrith slowly got to his feet. Then a broad smile spread across his face. "Coifi," he said, "the mind of the god is opaque to me, which is why we have you as priest: to interpret wyrd and its workings for us. I have no idea what the answer is." He turned to his brother. "I think we both owe Coifi two white mares."

Despite himself, Coifi gasped. His already pale skin went white and the bone rattle shook in a suddenly palsied hand. Four white mares were riches that only a king might dream on.

Noticing the priest's surprise, Eadfrith said, "Surely you saw what wyrd had weaved for you before you told this riddle?"

But Coifi's eyes rolled up until only the whites showed, froth spewed from his lips and his limbs began to shake like a man struck on the helmet in battle.

Edwin sighed. This always happened when one of the gods entered the priest, but if the god remained in possession they would never find out the answer to the riddle. They could simply wait for the god to leave, or they could take more direct action. Edwin signed to a servant carrying a bucket of water. Direct action.

Coifi came spluttering out of his trance. The raven feathers hung lankly about his shoulders and dripped upon the floor. He stared open mouthed at the high table.

"Did you say you would give me four white mares?"

Eadfrith laughed. "Well, brother?"

But before Osfrith could answer, Eumer, the messenger from the West Saxons, stood up.

"Can a stranger and visitor enter the riddle contest?" he asked.

Eadfrith turned to Eumer. "Of course," he said.

"What?" shouted Coifi. "No! No, he can't. I won fair and square. He can't…"

Edwin signed to a servant, and a second bucket of water splashed square in Coifi's face, leaving him gasping and breathless.

"Mayhap you will still win the wager, Coifi," said Edwin, "but let us hear the guess of our visitor. Eumer of the West Saxons, what say you?"

"I say it is a storm, a great storm of thunder, lightning, wind and rain. What say you? Do I speak truth?"

Coifi gaped like a stranded fish. The whispers of delight that accompanied a true guess began to sweep around the hall. In his mind the priest saw the unimaginable wealth represented by four white mares being ridden south, away from him. But he would not let the treasure be taken so easily. "You did not answer 'who drives me forth on my way'. That's part of the riddle too."

"*You* want to know who sends forth the storm?" Eumer laughed. "Thunor, of course."

"Ah, ah," said Coifi, waving his bone rattle, "of course he does, but the king has allowed men in this hall who deny the gods; men who do not believe that it is Thunor who sends the storm."

Edwin stared grimly at the priest, but Coifi, in the agony of his lost wealth, did not mark the king's regard.

"So who do these men say sends the storm if it be not Thunor?" asked Eumer.

"I do not know. But according to them it is not Thunor. That means that not everyone agrees you have given the right answer, so therefore you have not won and the horses belong to me. Those are the rules of the contest!"

"Where are these men? Let them speak for themselves," said Eumer.

Coifi made to send a slave for Paulinus, but Edwin held up his hand. "No. The priest prays to his god, and the god of my wife, for her safe delivery from labour. He is not to be disturbed."

Eumer turned to Edwin. "Your wife is in labour? That is wonderful news! Whence came she?"

"She is the sister of Eadbald, king of Kent."

"Kent? Northumbria waxes great indeed. The kingdoms of Elmet, Rheged and Lindsey, the isles of Man and Anglesey all already hold Northumbria as lord."

Edwin ignored the messenger's statement. Instead, he turned to his sons. "When Eumer returns to the West Saxons, he takes with him two white mares from each of you." Before Coifi could protest, and without looking in his direction, Edwin added, "We may send Cwichelm a priest too."

Suddenly deflated, Coifi sat down. A sympathetic hand passed him a cup of beer. To have such riches snatched away... The priest drained the cup and held it out again. This time wine, rich red wine brought by boat across the narrow sea from the sun-drenched lands of the Franks, filled the cup. Coifi drained it but he barely even noticed the richness of the wine. He sat hunched by the fire, a black and brooding figure, the flames reflected in his eyes, as he sought in vain for some intimation of the wyrd that had snatched wealth unimaginable from his arms.

"Forthred, call forth the feast," said Edwin. "I am hungry, for food and for news from the south, and the latter waits on the former."

The feast was no elaborate affair since, being prepared at short notice, it was the normal fare of the day with whatever dishes the servants could cook quickly to honour their guest. But drink, requiring no preparation, was easier to lavish upon an unexpected guest, and cups were filled with beer, ale, mead and wine, whatever was asked for and however many times thirst called for more. Even Acca, hearing the sounds of feasting from his sick bed, rose and tottered into the hall to partake of some medicinal wine. By the third cup, his voice was restored and by the seventh he could hardly be persuaded to allow anyone else to sing.

The men and visitors having eaten and drunk their fill, and with the early March night already drawing its thick cloak over the land, further torches and lamps were lit, filling the hall with the red gold glow that Edwin always associated with tales told and songs sung. This was the quiet time of reflection, when talk murmured through the hall, in and around the moving shadows, while some men stared into the shifting heart of the fire and others eased themselves into sleep. This was the time for conversation, for news of distant parts and the breaking of messages.

But first, Edwin sent for word of his wife. The servant returned shaking his head: the queen still laboured, but the midwife had said there was no need for worry.

"It has been many hours now," Edwin said.

"Cwenburg laboured two days to bring forth Osfrith," said Forthred.

"I remember." Edwin fell silent, staring into the fire. Then he shook his head like a dog shaking water from its fur, and turned to Forthred. "It is time to hear what messages come from the West Saxons. Call this Eumer to stand before us."

As Forthred, who had as usual drunk little and therefore walked more steadily than anyone in the hall, went to fetch Eumer from where he sat at table further down the hall, Edwin called his sons to attend.

"Listen well to Eumer's message. I have heard that Cwichelm, his king, is a subtle one who achieves as much through cunning and trickery as through strength of arms. Words can be as slippery as fish – grasp these tight and do not let their meaning twist away from you."

Forthred led Eumer to the high table and stood beside him as the messenger from the West Saxons came to a halt in front of the king; Eumer pressed his forearm to his chest in salute.

"To Edwin, lord of Deira and master of Bernicia, the king of Northumbria, of Lindsey, of Elmet and Rheged, of the western isles of Man and Anglesey, I bring greetings from Cwichelm, king of the West Saxons."

The king sat, chin on hand, his eyes shadowed as they surveyed the man in front of him. Edwin inclined his head in acknowledgement of the greeting, but he noted that Eumer's formal opening address had not included Edwin's claim to the high kingship of Britain, but instead merely listed the kingdoms that he explicitly ruled. Edwin nodded to Forthred to reply on his behalf.

"Edwin, High King of Britain, greets the messenger of Cwichelm, king of the West Saxons, and bids him deliver his message."

The slightest of glances conveyed to Forthred Edwin's appreciation: the thegn had heard the omission in Eumer's greeting and corrected it in his response.

"My message is in two parts: the first is a proposal and the second is tidings." Eumer, in his eagerness to deliver the proposal, stepped closer to the table. Forthred stepped up beside him.

"Cwichelm, my lord, king of the West Saxons, proposes an alliance between the West Saxons and the Northumbrians, and as pledge and surety of this alliance he offers his daughter in marriage to your eldest son, and his sister's son in hostage to you, to be raised by you, his blood and his breath to be forfeited should Cwichelm break his solemn oath to you. What say you, Edwin, king of Northumbria?"

There was not a trace of movement on Edwin's face. Osfrith's face, on the other hand, betrayed his dismay, but he made no sound, and waited upon his father to answer, although dread had clutched his heart.

"I say it is a fine and generous offer, but one to which I must give much thought before I can give answer. But first I must ask a question of you. How old is this daughter of Cwichelm, king of the West Saxons, and what will be her marriage portion?"

"She is still young, that is true, but her marriage portion will be great: eternal alliance with the West Saxons, five horses, one hundred pounds of gold, two hundred pounds of silver, and much more besides, including the finest cloths from the kingdom of the Franks and silks from the lands beyond the middle sea."

"You say she is still young. But how young?"

"Lord, I do not know her exact age."

"Has she, for instance, been weaned?"

"Oh yes, of course she has been weaned."

"Then has she begun to bleed?"

"No, not as yet."

"Does she have adult teeth then?"

"Oh yes, some adult teeth."

"But not all?"

"Probably not."

"I see. Then most likely she is about so high?" And Edwin held his hand about three feet from the ground.

"Yes, that is about right," said Eumer. "But of course her age does not affect her marriage portion. That will be great indeed."

"I was going to come on to that. This marriage portion: will it be payable on betrothal, or upon the consummation of the marriage?"

Eumer's eyes narrowed slightly. He stared straight at Edwin, then lowered his gaze.

"Upon consummation of the marriage."

"But of course I will be sworn into eternal alliance with Cwichelm of the West Saxons from their betrothal."

Eumer made no reply.

Edwin nodded. "And then what would happen if, after ten years, when this princess is old enough to marry, Cwichelm of the West

Saxons should find another husband for her? I would have given ten years' alliance to him and received nothing in return."

"There is his sister's son – hostage to you. His blood and life would be forfeit should my king break his pledge to you."

"I usually find it difficult to execute a boy who has been my guest and as a son to me, no matter how grave the offence of the oathbreaker. Besides, I hear that Cwichelm has eight sisters and more sister sons than he can count. A faithless king – although I am sure Cwichelm is not such a one – might not miss one among so many."

Eumer's lips grew pale. "I did not come here to hear my king insulted and his generous offer of alliance, friendship and marriage traduced."

But Edwin answered in a voice that was like the whisper of frost in the night.

"And I did not expect to be insulted in my own hall by the messenger of the petty king of a paltry kingdom."

Eumer began to answer in blood and heat, and then stopped. He passed a hand over his mouth, as if sealing the words in, and the flush of anger that reddened his face dropped away.

"My king, Cwichelm of the West Saxons, earnestly seeks your friendship and alliance, and he sent me here to achieve that. Tell me then, as you reject his offer, what must my king do to earn your friendship and alliance?"

Edwin stared at the messenger with hooded eyes. "Do you know what we are?" he asked eventually.

"Lord?"

"We are all petty kings of paltry kingdoms. We fight like dogs over scraps thrown from the tables of the Franks and the Goths, and the leavings of the Romans of the East. We squabble among ourselves while the Britons plot to push us back into the sea and, from the north, the painted people, the Picts, raid us and burn what they cannot carry off. You come offering great treasure: five horses, one hundred pounds of gold and two hundred of silver, but the very servants of the emperors of old knew such riches! Now we scrabble for the leavings like rats in a bag and all our valour is spent on staving off our fellow kings – for a while, until ill chance and wyrd bring us down and raise a new king in our place." Edwin gestured a servant to bring his standard over.

"You see this?" Edwin stood and took the strange device from the servant. "This is the tufa. See, it is round like this middle-earth, and it bears four boars' heads, looking to the four corners of the earth, as did the emperors of old. Tell Cwichelm of the West Saxons that he will have my friendship when he swears loyalty and honour to me. For I am High King of these islands, and those who do not bow before the tufa will be broken by it."

Eumer stared up at the tufa, wide eyed, then looked to Edwin. "You aim to bring all the kings of the Saxons, the Jutes and the Angles under your rule?"

"Yes."

The messenger inclined his head. "I will give word to my king."

"When the Saxons, the Jutes and the Angles acknowledge me as High King, then we shall call on the Britons, the Picts, the Scots and the men of Strathclyde to do so as well. For this is one island and it should have one king – and such a king would be a mighty king, able to stand as equal to the king of the Franks and even the emperor of the Romans."

The messenger stared at the king, his eyes wide. "Your ambition is so great?"

"Yes. But tell your king that this is no desire for glory and wealth on my part. Only if we achieve unity in these islands will we be secure. If we do not, then in time new raiders will come and we will be as the Britons were: dispossessed and pushed into the corners of our own land. For after all, our forefathers came here first as guests, hired warriors in the game of war between the contending kings of the Britons. Think you not that others wait beyond the seas, watching this rich land with greedy eyes? Would you give it them?"

"Who are these raiders you speak of?"

"The West Saxons live far from the sea. But for the Northumbrians, the sea is road and home. Many strange, wonderful and terrible things are cast upon the beach after a storm, and some of these are men, come to us over the waves with wares to sell and questing, calculating eyes. I have seen them, Eumer, standing before me with furs and amber in their hands but guile in their hearts, taking stock of our strength and our weaknesses. They will come, believe you me, they will come."

Eumer, his eyes now as hard and clear as new ice, nodded. "My king will hear of this."

"Very well. Take Cwichelm our demand, and return with his reply. Then we will talk of betrothals and marriage portions; not before. But you said you have news as well. I would hear that now."

Eumer looked around the hall. "There are two stories I must tell, king. The first shall no doubt soon be known to all men in these islands, but it concerns you greatly. However, as for the second... it may best be told in secret."

"Speak on the first. As for the second, that shall wait."

"Very well." Despite his assurance that all would soon know his first item of news, Eumer lowered his voice. "There is a new warrior among the men of Mercia: Penda. He has won many battles for his king – even defeating my own lord, Cwichelm, and wresting from him lordship of the land of the Hwicce. Although he is not related to Cearl, the king of Mercia, he takes the air of a man destined to be king, for the last of Cearl's own sons died recently, in battle against the men of Powys. Penda is descended, on his mother's side, from the Britons and he has sworn friendship to some of the kings of the Britons, notably Cadwallon of Gwynedd."

Edwin, who had been staring into the fire as he heard the news, looked over, startled despite himself, at Eumer when he heard that name.

"We left Cadwallon for dead, cast upon the seas."

"The sea did not take him, but carried him to Ireland, where he raised a new army from among his relatives there."

Edwin hissed air through his teeth. Forthred smacked fist into hand. "We should have killed him when we had him, lord."

"His god is more powerful than I believed." Edwin stared into the distance, calculating numbers and alliances. "You say Cadwallon has allied himself with this Penda of Mercia?"

"Yes," said Eumer.

"But Cearl still rules there, does he not?"

"Yes, Cearl still rules Mercia."

"Then Cadwallon will gain little from this alliance, for Cearl is my friend and exile father of old; he gave me his daughter, Cwenburg, in marriage when I lived with the Mercians, and Osfrith and Eadfrith are her sons."

"Our land abuts that of the Mercians, and we hear many rumours and tales from that people. It may be that Cearl will not rule Mercia much longer – Penda is gathering men to him, for he gives great gifts as freely as any king and not a season passes without war, from which more treasures flow."

Edwin and his sons and counsellors exchanged looks. Osfrith made to ask a question and then fell silent. Eadfrith, however, grinned. "We defeated Cadwallon before, father. We can do so again."

"No doubt, but I do not like this talk of alliance between Gwynedd and Mercia. If Cadwallon has returned, then Anglesey will be hard to hold."

"That may not be much of a disadvantage, lord," said Forthred. "Its render has always been difficult to collect, and the ships bringing it vulnerable to Scots and Pictish pirates."

"That may be so. But I would not that Cadwallon had its wealth to call on, for with it he may buy alliances that would not be given otherwise. We will see what the new season brings." Edwin turned to Eumer. "What of your second item of news?"

The messenger glanced around the hall. "Unless the king knows every man here and can swear to his probity, it may be better if I tell him this news in private."

"I keep no secrets from my sons, nor Forthred my friend and advisor."

"Of course not. But can all here be trusted as these are? Some, at least, owe allegiance to other kings and different lands."

"Speak you of the men of Kent that accompanied my wife?"

Eumer's silence gave answer.

"They have proved faithful in all things."

"But surely there are others here, maybe even one of those men you spoke of from over the sea. It would be wise for such as them not to hear what I have to say."

Edwin scanned the hall. Most of the men were near as familiar as his own sons, but it was true there were some visitors: traders and merchants, a thegn from the East Anglians and one or two travellers from across the waves, made welcome for their tales and their news as much as for their wares.

"Very well. Come, sit beside me. Those who should hear are all around; those who should not are beyond hearing."

Eumer thrust his forearm against his chest in acknowledgement of the honour Edwin did him. The king looked to Forthred.

"Come, join us too. I would hear your opinion of this news."

So Forthred followed Eumer as he made his way around the length of the high table. As usual, Forthred had drunk little and his head was clear. Following Eumer, he noted without thinking the way the West Saxon held his right arm stiffly by the side of his body. It looked as though an old muscle wound hampered the arm's movement. But then as Eumer approached the place where Edwin sat talking with his sons, Forthred saw his arm dip beneath the folds of his cloak, moving easily and freely. The thegn moved closer, and then he saw Eumer raise his hand and in it was a dagger, double edged and coated with a thick, viscous paste. Poison.

Forthred saw all this in an instant, and knew that Eumer meant to assassinate Edwin, and that there was no one within range to stop him. Edwin and his sons had their backs turned and the king's bodyguards stood too far away. There was only him, and his hand went for the seax at his belt only to find the loops empty. The seax was where he had left it, on the table.

There was no longer time to think. As Eumer stabbed downwards with all his might, Forthred threw himself forward, grabbing for the knife arm and putting himself between assassin and king. But the rushes beneath his feet shifted, throwing him slightly off balance as he jumped, and his grab missed. Time, as it had done so often in battle, slowed down. Forthred saw everything with absolute clarity: the black knife descending, the fierce concentration in Eumer's eyes, the sewn pocket in his tunic that had concealed the dagger. And the slow down in time allowed a mind that had been tutored since infancy in the calculation of angles of blow and degrees of deflection to see that the only remaining shield between Edwin and the knife was Forthred's own body. Thought and action were simultaneous. Forthred twisted round and up, bringing himself between knife and king. He reached up as he fell backwards, landing upon Edwin's shoulders, trying to gouge Eumer's eyes, but the knife fell faster and it struck Forthred, piercing his side with a blow like a club, and he felt it go deep, deep through flesh and muscle, sliding between bones, and out through his back and into the back of the king. Forthred reached palsied, strengthless arms up, trying to push Eumer back, but the assassin put all his weight onto the dagger, driving it further through the thegn and into the king.

Edwin, crushed beneath his thegn and with Eumer putting all his weight into the blade, struggled to push himself aside. Yells, shouts, alarms rang out throughout the hall. Osfrith and Eadfrith hurled themselves at Eumer and pulled him off the king, but neither was armed and the assassin, regaining his balance, held the black knife in front of them.

"Come on," he said, moving it back and forth like a questing snake, "come on, try me."

Before either brother could move, one of Edwin's bodyguards hurled himself at Eumer, sword upraised, but the assassin moved easily aside and jabbed the knife into the man's neck. There, for an instant, it stuck fast. Osfrith and Eadfrith leapt as one, the elder breaking the assassin's hold on his blade, the younger slamming into him and knocking him down. Osfrith followed, wresting the man's arm behind his back, pushing it up and up as Eadfrith throttled him.

"Stop!" Edwin stood swaying above them, his shoulder red with blood. "I want him alive."

Eumer thrashed in their grasp. Eadfrith squeezed the air out of his throat until the assassin went limp. Then taking some rope the brothers swiftly and securely bound the man. Edwin, clutching his shoulder, staggered to where Forthred lay upon the table, staring up at the ceiling. The king looked down into the face of his old friend but it had become as wax, stiff and unmoving. Wyrd had done for him and the fate singers had cut the thread of his life.

Edwin felt his legs give way. The world was going dim, indistinct around the edges, and in the decreasing part of his mind that was still functioning clearly he knew loss of blood would soon take him down into unconsciousness and then death.

"Eadfrith," he croaked. "Help me."

The young man sprang to his father, swept the table clear and lay him out upon it. Guthlaf, the warmaster and a man most experienced at dressing battle wounds, ran over, ripping cloth as he came. They cut the tunic from Edwin's back and Guthlaf pressed the wound shut with pads of cloth. Edwin lay upon the table, his mind drifting into mists of forgetting, but just as he was about to be lost in the fog, he focused on Forthred, also lying sprawled on the table, and anger and revenge cleared the mist away. He would not die until he had seen Forthred's killer dead, and the king who had sent him destroyed.

"Press this down," Guthlaf told Eadfrith, moving his hands onto the cloth pads. While he did so, the warmaster removed an oyster-shaped fungus from a pouch on his belt, together with a fine bone needle and finer thread. Seeing Eadfrith's question, Guthlaf said, "Birch fungus. It will help close the wound, and its virtues stop the black rot." The warmaster cut thin slices from the fungus with his seax and laid them out next to Edwin on the table. He quickly looked up from his work. "Osfrith, bring me clean linen, clean water and a hot iron. But first, find me the knife."

Osfrith cast around until he found the double-edged blade on the floor, kicked away under the table. He handed it gingerly to Guthlaf, making sure to keep his fingers clear of the black coating that covered the twin cutting edges. "Poison?" he asked Guthlaf.

The warmaster sniffed it and grimaced. "Poison," he confirmed. "I hope the bleeding has washed most of it from the wound."

The clean linen found, Guthlaf eased Eadfrith to one side. "When I say, remove the pad. Osfrith, stand ready with the iron and the linen."

Edwin lay face down upon the table.

"Remove the pad."

The wound began to bleed again. Guthlaf, lips pursed in concentration, washed away the caked and drying blood, then held out his hand for the hot iron.

"Hold him down if he moves."

Eadfrith and Osfrith laid hands on their father. The warmaster, his thick, scarred fingers moving as surely as those of a weaver, took the iron and pushed it into the wound. Despite his sons holding him, Edwin jerked as the muscles in his body spasmed.

"Hold him!" Guthlaf grunted.

The brothers renewed their efforts, pushing down with their whole weight, and the air was quickly scented with the sickly sweet smell of burning human flesh. But the cauterizing took only a few moments – Guthlaf sought rather to burn out the poison than burn the wound closed. He dropped the iron, and with swift, sure movements stitched the lips of the wound closed. Osfrith and Eadfrith continued to hold their father, but he was no longer struggling. So still did he become that Osfrith, who could not see his face, asked Eadfrith, "Does he yet live?"

"Yes, he lives," said Eadfrith.

The wound stitched, Guthlaf laid the strips of birch fungus atop it in a cross-hatch pattern. And as he worked, he taught.

"The best place to find this fungus is on dead or dying birch trees. Cut it from the tree whole; it keeps well. For wounds, cut thin strips from the fungus, lay them over the wound as I am doing here, and then bind the wound tight. The virtue of this fungus lies in it helping to stop the black and green rots setting into the wound. Keep the fungus on the wound until it is healed."

Guthlaf finished binding the wound and tied off the linen

bandages. He nodded to the two young men who, as gently as possible, lifted Edwin up from where he lay face down on the table.

"The king should rest," said Guthlaf.

"No," said Edwin, "not yet." But his voice was a whisper of its usual strength and his face as pale as a winter sky.

The brothers looked at each other over the head of their father, then Eadfrith began, "But, father…"

The king, his face deathly pale, began to sweat. "My blood burns."

"The knife was poisoned," said Guthlaf.

The king looked up at the warmaster with blurring eyes. "Did you burn it out?"

"As much as possible. But some is in your blood."

The king nodded. "Wake him," Edwin whispered, indicating Eumer with his eyes. "I – I would know why he sought to kill me, knowing his own death must surely follow."

While servants were sent to fetch buckets of water, Edwin, supported by his sons, stood over the body of Forthred. The king said no words, but simply looked into the eyes of the dead man. There was no recognition there, no reflection. The spirit had gone out of him and only the body remained – he was as lifeless as any man left for the crows and ravens on the battlefield. Yet Edwin knew that he lived now only through the sacrifice of his oldest and most faithful friend.

"Though you do not hear, let this be known through all the high halls of the gods and in the weaving place of the fates: I will avenge you, Forthred."

"The ravens will carry your message to Forthred and he will hear your pledge in the mead halls of Woden," said Osfrith.

Edwin weakly shook his head. "He – he did not die in battle. Only warriors who die in battle are taken to the mead halls of Woden." The king saw that the servants were waking the assassin. "Bring him before me."

With his sons supporting him, Edwin staggered to the judgement seat, the painted wood and stone throne that stood at the top of the great hall, and took his place there.

Eumer was thrust down upon his knees in front of Edwin. The king stared at him.

"You must have known that even had you succeeded in killing me you would die," Edwin said. "So why did you attempt this thing, against all laws of hospitality?"

The assassin looked up. His face was blood smeared and bruised, and one eye was half closed, yet Eumer still managed a death's head grin.

"My knife was poisoned – you may yet die."

Guthlaf struck the man down and kicked him in the ribs. "I burned the poison out. The king will live."

Eumer coughed, and spat a mixture of blood and phlegm before forcing himself back upon his knees. "We all die," he said.

"We do," said Edwin, "and your death is near, Eumer of the West Saxons. But it is in my power to make your death swift or long. Now answer me: why did you try to strike me down?"

"Do you remember Eohric, son of Dearlaf, a thegn of Mercia and companion to the king?"

"No," whispered Edwin.

"He was my father, and you killed him. Kings pay no weregild, they accept no fault for the blood they spill, but their blood is as red as any man's and it flows as freely. Would only that I had spilled more of yours."

"I – I do not remember him."

Osfrith drew his sword. "Father, shall I kill him?"

Edwin swayed upon the judgement seat and Eadfrith had to stop him falling from the throne.

"No – not yet," said Edwin in a voice that was growing steadily weaker. "Wh-why did Cwichelm send you against me?"

Eumer swayed, but forced himself to remain upright. "You would make us all your slaves. But the West Saxons will never, never kneel before you, and nor will the men of Mercia, or the Hwicce, nor the East Folk or the South Folk."

"Th-the world is changing, Eumer. The ways of our fathers, those ways gave us the strength to take this land, but they will not give us the strength to hold it. If you do not bow to me, you will bow to others, and worse, and they will burn your halls and take your women."

Eumer made to spit, but Guthlaf struck the back of his head and the man pitched forward. Osfrith's sword pricked his neck but Edwin signed him to hold.

"Le-let him see me live. But if I die, make his dying long."

"Oh, we will, father, we will." Osfrith signed to Eadfrith. "Help me." And the brothers helped their father, the king, from the great hall to his chamber, while Guthlaf saw to the prisoner and the dead.

# Chapter 10

Edwin's eyes snapped open.

Osfrith, who had been dozing, saw the movement and stooped over his father. The pupils were dilated, great black pits that filled the king's eyes. He looked questioningly to Coifi, who squatted by the fire, passing his hands through the smoke.

"What is it?"

But before the priest could answer, the king began to tremble, starting in his extremities, but moving inwards, to the core.

"Help me," said Osfrith.

Coifi stared at the thrashing figure of the king. "A god has taken him," he whispered fearfully.

"I need your help," said Osfrith.

The priest shook his head dumbly, backing away, his eyes as wide as the king's.

"Eadfrith," called Osfrith. "Eadfrith, get in here."

The younger brother rushed into the chamber to find Osfrith holding Edwin down as the man convulsed upon the bed, his body jerking and heaving despite Osfrith putting his full weight upon him. Eadfrith threw himself upon the king's lower half and the brothers together managed to hold the convulsions. Slowly, slowly the king subsided into a sweat-stained, shallow-breathed rest.

"Can you help him?" asked Eadfrith. "There was poison on the knife."

Coifi licked his lips. Thoughts flashed through his head. What would happen to him if he tried to cure the king and he died? Would the princes exile him for failure? And what could he do? A god had taken the king, he could see that, but he did not know which one. Unless he could find out, there was nothing he could do.

"Coifi?"

The priest, shivering with fear, turned to the fire. "Let me see, let me see," he mumbled, as he cast the seeds of poppy and henbane into the flames, searching for the weavings of wyrd in the perfumed smoke that twisted through the room and upon the shifting faces of the burning logs.

"What do you see?" asked Osfrith.

"I – I…give me time. The gods – "

"Leave him," said Eadfrith. "He knows nothing. I will call on the queen's priest. Maybe he has knowledge, for he comes from the land of the emperors."

"No, I will find the answer…" began Coifi.

"While you are looking I will bring Paulinus. In any case, two priests must be better than one. He can pray to his god and Coifi can pray to our gods."

Eadfrith hurried in search of Paulinus, leaving Osfrith tending to Edwin and Coifi swaying in front of the fire, occasionally throwing seeds and minerals upon the flames. Servants and slaves scurried in and out of the room, bringing water and burning sweet-smelling perfumes and heating oils. A miasma of heady scents filled the room and leaked out into the great hall, where the men waited in whispering, anxious groups.

"Here he is." Eadfrith led Paulinus into the room. "The king sleeps now, but he went into convulsions a short time ago. It was all we could do to hold him down."

Paulinus went down on one knee next to Edwin. He took his wrist and felt the king's pulse, then laid his hand on his brow. His fingers came away sticky and wet.

"The knife was poisoned," said Eadfrith.

"Where is it?"

Eadfrith looked to his brother, who gingerly handed the knife to the priest. Paulinus stared at the black ichor coating the blade, twisting the handle so that it caught the light at different angles. Then he sniffed along the blade. Finally, and very carefully, he scraped a tiny amount of poison onto his fingertip and touched it to his tongue.

"Belladonna," said Paulinus, getting to his feet. "The beautiful lady of death. The women of my home, they put the belladonna on their cheeks to give them a beautiful blush, and in their eyes to make them dark and beautiful. But when she gets into the blood, the beautiful lady is deadly."

"Can you help?" asked Osfrith.

"Maybe – I will try." Paulinus turned to a servant. "Go, get my satchel. James knows where it is. And I also need wine and a pot to heat the wine in."

"I will get the wine," said Eadfrith.

"And I will bring the pot," added Osfrith.

That left Paulinus alone in the room with Coifi and the unconscious king. Paulinus knelt again beside the bed, but did so in such a way that he could keep an eye on Coifi while he soothed Edwin's brow. For his part, Coifi remained squatting in front of the fire, swaying and staring into the coals, mumbling low incantations and occasionally passing his hands through the flames.

"A god has taken him," Coifi muttered without turning round. "He will not give him up."

"You serve demons, not gods, as the Canaanites served Moloch and sacrificed their children to him."

"If we did not make sacrifice to the gods, they would take what they wanted and give us back nothing in return."

"My God sacrificed himself for us and he asks our service in return." Paulinus paused as an image entered his imagination. "It is like this: imagine you are in battle, in the shieldwall, and your enemy is about to strike you down. Then your king puts himself between you and your enemy; he takes the blow and is struck down. But the king lives! Would you not owe such a king every service from that day forth?"

Coifi passed his hand through the flames. The yellow tongues licked over his rough fingers. "The gods are not like that. They give to the strong and they take from the weak. The gods are kings who cannot die."

"I thought the gods will die," said Eadfrith, returning with the wine, "when the serpent rises from the sea and the wolf comes from the north."

"There is only one God," said Paulinus, "and he has defeated death already."

Eadfrith looked at the priest. "Tell that to Forthred," he said.

Paulinus shook his head. "Forthred did not believe. But those who do believe in the one God, the true God, they shall rise again with him who has already risen from the dead. Think you: a king gives gifts to his bondsmen, and to the most favoured he gives the greatest gifts, yes? Our God gives life to his bondsmen – life indeed, in this world and the next world, for he has proved he has power over death by breaking forth from the underworld where wicked and cruel men had delivered him."

Osfrith and the servant – who had sprinted all the way from and to the king's room – returned with satchel and pot.

"Heat the wine," said Paulinus, as he took the satchel and searched through it. "I know – I know I brought some... Ah, here." Paulinus poured a handful of striated seeds from a leather pouch and smelled them. "Yes, they still have their virtue. Here, smell." He held the seeds out to Osfrith and Eadfrith, who both sniffed. "As long as the seeds retain their aniseed smell, they will work. I tried to grow some, but there is not enough sun for any civilized plant to grow here. My vine died too." Paulinus turned to the fire. "Is the wine hot yet?"

The heavy fumes rising from the pot gave answer. Paulinus added the seeds to the hot wine, chanting in a low voice as he did so. Coifi, who had been pushed away from his berth by the fire, squatted in the corner, his raven cloak pulled around his shoulders. He too began to croak an incantation, shaking his bone rattle, but when Paulinus heard, he turned sharply on the priest.

"Silence!" he said. "Do not invoke demons and devils while I pray for the king's deliverance."

Coifi looked to Edwin's sons for support. "I was asking the gods' help to change the wyrd that has afflicted the king."

"If this does not work you can call on the gods later," said Eadfrith. "For now, let Paulinus work alone. It does not do to have two commanders in battle nor two priests in prayer. The gods will not know which to listen to."

Coifi slouched down into a ragged pile of black feathers. Paulinus, finishing his prayers, filled a cup with the hot, flavoured wine.

"Help me get him to drink," he said.

Osfrith and Eadfrith lifted their father up. He moaned and shifted in their grasp, but the fierce strength that had sustained him through his years seemed gone; they had no need to exert themselves in order to hold him steady or to open the king's mouth.

"You must drink this," said Paulinus, holding the cup to Edwin's lips. "It will help against the poison."

Edwin's gaze, which had been rolling wildly around the room, slowly focused on Paulinus.

"Baby?" he asked.

"A – a beautiful baby boy," Paulinus said, his thin face flushing red as he spoke.

"A son," whispered Edwin.

"You didn't tell us," Osfrith hissed, but Paulinus did not look at the prince.

"Drink, lord, and see your son." The priest tilted the cup. At first the wine rolled from Edwin's lips, but the strong scent seemed to prick at his nose and the back of his throat. The king's mouth began to work, and the next sip made its way to the back of his mouth and down his throat. The priest gave more, and a little more, and the supporting princes could see their father's throat working as he swallowed the wine.

Edwin choked, coughing out the next sip, and his sons leaned him forward, so he might better clear his lungs. The first hint of colour appeared on his pale lips.

"It's working," said Osfrith.

But Paulinus shook his head. "Not yet. He must drink this all, or the poison will return." So, slowly, sip by sip, Paulinus gave Edwin, king of Northumbria, the cup of wine. By its end, much colour had returned to Edwin's face, and the cold sweat that had plastered his hair to his scalp was drying.

"Lie him down and let him rest," Paulinus said to Osfrith and Eadfrith.

Edwin gripped Paulinus's arm. "My wife?"

The priest blushed furiously once more, but his voice was low and steady. "She is well, lord."

The king fell back on the bed and closed his eyes, but the men watching could see that he slept a healing sleep and the poisonous delirium no longer gripped him.

"He can sleep now," said Paulinus, "but he must be watched."

"And guarded," added Osfrith. "I will remain until he wakes."

"I too, brother," said Eadfrith. "Or at least we will keep watch in turns. But first…" Eadfrith took Paulinus's arm and drew him over towards the door. "Why did you not tell us the queen had given birth to a son?"

The priest glanced furtively past Eadfrith to where the king lay sleeping. "Ah, please to come outside." He lowered his voice. "Where he cannot hear."

A puzzled Eadfrith signalled for his brother to follow. Outside, and although the noise of the great hall masked their conversation, the priest gestured the princes closer.

"I do not know if the queen gives birth or not," he said.

"But – but you said she'd had a son," said Osfrith.

"Your father, he was this close," Paulinus held his thumb and forefinger so near they were all but touching, "this close to death. Then he asked me if his wife has baby yet." Paulinus made a moue with his lips. "I do not know; all day we have prayed for the queen, but I have heard nothing. So when the king asked me, is his baby born, I, may God forgive me, told him he has a son, so he will come back and not die. What man wouldn't want to see his son?"

"So you don't know whether it is a son or a daughter?" asked Eadfrith.

"No, I do not know," said Paulinus.

"What if it's a girl?" asked Osfrith.

"I hope the king will not remember what I said. If he does," Paulinus shrugged, "he already has two sons."

"We should find out," Eadfrith said, turning to his brother.

"You go," said Osfrith. "I'll stay with Father."

"I also," said Paulinus. He glanced back into the room, where Coifi still squatted blackly in the corner. "I do not trust your priest. When the king wakes, maybe he will try to say his gods helped the king. They did nothing."

\*

Eadfrith returned, beaming.

"Good news?" asked Osfrith, getting up. "Though in truth I am not quite sure what good news is here."

Eadfrith's grin grew broader. "Yes, I think it is good news in this case, brother. And amusing too, for us at least, though mayhap not for the priest here." The young man smiled at Paulinus. "It's a girl," he said.

"The queen?" asked Paulinus.

"She is well."

"Thank God," Paulinus said fervently.

"She is weary, I was told, but well. The midwife said that for a first labour Æthelburh did not suffer too much. I did not say about what happened to Father."

Paulinus blew air through his teeth in relief. "God heard our prayers."

Eadfrith laughed. "You sound surprised."

"Relieved."

"But I thought your god answered your prayers?"

"Oh yes, he answers our prayers, but not always in the way we wish. For instance, ten years ago I prayed to God to remove me from my bishop, who was an angry and difficult man, and God sent me here!" Paulinus shrugged. "God answered my prayer, but I hoped for a nice parish near Ravenna where I can grow my vines and instead he sent me here, where it is so dark no vines will grow and I must wear wool drawers to stop my legs freezing!" At this point, and somewhat to the alarm of the two young men, Paulinus drew up the hem of his robe to reveal the long woollen tubes that encased his legs. His secret revealed, Paulinus took the opportunity to scratch his legs.

"They are warm, but so itchy."

"What is so itchy?"

The voice was weak but clear. The three men spun around, only to find Coifi already by the king, one hand upon Edwin's brow while the other weaved his bone rattle above him.

"The king wakes," Coifi said.

"Father." Eadfrith ran to the king, taking Coifi's place at the bedside. A pale Osfrith, struck dumb with relief, stood silent and still.

"What is so itchy?" Edwin repeated, struggling to sit up a little. Eadfrith gestured for his brother to help, and together they lifted him.

"My, er, drawers," said Paulinus.

Edwin raised an eyebrow.

"The wind, it is so cold, not like in my home."

The king was about to answer, when Coifi fell on his knees, arms upraised, and shouted out, "May the gods be praised! You are well, lord, and you have a son!"

"A son?" Edwin turned to Eadfrith and Osfrith, his face shining. "A son. So it was true what I heard before. I thought it might have been the fever."

"Ah," said Osfrith.

"Er," said Eadfrith.

The king went pale. "It's not the queen?"

"No, no, the queen is well, father," said Eadfrith. "It's just… You tell him," he said, looking to Osfrith. "You're the elder."

"Tell me what?" asked Edwin.

"Um…" began Osfrith, and then his voice trailed away.

"Is there something wrong with my son?" asked Edwin.

Osfrith stared across helplessly to his younger brother. The king looked from one to the other, searching for an explanation. As one, the princes turned on Paulinus.

"You tell him."

"After all, you started it."

Edwin, baffled, looked to the priest. "Started what?"

"Lord…" Paulinus swallowed. "Your son is a daughter."

Edwin made to answer, then shook his head. "What did you say?"

"The baby – it is not a boy, it is a girl."

"But…didn't you…?"

Paulinus blushed even more brightly. "I did."

"The stranger lied to you, lord." Coifi pushed past the princes. "He said the baby was a boy."

Paulinus hung his head. "May God forgive me."

But Eadfrith began to laugh. "Father, he only told you it was a boy because the fever had gripped you and the news pulled you back. If it was a lie, we should get you to tell some more, priest."

"So my son is my daughter…?" The king looked for confirmation, and three heads nodded vigorously.

"But the queen is well? That part is true?"

"She is well, lord," said Paulinus.

Edwin breathed out a long relieved sigh. "Thank the gods."

"Yes, yes, thank the gods!" echoed Coifi.

"Ahem." Paulinus coughed. "The gods, your gods, had nothing to do with it, lord. Ask your sons – who was it who called you back from the banks of the black river? Was it the priest of vain gods of dead wood and dumb stone, or the minister of the living God, the true God, who hears and answers our prayers? Tell." Paulinus looked to Osfrith and Eadfrith.

The brothers grimaced at each other. "It's true," said Osfrith.

"The assassin's knife was poisoned," added Eadfrith. "Coifi was no help, but the queen's priest knew the venom and he cured you."

"Through God's grace," added Paulinus.

Edwin looked long at the priest. "I thank you," he said.

"The thanks are not due to me, lord, but to God. He is power and truth and wisdom."

Edwin fell silent, his face withdrawn. To his watching sons it was clear that he was thinking hard. Then he looked up at Paulinus.

"Will your god give me victory over Cwichelm and the West Saxons? Has he the power?"

"Lord, my God threw down Pharaoh in all his strength and magnificence. He will give you victory over this king."

"If he should, then I will follow him."

The room fell silent. Coifi shrank into the black embrace of his raven-feather cloak. Osfrith and Eadfrith stared at their father, for where the king went they needs must follow.

"My God is a jealous God, lord. He is not one among many, but reigns alone. He will not accept you if you worship him among other gods. You must reject and abandon the vain gods of wood and stone, these demon offspring that tempt you and taunt you and threaten you." Paulinus, his face pale and thin, his hair startlingly black against his skin, stared fixedly at the king.

"The god that gives me victory is the god I will follow."

A profound silence filled the room.

"You must pledge it," whispered Paulinus.

"I so pledge," said the king.

Paulinus breathed out a breath as long as the wind.

"As surety, I give my daughter to your god. Consecrate her to him."

Paulinus bowed. "I – I will tell the queen."

"When she is able, ask her to bring my daughter to me. I would see her."

"Yes, lord, certainly." The priest bowed his way from the chamber. Coifi made to say something, but Eadfrith, seeing him, held his finger to his lips.

"Leave us," he said.

Coifi shuffled from the room, his cloak trailing upon the ground like the feathers of a bedraggled bird.

Eadfrith waited until Coifi was out of earshot before turning to Edwin. "Is this wise, father? Many of your thegns follow Thunor, or Tiw, or Woden. They will not easily acknowledge a new god."

"I know my thegns," said Edwin. "They will follow the god that gives them victory. We will see if this new god is more powerful than the old gods." The king began to cough, his body wracked by the fit.

"You should rest, father," said Eadfrith.

"Yes," admitted Edwin, laying back on the bed.

"One question, father," said Osfrith. "What should we do with Eumer?"

"Give him to Guthlaf," said Edwin. "He will find it useful to have someone alive for his exercises with the men. When he's finished with Eumer, tell Guthlaf to feed his body to the dogs."

# Chapter 11

"Are you well?"

Æthelburh looked up, surprised, from the baby nursing sleepily at her breast, and shaded her eyes against the morning sun. She sat upon the platform before the great hall, taking for herself and her child the new warmth of the spring sun.

Eadfrith stood before her, shifting slightly from foot to foot. "And the baby? Is she well?"

Æthelburh looked down at the baby and smoothed her hand over the head. "She is well." She squinted up at the young man. "You are in the sun."

"Oh. Sorry." Eadfrith shifted to his right, coming into the shade beneath the eaves of the hall. "Er, does she have a name yet?"

"Eanflæd. If my lord wills. How is the king?"

Eadfrith shifted again, like a man skipping from foot to foot in the shieldwall. "That is why I have come to see you. The king... weakens. The poison saps his strength. He drifts between dream and sleep. Perhaps if you could come, and the baby, you might call him back from the shadows."

Æthelburh looked down upon her child and made no answer.

Eadfrith, his lips tight with contempt, turned to leave.

"Did you not think that I, his wife, should see the king and know his health before?"

Eadfrith turned back to see the queen, her face set with fury.

"How long have I sat waiting upon news of my husband, told that he was too ill to see me – to see us – and now, now only, you tell me he is passing into the shadows." Æthelburh unlatched the baby from her breast, paying no heed to her squawk of protest, and passed the child to the wet nurse who waited upon the queen's command and the baby's need.

"I – we – thought he was getting better," said Eadfrith.

"Pray that you are not mistaken." Æthelburh fixed her veil in place. "Let us go to him. Godwif, bring the baby. And Eadfrith…"

The young prince paused in mid step. "Yes?"

"When next you come seeking me, you will call me 'queen'."

Eadfrith stared at the woman, younger than he was himself, but Æthelburh returned his gaze with a self-possession he had not seen before. "Very well."

"There are enemies who seek ill for your father, Eadfrith, but I am not one of them."

"So you say. Queen."

Æthelburh made to answer, but then shook her head. "Let us go to the king."

Eadfrith led the way, but he paused upon the threshold of the king's chamber. "Be not shocked when you see him."

Æthelburh pushed past the prince and entered the room. The king lay unmoving upon the bed, his body covered in furs. His eyes were closed, but his lips moved weakly, although he made no sound. The flesh had drained from his bones, leaving him as a man of famine. The room reeked of smoke. Coifi, squatting by the fire, hissed at the interruption. He passed his hand through the flames, and sparks flew, spewing fresh smoke into the thick air.

"What is this?" Æthelburh looked to Eadfrith.

"Coifi searches for the king's spirit, to call it back to his body."

The priest hissed again, his eyes rolling white.

"No, no, no," said Æthelburh. "There is no air here. Bring the king forth, let him breathe the spring."

Eadfrith looked from the queen to the priest, torn between the two.

"His spirit drifts away from life," said Coifi. "Would you stop me calling him back?"

"He needs air." Æthelburh turned to Eadfrith. "Bring the king out."

Eadfrith called the guards from outside the room. "Carry the king without." He turned back to Coifi. "You have been trying to call the king's spirit back these past two days."

They lay Edwin down where Æthelburh had sat before. A quiet ring of fearful, mourning people formed around the bier, but none dared to approach closely, for the queen sat beside him, with her child, while Eadfrith waited next to them.

"Edwin." Æthelburh smoothed the hair from his forehead and, doing so, the touch of his fingers on her face during her labour came back to her. "Edwin."

The king's eyes opened. They rolled, then slowly settled on the queen. Edwin's hand flopped upon the furs that covered him, as if he tried to raise it but had not the strength. Eadfrith, seeing his father wake, came closer.

"Cwenburg?" Æthelburh stiffened. The smile that had greeted the king's waking froze upon her face.

"No, father…" Eadfrith began to speak but Æthelburh shook her head. She looked fiercely at him, holding finger to lips for silence, then stroked the king's cheek. Edwin's eyes fought for focus, trying to steady themselves on the shadowy face before him.

"Cwenburg?" he repeated, his voice fainter.

"Yes," said Æthelburh. "Yes, I am here."

The king's eyes slowly closed. But now he slept the sleep of healing.

Eadfrith looked over the still but now calm body of his father to the queen, gently drawing a damp linen over his brow.

"You let him think you were my mother."

Æthelburh did not look up, and only a break in the rhythm of her movements showed that she had heard Eadfrith's words. Her face was pale.

Eadfrith took Edwin's hand in his own. "You brought him out of the shadows."

Æthelburh shook her head. "Not I. It was the memory of your mother that brought the king back."

"Nevertheless, I thank you." The prince released his father's hand and stood up. "You said earlier that you were no enemy of ours. I see now that you speak the truth."

Æthelburh looked up at him. "It has taken you long enough. I pray for all our sakes that your judgement in other areas is swifter."

"I trust it is." A grin twitched Eadfrith's lips. "At least, it is faster than my brother's."

"You could tell him not to fear me."

Eadfrith nodded. "I will, my queen. But…" he shrugged. "It will take time. Osfrith honours our mother, and remembers her. He is also stubborner than a mule and but a little cleverer. But I will bring him round. I always do." Eadfrith's grin grew broader. "It will be easier for the baby being a girl."

"I love her not the less for that," said the queen.

Eadfrith looked to where the babe lay sleeping in the arms of her wet nurse, a bubble blowing upon her lips. "I as well." He turned back to Æthelburh. "But make the next a boy – then I would have a brother I could order around!"

A blush coloured the queen's answering smile. "I – I will try, if God wills, and may he be as biddable to his elder brother's will as you are to yours!"

# *Chapter 12*

The bleak cold of the year's early Easter had given way, forty days later, to sunshine and warmth. Edwin, still recovering from his wound and the effects of the poison, sat in the sunshine upon a stool beside the River Derwent. Despite the warmth, he drew his cloak around his shoulders. Since Forthred's death, a chill had entered his body and not even the early summer sun was able to displace it. Most of his men were out hunting or bringing in food renders from the more distant farms. Because of his convalescence, the royal party had stayed at the vill on the Derwent far longer than normal, and the food stores, collected and preserved by the local thegn, had become depleted.

Some of the men remained, however, and they had gathered around Edwin in curious silence to watch what their king too was watching. Eadfrith was with him, but Osfrith had averred that he had to see to his horses, one of which had gone lame. The king had not insisted he stay.

Paulinus stood up to his thighs in a natural shallow pool of the river. He had tucked the end of his robe into his belt, to stop it trailing in the river, but still the wool was darkening as water soaked into it. The queen, with the people of her household, stood upon the small beach that led to the pool, and she carried her baby, Edwin's baby, in her arms.

Paulinus turned to face the silent, watching men. He had taken the precaution of facing away from everyone when he first entered the river. The precaution had been wise: the water was colder than even he, a child of the south, had imagined. He had managed to lock his mouth against any exclamation, but he feared his expression had not been so disciplined. But now, used to the cold, or at least with an increasingly benumbed lower half, Paulinus looked up to where the king sat with his men around him.

"Today is the great feast of Pentecost, when God descended as fire upon the apostles, the first messengers of his good news to the world. I, an unworthy priest, yet am a descendant of these same apostles, and I bear witness to the good news they brought to the world: God, the very God who made all things and holds them in his hands, became man that he might take the weight of our sin upon his back, the punishment for our evil in his flesh, and win for us a new kingdom, God's kingdom."

Paulinus held out his arms. The queen stepped forward. She did not stop at the water's edge but walked into the pool, until the river came up to her knees. Æthelburh removed the shawl and gave her baby into the priest's arms. The child slept peacefully, unaware of the attention concentrated upon her.

"Here in my arms is the first-fruits of the good news in this kingdom. This child, this baby shall be named Eanflæd. By the wish of her mother and through the will of the king, Eanflæd is to be consecrated to Christ. I will now wash away her old life and bathe her in the waters of life eternal."

The priest held the baby up for all to see. Then Paulinus bowed and held the child over the water.

*"Ego te baptizo in nomine Patris…"*

And as he invoked the Father, he plunged the baby beneath the water and brought her up. Eanflæd, suddenly, rudely awake, made to scream, but Paulinus dipped her into the river again.

*"… et Filii…"*

For a second time the baby prepared to howl, but the priest immersed her once more, stifling the scream.

*"…et Spiritus Sancti."*

Eanflæd emerged a third time and this time, given opportunity to draw breath, she screamed, her little body flushed red with the shock of what had just happened to her. Paulinus passed the wriggling, outraged baby back to the queen, who wrapped Eanflæd in the white shawl and soothed her on the breast. Hugging the baby tight, Æthelburh waded from the river and bowed to the king.

"Thank you for giving life to our daughter," she said.

Edwin inclined his head, but made no other reply.

Paulinus remained in the river and now, one by one, other members of Æthelburh's household came forward to receive baptism: women and men, old and young, they walked into the river, and the priest, now up to his waist in the cold water but no longer feeling its chill as a fire of faith lit him, laid them down beneath the surface, only for each to emerge spluttering, sometimes coughing, sometimes laughing but in all cases radiant.

"At least these ones aren't howling," Eadfrith commented. "But the queen's baby did not seem too pleased about being given life eternal."

"Quiet," said Edwin. Eadfrith was on the point of giving a brisk retort when he looked at his father; Edwin was watching the proceedings with the concentrated intensity that he normally reserved for war. Eadfrith stayed the words in his mouth and looked again, trying to see what his father was seeing. But to him it simply looked like a group of people getting wet.

As the baptisms drew to a close, most of the watching warriors drifted back to the royal vill, passing jokes with the gate keeper as they went through the stockade. Edwin remained, however, with Eadfrith lingering nearby. The young man did not know why he remained, yet he could not pull himself away.

As the last of the baptized emerged from the river, shivering and smiling at the same time, and was wrapped in clean, white cloth, Æthelburh approached the watching, silent king. Eadfrith moved closer while pretending an interest in a boat approaching up the river.

Æthelburh gave an uncertain smile. Edwin remained blank, a watching, brooding presence. The queen came closer, holding out the baby to Edwin, but he did not take her.

"She is one of you now? A Christian. Like the Britons."

"Eanflæd is a Christian, yes, like me. And like my mother's people, the Franks, and like the emperors and like the pope. Eanflæd is a Christian, and I am a Christian too, husband, and I have not changed into someone else before your eyes this day, so why do you look at me this way?"

Edwin made to answer, then fell silent. "Eadfrith asked a question – one I think worthy of answer. Why did the child cry so when the priest gave her eternal life? Should she not have laughed and smiled and cried with joy?"

At this question Æthelburh laughed.

Edwin stared at his wife, his face hard. "Is my question so funny?"

The queen shook her head. "My husband and my lord, you would not ask such a question had you been there when your daughter was born. She was born into this life screaming. Is it any surprise she should cry when she enters a new life? Besides, in baptism the sin she carries from our forefather of old, the bloodguilt of his oathbreaking passed down through all the generations, is torn from her, like a diseased scab torn from a wound, that the flesh underneath may heal. Of course she cried today, lord. I would have been more worried if she had not." Æthelburh smiled in memory. "You should have heard her scream when she was born. She shouted so loudly I was sure you must hear her and come. It was only later that I learned you lay in a fever dream and could not come."

Æthelburh held out the baby again. "Here, my king, my lord and my husband, will you take your daughter, Eanflæd, and give her your blessing?"

For a moment the king did not move, and the smile on the queen's face began to strain. But then Edwin held out his hands and took his daughter in his arms.

"She does not feel any different," he said.

"Do I?" asked Æthelburh archly.

Edwin, seeing his son watching, almost blushed.

"No. But I thought, after this baptism, she might."

"Give Eanflæd your blessing, lord."

Edwin looked down at the baby girl, asleep now in his arms, wrapped in a white shawl. He moved his head to shade her face from the May sun. Eanflæd stirred, then settled again, and a smile tugged gently at the king's winter face.

"Eanflæd, I give you my blessing, and that right gladly. May you find favour before God and know no treachery from men." Then Edwin handed the baby back to her mother.

"Thank you," said Æthelburh.

Paulinus was leading a procession of the newly baptized back into the royal encampment. Edwin nodded towards it. "Go, Æthelburh, and join the celebrations of your people."

The queen held out her hand for him to follow, but Edwin shook his head.

"No, I have much to think on. I will stay here."

Æthelburh's face stiffened, but she bowed before the king and went to join the chanting, singing procession.

Eadfrith came over to join his father. They watched the newly baptized process through the gates, neither speaking to the other until the procession was out of sight, although the sound of its singing still reached them by the side of the river.

"You blessed the child by their god, not ours," said Eadfrith.

The king looked up at his son. "You have sharp ears, Eadfrith." Edwin turned his gaze back into the distance. "Osfrith should have been here."

"He honours our mother; it is all he can do to speak to the queen. He could not come here."

Edwin stared out over the river, watching as a wind-blown twig twisted upon its waters as the current tugged it downstream to the sea.

"I honour your mother too. But a king marries for power and alliance and riches; Æthelburh brought all those, though Cadwallon stole most of the gifts."

"She is young too. And beautiful."

Edwin's face twisted, the expression somewhere between a grimace and a smile. "An advantage and a disadvantage."

"She has brought her religion too."

Edwin watched the twig as it drifted out of sight.

"Likewise," he said.

Eadfrith stood beside his father for a while, but when it became clear that the king had nothing more to say, he made to leave. But after he had taken a few steps, he returned to the king's side.

"There is something I should tell you. The queen's priest saved you from the poison in Eumer's blade, but afterwards you drifted into the shadows and it seemed you would not return."

Edwin continued to stare out over the river. "It was cold there. And dark."

"Coifi tried to call you back, but could not. In the end it was the queen who brought you back from the shadows. Æthelburh. Only, you thought it was Mother."

Edwin looked up at his son. Eadfrith nodded. "It was Æthelburh you heard amid the shadows, Father."

The king turned back to the river. "Thank you," he said. Eadfrith waited upon him, but he spoke no more, and the prince withdrew.

From the queen's quarters came the sound of singing and much joy. On the training grounds Guthlaf put the men through their exercises. Everywhere there was bustle and movement, as servants and slaves hurried to and fro, carrying pots and cloth and weapons and food, and petitioners arrived to put their cases to the king.

But the king himself sat in solitude upon a stool by the river, his eyes looking out and his mind turned within. He sought the memory of Cwenburg, striving for the look of her face, the smell of her hair, the touch of her fingers. But it was gone. Only shadows remained, the memory of a memory. Instead, unbidden, there came to his mind the image of Æthelburh, sitting beside him at the high table, handing the cup to men who came for audience and fellowship, smiling, bringing cheer. The pall of gloom that had hung over his companionship these many years since the death of Cwenburg, a dourness that had become so ingrained that he had not even noticed it, had lifted and his hall had become again a place of laughter and song, of warmth and light. But the change had come so gradually he had not even realized it.

Unconsciously, Edwin twisted the garnet-encrusted gold band that encircled his forearm. The interlaced animals – serpents and eagles and creatures of the sea – ran around his arm in continuous whorls that twisted as he slowly rotated the band. The bracelet had been Forthred's. Edwin had given it to him many years before, the richest gift from the spoils won when taking the kingdom of Lindsey under their control. The king still sometimes marvelled at the wealth they had found in the hall of the marsh king – wealth that had made the miserable campaign, waged through swamp and water and mud, suddenly and gloriously worthwhile. In memory he saw the laughter in Forthred's face as he had held up handfuls of treasure, his arms dripping with gold and silver and jewels.

"Who would have believed the king of so mean a place could be so rich?" Forthred had said.

Edwin remembered his own delighted laughter, and giving the armband, the richest he had ever seen, to Forthred as a gift. And he remembered taking the band from Forthred's arm as he lay upon the pyre, clad in the finest cloth, his weapons about him. The gold had been as cold as Forthred's flesh. He had replaced the band with one taken from his own arm, then he slid Forthred's bracelet up over his hand and wrist onto his forearm. His old friend had stared up with sightless eyes at the grey clouds scudding low overhead. The wind, a cold north-easterly, was sending them in from the sea, and Edwin could smell the rain that would fall later that day, extinguishing the ashes of Forthred's pyre. The body lay upon crossed logs outside the encampment and on the banks of the Derwent. Coifi had carried the urn that would take the gathered ashes when the fire had eaten its fill. The king had drawn his hand down over Forthred's face, gently closing his eyes.

"Rest well, old friend," he had said, but the words sounded hollow in his mouth. For warriors who did not die in battle, there was only Hel, the shadow world, where ghosts slowly gibbered their way into nothingness through the long, grey ages. Forthred had sacrificed his life for him, but there would be no gift giving for the great service he had rendered his king. Gifts stopped with death. Maybe the gods would look kindly upon him, for Forthred had been a brave warrior, and a wise and cunning counsellor, but wyrd had taken him, and against the fate weavers the gods themselves fought in vain.

Taking the brand, Edwin had thrust it into the pyre. The logs, dry and packed around with tinder soaked in wax, had turned quickly to flame, the yellow tongues licking up over the body. The king had stood close to the pyre – so close that he felt the hair on his arms crisping – but he did not step back until the flames had closed over Forthred, enfolding him like a flower closing for the night. The body had shifted as it burned, the collapsing logs beneath it at one point making it seem as if the charred black remains were trying to sit up. But the body had fallen back into the flames, sending a gout of red sparks flaring through the air.

As the fire died away into a sullen, cloudy evening, and the first rags of rain whipped in from the east, Edwin had allowed the rest of the royal household to return to the warmth of the fires in the great hall. But he had remained by the pyre until the scudding showers had doused the flames.

"Collect his ashes," Edwin had said to Coifi. As the priest scuttled forward with the urn, Edwin added, "Make sure his treasure is with him."

The urn still resided in the great hall, but when the royal household finally left to make its way to York, the urn would be buried, where Forthred had burned.

Wrapping his cloak about his shoulders, for with the sunset a cool wind blew inland from the sea, Edwin stood up and walked over to his old friend's final resting place. The earth lay fire bare, save for some scattered ashes, and for many feet around and beyond the grass was yellow and dead.

Edwin squatted on his haunches and laid his hand upon the scorched earth. Forthred had sacrificed his life that he might live, and there was no repayment he could make or treasure he could give to equal such a gift. Though he was a king and Forthred his follower, yet his man had been more generous than he.

"Will you not come and join us?"

Edwin turned to look and saw the queen, her cloak drawn around her and her face veiled. He stood up, and the dust of Forthred's pyre fell from his fingers.

"This celebration is yours, my queen. I cannot join it."

Æthelburh nodded, her face in shadow behind her veil, and turned away.

"Wait."

The queen stopped, but she did not look back to the king.

"Eadfrith told me that it was you who called me back from the shadows, not Cwenburg. Why did you not tell me?"

"I – I feared if you knew it was me who spoke to you, not Cwenburg, you would not come."

"In the shadow world, I wandered in memories. But know this, Æthelburh of Kent. Here, now, in the world of the light and the living, you are my wife and my queen and I would have no other."

Æthelburh turned her face back to Edwin.

The king saw that she trembled. "Are you cold?"

Æthelburh laughed, but her eyes were filled with diamond tears. "No, I am not cold!" She laughed again, and there were no tears this time. She held out her hand. "Now will you join us?"

And Edwin took her hand.

# Chapter 13

"You want vengeance."

Edwin did not look around. He had heard Wældhelm's approach. The smith's lameness made him drag his foot along the ground.

The king's recovery dragged on, and oftentimes, when the sun was warm, he would bring a stool to the hard-packed earth where Forthred had burned from the world and sit upon it, drawing his cloak about his body and his plans about his mind.

"Yes," he said.

Wældhelm stood beside the king, looking down at the burned earth.

"Destroy your enemies, kill their children, salt their earth and let the last sound they hear be the screams of their women. It is as the gods would do."

Edwin slowly stood up and turned to the giant smith.

"The god of the queen tells us to eschew vengeance. He tells us to love our enemies."

The giant smith began to smile, but when he saw no answering laughter from the king, the smile died away.

"Are you joking, lord?"

"No. No, I am not joking. That is what the queen told me this new god teaches. I could not believe she spoke truly, so I asked her priest. It is true. That is what her god commands."

The smile spread again across the smith's face and creased into laughter, the deep laughter that creaked in his forge as things that were once as solid as rock were made to run like water. Wældhelm wiped the tears from his eyes.

"That is a religion for women," he said at last. "And Britons. No wonder we took this land from them."

"It is the religion of the Franks, and the emperors, and more peoples than I have heard of too."

"But our gods are the gods of our fathers." Wældhelm shook his head, still marvelling at this new doctrine. "This is how our gods take vengeance, lord. The fame of Wayland the smith grew so great that King Nidud determined that he must have him as his royal smith, to make wondrous weapons for him. So he tricked Wayland into coming to his court, and he feasted him, but the mead that trickled down Wayland's beard was laced with a sleeping draught. When Wayland woke, he found himself imprisoned on a lonely island, along with his brother, and to ensure that Wayland could not escape, King Nidud had hamstrung him.

"Wayland's brother, Egil, collected feathers from the seabirds that nested on the island, and Wayland, in between forging swords and torcs and spears for the king, made wings. With the feathers stuck into them, the brothers were able to fly, and escape the island. But Wayland did not escape. Instead, he tricked the king's sons into coming to visit him, and when they were inspecting his latest wonders, Wayland slaughtered them and, stripping the flesh from their bones, he made their skulls into jewel-encrusted goblets, and their teeth into a beautiful necklace. Then he brought these latest, most exquisite works of his craft before the king. Nidud was so delighted with the goblets he immediately began to drink from them, and the necklace he hung upon his beautiful daughter, Beahilda.

"But Beahilda, like all her family, was greedy, and she stole away to Wayland's island later that night to garner further treasures. Wayland raped her and got her with child, and only then did he strap on his wings and make his escape. But before he returned to his home forge, he flew on his iron wings to King Nidud's palace, and shouted to the king the news of what he had done."

Wældhelm the smith, the lame servant of a lame god, who had told the tale while staring out over the river vale, turned to the king and his smile was fierce.

"Thus does a god take vengeance, lord. And if you would take vengeance for Forthred, I have forged a sword for you that is the greatest I have yet made – there is no blade finer. It will cut through a shield of green limewood and yet sit as light in the hand as a child's seax. Would you see it, lord?"

"Yes, I would see it."

"Then I shall take you to my forge, lord, and you shall see it."

Edwin looked in surprise at the smith. "But you allow no man to come to your smithy."

Wældhelm grinned. "The labour is done, lord, and the sword made. You may see my fires, but you will not see my secrets."

"Lead on," said Edwin. The king followed the limping smith as he painfully made his way upstream along the river path to the stand of trees in the midst of which stood the smith's forge. Every smith lived apart from other men, bringing his wares to the village or the court, and receiving visitors in turn, but always remaining apart, as befitted a man whose art was to turn brute rock into flesh-biting metal.

The trees, a copse of alders that sank their roots into the damp riverside earth, were old and twisted, the leaf fall of years caught in flares of mistletoe. Each breath of wind made the dead leaves rattle, like Coifi's bone rattle. Edwin found himself startling at the sound, and more so once they had entered the copse proper, and he found that the scrub of hawthorn and blackthorn, mixed with yew and holly, growing beneath the alders cut off any view of the outside world. It was as if he had entered a forest, yet approaching he had seen it to be no more than a stand of a few dozen trees.

Wældhelm limped along a path that cut between the bushes. Edwin followed, wondering at how long they had already been walking in this tiny wood. He smelled burning, the pervasive wood smoke of charcoal burners, and then finally they came out into a clearing. In the centre of the clearing, as far from the trees as possible, was a hut that steamed, leaking smoke through its walls and roof. By the trees' edge was a house.

"Daddy!" A boy of maybe eight winters came running from the thatched house that backed against the trees at the clearing's edge, and threw his arms around Wældhelm. Edwin noted that such was the girth of the smith that the boy's arms did not meet.

Wældhelm ruffled the boy's hair and turned to the king. "My eldest son. When he is older, I will cut him."

"Cut him?"

Wældhelm looked at the king through fire-narrowed eyes. "To know Wayland's secrets, he must know Wayland's pain." The smith pushed the boy on. "Come, lad, show the king the sword I have made for him."

Beaming with pride, the boy ran to the forge. He emerged a moment later with the sword in his hands and, still smiling shyly, he came up to the king and held it out for him.

Even at first glance Edwin could see that this was a weapon of extraordinary craft. The blade was etched with flowing lines, but its twin edges shone, clean and clear and hard.

Edwin looked questioningly at Wældhelm.

"Take it," said the smith. "Feel its weight in your hand, its cut through the air. Try the edge and think of it upon your enemies."

Edwin grasped the hilt of the sword. He held it outstretched and felt the weight of the blade pulling his arm downwards; this was a sword that wanted to slash through the air and come down upon the weak place where helmet met mail shirt. Giving the sword its desire, Edwin carved it through the air, taking it through the patterns that he had learned in a lifetime of combat. Wældhelm watched Edwin as he made the blade hiss, grinning broadly through his beard.

"I made it for you," said the smith, "and I made right."

Edwin, sweat beginning to prick his forehead, brought the sword to a halt. It quivered in the air, like a horse eager to have its head.

"Let me see how it cuts," said the king.

"Fetch a shield, lad." Wældhelm sent his son off to the family house with a friendly cuff around the back of his head. The boy, expecting it, managed to dodge most of the blow, and what did land only made him stumble a little. He ran back with a raw limewood shield, edged in iron but bare of the usual leather cover.

"This is new, green limewood," said Wældhelm, taking hold of the shield. "It's still so full of sap that it would grip any ordinary sword that cut into it tighter than a clam."

"Then a quick half-turn of the shield, and you've disarmed your enemy. I've seen it happen many a time."

"Probably the last thing those warriors saw was their sword disappearing," said the smith.

"In most cases."

"Try this blade. It will not suffer itself to be held by any wood, not even raw limewood." Wældhelm propped the shield up against a sawn-off tree stump.

Edwin looked at the smith. "You're not going to hold it for me?"

Wældhelm laughed. "And have you cut me in half too? No, lord, you will see the wisdom of what I do when you try the sword."

The king assayed the weight of the blade again, then in a single, smooth overarm chopping motion he brought it down upon the rim of the shield. It sliced clean through the iron edging hoop, transmitting scarcely a judder up into his arm, and sliced deep into the wet wood, splitting it asunder as neatly as a woodsman's axe.

Edwin inspected the sword, holding it up in front of his face. The intricate patterns of its forging whorled along its length, catching the eye into visual riddles as it sought to find the start and end of the pattern. He put his ear next to the sword.

"Listening for the blood music?" asked Wældhelm. "Though I have whetted the sword, I have not yet wetted it. It will not sing yet."

"It is true then?"

"The blood music? Oh aye, it is true, though the blade that makes it is rare indeed. I have known only two swords to do so."

"Which were they?"

"The sword of Æthelfrith, called the Cutter, and the sword of Ida, which was lost."

"Æthelfrith's sword did not sing the day we killed him."

"Mayhap it did, but its music was for Æthelfrith alone. Know this: a sword that sings will take its price; it gives victory, but one day it will sing the song of its wielder's death."

"Everyone dies – even the gods." Edwin held the sword in front of his face and looked it up and down. "Will this sword sing?"

"It will sing, when it has been wetted." Wældhelm held his hand out for the sword and Edwin reluctantly gave it back to him. "It is time I cut my son…"

"No," Edwin said, surprising himself and the smith. "No," he repeated, more quietly this time, so that only Wældhelm could hear. "He is a good boy – let him run a while longer."

"It does no good to be soft with children, but if you command it…"

"In this I ask, I do not command."

Wældhelm snorted. "A king's request… Not many kings take kindly to their requests being refused. But if you do not want the boy cut to blood the sword, I have a slave who stole a comb from my wife; I will wet the sword on her."

"Should not the sword's first blood be that of a free man rather than a slave?"

"You might think so, lord, but the sword does not care – it is blood it wants and the sword will happily shed it all, be it slave or free man, king or bondsman." Wældhelm turned, looking for his son, then spotted him lingering and watching the grown-ups from the doorway of the house. "Hey, lad, get your mother to bring out Gwen. It's time I punished her for stealing."

Edwin was curious to see what manner of woman the smith had taken for a wife. So when two women emerged, he looked carefully at the one that followed, beating the first forth with a switch of hazel branches. She was a small woman, black of hair and blue of eye, with the quick, darting movements of a dunnock. But she wielded the switch with a furious energy, beating the crying slave girl out of the house amid a torrent of abuse for the girl's theft of a comb. Edwin could hear at once that both women were Britons – his years at Cadfan's court had made him fluent in their tongue. No language he knew made insult sound so poetic, and he enjoyed listening to the stream of invective the smith's wife poured upon the slave girl. With a final flick of the hazel switch and a resounding denunciation of the girl's malfeasance, the smith's wife sent the slave girl onto her knees in front of Wældhelm, who stood in front of her, as massive as a bear, fingering the edge of the newly forged sword.

Seeing it, the girl immediately burst into tears and tried to throw her arms around the smith's knees, but Wældhelm, with one eye on his watching, toe-tapping wife, moved out of the way with surprising speed for a lame man. The slave girl tried to crawl after him but Wældhelm said, "Now, now, Gwen, you stay put, you hear."

The girl squatted upon her heels, her eyes red with tears, and looked beseechingly up at the smith. Edwin, noting the furious expression on Wældhelm's wife's face, wondered if that had been Gwen's best course of action. The smith's children, all of them, had crept out of the house and were now capering around the clearing in excitement.

"I didn't steal the comb, master; honest I didn't. I just borrowed it so's I could comb my hair, because I heard you say that Master Bebba was coming and if he was coming, then I thought maybe he'd have Owain with him…"

"You're not going to listen to the little strumpet, are you?" said the smith's wife. "Honest, if you do, I'll turn my switch on you." And to Edwin's suppressed delight the little woman began to raise the hazel twigs against her husband.

Wældhelm raised his hands placatingly. "Nia, don't take on so. Of course I won't listen to her."

"Good." The smith's wife glared up at him and the huge bear of a man quailed. "Otherwise I'd be thinking you were getting ideas you shouldn't."

"No, no, of course not. Definitely."

"Well, then. What are you going to do about her stealing my comb? It's my favourite comb too, the one you carved for me after Deor was born."

Wældhelm held up the sword. "Um, well, this sword needs to be wetted and I was thinking of cutting off her hand."

Nia tutted angrily, while the slave girl whimpered in fear. "And what use would she be to me with only one hand, you great clumsy idiot!"

"Her foot?"

"And have her hopping around and falling over whenever I send her to do some work. Very clever."

"Er… her nose?"

The slave girl gave a little shriek and clapped her hands to her face. Nia, on the other hand, looked thoughtful. "She'd still be able to work, true, but no. You've heard old Gyrth's slave, the one without a nose: he sounds like a wet fart. We'd never get any sleep with her going on like that."

"Well, what then, woman?"

Nia thought for a moment, then her eyes lit up. "Her ear. Cut off her ear – it'll bleed well too, so the sword'll be properly wetted. Stop snivelling, you stupid girl," she said to the slave. "With your scarf, no one will even know it's gone and you can still make eyes at Owain. Stop snivelling, right, or I'll tell him to cut off your hand, like the law says."

Gwen the slave girl wiped her eyes with a trembling hand. "I think I'd rather you cut my hand off, mistress. If it were this one," she held up her left hand, "I could still work."

Wældhelm shrugged. "Maybe I should cut them both off."

Edwin held up his hand. "Since the sword is to come to me, I should prefer if it were first employed on a nobler task than cutting a thieving slave girl."

"You got anyone, lord? All I have is her, or there's my lad…"

"What?" said Nia, outraged. "What were you going to do?"

"Now hold on," said Wældhelm, holding up his hands. "You know I'm going to have to cut him some day if he's to learn my business."

"Don't you dare!" said Nia, trying to grab the boy.

But the lad himself danced away from her embrace. "Ma, I want him to cut me. I want him to."

"Come here." Nia grabbed after the boy but he skipped nimbly away.

"Ma, I want Da to cut me. Please."

Wældhelm grinned broadly as the boy continued to elude his mother. "There, see Nia, he wants me to cut him – he's ready too."

Nia came abruptly to a halt, breathing hard. "Very well, let him cut you. That way I can be sure of catching you in future."

The boy stopped his capering. "I hadn't thought of that," he said.

"Just as well there's someone around here to do the thinking," said Nia. "I could have said the king wouldn't want a slave wetting his new sword too." She turned to Edwin and made the courtesy. "Have you anyone more suitable, lord?"

Edwin smiled bleakly. "I may have. I believe Eumer is still alive. Guthlaf has had sport with him, but he is tough and lives yet. So I'll give him to you to wet this blade, Wældhelm. It is right that the assassin's blood should feed it first, for once it has drunk its fill of him, there will be much blood for it to drink when we ride against the West Saxons."

The smith looked from king to wife and back again. "Is that all settled then?"

Edwin began to nod, then glanced at the slave girl. "You have your comb back?" he asked Nia.

"Yes, lord, I got it back."

"Then give her a good beating and leave matters there. If she steals again, hang her."

Nia began an answer, thought better of it and made obeisance. Gwen, deciding it better not to be noticed again, abased herself.

"Come," said Edwin to Wældhelm. "Bring the sword. Once I hear the blood music, I will know it's time."

# Chapter 14

"Eumer said the West Saxons would never kneel before me." Edwin looked down at the man before him. "He was wrong."

The man began to look up. Guthlaf struck the back of his head with the pommel of his sword, sending him face down into the blood-soaked mud.

"You look up when the king tells you to look up," said Guthlaf.

The man groaned. His mail shirt, and it had once been a fine shirt, was ragged, and the leather jerkin that covered it had been all but cut to pieces. Cuts covered his arms and hands, and though none were life threatening, congealing blood coated his limbs. Flies, black and blood drunk, crawled over him.

"Get him up," Edwin said to Guthlaf, and the warmaster set about slapping the man back into consciousness. As he did so, Edwin looked about him, swaying with weariness.

The battlefield had become a place of slaughter. The dead lay scattered upon the rutted turf by the ford, for Edwin had come down upon the West Saxons at the only place where men could cross the River Thames on foot, and set upon them in the loop of the river there, so that the waters hemmed them in on all sides. Once the shieldwall of the West Saxons had broken, the killing had begun in earnest; men running, cut down as they fled, Eadfrith and Osfrith and their households taking to horseback and pursuing the routed West Saxons across field and into copse and wood, for the battle thirst was on them fiercely. Edwin had let them go. It had been many years since the red rage had descended upon him; too many battles, too many dead meant that he fought coldly now, without emotion. Once the battle was over, he had no desire to gallop madly after the enemy; that was for the young men, with their blood up, still thirsting for riches. Besides, he had his enemy here.

Guthlaf hauled the swaying, semi-conscious man to his feet. Edwin signalled for his horse to be brought over and he unhooked a leather sack from the saddle.

"Wake him," Edwin said.

Guthlaf relieved one of the men stripping corpses of their armour of the helmet he had acquired and, filling it from the river, he dashed the water into the man's face. His eyes finally came into focus as he stumbled to his feet, but the warmaster could see in them the mistiness of a man waking to a reality he would much rather hide from, be it in unconsciousness or death.

"Kneel to me, Cwichelm," said Edwin.

The king of the West Saxons blinked at Edwin, but he remained standing. Guthlaf kicked the back of his knees and his legs collapsed.

"You kneel when the king tells you to kneel."

"Here," said Edwin, "catch." He lobbed the sack towards Cwichelm. "Now, open it."

The West Saxon began to open the sack, then dropped it with disgust.

"Take it out," said Edwin. "Hold it up."

When Cwichelm hesitated, Guthlaf cuffed him around the head. The king of the West Saxons drew the head of Eumer from the sack.

"I fed the rest of him to the dogs," said Edwin, "but I kept the head for you."

Cwichelm began to let the head down, but Edwin struck his arm back up.

"Look at him!" he shouted. "Look at him."

The face and head were marked, scored with the ill use that had filled Eumer's final days.

"He died cursing you," said Edwin. "He died cursing the king who betrayed him. He died as these other men are going to die: spitting your name in blood." Edwin turned to the guards. "Bring them here."

The captured kings and thegns of the West Saxons were hustled towards Edwin. They were either naked or stripped to their trousers, with all the riches of their rank having been taken from them. Those who could still walk were prodded onwards at sword point; those unable to hobble were dragged.

Edwin pointed to where Cwichelm swayed upon his knees, still holding Eumer's head.

"This man brought you to this," he said. "A liar, a traitor, a deceiver. This man has made your wives widows and your children orphans. You die for him. Take his name to your graves." Edwin drew his sword, the sword that Wældhelm had forged for him. He had heard the blood music earlier; he had heard it singing as he cut through flesh and bone and tendon. But as the battle ebbed and the enemy ran, the blood song had died. Now he would make it sing again.

"You." Edwin pointed at the nearest man in the group. "You first."

The man glanced around, then realized that it was indeed him. He paled slightly, but otherwise gave no reaction, and he limped into the gap between the group of captives and the kneeling king of the West Saxons.

"Kneel."

The man, his eyes fixed upon his king, knelt.

With a single smooth motion, the blood music already beginning to sing, Edwin brought the sword around in an arc. Bone and flesh barely slowed the blade. The man's torso remained kneeling for a moment before it fell. The head rolled towards Cwichelm.

"Pick it up," Edwin said. When the king of the West Saxons did not respond, Edwin screamed, "Pick it up!"

Such was the fury in his cry that Cwichelm, on his knees, shuffled to where the new head lay and picked it up.

"He was a better man than you. Lay him with Eumer." Edwin turned to the silent, waiting group of men. "You are all going to die. You are going to die because this king did not have the courage to meet me in battle, but sent an assassin to kill me by stealth. But know this: you fought well, and bravely, and your sons and wives will live. This man here, this coward, this villain, he is going to live, but know this before you die – he will live but his sons will die and his women will be slaves. Die well, then, and curse him as you go

196

down." Edwin waited. The captives shifted and then one of them, a man who could barely walk, so badly cut was his leg, stumbled forward. Edwin nodded to him as he made his way forwards.

"I will die standing." The man spoke to Edwin, but his eyes were fixed on the kneeling, broken figure of Cwichelm.

The blood music hissed. The man fell. Cwichelm, without being asked, scooted forward on his knees and collected the head, laying it with the first two.

Edwin looked at the captives. There were another five men to go. Each of them met his eye steadily. Certainly there was fear there, but it was the controlled fear of acceptance. These men had seen death often enough to know that one day it would come for them. Now it was here, and Edwin was cloaked in its grey mantle.

But he had had enough. The cold rage that had driven him through the previous days of hard riding and harder marching – that had given him a terrible clarity as he positioned his men for battle and had remained with him through fighting and slaughter – suddenly dissipated. He had for a while become death, but no more. However, the necessity remained: more men had to die so that Cwichelm and the West Saxons should be reduced to abject vassals. But he had done enough killing.

"Guthlaf, finish the rest. Make it quick for them."

The warmaster looked at the king, kneeling, head down, beside the growing pile of heads.

"Leave him," said Edwin. "I will deal with Cwichelm, king of the West Saxons."

Unsheathing his sword, Guthlaf strode towards the prisoners.

"I have seen enough death for this day," Edwin said to Cwichelm, "but you will watch your men die." He lifted the king's downcast head with the tip of his sword. "Watch them."

Although he had his back turned on the executions, Edwin heard the hiss of sword and the drop of flesh to ground, and he saw the reaction on Cwichelm's face, each death reducing the man further. When the last man lay dead, Edwin called for a spade and threw it upon the ground before Cwichelm.

"Get up," he said, "and dig your men's graves. They deserved a better king than you; at least bury them properly."

While the king of the West Saxons laboured, and Guthlaf and his men saw to the minor wounds of his own warriors, Edwin paced beside the river. The banks here were lined with willow, mostly crack willow, and alder. Already the river creatures that had fled into hiding with the noise and fury of battle were emerging. He watched as a grass snake twisted greenly through the water, swimming to the far bank.

Osfrith and Eadfrith and their men straggled back to the battle site – their horses laden with plundered booty: swords, helmets, armour and hack silver and gold – when their beasts were simply too laden to carry any more. The two young men rode to their father, their faces still alive with the glee of such wealth and the flush that came of battle ending and still being alive.

"We harried them through to the forest yonder," said Osfrith, pointing at the distant line of trees that covered the rising downs to the south. "I doubt more than one man in ten escaped us."

"It will have been more than that," said Edwin. "It is always more. But no matter. We killed the ones we needed to kill."

"What did you do with Cwichelm?" asked Eadfrith.

Edwin pointed. The brothers turned to see the pit and the corpses lying alongside it, and the head and shoulders of the man digging.

Eadfrith began walking towards the pile of corpses. "Which one is he?" he called back.

"He is the one digging," said Edwin.

Eadfrith stopped, then backtracked to his father. "He's still alive?"

"Yes," said Edwin.

"I'll kill him," said Osfrith, beginning to unsheathe his sword.

"No," said Edwin. "He lives."

Osfrith stared at his father uncomprehendingly. "But I thought all this," he gestured around at the battlefield, at the stripped corpses lying on the ground and the gathering carrion birds, "it was to kill him, to avenge Forthred."

"It was to avenge Forthred and to destroy Cwichelm and the West Saxons." Edwin pointed at the man labouring in the pit. "He is destroyed. He lives by my sufferance, and he knows it and his people know it. The power in this land now lies with me, with us; the king is ours to command – and we did not even have to buy him with treasure or a bride. All it cost me was the pleasure of spilling his blood now – and his blood is not worth the spilling. Do you begin to see?"

Osfrith still looked puzzled, but Eadfrith was grinning like a thegn who had just seen the solution to one of Acca's riddles.

"But once we have gone, surely he will rise against us?" asked Osfrith. "Even if he should not, he killed Forthred; his blood should flow for him."

"No, he will not rise against us, for in doing so he would lose our protection, and all the kings around him, the kings of Hwicce, of Kent, of Essex and Sussex, would smell the blood and close upon him, like hounds after a wounded hart. Cwichelm's rule would not survive the month. No, there is no threat there, Osfrith, but what you say concerning Forthred is just. His blood calls vengeance. But I knew Forthred of old, and I know he preferred to take his vengeance cold. We will bleed this land, take its fat and make it ours, and turn its men into our men." Edwin paused, and his sons, knowing the look of old, saw that he was weighing in his mind what to say to them. "There is another consideration: in this campaign, I put the power of the new god, the god of my wife and Kent, to the test." Edwin looked around. "It appears his power is great. But if it be so, then I must needs take some note of what Paulinus teaches about this new god: apparently, we should want good for our foes."

The two young men stared incredulously at their father. "What should we want?" asked Osfrith.

Edwin grimaced. "It was worse than I said. Paulinus's exact words were: we should love our enemies and do good to those that attack us."

Eadfrith laughed. "This is a jest, surely?"

But Edwin shook his head. "That is what I thought at first, but it is no jest. That is what we should do, according to this new god."

"That – that is nonsense," said Osfrith. "That means if Eumer had killed you, we should have given him food and drink and let him go?"

"No. That is what I asked Paulinus, and he said the first task of a king is justice and the second is to defend his realm. So we may punish wrongdoers and do battle with those who attack us, but still we should exercise mercy towards our enemies."

Eadfrith stared at his father in amazement. "Woden would give no mercy to such as Cwichelm."

"But which is more powerful? Woden or the new god?"

Eadfrith shook his head. "Surely you do not believe all this, father?"

In reply, Edwin gave a snort of laughter such as his sons had never heard before, and his skin flushed darker. "No, no, of course not. Not really. But… We have victory here, and do either of you remember a battle won so overwhelmingly, with such little cost to us and so much devastation to the enemy? I do not."

"No, no, no," said Eadfrith. "This is wrong. This is not the way of our fathers; this is not how we took this land and made it ours. The new god – is he not the old god of the Britons? If he is so powerful, how could we have taken this land from them?"

"I have lived a long time, Eadfrith, and I have seen the world move on. This god that Paulinus brings with him, he is the god of the Franks and the Goths and the emperors and the pope. Woden is the god of…us."

"There are the Geats and Swedes and Danes, and the other tribes that take the sea road to trade. Their gods are like ours."

"And they are like us as well: petty, squabbling kings of insignificant kingdoms. The emperors of old claimed sovereignty of the whole world, and Paulinus tells me that the pope has sovereignty over the next life, for his god has given him the keys of heaven."

"What is heaven?" asked Osfrith.

Edwin shrugged. "Paulinus was not so clear about that, but it seems to be like the great hall of the gods, although in this heaven there is no fighting."

"Who would want to go there?" said Osfrith.

Edwin looked at his sons, still young, still so eager for battle glory. They would not understand. But for himself he remembered that when Paulinus had told him of heaven, of a place of perfect peace, his heart had lifted for a moment at the hope that such a place could be. He looked down at his hands. The gore of battle and execution clung to them, but even washed they had shed so much blood. It was good that they might be clean again. That he might be clean again.

"No matter," said Edwin. "We will speak on this later. For now, know that there is another reason I have chosen to keep Cwichelm alive. Think well on this: which kingdom abuts this land of the West Saxons?"

"Mercia!" answered Eadfrith, his eyes shining with sudden realization.

"Yes, Mercia," said Edwin. "The only kingdom now that does not acknowledge me as overlord. The only kingdom in this land that I cannot ask to acknowledge me as lord, for Cearl its king is your grandfather, and father to Cwenburg. It would not be meet for him to bow to me, although Cearl surely knows that Northumbria is the master of him. But Cearl is old now, and Eumer brought me one item of news that I had not known, before he tried to kill me: Cearl's last son died in battle against the men of Powys. Cearl has no heir." Edwin looked at his sons. "Save you."

Osfrith looked from brother to father. "Which of us takes Mercia?"

"You, as elder, shall take Northumbria, of course," said Edwin.

"What about…" Osfrith began, then stopped, blushing.

Edwin looked at him curiously. "What is the matter?"

Osfrith shook his head. "Nothing." But still his face flushed red.

Eadfrith grinned. "I know," he said. "It's the queen, isn't it?"

Osfrith flushed redder, but having been confronted, he forced the words out. "What if, if you and the queen…"

Edwin tried not to smile. He all but succeeded. "If we have a son?"

"Yes. What then?"

"Then you will have a brave young warrior for your warband – when you are my age." Edwin's face grew serious. "Know this: you are my son. I stand beside you always. This will never change." He reached out and grasped Osfrith's shoulder. "Know this too: the queen has never tried to supplant your mother in my memory, let alone my sons. There are many who would intrigue and plot to advance their own, but she is not of that kind." Edwin let Osfrith go. "Satisfied?"

The prince nodded, still too embarrassed to speak.

Edwin turned to Eadfrith. "As to Mercia, that shall be my gift to you."

Eadfrith bowed to his father, then turned and clapped Osfrith on the back. "You know, this means I won't have to kill you."

"What?" said Osfrith. "Why would you kill me?"

"Younger son, father's death, kingdom to divide – it happens all the time. But now, you have Northumbria, I take Mercia, and then we take the rest of the land for ourselves – you have the north, I take the south."

Osfrith shook his head. "I still don't understand. You wanted to kill me?"

"Of course I did not want to kill you – you are my brother, after all. But I would have had to." Eadfrith smiled brightly. "Now I don't."

Osfrith looked at him suspiciously. "You are joking?"

For a moment Eadfrith remained impassive, then he dissolved into laughter. "Of course I was joking," he wheezed in between guffaws.

Osfrith looked at his father and shrugged. There were times he did not understand his brother. Edwin, though, did not laugh. Dissension and division between his two sons had always been his greatest fear. To counter this, he had kept them with him as they grew, rather than sending them at seven or eight to a neighbouring kingdom to spend their formative years learning the skills of a warrior and forging valuable alliances. So far he had been pleased with what he had seen between his sons: the natural rivalry between brothers had been offset by the profound difference in their natures, ensuring that they seldom pitted themselves directly against each other. Eadfrith's jesting with his brother was, in that respect, a relief – although Edwin knew his younger son to be far more capable of subterfuge than Osfrith, he doubted whether

Eadfrith would joke about something that he had at any time seriously considered.

"When you have recovered from your joke, Eadfrith, tell me why this explains my keeping Cwichelm alive?"

In between the occasional juddering inbreath, Eadfrith said, "It's easy. Cearl may want me – us – to inherit, but there will be some among his thegns who see themselves as better kings of Mercia; maybe this Penda that the assassin spoke of, or someone else. With Cwichelm as our ally in the south and Northumbria to the north, any thegn seeking to claim Cearl's throne would find little support from the warriors of the king's household."

"That is correct. But be not so sure that wisdom will prevail – the ties of place are strong, and though you are in part of Mercian blood, neither of you has grown up on its soil or shared feast with its men. They may still prefer one of their own. So we shall have to introduce you to the men of Mercia, and let them see you, when we explain to Cearl who the proper heir to his kingdom should be. For now, go and see how our new ally is doing with the task I left him. For myself," and here Edwin, suddenly drained after the exertions of the previous weeks and the bloodshed earlier, sat down upon a log, "I will rest a while."

"Some food and water for the king," Eadfrith called. Slaves, the camp followers who drove the wagons and attended the horses while on campaign, came running, bearing water skins and dishes filled with the pottage that they had been cooking upon wood fires.

While Edwin took food and drink, the brothers walked to the pit. Cwichelm still dug within it, for it was not yet deep enough to take the executed men.

"We are the sons of Edwin," said Eadfrith, and the mud-smeared man in the pit stopped his labour and looked up. He barely looked human any longer, so covered in earth and blood was he, but rather a wight of swamp and marsh caught wandering in the day.

"You will kneel to us too, king of the West Saxons."

And slowly, Cwichelm, king of the West Saxons, went down on his knees in the mud and slime at the bottom of the pit.

# Chapter 15

Having sat upon a horse for three days, Osfrith's legs were sore enough for him to voice his complaint.

"Why did we not take ship back to York? We were upon the Thames already. We could have taken all the men and horses and slaves on ships, and allowed the river to take us down to the sea, and then sailed up the coast. Instead, the insides of my legs feel as raw as chopped liver."

"That is because you ride a horse like, well, like an Angle," said Edwin, who sat upon his own horse as easily as a leaf upon a tree. "You sit upon it as a sack sits upon a wagon. When it comes to riding a horse, look to the Britons. They sit upon their horses so lightly it is as if man and animal were one."

"That's all very well for you," grumbled Osfrith. "You lived among the Britons when you were young. All we do nowadays is kill them."

"And take their land," added Eadfrith.

Edwin laughed. "Would that it were so! What land they have left is barren and mountainous, the haunt of wolves and wights and terrible things. Let them keep it. It is the same with the painted people; nothing but rock and rain and wind. No, I fear the battles we will fight in future will be against our own people. The Britons are finished."

"That's all very well, but you still have not said why we come this way when we could have taken ship," said Osfrith.

"That is why," said Edwin, pointing ahead as they breasted a rise in the land.

The ground fell gently away before them into a broad plain. To the north it rose again, but in the great bowl before them the ground was clothed in thick oak forest on the sloping sides of the plain and in the flood plain with a greyer blanket of alder and willow.

Cutting blue through the green were two rivers, one running east to west, the other south to north, until they met and continued north, united. At their confluence, there was a great clearing in the forest, made first by marsh and reed where the rivers ran shallow and broad, flooding out forest, and then latterly by axes, clearing and cutting for the great hall, stockade, village and fields that lay in the crook of the two rivers.

"That," said Edwin, pointing to the east–west river, "is the Anker, and that," to the river running from the south, "is the Tame. They run together into the Trent and that river flows north-east into the Humber. You will get your wish, Osfrith, for once our task is done we will take ship home. But this is the reason why we have come here." Edwin pointed at the great hall set among the surrounding forest. "That is Tamworth, great hall of the Tomsætan, and the first and greatest home of the kings of Mercia."

"Ah, that explains it," said Eadfrith. "For the last few miles, as we were riding through the forest, I suspected there were men watching us. They would be the woodsmen, taking word to their king of our approach."

"I did not see anything," began Osfrith.

"Of course," said Eadfrith.

"But I did hear movement," continued Osfrith, "and the woods were too quiet, too still – when the birds and animals are so quiet, it means there are men afoot among the trees." Osfrith rode his horse closer to his brother and rapped his knuckles on Eadfrith's helmet. "You might hear some of this if you did not insist on wearing that all the time."

"If you had won a helmet this magnificent in battle, you would wear it too," said Eadfrith.

Osfrith held his hand up and whispered, loudly enough so that everyone could hear, "I've seen him sleep in it."

Edwin left his sons to their chaffing, letting his mind drift with the rhythm of the horse as it slowly descended the forest road into the vale below. As the Northumbrians came onto the flat ground, the trees thinned out. The road stood proud of the surrounding marshy land. It was a causeway, made from many thousands of logs sunk deep into the mud. It was summer, and the plain was still lush green, studded with grazing cattle and sheep, but the tussocky grass and occasional green pools foretold winter flooding. He suspected that if he should return when the days were short, he would find the causeway to be a straight, dark line through wide silver sheets of water. Edwin nodded approvingly. The Mercians had chosen a good defensive position for this royal vill.

As they drew nearer, the great hall grew larger, and the men fell silent. It was a huge structure, as large if not bigger than their own palace in Ad Gefrin, and made to seem larger by being set upon a huge platform of dug earth, walled with thick planks. The area around the platform was covered with workshops, barns, sheds and some small houses, while the whole area north of the rivers' confluence was surrounded by deep ditches surmounted with stockades. The stockades ran along the river's edge to the south as well, but there was a gate at the jetty. There were many small craft, rowing boats and coracles mostly, tied to the jetty, as well as two short-masted river boats. But on the near bank of the river at the end of the flood plain causeway, where the road came to the river, there was a raft waiting.

As the Northumbrians rode closer they saw the rafter pulling his craft into the middle of the stream using ropes slung across the river. There in the centre of the river he remained, holding the raft against the flow with the ropes and shading his eyes against the sun so that he might more clearly see the approaching riders.

"Who be you?" the rafter called to the Northumbrians as they reined in at the water's edge.

Edwin nodded to Guthlaf, who urged his horse to the shallows.

The rafter, seeing the horse move closer, began to pull towards the far shore, but Guthlaf stopped when his horse's hooves splashed into the water. The warmaster raised the tufa that he bore for the king when they travelled, lifting the winged globe upon its gilded pole.

"Edwin, king of Deira, sovereign of Bernicia, ruler of Lindsey and Elmet, lord of the isles of Anglesey and Man, by right Bretwalda,

High King of Britain, brings greetings and gifts to Cearl, king of Mercia."

The rafter made the courtesy but he did not move his craft any nearer. "Hail, Edwin, Bretwalda, High King. Cearl, king of Mercia, greets and welcomes you. He is eager to meet with you, for well he remembers the kindness you ever showed his dearly missed daughter."

"For his part," Guthlaf answered, "Edwin, High King, is ever desirous to speak with Cearl, king of Mercia, and waits upon this shore, ready to pass over into Tamworth."

"I stand ready to bring the High King over the river, and his sons if they be here, and in turns the rest of the High King's party so long as they be willing to deposit their swords and spears with the king's door warden before passing into the royal precinct."

"Is this the courtesy shown to the High King? That he be asked to leave his sword at the door, as if he were a travel-stained rapscallion of no worth."

The rafter spread his hands placatingly. "There is no insult here – the king's warmaster, with the king's blessing, lays down this law upon all so that in the heat that sometimes comes upon men with feasting and drinking, there be no blood spilled and feuds entered, but rather friendship and good cheer."

Guthlaf began to answer but Edwin held up his hand. "We will leave our weapons with the king's door warden, so long as he undertakes upon his blood to care for them and return them when we ask."

"He will undertake that right gladly, lord," said the rafter, bowing his head to Edwin.

"Then we stand ready." Edwin dismounted, and his men followed suit.

The rafter pulled his craft back across the river and grounded it upon the bank. It was broad enough to take three or four horses and men, so Edwin, his sons and Guthlaf led their animals upon the planks.

As the rafter strained to pull the now heavy laden raft off the bank, Edwin soothed his horse. Guthlaf, seeing the man struggle, gave his horse into Eadfrith's charge and laid hold of the rope as well. Together, the two men hauled the raft back into the stream, whereupon the rafter pulled it to the far bank.

The Northumbrians led their animals ashore. The rafter made the courtesy, then pulled back across the river to start the task of relaying the rest of the party across the Tame.

Edwin, his sons and his warmaster led their horses to the gate in the stockade. The door warden made his courtesy, then accepted their swords gravely. His eyes widened when Edwin handed him the blade forged by Wældhelm, and this sword he laid carefully down, apart from the others.

"You need have no fear, lord," he said. "I will guard your sword well, with my own blood."

"I would have your blood if it were lost," said Edwin.

"I would give my blood right willingly if I lost it," said the door warden. "Now enter, for the king is expecting you."

"Send the rest of the men after us when they have crossed the river," added Guthlaf.

Passing through the gate, they entered the royal compound of Tamworth. Ahead and above them, standing high upon its platform, was the great hall, the gold and red painted designs on its great timbers gleaming in the sunlight. As they walked across the wide expanse of the compound, their practised eyes took in the encircling palisade, the workshops and smithy, the barns and dwellings, the well and the foodstores that made Tamworth both a grand royal dwelling and one well able to withstand a siege. The men, women and children working and playing in the compound all stopped what they were doing to watch as the small company strode across the flagstones towards the great hall and climbed the steps up to the platform.

The door to the great hall stood closed and before it stood four guards, fully armed. Although none of the men drew their weapons, they stood with hands upon hilts, ready.

"Who seeks audience with the king?" asked the hall warden.

Guthlaf again stepped forward, it not being meet that a king should announce himself.

"Who are you to ask this?" he said.

"I am Beocca, hall ward to Cearl, king."

"Know this then, Beocca, hall ward of Cearl, that here stands Edwin, High King, lord of Deira, lord of Bernicia, king of Northumbria and Elmet and Lindsey, master of the islands, and he comes not to seek audience but to grant it."

Beocca's grip on his sword hilt tightened, but he did not draw it.

"This is the great hall of Cearl, king of Mercia, lord of the Tomsæte. He alone is king in these lands."

"And he was once my father-in-law." Edwin stepped forward. "You may not remember me, Beocca, but I remember you: so short, I had to lift you up on your horse and then you fell off the other side. How you howled!"

The other three guards strove to keep their faces straight, and failed. Beocca blushed beneath his helmet.

"However, you got straight back on the horse again, even though you were still crying. You were a brave boy and I see you have become a brave man; few others would keep me standing at the door. Whose command do you wait upon? Cearl would not have me shuffling my feet on his doorstep."

Beocca made the courtesy, clashing his forearm against his mail.

"Your pardon, lord, but the king's warmaster gave orders that none should be admitted into the king's presence without his leave."

"And who is Cearl's warmaster now?"

"It is Penda, lord."

"Ah, Penda. I have heard tell of this man. I would meet him, but after I have met the king. Stand aside, Beocca son of Berhtred. You have done your duty and more, but it is time now for kings to take counsel with each other."

Beocca hesitated, then bowed his head and stepped back. "Enter, lord, and may you find the king willing to greet you."

The Northumbrians entered the great hall. Light streamed through the door after them. Pillars of wood marched down either side of the hall; tall smooth beech trunks painted in intricate designs of gold and red and blue were interspersed with broader oak pillars hung with rich cloth. Rich tapestries dangled upon the walls, telling in pictures the deeds of the ancestors of the kings of Mercia, stories of the gods and the victories of Cearl and his forefathers. A great fire burned in the centre of the hall, even though it was summer, and the air within sweltered, heavy with smoke and sweat. Slaves and servants moved silently around the edges of the hall, but there were few men seated at table or gathered in conversation. Those who were there stood and watched silently as the Northumbrians advanced down the centre of the hall, walking between the flanking rows of pillars.

At the head of the hall another fire burned and behind it, beyond the high table, sat the king, flanked by his bodyguards. Cearl's head rested upon his hand and his eyes were downcast, covered in shadow, so that he seemed a man in deep thought, but he did not stir as the Northumbrians approached. Despite the warmth in the hall, Cearl had wrapped around his shoulders a cloak, trimmed with wolf fur, and fine leather boots, also fur lined, upon his feet. He was seated upon a wooden throne, carved from a single trunk of oak and scored with intricate patterns, leaping animals chasing each other around his head, their eyes inlaid with garnets and emeralds, their limbs leafed with gold. In the firelight the throne glistened.

The Northumbrians stopped before the throne. In the hall all movement had ceased. Even the slaves stopped to watch. From outside there came the noise of dogs barking and distant conversation, but all was silent in the great hall.

"Cearl." Edwin spoke. "Wife father."

The man upon the throne slowly raised his head. Although in truth he had been asleep a moment before, there was no befuddlement in his eyes.

"Edwin," he answered. "Daughter husband."

Cearl's recognition of the visitors brought a slackening of the tension in the hall. Conversations resumed. Slaves returned to their tasks. The hands of the bodyguards rested more lightly upon their sword hilts.

Cearl held out his hand towards Edwin. It trembled slightly. Edwin stepped forward and took the hand in his own. The skin felt dry and cracked, like a leaf when no rain has fallen, but the flesh was cold.

A tear pricked the corner of Cearl's eye.

"Would that you had not come, daughter husband, and seen me like this: old, unmanned." The king spoke in a whisper so that only Edwin might hear his words.

But Edwin gripped the old man's hand more fiercely. "Cearl King, you alone of all the monarchs in Britain pay me no homage."

"That is in honour of Cwenburg, my daughter and your wife, and for no other reason, Edwin, as you well know."

"In part it is for her honour and memory, but it is also for the home you gave me when I was in exile, and the kindness you showed me, and the escape you allowed me when Æthelfrith demanded my head."

Cearl brushed the tear away before it could fall. "I miss Cwenburg still, Edwin. Do you?"

The High King fell silent for a moment. Here, in this hall, where he had first met Cwenburg, her memory still lingered, though it had faded under the abrasion of events.

"Yes, I miss her."

"It is not right that a man should outlive all his children, Edwin, but I have outlived all mine. All dead; all dead save me, their father. I have known sixty summers, but in truth they feel like sixty winters, and their chill never leaves my bones, nor their frost my hair." The old king stared into Edwin's face, his eyes showing the first rheum of age. "Why am I still alive when they are all dead?"

"Not all," said Edwin. "For in the child, the parent lives on. Wife father, here are the sons of Cwenburg, my sons, princes of Northumbria, heirs to the High King: Osfrith and Eadfrith."

On cue, the two young men bowed to Cearl. The old king beheld them in wonder, his eyes moving from one face to the other and back again.

"Yes, yes, I can see her, my beloved Cwenburg. I can see her in you." He held out his arms and now they were trembling with emotion, not palsy. The two young men approached and the old king embraced them, smoothing their hair with his hands, taking their faces each in turn and holding them close that he might see them the more closely. "Not only Cwenburg; I see in you boys how I used to be when I was young and strong, and all men feared me. Now age sits so heavily upon me, and the young men no longer come to me, ring giver, for glory and war, and my hall is empty save for the most faithful of the faithful." Cearl shook his head. "I do not know what would have happened, Edwin, daughter husband, if it were not for the valour and ardour of my warmaster, Penda. Young men flock to him, for they know he will fill their arms with rings and their glory with war, but he does all this still in my name."

"That is – remarkable," said Edwin. "I have heard of your warmaster from other sources too. Come, where is he, Cearl. I should like to meet him."

"He should return soon, for he has been out raiding and receiving the tribute that is yet given to me, but we were given word that he should be returning this day. Come though, let us eat and drink, that I may speak with my grandsons and see reflected, if only dimly, my Cwenburg for a while."

"That would be welcome indeed, grandfather king," said Eadfrith, "for we have ridden far."

"And riding is thirsty work, particularly for me," said Osfrith.

"He rides like a sack of oats," Eadfrith added, to the old man's evident delight.

"Come, come," said Cearl, "mayhap it is the horse and not the rider. After we have taken our fill, I will show you my horses, that you might take your pick. They are fine animals, and on them, I'd wager, you would look like a king." Cearl looked around for a slave and clapped his hands. "Food and drink for our guests." The slave was about to rush to the kitchen when Cearl stopped him. "And bring me word when Penda returns – he must meet my heirs."

That single word rippled around the great hall. Heirs. Cearl, king of Mercia, lord of the Tomsæte, was acknowledging his grandsons as his heirs. Slave whispered to servant, bodyguard to thegn, priest to scop, and they all turned to examine the new heirs to their king.

For his part Edwin said nothing. He had expected to have to work his way towards Cearl accepting his sons as heirs, rather than having the kingdom presented to them while he was still making his greetings, but he was not about to question such a turn of fortune. Indeed, it seemed that all had gone well since he had invited the new god of the Christians to demonstrate his power. As slaves and servants brought drink – wine, mead, beer and ale – and food in ever increasing amounts, laying them on the high table and filling those tables in the great hall that had men attending them, Edwin settled to eating and drinking quietly, allowing his sons to monopolize the conversation with Cearl. After all, they had to learn the ins and outs of the kingdom that would one day be theirs. Guthlaf sat in silence with the king, filling his stomach with food and drink but stocking his memory with details of the hall and the men in it, from which hand they used for the knife to the location of the subsidiary smoke holes in the roof. Although Cearl was embracing his grandsons with all the fervour of an old man not long for life, the workings of wyrd and the caprice of the fate singers could mean that in a year's time they would be trying to burn down this hall rather than being received in it.

The meal slowly turned into a feast. Edwin's own men joined the lower tables, doubling at a stroke the number of warriors in the hall. There were still many empty tables, however, and Edwin and Guthlaf noted the lack of warriors in the king's household. Cearl, seeing Edwin's appraising glance, nodded.

"It was not as this in your day, was it, Edwin? Then young men came from all over this land, and from over sea, hungry for glory, greedy for gold, and my hall rang with song and story and boast. But as the years covered me and drained the strength and vigour from my marrow, the young men came no longer, and these halls grew quiet and drear. My heart beats proud now to see my grandsons, the image of my beloved daughter, filling the hall with laughter and cheer and promise." Cearl leaned closer to Edwin, and while to any watcher he appeared to be speaking normally, he whispered, "Some among the men of Mercia will not welcome sons of Northumbria as

213

lord – tell them to be on guard against Smala and Selred and Cutha – but they, and you, can rely on Penda. He will bring the men of Mercia around to you."

"I look forward to meeting this Penda. It is… unusual to find such devotion today."

"That is what I tell myself, and give thanks each day to the fates that in my old age they sent me such a man to keep my kingdom safe and hand it on to my grandsons." Cearl peered towards the end of the hall, blinking. "He has arrived. He is here."

A party of men were advancing up the centre of the hall, stained with the dust and sweat of summer travel. Whispers and greetings followed them as they went. King Cearl's champion, his warmaster, had returned. At the head of the group was a man of normal stature, certainly not a giant like Wældhelm the smith, but Edwin noted the vigour of his tread and the fluidity of his movement. In battle, Edwin thought, such a man would favour speed over strength, feint over ferocity. His companions, his hearth troops, were men of similar mould, lithe and quick stepping, their travelling cloaks trimmed with fur and edged with gold. They wore rich buckles, and their cloaks were pinned with gold and garnet, but Penda's own clothes were plain and he wore only a simple buckle made of iron. It was his bearing that told of his leadership, not his accoutrements.

Penda walked rapidly up the hall, and swiftly, fluidly, went down on one knee before Cearl, bowing his head, then raising it to say, "Hail, Cearl, king."

"You are right welcome, Penda, warmaster, most faithful and trusted of my thegns. Stand and greet our guests."

Penda rose to his feet with the same physical grace that he had shown when kneeling. He looked curiously towards Edwin and the other Northumbrians at the high table, in particular at the two young men seated on either side of Cearl, but Edwin could see no trace of rancour or ill will upon his face, only natural inquisitiveness.

"Penda," said Cearl, "warmaster, counsellor, friend, I present to you Edwin, daughter husband, whom I received in his exile many years ago, when I was as you are now, a man of strength. I gave to him in marriage my most beloved daughter, Cwenburg, and he returned to the glory that was his, reclaiming his throne and much more besides, as you no doubt know."

Edwin, who could tell that the old man was enjoying himself, watched the warmaster closely throughout Cearl's oration, but there was again only pleasant interest.

Penda made the courtesy to Edwin, but then he went further and bowed his head.

"High King," Penda said, "I greet and welcome you."

Edwin got to his feet. He was, he saw, half a head taller than Penda. The warmaster had the dark hair and build that was common among the Britons, but the ruddy complexion and pale eyes of a Saxon or Angle. The Mercians were Angles, but Penda looked only in part Angle to Edwin's eyes. Whatever his background, the warmaster showed no sign of discomfort under Edwin's scrutiny, but returned the High King's gaze naturally and openly.

"Penda, I give you greeting," said Edwin, "and my gratitude for your care and valour in defence of the realm of Cearl, wife father. We have come from the land of the West Saxons, where we slew their underkings and received the fealty of Cwichelm, their overking." At this news Edwin at last saw a reaction from Penda: a slight tightening of the jaw and narrowing of his eyes as the implications of the Northumbrian victory became immediately clear to the warmaster. Edwin was nonetheless relieved: if he had been unable to perceive any reaction to such important news, he would have had to conclude that Penda was entirely unreadable and therefore a threat so great that he would have had to be removed forthwith. But now that he had seen behind Penda's mask, he could consider allowing the man to live.

"In view of your valour in service of Cearl, wife father, I give this ring, taken from the West Saxons, your enemies of old, now defeated, and pass it to you, Penda, warmaster, thegn to the king." Edwin drew from his arm the richest, most intricately carved and thickly jewel encrusted of all the armlets that had been stripped from the dead at Duxford and held it out to Penda. Looking past the gift held in his outstretched hand, Edwin saw the gold lust glitter in

Penda's eyes, the dark and deep desire, slower burning but fiercer even than the woman fire. But Penda too looked past the gift into Edwin's surprised eyes, and as quickly as the fire had sparked it was extinguished, to be replaced by a cool amusement.

In one smooth movement, Penda took the armlet and placed it on the table in front of Cearl.

"This gift is truly that of a king and worthy of a king, so I pass it to my lord, Cearl, king."

The old man stared at the armlet. It glowed and glistened in the firelight, the inset jewels casting shards of brilliant red and blue light upon the rich, deep gold. Cearl reached a trembling hand towards the gift.

"This – it has been so long…" He looked to Penda and began to speak, to ask permission, but the warmaster answered the question before it could be asked.

"It is yours, lord. Put it on."

Cearl drew the band over his hand and pushing up his loose sleeve he moved it upwards. The muscles of his forearm were too wasted now to hold the metal, so Cearl pushed the armlet past his elbow. He stared down at the armlet with the wonder of a boy receiving his first seax, turning the ring first one way and then the other.

"Penda, you are a good and faithful thegn, and if you were of my blood you would be my heir," said Cearl, stroking the armlet now as gently as a man might stroke a woman. "Ever have you served me faithfully, and I am right glad that you have come this day, that you might see and meet and make obedience to the heirs of my blood, the sons of my beloved daughter." The old king left off fingering the armlet and put his arms around Edwin's sons. "These two young men are Osfrith and Eadfrith, sons of the High King, sprung from Cwenburg, brave warriors, leaders of men, my heirs and your future king. What a kingdom they will wield, uniting the thrones of Northumbria and Mercia; all the thrones in the land must needs bow before them. Therefore, I ask you, give them your welcome and pledge them your allegiance, Penda, warmaster of the kings of Mercia."

While all other eyes were on Cearl, Edwin watched Penda throughout the old king's speech. The warmaster's gaze had flicked from Cearl to the two young princes, but then it had returned to Cearl, where it remained. Penda's jaw had tightened as Cearl proclaimed the young princes his heirs. Watching, Edwin could feel the tension in the man, the almost overwhelming desire to look at him, Edwin, the architect of the sudden elevation of two unknown princes into heirs, but not once did the warmaster's control weaken. His eyes remained fixed on Cearl throughout. And then, when the hall fell silent, waiting upon his reply, he still kept his gaze upon the king.

"This… I admit, this is a surprise. I had hoped…but no, of course not. It would not be meet for the son of a thegn and a slave woman to think on thrones…" Penda turned his head smartly, sharply, from Osfrith to Eadfrith, nodding to each in turn. "I greet you, Osfrith and Eadfrith, sons of Northumbria, heirs to Edwin, High King." Penda turned back to Cearl. "Of course, if you have nominated these Northumbrians as your heirs, I will follow and serve them, lord, and I will strive to ensure that the witan of your people, the people of Mercia, accept and acknowledge them as your heirs and successors." Penda gave a slight shrug. "After all, as you know better than anyone, the Mercians can be a stubborn people. Some may be reluctant to accept outsiders as king."

"But you will speak for them, Penda? The people, my thegns, they fear and admire you; if you stand before the witan and announce that you will follow my choice and accept these young men as my heirs, then many others will follow your lead."

"Of course I will carry out your wishes, Cearl, king, for have they not always been as commands to me, dearer than the orders of a father?"

The old king smiled. "You have been better and more faithful than a son to me, Penda. Would only that you were of my blood too, that you might share in the kingdom."

Penda smiled ruefully. "The fate weavers wove, and I came out from the wrong side of the bed." He turned to Edwin and his sons. "But for those born to the throne, I pledge my strength."

Edwin and his sons rose. "I would have pledge of your wit more even than your strength," said Edwin.

The warmaster looked up at the king with unruffled eyes. Edwin could see no trace there of the bitter disappointment that must have come from hearing Cearl announce his heirs. But nor could he discern anything at all below the surface calm that Penda chose to present to them. The warmaster might have pledged his allegiance, but he warranted attention; Edwin found it difficult to believe that Penda would relinquish being the effective power in the kingdom so easily.

"I pledge my wit," Penda said.

Edwin inclined his head in acknowledgement, turning over possibilities in his mind. There was a formidable cunning to this young man – he could see that already. It would be meet to co-opt him, rather than have Penda acting against their interests when they returned to Northumbria and waited upon Cearl's death to claim the inheritance.

"And I vow that you will remain warmaster of Mercia and, should wyrd work to our favour, be king under us as well."

Penda bowed gracefully to the High King.

"I had heard that Edwin was generous as well as wise; now I see the truth of it."

Edwin would have liked to step forward at that point, to stand eye to eye with Penda, as a man fought an enemy in the shieldwall pushing tight against him in the embrace of death, for there was an edge of steel to his pleasant words, a gall in the honey of acceptance, but one he could not locate. However, the width of the high table was between them, and Penda was stepping back from it, increasing the distance between them.

"Penda, join us in feast," said Cearl.

"Of course, lord, and gladly. Allow me first to wash away the dust of travel, then I fancy I will drain a cup of ale faster than any man in this hall." As Penda made this boast, his voice rose, spreading through the gathering and drawing a ragged cheer.

"This torc says you won't," called out one of the king's retainers, taking it off and waving the gold ring above his head.

"And this parsnip says I will!" In one swift movement, Penda grasped a raw parsnip from the king's table and threw it through the ring. The innuendo was clear, the laughter instantaneous – even the man who had challenged Penda started laughing.

The tension in the hall broken, Penda departed to wash, swapping words and laughter with one or two men as he left. Edwin watched him go, then turned to Guthlaf. Cearl was telling tales of his youth to his grandsons.

"What do you think?"

Guthlaf picked up a parsnip, tossed it in the air and caught it. "If Penda throws a spear as well as he throws a vegetable, he will be a fine ally."

"Or a dangerous enemy."

"Indeed."

Edwin dropped his voice further. "When Penda returns and he has drunk his fill, duel him. I want to see how he fights."

Guthlaf nodded. "What sort of duel?"

"Three shields, but no blood. A trial of warmasters."

"Very well." Guthlaf smiled. "Now at least I have something to look forward to tonight."

# Chapter 16

Penda won the ale-drinking contest – at least, the first one. He won the second too, and the third, but the fourth saw him bested by an old grizzled warrior who warmed his bones by the fire in winter and sat in the sun through the summer. Edwin noted that Penda took the defeat in good heart and gave the old man more than he had bet. The aged retainer's face broke into such a beam of delight as he slipped the arm rings on that Edwin saw echoes of the boy and youth he had once been breaking through the lines of age. He marked well the few quiet words Penda shared with the retainer when the cheering had died away and the men in the hall went back to their eating and drinking and talking, and the way the old man grasped Penda's wrist in thanks. Edwin looked to Guthlaf.

"Formidable," said the warmaster.

"Show me how he fights," said Edwin.

Guthlaf nodded.

"But later, when the men are in their cups and ready for some entertainment."

Guthlaf drained his own cup and made a face. "There'll be more entertainment from a duel than from this Mercian beer. Our beer is much better."

"The waters of Deira are sweet waters," said Edwin.

"'The land of the waters' indeed. Even now I still taste the sweet and cool water of the River Wharfe, and remember how we used to splash and play in it like young otters on hot summer days, my brothers and me." Guthlaf grimaced at his empty cup. "And it makes better beer too."

"Deira is my home too." Edwin looked into his memory hoard. As he grew older he realized that he guarded this treasury more closely than any gold, returning to it when alone, or in company, and running his fingers over its accumulated riches. "For my part, it is the Don that I recall, and the Ouse, of course; stealing my brothers' boat and setting off to sea – I was five at the time. How they beat me when they caught me! I went howling to my father. When I said I was sailing for the sea, he asked me how far I had got. 'Fulford,' I replied. How my father laughed. 'Next time you set sail for the sea,' he said, 'at least make it as far as Thorp!'" Edwin smiled at the warmaster, taking Guthlaf by surprise. "I wonder what my sons will remember of me when I am dead."

"May the fate weavers give them many years to remember you through." Guthlaf held out his cup to a slave for it to be refilled, however poor the local beer might be. "Do the shades in the underworld remember their fathers? My boys were bare old enough to walk when the flux and the pox took them." Guthlaf took a swallow of the beer, not noticing its thinness. "Will I even know them when my shade goes down into darkness?"

"My friend, the All-Father will surely send his daughters to take one such as you, a great warrior, to his halls when you die."

Guthlaf stared truculently at his king. "My sons have no place in the feasting hall of Woden – they died before they were old enough to wield even a wooden sword. But lord, when I die I would rather be where they are than feasting with the gods."

Edwin looked in surprise at his warmaster and saw that he was serious. "In Woden's halls, they say, there is feasting and battles and deeds until the seas rise and the moon falls. You, a warrior through and through, would you not be there?"

Guthlaf swallowed his beer and grimaced into the cup. "It does not get better with drinking."

"Guthlaf?"

The warmaster looked to the king. "As you say, lord, I have been a warrior through all my days. But in death, if it were possible, I would be a father, as you have been to Osfrith and Eadfrith."

"Do those who die as children… do they grow older?"

Guthlaf shrugged. "The stories do not speak of such matters.

I have asked Coifi, and sometimes he says one thing, sometimes another. If he knows the answer, he has not told me."

"When he first entered my service, the gods spoke often to Coifi, and sometimes clearly. But now, I fear, it has been long since the gods spoke to him. His answers, when I ask him of the weavings of wyrd, are in his own voice, not that of the gods."

Guthlaf nodded. "The queen's priest has the best of it there, for if his god is not speaking to him, Paulinus can find the answer in his book. But for Coifi, when the gods are silent…"

"Not that the gods' silence renders Coifi mute." Edwin winked at Guthlaf, who grinned back.

"Would sometimes that it did."

Edwin looked over to where Penda was sitting at the other end of the high table, with his friends and retainers clustered around him. They had eaten and drunk in apparent good spirits initially, but there had not been the usual laughter, boasting and insults that accompanied the best spirited of feasts. Now, with the food mostly eaten, Penda's men sat over their cups, joining in quiet conversation or listening to Cearl's scop as he told a long and involved tale of their forefathers.

"I think the time is right," said Edwin.

Guthlaf swung his legs off the bench, stood, stretched and belched, loudly enough to garner some appreciative grins.

The arm ring, a band composed of interwoven strands of gold ending in the twin heads of serpents, rattled onto the table among the cups and knives of Penda's men.

"Time for some proper entertainment. This arm ring, taken from a West Saxon king, for a three-shield duel, Penda. One warmaster to another. What do you say?"

The hall fell silent. Even the scop, in the midst of telling how Cearl's grandfather, Creoda, had first fortified the mound by the confluence of the rivers Tame and Anker when he was attacked by the men of Rheged, stopped his telling.

Penda picked the arm ring up and dangled it from his finger, feeling its weight.

"Gold?"

"The dearest love of kings," said Guthlaf.

Penda smiled. "Mine, however, is fighting: the play of swords, the hiss of spears."

Guthlaf nodded. "That is why we are not kings. Let us make sport."

The Mercian swung up from the bench and sent one of his men to the back of the hall. "He will bring us duelling swords, and shields." He looked to the centre of the hall, where the men were already gathering and making excited predictions about the contest, with many a whispered wager being laid. "Make room, and someone, lay out the ground."

There was no shortage of men eager to lay their cloaks upon the ground as the duel arena. Penda, receiving the duelling weapons, carelessly took the first that came to hand and passed the rest to Guthlaf for his selection. The habit of years meant that Guthlaf carefully weighed each sword in his hand, holding it out level to feel its balance and whipping it through the air to test its flex. They were all workaday swords, their points and edges dulled, good for practice duelling but little else. Choosing a plain but reasonably well-balanced sword, Guthlaf followed Penda to the centre of the hall.

"Shield." Penda held out his arm and a leather-covered limewood shield, painted the blue and yellow of Mercia, was handed to him. A yellow dragon writhed upon the shield given to Guthlaf. The warmaster grasped the leather strap over the hand space. It was a good, round shield, light, but with enough flexibility to absorb most blows. Guthlaf consciously relaxed the muscles in his arm. The trick was to absorb the blows with a loose arm, allowing the wood to do the work, rather than tense up and stop the force with your own strength.

The two men took up positions on either side of the pegged-out cape. Stepping off the cape, either through being forced back or from being unaware of its position, meant a shield loss. The shield itself cracking or breaking was a point lost, as was having a knee forced to the ground.

At the high table, Cearl stood up for a better view. Osfrith and Eadfrith stood too, but Edwin left the table and pushed through the crowd so that he could watch at close range.

Guthlaf and Penda faced each other, sword in one hand – they were both right handed – and shield in the other. Neither was helmeted, nor were they armoured.

"Ready?" asked Guthlaf.

"Ready," said Penda.

The swords clashed in the space between the two men, the iron clang ringing through the hall to announce the start of the duel.

The opening, time-hallowed move made, both men settled back into low stances, shields held up to the neck line, swords steady and poised. Already, from the weight of the initial exchange, Guthlaf knew that he had the weight on Penda, but he had known that would be the case simply from looking at the smaller man. Their quickness of hand was similar, but he suspected that Penda's sword might be slightly quicker through the air. The younger man was certainly faster, but he was not as strong, a deduction Guthlaf tested with his next blow, a heavy overarm slash onto Penda's shield. The shield took and deflected the blow, as Guthlaf had expected, but he had struck downwards to test Penda's upper body strength. The slight give in the shield and the way Penda turned it to deflect rather than absorb the blow suggested considerable but not excessive strength. Guthlaf stepped back, satisfied with his first, probing attack, then had to bring his shield sharply down to block an underarm slash at his knee. He only just brought the shield down in time. Gods, the man's sword arm was fast.

Guthlaf nodded his respect to Penda, but the Mercian's face remained blank and unmoved, his eyes like dull, uncut jewels. As they circled slowly over the pegged-out cloak, Guthlaf realized that Penda was one of the bare handful of warriors whose face could not be read. Most men found it impossible not to foreshow their attacks in some way, be it through eye direction, shifts in body weight or alterations in their stance. Penda, though, gave no indication whatsoever of where his next attack would be directed. It was only because he was scrupulous about maintaining distance between them that Guthlaf had been able to block his first few strikes.

Now, however, it was time for the warmaster to impose himself upon his opponent. Guthlaf, who had been careful to subtly signal his initial attacks, struck in fast, heavy succession overarm and roundarm blows to the upper body and head, forcing Penda to raise his shield, and by upping the rate at which he struck, Guthlaf made the Mercian raise his shield that fraction too far, so that it slightly blocked his eyeline. The mistake made, Guthlaf immediately followed the next sword strike with his shield, putting his weight into the hard iron boss at its centre. Catching Penda off balance, the shield advance left him no option but to step back to retain his footing, and the shout that resounded around the hall told the tale: Penda had stepped out of the ring.

Guthlaf nodded at the Mercian and moved back to the far side of the duel arena. Still expressionless, Penda returned, but the men of Mercia urged him on, shouting his name – although not a few took the chance of the break to lay wagers on Guthlaf, now that they had seen his mettle.

Guthlaf backhanded the sweat from his eyes and, before he knew it, found his right leg swept out from under him and his bottom on the floor. He stared up at the sword held in front of his eyes, and his eyes travelled along its length, up the arm holding it, to Penda's face. The Mercian allowed himself a slight, tight smile.

"One all."

Cheers rang out around the hall, while some of the more vacillating of the spectators attempted to rescind their recently placed bets on Guthlaf.

The Northumbrian got up. He no longer had the spring and elasticity of a young man, so his getting up was more laboured than it might have been, and Guthlaf played that up, grimacing as he straightened his back and kicked a kink out of his knee joint.

The two men resumed their positions on the cloak. Sweat was pricking through their skin and leaving tracks down the sides of their faces. Guthlaf smiled; he was enjoying the contest. It had been a while since he had faced a worthwhile opponent. Penda's face remained blank, however.

It was that very blankness that gave Guthlaf the clue to the next attack. Penda sprang forward, using his shield to push Guthlaf's blade out of position while his own sword swept underneath the wood, aiming to knock Guthlaf's leading leg from under him. But Guthlaf was not there. Anticipating the attack, he had sidestepped it and, using his own shield, he drove it against Penda's, sending him stumbling forward and out of the ring.

As Penda caught himself, and cheers and groans echoed around the hall, Guthlaf saw the first appearance of emotion in the Mercian. A compression in the man's lips, a whitening of the cheeks and a tightening of the eyes. Guthlaf put the knowledge away for future use: Penda was a man whose anger burned cold. They were, in general, more dangerous than the men who burned.

Penda walked back into the duelling ring. Guthlaf made himself ready. The hall went quiet. The Northumbrian only needed one more point for victory.

But that point proved hard to win.

A succession of blows traded and blocked, swords moving faster than the eye could follow, left both men sweat streaked and breathing hard, but neither was forced from the ring, or blooded, or put upon their knee. And, as happens in battle, without word they both fell back to the edge of the ring to gasp air into lungs.

"What… do you say… to a drink?" asked Guthlaf.

"I… say…yes," said Penda.

Guthlaf, too out of breath to say more, signed and a slave rushed to them with cups of beer. This time the Northumbrian drained his cup without any complaints about the quality of Mercian beer. Penda, having drunk too, called for water and splashed it over his face and hands. Seeing him, Guthlaf called for water as well, but he, to the laughter of the watching men, upended the bucket over his head. From where he was watching, Edwin stifled a smile. There had been a risk that calling a duel between the two warmasters would raise tensions between Northumbrians and Mercians, but Guthlaf was playing his part perfectly, ensuring that the contest was seen as a good-humoured trial rather than battle by proxy.

Guthlaf squelched back into the ring. Penda followed.

"Re – " The word was not out of Guthlaf's mouth when Penda swept his sword in an arc under the Northumbrian's shield, catching the side of his knee and sending him, grunting with pain, to the ground.

Cheers and catcalls went up from the watching men, depending on where their allegiances and their money lay. Those who had laid more on Guthlaf shouted that the attack was unfair, but Guthlaf himself merely grimaced as he used his sword to push himself back to his feet.

Keeping a wary eye on Penda, the Northumbrian retook his battle stance.

"Two each," he said. "Next one wins."

Penda gave the slightest of nods, but his face and eyes remained impassive. Guthlaf realized that there was no reading the man in combat. He could either wait and attempt to counter whatever attack Penda made – but that strategy ran the risk of failure because of the Mercian's great speed of hand – or he attacked himself, forcing the duel to a conclusion, one way or the other.

Guthlaf grinned. Penda saw the warmaster's amusement.

"If you wonder why I smile," said Guthlaf, "it is because this is the first duel I have fought in a long, long time where I do not know if I will win." Guthlaf's grin grew wider. "Thank you for that, Penda of Mercia." And with his thanks, Guthlaf launched his attack.

He based it on weight of blow and weight of shield, raining strikes down upon Penda one after the other, interspersed with shield thrusts, using each to push the man back, and back, and back. Every readjustment of Penda's stance brought his rear foot closer to the edge of the arena and the sheer ferocity of the attack was beginning to crack his shield, forcing him to rotate the wood so that fresh wood took successive blows. But there was a limit to how far the shield could be turned without putting such strain on the shoulder that the shock of absorbing the blows would dislocate the joint.

The Northumbrian expended energy prodigiously, using every ounce of his weight to force the Mercian back, but Penda defended tenaciously, economically, attempting as far as possible to hold his ground until the inevitable lull, when his opponent's breath failed and muscles cramped, when he might launch his own counter-attack.

With a final, lung-bursting effort, Guthlaf rained a flurry of blows, using both sword and shield, upon Penda. Any ordinary man would have fallen long since and even extraordinary ones would have been forced out of the ring by that final prodigious effort, but Penda absorbed, deflected, survived, to the accompaniment of an increasing chorus of gasps and shouts from the watching men who, realizing what they were seeing, would have cheered had they not been so absorbed by the contest.

The storm slackened. The rain of blows lessened. No man could continue at the pace Guthlaf had set. The watching men knew that, and so did Penda. Now was his chance.

With the pressure slightly reduced, the Mercian sidestepped, allowing Guthlaf's last flurry of attacks to carry him forward and off balance, while he aimed a roundhouse blow to the back of Guthlaf's head, intending to send him toppling forward and out of the ring. Of course, in battle Penda would have chosen a straight thrust to the exposed armpit or the side of the neck, but this was a duel. And Guthlaf knew this.

Anticipating the strike to his back, Guthlaf ducked beneath it. Then, rising again, he pushed Penda's extended arm onwards, taking the man tumbling with it over the pegged-out limits of the cloak onto the rush-strewn floor of the great hall.

As one the spectators of the fight drew in breath, then they gave a great roar, the men of Northumbria loudest among them of course, but not a few of the Mercians, who looked to profit from Guthlaf's victory, matched their cheer. Even those who had lost, and lost money, banged their cups upon the table and gave voice. This had been a great contest, one whose equal few in the hall had seen before, pitting two warriors at the peak of their respective strength and experience against each other.

As the hall cheered, and Guthlaf raised his arms and turned in acknowledgement of the praise, Edwin kept his eyes upon Penda. On falling out of the ring, the Mercian had nimbly rolled back onto his feet, his sword and shield out. Edwin waited for defeat to cast its bitter cloak over Penda's face, but even as the acclaim for Guthlaf rang out, and Penda slowly lowered shield and sword, the Northumbrian could see no trace of anger in the Mercian's appearance. Instead, Edwin caught the slightest of nods he cast towards his own retinue of warriors, and the answering acknowledgements, before Penda put down his weapons and took one of the plain rings from his arm.

The Mercian approached Guthlaf, still standing with arms upstretched, and handed him the ring.

"Good fight," said Guthlaf, slapping Penda's shoulder as he took the ring. "You are one of the best I have fought."

Penda took Guthlaf's wrist and raised his arm.

"And this man is the best I have fought! Praise him!"

The men around the hall stood and cheered, banging cups and seax handles on the long wooden tables.

"Praise him!" Penda pushed Guthlaf's arm higher and renewed shouting filled the hall.

"Praise him!" A final, tumultuous cheer rang out. Guthlaf and Penda spoke, but their words were drowned beneath the applause. Edwin watched the two men exchange arm rings, Guthlaf giving the Mercian one of his richest in exchange for the relatively plain ring Penda placed upon his arm, and then the two men returned, amid much back slapping and congratulations, to their respective places in the hall.

Cearl rose to his feet amid the delighted hubbub of post-duel conversation.

"Men of Mercia, my men, let what we have just witnessed be a sign and signal for the future friendship between Mercia and Northumbria. For the victor…" Cearl took a gold and garnet ring from his thumb and placed it in Guthlaf's hand, amid further cheers. "And for Penda, my faithful servant and faithful servant to my heir when I am gone…" Cearl took a garnet-embossed arm ring from his wrist, the jewels making the eyes of a lithe hunting dog that pursued itself in an endless circle, and gave it to Penda.

With a grunt, Guthlaf sat back down next to Edwin and reached for his cup. While Cearl commended the two warriors, Edwin leaned closer to his warmaster.

"Well?"

"In five years, he will have the beating of me," said Guthlaf.

Edwin raised an eyebrow. "So long?"

Guthlaf grunted in laughter. "You're right. Three." The warmaster grimaced, then looked questioningly at Edwin. "How did the duel look to you?"

"A close contest between two fine warriors."

"Too close." Guthlaf lowered his voice. "I am not sure he did not have the beating of me."

"Why would he lose deliberately?"

"You tell me."

The two men, king and warmaster, looked to where Penda sat among his retainers. The men were laughing and talking among themselves, seemingly unaffected by their lord's defeat, but the Mercian sat silently in their midst. His gaze met the Northumbrians', and he raised his cup to them. They in turn saluted him.

"Will such a man stand aside for Eadfrith when Cearl dies?" asked Guthlaf.

"No," said Edwin. "But he has given Cearl no reason to doubt him, and the old king will cling to his warmaster through his remaining years. We will have to win Penda over to our service."

"Or kill him."

"Yes. Or kill him."

"That would be easier. And cheaper."

Edwin pursed his lips in thought. "The killing would not be so straightforward. We are in Mercia, and if he died while we were guests in the hall, we would not escape with our lives. Cearl no longer has the strength and authority to hand Penda over to us, and if he attempted to do so, Penda would take Mercia from him. No, we must attempt to win him."

"How do you do that?"

"How do you win any warrior? Gold and glory." Edwin laughed.

"What's so funny?"

"We are neither of us young, Guthlaf. Someday I will have need of a new warmaster. You have found him for me."

Edwin rose from the bench and made his way round the hall to Penda. The Mercian, seeing him approach, stood up and made the courtesy. Edwin returned the greeting and took Penda's arm, leading him to a quiet corner of the hall.

"Pledge yourself to me and I will give you glory," said Edwin.

"I am Cearl's man, professed and true," said Penda.

"Of course, and that is as it should be. But when the day comes and Cearl's grandson takes the throne, know that I will make you warmaster of Mercia and Northumbria. Before our warriors, all the kings of this land will offer fealty. They will bow to us, as they did to the emperors of old."

Penda's eyes narrowed and for a while he made no answer. Then he said, "That is a mighty dream."

Edwin gripped Penda's forearm. "With you, it will be a true dream. As long as we are divided, we are weak. We took this land from the Britons, for their kings fought among themselves. Now we in turn fight among ourselves. If this continues, sooner or later hungry eyes will turn upon us. Do not think we are so strong that we could withstand our cousins from across the cold sea, raiding in their dragon-prowed boats. The rivers cut into the country's heart, waiting only for a sea pirate bold enough to sail them, and he will have rich pickings. Mercia is far from the sea, but my land is wave lashed along its length, and I tell you, sea wolves there are, prowling the whale roads. Let them gather in packs and we would be hard pushed to defend what is ours. That – that is why we need unity, we need the kings of this land to bow to one king, or they will find new kings taking their thrones."

"You will be that king?"

Edwin shrugged. "There is no one else."

Slowly, Penda nodded. "You are right. There is no one else." The Mercian grasped Edwin's forearm. "When the time comes I will stand with you."

Edwin made to remove an arm ring, but Penda stopped him. "No," he said. "Not yet. I am Cearl's man for now, but when the time comes I will take your rings, Edwin, king. I will take them right gladly."

# Chapter 17

As the boat slipped down the River Tame, Edwin and his sons stood looking back at the men gathered on the quay bidding them farewell. Despite the heat of the summer's day, Cearl, king of the Mercians, stood wrapped in a heavy cloak. Penda was beside him. The old king had wept when his grandsons took their leave. He had held their faces in his hands and stared at them, trying to drive their images into his memory. But as he let them go, Cearl shook his head.

"I think I will not forget, but I know that as soon as the boat has taken you from sight, your faces will fade. In time everything fades away and only shadows are left."

Osfrith and Eadfrith embraced their grandfather. Edwin kissed the old man's brow. Cearl took Edwin's hand and pressed it between his own.

"They are good boys," he said. "So like their mother."

"Yes, I know," said Edwin. "You will not forget?"

"I will not forget," said Cearl.

But standing upon the boat as the slow-flowing Tame took it downstream to the confluence with the River Trent and then the journey across country to the Humber, where flowed also the River Ouse, allowing a short pull upstream to York, Edwin's eyes were upon the man who stood next to Cearl.

"Can we trust him?"

Edwin looked around.

Eadfrith, putative king of Mercia, still had his hand raised in farewell, but it was he who had asked the question.

"Cearl?"

"No, not Cearl. Penda."

"For now, yes. He will not raise his hand against the king. But when Cearl dies?" Edwin shrugged. "In one sense, it does not matter.

We have Lindsey, Elmet, Kent, the West Saxons and East Angles with us. We are masters of Man and Anglesey. The painted people of the north fear us still. The men of Strathclyde and the kingdom of Dal Riada will not take arms against us. Who else is there for Penda to ally himself with?"

"Powys? Gwynedd?"

"Cadwallon is defeated, even if he is not dead. No, there is no one to stand with Mercia against us. Penda is no fool. When Cearl dies, the throne will come to you."

"What do I do with Penda then?"

"As king, I leave that to you."

Eadfrith grinned. "And as king I naturally turn to my oldest and wisest counsellor. What would you do if you were me?"

But to Eadfrith's surprise, his father fell silent. The oars creaked in the rowlocks as the men rowed downstream. Soon the Mercians had dwindled into tiny figures almost lost against the high jutting timbers of the great hall upon its platform. Then a bend in the river carried them out of sight. The Northumbrians settled down for the journey, finding space among the coils of rope and bales of produce that filled the flat-bottomed boat. The horses, tethered and fed, stood calmly chewing in the centre of the boat, enjoying the journey.

Edwin squatted down next to his younger son.

"You asked what I would do."

Eadfrith, rousing himself from a doze, nodded.

"Once, not long past, as soon as I had secured the kingdom I would have had Penda killed. But now…" Edwin flicked a stray stone over the side of the boat. It splashed in the river and was gone.

"You'd let him live?"

Edwin sighed. "It is seventeen years since your mother died, Eadfrith. Our lives are short and we are a long time dead. But maybe the priest is right. Maybe there is a new life for men who swear fealty to his new god. If that be so, then I must needs have a care before I spill men's blood, that they might have the chance to gain this life. Besides, I have seen few, very few, warriors to match Penda. Even Guthlaf was not so good at his age. Think what you could do with his help."

"But would Penda be content to remain warmaster?"

"That is up to you. A king may take the throne by force, but he remains there through love. Unless men will follow you, stand shoulder to shoulder in the shieldwall with you and sell their lives for you, you will not endure long as king, and nor should you. Ring giver, praise giver – such do the scops call kings, but I tell you truly: it is friendship and love that forges a kingdom and unites a warband."

Edwin stood up. The river ran smooth and slow through water meadows. Sheep and the occasional cow watched as the boat creaked past, tended by boys who shouted comments and insults and requests to the passing vessel. The men, at least those who weren't sleeping, swapped retorts with the boys or flirted with girls drawing water from the river. This land of the Mercians was a rich land, green and fertile. Thick woods shaded the hills; the valleys, threaded with rivers, were ploughed and cleared, studded with homesteads and farms. It reminded Edwin of Deira, the kingdom of his home, the land of waters. But it was richer and fatter than Bernicia, the land of the mountain passes, Æthelfrith's old power base. The king of this land would have much gold to distribute, many rings to give to restless young men drawn by the prospect of riches and glory.

The sun drew higher in the sky and a dragonfly hovered, unmoving, in front of Edwin, its jewelled eyes fixed upon the king before flicking out over the river and hawking a somnolent fly from the air. The dragonfly settled upon a willow and began, slowly and methodically, to consume the fly.

# Chapter 18

"The king will not accept baptism."

Paulinus was walking up and down outside the queen's quarters. Æthelburh herself sat outside the building in the evening light, cradling her baby in her arms and rocking the little girl to sleep. The baby's wet nurse sat upon a stool nearby, taking some thick, sweet mead to help replenish her milk.

Paulinus stopped his pacing and stood in front of the queen.

"He promised. The king promised he would accept baptism if God gave him victory against the West Saxons. God gave him victory, but when I asked the king when I could baptize him, he told me not yet. He said he had to think about it. Think about it!" Paulinus threw his hands up to the sky. "What is there to think about? I offer him the gift of eternal life, and he has to think about it!"

Æthelburh looked up at the priest, holding a finger to her lips.

"Shh," she said.

"What?" said Paulinus.

"Shh," repeated the queen.

"This is the king's eternal soul, and you want me to be quiet?"

The baby squawked, almost settled, then began a long, reedy cry.

The queen glared at the priest. "I was trying to get her to sleep."

Paulinus blushed. "I am sorry."

Æthelburh, pursing her lips, tried to settle the baby, but the little girl would not be quieted and in the end the queen signed for the wet nurse.

"You take her," she said, handing the swaddled infant to the wet nurse.

Clucking to the child, the wet nurse put the little girl to the breast. Æthelburh smoothed her dress over her knees and adjusted her veils.

"You were saying?"

"I – I am sorry. For waking the baby."

"It is too hot for little Eanflæd." Æthelburh fanned herself. "It is too hot for anyone."

"But what are we going to do about the king?"

"What do we need to do about him?"

"About his baptism, of course."

Using her veils, Æthelburh fanned herself further. "We wait and we pray. The king is not a man to be hurried, but he is a man who keeps his word."

"But everything rests on him. If the king accepts baptism, then his thegns will too, and the people after them. Before long the whole kingdom will have been won for Christ. But as long as he waits, so will everyone else."

"That is why he waits, Paulinus. If the king is baptized, then so is the kingdom. Edwin cannot accept baptism until he is sure that his thegns will follow him. Too many of them still follow the old gods, but many of the younger men are interested in your teaching, father, for they can see its fruit."

Paulinus grimaced. "Bloody fruit. Victory over petty kings, treasure stolen and slaves taken. That is what they see. A battle god stronger than the old battle gods. But if that is all they see, I fear most dreadfully for the faith here in these lands. Yes, God gives victory to the righteous, but he tests them too – and did not the most righteous one of all die upon a cross? If faith be tied solely to victory in battle, I fear the fortunes of war will tear as many men from the church as bring them to her."

Æthelburh shook her head. The gold and silver about her neck rang out the motion, the deep register of the sound revealing the weight and purity of the jewellery she wore.

"Father, have more faith! Honestly, I cannot believe I have to tell you this, but have more faith. Once men have been baptized, and the fire of the Spirit warms their cold souls, they will not abandon what they have been given. No! Not if they lose ten battles will they give it up. I would not."

Paulinus bowed his head to the queen. Looking up, he was reminded by the freshness of her face that she was still so young. But ever since Æthelburh had married Edwin, and even more since she had been delivered of her baby, the young girl he had escorted north from Kent had become truly a queen, wise and courageous, and not above telling him, and others, where they were going wrong.

"It is I who should be exhorting you to faith, my queen; not the other way round."

Æthelburh tried to look grave and magnanimous, but the effort collapsed into giggles. "Oh, Paulinus, to think I should be telling you off for anything! You used to terrify me when I was little, and my mother would say you were coming to teach me about God. I always tried to hide. You know, and God forgive me, I think I thought you actually were God, so much did you scare me."

"Oh, *mater Dei*." Paulinus crossed himself, his discomfiture serving to set Æthelburh laughing again. The priest waited while his blush paled and the queen's mirth died away. The wet nurse looked up from the nursing baby and signed that she was sleeping. Æthelburh smiled her thanks and got up to look at the contented little one.

"Shall I put her down?" asked the wet nurse.

"Yes. Stay with her. I will come in soon."

Cradling the sleeping baby the wet nurse went inside, and from outside queen and priest soon heard the rhythmic creak of the cradle and the softly crooned words of an old lullaby.

"Do you know when the king will return?" asked Paulinus.

"He should be back soon. The hunting must have been good for them to stay out so late, but the evenings are long at this time of year."

Paulinus nodded.

"Why do you ask?"

The priest smiled. "I have something for him." His smile grew broader, transforming his narrow, ascetic face. "And for you."

Æthelburh clapped her hands excitedly and the priest reflected that one reason she was so laden with jewellery and gold must be that her husband took pleasure in giving her gifts and seeing the joy she got from them. Now it was his chance to give the queen a gift, and this a gift like no other.

"What is it?" asked Æthelburh.

Paulinus tapped the side of his long, thin nose. "Not until the king returns."

"That is so unkind!" said Æthelburh.

"Patience is one of the seven holy virtues."

"And as my confessor you know perfectly well it's the one I struggle hardest to attain."

"As your confessor, it is my task to inculcate it."

Æthelburh pouted. Paulinus pointedly turned away, looking out over the palisades of the royal enclosure to the distant line of dark forest where Edwin and his men had ridden in the early morning. There were boar in that forest, and wolves; even rumour of bears. Now, approaching in the slanting evening light, he saw a long line of riders returning, their shadows stretching east over the fields.

"The king returns." Paulinus turned and smiled at the queen. "You will not have to wait long."

Æthelburh pouted again. "I am a queen," she said. "I should not have to wait at all."

"It is good for your soul," said Paulinus.

"But not for my humours. Can you not give me a clue?"

Paulinus shook his head. "No, my queen."

"But how did you get these gifts?" Æthelburh clapped her hands together. "It wasn't that little priest you met in York? The one with the strange accent, whom you shut yourself away with for hours on end?"

Paulinus tapped the other side of his nose. "When the king returns, all will be revealed."

"Oh, that is just not fair. It will be hours before they're back and ready to eat – before that there will be all the boasting about who killed what and which falcon brought down the biggest bird. You simply must give me some sort of clue or I will burst, and you don't want a burst queen on your conscience, do you, father?"

"True… A clue: these gifts come from far away."

"Kent? Was it Mother? Did she send the gifts?"

"Further than that."

"My grandmother, then, from the land of the Franks?"

"Even further."

"Surely not Burgundy?"

"I don't think you will guess."

"I will, I will. The land of the Visigoths? Aquitaine."

Paulinus laughed. "I can see you really will burst, my queen, if I do not tell you."

Æthelburh nodded rapidly, her jewellery adding its own assent. "I will, I really will."

"Very well. These gifts I have for you are from… are from…"

"Yes?"

"The pope."

Æthelburh suddenly went pale, and for a moment the priest feared she might faint, but the queen steadied herself by taking hold of the doorpost.

"Are – are you all right, my queen?"

"Did you say the pope sent these gifts? The pope in Rome?"

"Yes."

"You mean to tell me the pope, the successor of Peter, the man who can unlock the gates of heaven – the pope knows who I am?"

"Of course he does. And he prays for you every day."

"How do you know?"

"He says so in his letter."

Æthelburh suddenly sat down, hard, upon her stool. She was gasping. Paulinus crouched beside her and started fanning her face with the hem of his robe.

"My queen, are you all right? Should I get you something to drink?"

"I – I…" Æthelburh stopped talking and joined in the fanning, using her veils to send air over blush-red skin. When the flush had receded, Æthelburh held out her hand. "Help me up."

After smoothing her skirts, the queen ran her fingers over her cheeks and brow, rubbing away the sweat that had pricked her skin.

"Are – are you better?" Paulinus asked fearfully. He had not expected this reaction to his news.

"Am I better? After you tell me that the pope prays for me every day; that he has written a letter to me and sent me gifts? Of course I am better! I must make myself ready to hear his words and receive his gifts." Æthelburh turned to head inside. "When my husband returns, tell him you have important news for him and that I will join him to receive the news." She beamed at the priest. "He will be delighted."

# Chapter 19

"You have a message for me?"

Paulinus nodded, trying hard not to glance at Æthelburh sitting next to the king, for surely then he would begin to laugh.

"I do, lord."

"Who is it from?"

"The pope. In Rome. The, ah, chief thegn to our Lord, and the head of the church in this world."

Edwin looked around the hall. "Where is the messenger?"

Paulinus held up the parchment. "This is the messenger."

The king looked from the obscure markings on the parchment to the priest. "You have memorized the message?"

"There is no need to. The words of the pope are here, laid out on this parchment. His very words."

Edwin stared at the message. "How is this possible?"

"It's true, the pope probably did not write the message himself – he would have dictated it to one of his scribes, who wrote it on a chalk slate and then transcribed the words onto parchment. But yes, these are the words of the pope himself."

Edwin stared fixedly at the parchment. Paulinus, knowing that the king could not read, wondered why he was looking at it with such concentration.

"You said you are holding in your hands… words?"

"Yes, lord." Paulinus held up the parchment so that the king could see the writing more clearly. "These marks are words such as you or I speak, although of course the language is Latin."

"Ah, is it only that language, Latin, that can be preserved in such a manner?"

"No, I do not think so. Latin is the language of the church – it enables us to speak to each other, from one end of the world to the other, whatever our native tongue, but these marks represent sounds." Paulinus pursed his lips as he looked down at the script, before nodding and turning back to the king. "I think, lord, that it would be possible to write the sounds of your tongue in this script too. It would take work, but it should be possible."

"By such means I could be present where I am not," said Edwin. "My laws could be given to every thegn and council in the kingdom, the very laws themselves. We would not have to rely on the uncertain recall of some messenger."

"Yes. Yes, you could," said Paulinus, impressed with the speed at which Edwin had grasped the implications and potential of such an invention.

"Who has knowledge of this?"

"Most priests can read, at least enough to follow the words of the Mass, but reading is not enough. You need someone who can write. For that you need monks."

"What are monks?"

"I am a monk. As the role of a warrior is to follow his lord and fight, so that of a monk is to serve God and pray. But to pray the Holy Office, monks need books, so many monks are trained to write, and read."

"Can you write and read?"

"I read well. My writing is… adequate. I have no great hand."

Edwin nodded. "Let me hear what your pope has to say to me. But I think I will have need of monks in future."

Paulinus took a step back and held the parchment up so that he could read it better in the light.

"The message is written in Latin, but I will translate." He looked over the top of the parchment. The king was leaning forward in the judgement seat, concentrating fiercely.

"From Boniface, of the City and Church of Rome, the servant of the servants of God, to the illustrious Edwin, king of the English.

"No words of man can encompass the power of the high God, who abides in his own power, eternal, invisible, inscrutable. Yet through his humanity, God has seen fit to open the hearts of men to his presence and to reveal to us the secrets of his nature. As bishop and pastor, we now seek to make known to you the key to this knowledge, how through faith in Christ you may drink the cup of salvation.

"Our merciful God, who through his word creates and sustains the world, proclaimed the laws by which it exists; and through this word and in the unity of the Holy Spirit, he made man in his own image out of the dust of the earth. To man God granted the greatest privilege of all earthly creatures: that he might know eternal life through obedience to God's laws. This very God – Father, Son and Holy Spirit, the eternal, undivided Trinity – is worshipped by men from the rising of the sun to its setting. All royal power and authority on earth is subject to God, for it is from God that kingship comes. Such is God's mercy and concern for the well-being of his creatures that he has sent his Holy Spirit to warm the frozen hearts of the most distant nations.

"We trust that Your Majesty has heard how your neighbour and king, Eadbald of Kent, has through the mercy of our Redeemer been brought to knowledge of the light. We trust that God, through his mercy, will give this gift to you as well, more particularly since we learn that your gracious queen and true partner has already been blessed with the gift of eternal life through baptism. We fondly hope Your Majesty will renounce the worship of idols and the deceit of omens, and profess your faith in God the Father Almighty, his Son Jesus Christ and the Holy Spirit. This faith will free you from thraldom to the devil and, in due course, give to you the gift of eternal life.

"We send to you the blessings of Peter, Prince of the Apostles. We send also a tunic, ornamented with gold, and a cloak from Ancyra, asking Your Majesty to accept our gifts with the same goodwill with which they are sent."

Paulinus gestured James forward, and the deacon laid before the king the tunic and cloak. They were rich gifts, the cloak dyed the deepest imperial purple, but the king viewed them distractedly. His attention was still upon the message. The queen, standing beside

Edwin, saw well how he stared at the parchment Paulinus was holding and she chose to hold her peace and to allow the pope's message time to work its way into her husband's soul.

"Those are the very words of your pope, your king?"

"As if he were standing here himself."

"Delivered from the other side of the world." Edwin shook his head. "It is a world of wonders we live in. And this message he sends – if it is true, it is most passing strange: you say the God of the heavens, the maker of all, sent his Son among us? How did he come? Why did I never before hear of him, for surely he must have been the greatest of all kings? Was he one of the emperors of old? Did he raise the stone towns and towers, and lay down the straight roads that are about this land and, I hear from travellers, through the rest of this middle-earth?"

Paulinus shocked himself by blushing.

"Er, no, lord. The emperors of old, um, they killed him."

"Death in battle is glorious. The gods rain favours upon warriors who die in battle."

Paulinus exchanged glances with the queen. This was going to be difficult.

"Our Lord did not die in battle. He died upon a tree. He was executed. By the Romans."

"But how was he taken prisoner? What happened to his thegns? Were they all killed?"

"His men all abandoned him. They ran away and left him to be captured."

"No!" Edwin gasped. "The lord of all creation, and you say his men betrayed him?"

"Well, one, Judas, actually betrayed him. All the others ran away."

Edwin shook his head. "I would not have betrayed him. I would have stayed at his side."

Paulinus stared at the intense figure of the king, leaning forward upon the judgement seat, and he nodded. "I believe you would have, lord. But – ah, wyrd or, as we might say, providence – decreed otherwise. It was the fate of our Lord Jesus Christ to fall into the hands of the wicked and the evil, and to die at their hands, innocent and blameless, as a sacrifice made once and for all for the wrongs that we do. But here is the difference, and the proof of what I say. Lord, when you make sacrifice to your gods, what happens?"

"Coifi takes the animal – or it could be a slave or prisoner, although not often – and kills it, cutting its throat usually. Then he throws some of the blood before the god in the sacred grove, and burns the fat so the smoke goes up to the gods. Coifi then reads the runes, or travels in spirit, or uses the bones to see whether the gods are satisfied with the sacrifice. If the gods are satisfied, well and good. If they are not, we sacrifice some more."

As Edwin spoke, Paulinus nodded. "Yes, yes. But here is the difference, lord. When Jesus Christ offered himself as sacrifice for us, God showed that he had accepted the sacrifice not by the rattle of bones or the stink of spilled entrails, but by raising Jesus from the dead. For forty days he walked among us, talked to us, ate and drank with us, a man again, of flesh and blood, but transformed in a most marvellous manner. There is the guarantee of what I preach; there is the pledge of my words. Jesus Christ proved it himself, in his body, through God receiving his death and returning him to glorious life. And through faith in him we too can share this life."

Edwin nodded slowly, thoughtfully. "These are great matters of which you speak, Paulinus. But when I receive a messenger with an important message from a king, I require some proof of what he says, that he carries the true words of his lord. What trust can I put in your words?"

"I am an apostle of the apostles. Every word you hear from me I received from others, who in turn passed on the testimony of those who received Jesus Christ after his resurrection. Our Lord tasked these men with spreading the good news, the hope unbidden of life eternal in God, to the furthest ends of the earth and to every people, and they did so, laying down their lives and spilling their blood that everyone might hear and know that they too are invited to the feast; that they too have a seat at the high table beside our Lord. And the apostles wrote down the message in our holy book, and the words of the message are there, as Jesus himself spoke them, as the words of the pope in Rome were delivered to you just now."

"What holy book is this of which you speak?"

"The holy book is the Bible, the book of the words of God."

"I would see this book."

"Lord, the Bible has many, many pages and it is the labour of many months and many men to copy a new one. I do not have a Bible with me, although I have asked Bishop Justus that he might send the book to me and I hope, God willing, to receive it should you accept baptism and the gift of life. However, I do have a Gospel book."

"What is that?"

"It contains the four books telling the good news of Jesus Christ, but does not have the books telling the history of the people of Israel or of the early history of the church. James," Paulinus turned to his deacon, "run and fetch it."

"While we wait for him to bring the book," said Æthelburh, "do you want to see what the pope sent me?"

Edwin looked to his wife. "He sent you gifts too?"

Æthelburh beamed. "Yes, he did. And here they are."

While the queen showed the silver mirror and the beautifully worked gold and silver comb that the pope had sent her to the king, Paulinus stood fretting for James's return. He glanced around the great hall. As usual it contained knots of men sitting at table over cups of beer, scurrying slaves and, in one corner, Acca practising with his lyre while lining up a surprising number of empty beer cups upon the table.

But then Paulinus saw Coifi, hunched in his raven-feather cloak, a darker shadow within a pool of shadow. The priest was staring up at the high table, his face pale white against the dusty black of his mantle. His hands were moving in jerky rhythm, snaking the bird-bone rattle through the air, and his lips were moving. Paulinus knew well that sight: Coifi was praying to his gods. It was all Paulinus could do not to sign the cross in protection against whatever demons Coifi was calling up, but the Italian remembered well Edwin's fury when he had openly opposed Coifi before; he would not make that mistake again. Instead, Paulinus slowly and deliberately turned his back on the priest.

Coifi howled. He howled with the long, drawn-out ululations of women lamenting the dead and wolves welcoming the full moon. He howled with the desolation of halls burned down and fields laid waste. He howled, and the hall fell into silence. The few groups of gossiping men turned from conversation to stare at him. Slaves stopped in their tasks. Acca laid aside his lyre, picked up his cup and stood for a better view.

Paulinus stiffened but he did not turn round. He kept his back to the priest, but from the reactions of Edwin and Æthelburh he could tell that Coifi was approaching the high table. A surreptitious adjustment of the queen's mirror allowed him to see what Coifi was doing without giving him the satisfaction of seeing Paulinus turn to stare at him.

The priest was approaching the high table in little jagged, jerking runs, the movements mimicking those of a bird foraging for food: quick scuttles interspersed with moments of watchful stillness. Whenever he stopped, poised and alert, the priest's head snapped from side to side as if seeing sights not apparent to everyone else in the hall and he shook his bone rattle towards those unseen creatures as if warding them off.

For Paulinus, it was an appalling but fascinating spectacle, and in the end he could not help but turn to watch. However, he noticed that after the initial reaction, the slaves had returned to their work, and conversation resumed in the hall. It seemed that this sort of behaviour from Coifi was not unknown.

As the priest slowly approached the high table in juddering fits and starts, Edwin rose to his feet and Æthelburh stood beside him. Guthlaf, on the other hand, who had been sitting quietly at one end of the table, shook his head and reached for a cup of beer.

Coifi darted closer, rattle shaking, then as swiftly moved away, his eyes rolling up white into his skull and spittle leaking from the corners of his mumbling, trembling lips.

Æthelburh looked to her husband. "What's wrong with him?"

"The gods are speaking to him," said Edwin. His voice was neutral and his eyes veiled as he answered.

Guthlaf snorted and took another swallow from his cup, holding the emptied vessel out for a slave to refill.

Coifi rattled closer, his raven-feather cloak creaking as he approached, the feathers rustling like dead leaves. But just as he appeared to be coming to a halt in front of the king, he darted away again, apparently called by a whorl of smoke rising from the hearth fire. The priest passed his hands through the smoke thread, bathed his face in it so that his eyes wept, then turned the red-rimmed, weeping eyes to the king and queen. Æthelburh gasped. Red tears, tears of blood, were oozing down Coifi's cheeks, leaving their salt-thick tracks upon his face.

"Why?"

Æthelburh glanced at the king. Edwin was looking at Coifi calmly enough, but Æthelburh saw the tension in his jaw and the throb at his temple.

The king made no answer to the question, and Coifi swept closer, sending the feathers of his cloak rattling over the table.

"Why?"

Again the king made no reply. From the end of the table, Guthlaf belched, suddenly, explosively, and Æthelburh saw Coifi's red eyes flick in annoyance at the old warrior. The ghost of a smile tugged at the corner of Edwin's eye. Relieved, Æthelburh turned back to the priest.

Coifi shook his bone rattle at the king. Edwin did not flinch. In fact – Æthelburh glanced to make sure – the smile seemed to be tugging harder at his face.

"Why?" Coifi repeated. But this third time it lacked the sibilant menace of its previous iterations, sounding more like a querulous child than a wight whispering from a barrow.

Finally, Edwin reacted. "Are you threatening me, Coifi?" he asked.

The priest shrank back, blanching, as if it were he who now heard the wights whisper his name from the tomb.

"No! No, lord, never. Never." Coifi crept closer again, scuttling low, glancing around as if he were not already the centre of all attention in the hall. He sidled closer to Edwin, whispering, so that the king had to bend close to hear his words.

On one side, Æthelburh leaned in to hear the conversation, as did Paulinus on the king's other side. Guthlaf, however, made a show of picking his teeth with a bone needle.

"...if some others seek to lead you astray," Æthelburh heard, when she tuned her ears in to Coifi's voice, "to take you from the ways of your fathers and your fathers' fathers, let no one say that I did not speak, lord, and bring word to you: wyrd has made you great, lord, greater than any other king in the land, but the gods require honour and sacrifice, lest they take their favour from you. Do not go chasing after new gods, unknown to your fathers. Where was this god when Uxfrea took the whale road across the grey sea? Where was this god when Ælla took Deira from the Britons?" Coifi crept even closer to Edwin, like a dog sidling up to its master, and, laying his hand on Edwin's arm, said, "The old gods, the gods of your fathers, have been faithful to you, Edwin Ællason. Keep faith with them, and they will reward you mightily. Break that faith, and they will bring you and all your people down."

Æthelburh looked anxiously at her husband. Coifi was grasping his forearm and pawing at his belt with his other hand, but the king looked down at him as if paralysed. The queen made to speak, but Guthlaf caught her eyes and shook his head. She fell back. Waited. The whole hall had lapsed into silence; conversations stilled and work stopped as eyes, openly or surreptitiously, turned to the king and his priest, caught in a tableau of indecision.

Only one man moved.

Paulinus left his place at table. A bead of sweat pricked through the skin of his forehead and tracked down between his eyebrows and along the side of his nose. Guthlaf tried to attract his attention and stop him, but the Italian's dark eyes did not move from the king. It was as if he was in a trance, or walked asleep but with eyes wide. Paulinus stopped in front of the king.

"King Edwin."

The king, unaware of Paulinus's approach, jerked. Coifi, squatting beside the king, hissed and tried to paw his attention back, but Edwin brushed his hand away.

"Do you remember this sign?"

Paulinus stepped forward and laid his right hand upon Edwin's head.

Around the great hall, a gasp arose, and oaths, and whispers and murmurs, for it was a thing unheard that a man should lay his hand upon the head of the king.

But Edwin made no move in anger. He stared into the priest's dark eyes and his own face grew pale, as pale as winter's breath.

"I…I remember this sign," Edwin said, but his voice was a whisper as from the grave, and it seemed the strength of his limbs was upon the point of failing him, for he lurched as if to fall. But Paulinus stepped forward and took the king in his arms and lowered him gently to his seat.

Coifi hissed and lifted his rattle, but Paulinus turned upon him as a man turns upon a snake.

"Be gone! In Jesus' name, I command you: go!"

Coifi shrank back, but he did not go. He turned to Edwin.

"Lord?"

The king turned his pale face to him, and Coifi shrank from it, for it was the face of one who has seen his death.

"Go," whispered Edwin.

The priest, snuffling like a beaten child, scuttled from the hall.

The queen was chafing Edwin's cold hands, while an alarmed Guthlaf brought wine for the king to drink.

"What did you do to him?" Æthelburh asked Paulinus.

The priest himself seemed to shiver, and his eyes, which were before as distant as the moon, focused again on the queen. "I reminded the king of a promise he made, many years ago," said Paulinus.

Edwin turned to the priest. "So, it was your god that delivered me from my enemies and lifted me up above my fathers and my fathers' fathers."

Paulinus nodded. "God brought you forth from the hands of your enemies, when all hands were turned against you, and he has made you a king greater than any in this land. You promised, many years ago, when you stood in darkness by the sea in the kingdom of the East Angles, to follow the counsel of the man who promised you truthfully that this was what God meant for you."

"I so promised."

"Then accept the faith I bring you. Obey God's commands, be baptized, and the God who saved you from your enemies on earth will save you from your enemies after death and give you a place in his eternal kingdom."

Edwin bowed his head. Æthelburh, as still as a drawn bowstring, watched her husband.

Edwin raised his head.

"I will accept your faith," he said. The queen let out a long drawn-out breath. She lifted Edwin's hand to her lips and kissed it. But the king's gaze did not leave the priest.

"It is my will as well as my duty to accept your faith. But I am a king. I decide not only for myself, but for my people. To that end I will call together a council of all my people, and you shall put the truth of your – of our – new faith to them all, that they may be persuaded of its truth. Then my people and I shall enter into this new life together, and there will be no schism between king and people. Do you, Paulinus, understand and agree to this?"

"Yes," said the priest. "Yes, I agree."

"Very well." Edwin stood up, and his voice reached to every corner of the great hall. "Let the message go out to all men of Northumbria that they are to assemble for a great council, at York, six months hence at the feast of Eostre, there to consider the taking of the new religion that has come to us of late, through the queen and Paulinus her priest."

As Edwin finished his announcement, James finally returned, carrying the Gospel book.

"Did I miss something?" he said.

# Chapter 20

Later, when the night drew down and the hall had settled into a contented hum of conversation, James turned to Paulinus.

"With all that happened, I forgot to tell you something I saw earlier. When I had taken the Gospel book from its stand, and censed it, I came out and saw the priest, Coifi. He was in front of the old oak tree where he makes sacrifices, but there was something strange about what he was doing, so I must confess, father, I crept a little closer to try to see and hear better. Was that a sin?"

"No, no, of course not," said Paulinus. He leaned closer to James, lowering his voice. Coifi had not returned to the hall after Edwin had sent him forth. "What did you see?"

"The priest was squatting on the ground, and as I got closer I could see he was picking up handfuls of dust and throwing them over his hair and clothing, like a bird having a bath. I could hear he was talking, muttering, but I was too far away to hear clearly, so I went even closer, staying behind the stockade so he could not see me."

"Yes? Go on."

"I could only make out some of the words. At the beginning, I think he was chanting his genealogy, the names of his fathers and his fathers' fathers, but then he started snuffling and crying, like a little boy when his father has beaten him. Then he asked the tree – I suppose it must be his idol – why the gods no longer listened to him and why they did not help him. He asked if there was any sacrifice he could make to win back the gods' favour, and then he went silent, as if he was listening. I was just about to give up and come back when he jumped up and started striking the tree with his hands and kicking it with his feet, screaming at it, 'Why don't you answer me?' I thought he was going mad. I hope I did no wrong?"

"No, indeed," said Paulinus. "No wrong at all."

Further along the high table, Guthlaf saw the two Italians deep in conversation. He did not understand their language – no one did among the Northumbrians – and he was always suspicious of shielded talk; it could too easily turn to treachery. But the expressions on the men's faces were clear and without guile, and the way they held themselves suggested no perfidy. Putting away suspicion – for the moment – Guthlaf turned to Edwin.

Lowering his voice, so that their conversation might remain between the two of them, he said, "Are you sure about this new religion?"

Edwin glanced around to make sure no slaves were near.

"Forthred, if he were alive, would remember. When I was in exile, at Rædwald's court, Æthelfrith sent a messenger declaring that he would offer either riches or war for my death. Rædwald was minded to accept the riches – maybe I would have done the same, for the Twister had by this time twisted all the north to him, and many of the middle kingdoms. Forthred brought me word of my doom, and advice to take the whale road and pass over the grey sea to the courts of our kinsmen beyond."

Edwin stared into the hearth fire, his gaze focused upon the past. Then, looking at Guthlaf, he said, "I was tired. Weary past understanding. I had spent years running from Æthelfrith. After Forthred had told me that Rædwald planned to give me up to him I went to the shore. It was night, a clear night but dark, with only the star glimmer and wave glow to light the darkness. And when I was standing on the beach, a man came to me. At first I thought he was one of Æthelfrith's assassins, but wyrd – or maybe something else – stayed my hand when I might have struck him down. The man spoke to me, and promised that I would overcome my enemies and rise up, a king greater than any of my forefathers." Edwin looked back into the fire, and his voice was so low that Guthlaf, bending close, could barely hear it.

"Such I have become. And this… this man said he would give me a sign to show how these things he prophesied had come about, and to that end he put his right hand upon my head." Edwin turned and faced Guthlaf. "As the priest did today. That was the sign, the signal by whose power I was delivered from my enemies and raised high, and therefore that power belongs to the new god, not the old ones, and I would be a faithless man and king of no worth if I did not stand by my pledge, given in despair, those many years ago by the grey sea."

Guthlaf whistled softly through his teeth. "Is that what happened? Yes, I see now." He clicked his tongue against his teeth. "But I still think it will be difficult to persuade all the thegns to leave the ways of their fathers and follow this new religion."

Edwin looked at his warmaster. "And you, Guthlaf? What of you? Will you follow the new god?"

"Ah, there's a question." Guthlaf reached for his cup, but rather than draining it he turned it between his hands before turning back to Edwin.

"Maybe," he said. "Maybe."

Edwin nodded. "Thank you, old friend."

But Guthlaf shook his head. "If I abandon the ways of my fathers, it will not be for you; it will be because this new religion brings us new knowledge. Do you understand?"

"Yes, I understand." Edwin grasped Guthlaf's wrist. "I can ask no more, but for myself I no longer doubt that the new religion brings great knowledge. Think on the message sent to me by the pope. Could Coifi send such a message?"

Guthlaf's answer was a snort of laughter.

"But nevertheless, Coifi is still priest to my people and if I am to persuade them to follow the new god, it would be better if Coifi were persuaded first. Should he hold silence, or even speak for the new god, it would make the great council's decision all the easier." Edwin pitched his voice so only Guthlaf could hear. "Go to Coifi. Find his price."

Guthlaf nodded. "Very well."

# Chapter 21

"Why have you come seeking me, Guthlaf, son of Sigeberht?"

Coifi had not moved throughout Guthlaf's silent approach. The priest had remained, still, beneath the great tree, squatting in its shadow, a darker shadow of raven feather and sable fur, with his face turned towards the deeply folded trunk. He might have heard Guthlaf's approach, but he could not have seen it.

"Impressive," said Guthlaf, stepping out of the shadows and into the dappled light under the tree. "Even after many years, you still sometimes take me by surprise, Coifi. Did the gods tell you who approached?"

"The gods?" Coifi turned to stare at Guthlaf, his skin pale against his cloak. "What do you know of the gods, son of Sigeberht?"

"I am a warrior, Coifi. I know death and killing, and the edge upon which a man stands between bravery and terror. You are the priest; it is your job to know the gods." Guthlaf stopped outside the sanctuary that marked the sacred space around the oak. "What have they been telling you, Coifi? Did they warn you of the assassin Cwichelm sent? Have they told you of this new god from across the grey sea?"

Coifi shivered, his eyes darting about the grove, and he gave no answer.

"Did they warn you of this?" asked Guthlaf, and slowly, deliberately, he passed the line of standing, living willow poles that marked the boundary of the sacred enclosure.

Coifi gasped and made frantic shooing gestures, but Guthlaf stood his ground, although up and down his back he felt tingles of running fear, like bats' wings in the night. To the priest, though, he gave no sign of his fear.

"Go, go," whispered Coifi. "They must not see you here."

"What will happen if they do?"

"It will be terrible, terrible. They will bring the kingdom down; they will kill you."

Guthlaf looked up at the spreading arms of the oak tree and raised his own arms in answer to it.

"Here I am," he said. "Unhallowed, I stand on sacred ground. Strike me down. Strike me, if you have the power."

From the tree, as if in answer, a crow cawed, its harsh voice breaking the silence, and Guthlaf felt his bowels loosen in fear. Coifi looked around wildly, searching for the source of the sound, but the tree was still and there was no movement among its branches. The crow, if crow it had been, fell silent. Nothing moved. In the distance, smoke rose from the stockade around the king's hall, but the field strips beyond the fence were bare of men and animals. It was twilight, a liminal time, and Guthlaf could feel a fear that he had not known since childhood stalking him: the terror of shadow things, of creatures of swamp and barrow and deep dark forest. When he had grown to manhood and earned the right to wield and carry a sword, those fears had left him, for sharp, bright iron seemed to his young self proof against twilight fears. But now those fears gripped him anew, as shadows lengthened and leaves rustled and something moved without speaking above him. Coifi jerked this way and that, looking desperately around for the source of the movements, but he could see nothing, and Guthlaf could not move.

For how long they remained like that, perhaps neither could say. But night drew down, and the shadows spread and combined, and fear pooled and then slowly ebbed away. The gods had seen what Guthlaf had done – there could be no doubt of that – but they had done nothing. The old warrior lowered his aching arms. Nothing had happened. He felt suddenly foolish for his fears.

"There, what of your gods, Coifi?"

The priest was still looking around, staring into the dark but seeing nothing. He shook his head.

"I – I do not know. Once, I could see the weavings of wyrd everywhere, in the rise of smoke and the fall of leaf and amid the rattle of dice. But now I see nothing: only smoke and dead leaves and dry bones. The gods have gone silent. They ignore me, although I have been their faithful servant these many years. I do not understand why."

"The gods are old. When men grow old, they sit by the fire and mumble tales of their glory and seek no bother until it be time for eating. Maybe that is why we should follow a new god, a young god."

"Gods are not men; they do not age and die!" Coifi stroked his hand over the rough bark of the tree, then slapped it in disgust. "But they do, it seems, grow deaf!" The priest stood up, shaking out his raven-feather cloak. "It is no wonder the king himself is set to abandon the ways of our fathers."

"The king has called a great council of our people in a six month, at York. There the council will hear of this new god from across the grey sea and take thought as to whether we should leave the ways of our fathers and strike out upon a new path, as our fathers themselves did when they left the land of their birth and took the whale road to a new land."

Coifi glanced around. They still stood within the boundaries of the sacred enclosure, the living brands of sprouting saplings marking the edge of the grove. With a glance to Guthlaf, indicating that he should follow, the priest left the enclosure. The warrior followed, and as he stepped out of the grove he felt a weight, the weight of unseen eyes, fall from him. Guthlaf took a breath, only now realizing how shallow his breathing had been while he stood within the sacred grove, then followed the priest as he led him down the track towards the royal enclosure.

Once they were halfway there, amid empty fields and far from any grove of listening trees, Coifi slowed so that Guthlaf could walk alongside him. They meandered towards the great hall, to any idle watcher two old friends in earnest conversation.

# Chapter 22

The oars, working in unison, sculled the turbid water. Winter had been long and hard, and snow-melt still swelled the river. The first silver green flush of spring shivered through the trailing fingers of willow, but the men, who sat in lines across the boat, paid the promise of future warmth no heed. The work of rowing upstream against a fast-flowing current provided warmth and enough. Further boats followed, strung out along the river according to the water fitness of the vessel and the strength of the rowers. Standing behind the prow, Edwin looked ahead. He knew this river, its moods and its peace, better than anywhere else. Though he had travelled far, by boat and horse and foot, yet he still looked forward to each return to this melancholy, magical place.

As he knew it would, the river swept around a bend, the bank-lining willows gave way to rush and sedge, and the old broken-down city walls of York came into view, riding high over the low mist that swirled muddily over the fields outside the walls.

> *"Well-wrought this wall, wyrd broke it.*
> *The burgh broke, the battlements fell:*
> *The work of giants withers and decays."*

Edwin chanted the words under his breath as the ruined city came closer. Clustered around its broken walls were many small wooden houses. Smoke rose from the homes, ascending in straight fingers from those dwellings that had chimneys, or seething from the thatch of the ones without. Few people cared to live within the bounds of the old city, for its ghosts walked yet among the stone buildings and tumbled walls. But the land around the city was too rich and fertile to be left to return to wilderness, so over the years many families had built shacks and houses, clustering in the areas of slightly higher ground where, even when the river was in spate, the waters did not reach.

But Edwin knew the city well. His father had come often to York when Edwin was a boy, rowing upstream on the Ouse after sailing across the wide though treacherous currents of the Humber. Indeed, Edwin remembered the wide-eyed surprise of his younger self when his father had told him to lean over the side of their boat and taste the water. He could not believe an expanse of water so broad could be sweet.

Edwin's father, Ælla, had built a hall in York, by the river, ordering his men and the local populace to clear the ground of the old buildings that inhabited the site he had chosen. Edwin still remembered the week's long struggle to demolish and clear the ruins that Ælla wanted moved. None of the local people and few of the men had been willing to stay within the boundaries of the old city after nightfall, but Edwin loved to roam among the ruins. No one knew for certain how many generations of men had passed since the last emperor took the grey sea road and went south into the sun, but no man living could tell of those times, nor could any be found whose grandparents remembered when the walls were whole and high, and clear-eyed soldiers kept watch from them. Sometimes, Edwin would climb up decaying staircases or scramble over stone and timber to stand again upon the walls. Strange marks cut into the stone were to be found on many of the little towers. He would often run his fingers over the marks, wondering what they meant. If there was time, he could take Paulinus up onto the walls and ask him what the stone cuttings said, for he realized now that the marks were writing.

His father's great hall, built in wood rather than stone, stood out bright and alive, painted vividly gold and green against the grey backdrop of stone. Ælla had loved this hall more than all his others, and his son loved it too. Now, rounding the final bend of the River Ouse, Edwin saw the steeply slanting roof and upthrust timber finials, gold gleaming, and the deeply carved and painted pillars that held the roof up. The hall stood upon a raised platform of stone and earth, ensuring that even in flood the river did not wash into the building. A flotilla of boats bumped gently against the jetty, most of them gaily painted but with their sails furled. Some tents, as richly painted as sails, were set up on the level ground that surrounded the hall, although there were many more outside the city walls. Although his thegns and counsellors would come into the old ruined city to talk and listen and feast, many of them preferred to pass beyond its confines to sleep.

As they approached the jetty, the men at the front of the boat shipped their oars and made ready to make the boat fast, while the rowers to the rear kept the vessel slowly moving forward against the current. On the jetty, longshoremen stood ready with ropes to secure the king's boat. Edwin turned around to see Æthelburh speaking with Paulinus, pointing out the flags flying from the tents around the great hall and explaining who flew these banners. The queen was carrying their daughter. The baby, for she was not yet one, slept, but her rest was fitful, and the pull upstream had been accompanied by thin wailing that could only be soothed by putting baby to breast. Osfrith and Eadfrith followed in the other boats – the brothers had drawn lots for who should accompany the horses and who should bring the stripped-down wagons and carts. Eadfrith had won, leaving Osfrith to the muck and manure of the animal boat. The horses had been as skittish as usual, despite being blinkered and hooded, and more than one of the men on board bore the bruises of kicks, while Osfrith himself had disappeared over the side when a horse had lashed out against particularly irksome flies. It had taken two men to haul a spluttering, choking, half-drowned prince back into the boat, much to Eadfrith's amusement. Through the rest of the voyage upriver, he had kept reminding his brother of his early dip, until Osfrith, driven to distraction, caused his boat to fall so far behind that he could no longer see the rest of the party.

Now they awaited his arrival at the jetty. Edwin made his way to the hall, however, with Æthelburh, Paulinus and Guthlaf. News of the great council had spread wide, and many more people than would be attending had gathered around York, seeking news, alms, favour or simply the thrill of tales told from afar. The sick and crippled clustered around the gates to the royal enclosure, waving stumps and sores at the royal party as it passed.

Æthelburh looked in wonder and pity at them as they approached. "It is as if all the poor and crippled the length and breadth of the land have gathered at our door," she said to Guthlaf. "What brings them here?"

"You do," said the warmaster. "All the realm has been preparing for this council this past six month. The winter was hard, many have gone hungry and some have starved. All know, however, that there will be food and feasting here for the king and his thegns and counsellors; that all the wealth of the land was to be gathered here at the feast of Eostre. So, as dogs smelling meat gather to beg for scraps from the table, they come limping here to ask the scrapings from our feastings."

Æthelburh, looking past the men who pushed a path through the crowd of outstretched hands, caught the eye of a woman who also held a baby to her breast. But this baby lay limp in its mother's arms, and the woman's eyes were dull with exhausted hope.

"We must give them food."

Guthlaf nodded. "They can now the king has arrived. They could not do so before he had arrived, for it is his to give. I wonder how many died because we were delayed…"

As word of the king's arrival spread, the tents outside the city emptied, and thegns and counsellors and priests and scops made their way to the king's hall, there to give him homage and receive, in return, gifts from Edwin's own hands. This, the first stage of a great council, went on for two days, and it was as well that their boats had been heavily laden with treasure, for by the end of that time almost all the gifts had been distributed and, in a quiet moment, Edwin had dispatched Guthlaf to the merchants moored at the quay to acquire more rings and brooches and belts and buckles – indeed, anything so long as it glittered and its metal took a mark when bitten.

But such were the treasures they had taken in the last year that no one left Edwin's side unsatisfied, and most came away praising his open-handedness, for generosity was, with bravery and luck in battle, the truest mark of a king.

The preliminaries taken care of, Edwin gave word that the morrow would see the start of the great council. Then Edwin walked with his sons, Paulinus and Guthlaf to see the building he had ordered constructed.

It stood a little apart from the great hall, sheltered from its direct line of sight by the ruins of the greatest of the buildings of old. However, the way between the hall and the new building was still paved with stones that for the most part lay level. As they approached, they could see how far the timber building had already risen in two short days, for the wooden posts that would anchor it and provide support for the roof had been dug into the ground, and a start made upon the walls, so that they reached as high as a man's chest. James, with an excited foreman beside him to relay the orders, was supervising the work, but when he saw the royal party approaching he gathered up his robes and ran to them.

"W-what do you think?" James asked.

Paulinus pursed his lips. "When will it be ready?"

"We are going as fast as we can."

"When?"

James licked his lips. "Um, two weeks?"

Paulinus shook his head. "You may have two days."

"Two days." James briefly closed his eyes. He was pale and his lips moved silently.

"What is he doing?" Osfrith whispered to his brother. "He looks like Coifi when he is searching for wyrd."

"I think he is praying," said Eadfrith. "Yes, look," and he pointed as the deacon marked out a cross over his body, drawing from forehead to belly to each shoulder. "They do that when they pray."

"He'll need his god's help to get that finished in two days," whispered Osfrith. "Do you know what they're making?"

"It is a building for the new religion. Our fathers spoke to the gods outside, under trees and in groves; if the council decides, we will listen to our new god inside, under a roof."

Osfrith nodded. "It will be drier."

"Warmer too," agreed Eadfrith.

They both turned to look at the shell of the building in front of them. "But not for a while, I think," added Eadfrith, pulling his cloak more tightly around his shoulders. The wind, blowing in from the north-east, still carried winter's lash. Leaving Paulinus behind to further encourage James and his workforce, the rest of the party headed back to the great hall, looking forward to its warmth.

As they went, Edwin pointed out parts of the city where he had played as a boy. Now, at twilight, the ruins appeared to close in around them, the empty doors gaping darkly as if opening into a night that had no day. But Edwin knew the city of old, and it held no fears for him. He had often crept through it at night, when his only companions were cats and other night creatures. Now, even fewer of the buildings retained their roofs, but the geography of York remained printed on his soul.

"My father made the first building here since the time of the emperors," Edwin said, pointing to the great hall as they rounded the corner to see its watchfires blazing. "Now we are building the second. We are raising it in wood, that it might soon be ready, but if the council agrees that we adopt these new ways – and I trust that it will – then we shall see something that has not been seen on this island for generations." Edwin looked to his sons, to make sure they were listening. "We shall raise a building to our new God and we shall raise it in stone, as the emperors did of old, and it will last for a thousand years or more, as their buildings do, even though the men who raised them are dead these many generations past." The king stopped. "Now do you understand the importance of this great council?"

Osfrith nodded his understanding. Eadfrith whistled through his teeth, his eyes widening as he realized what his father planned.

"You will be like one of the emperors of old," he said.

But Edwin shook his head. "They ruled all the world, and this city was but a tiny part of their realm. I am no emperor, but Paulinus tells me that the emperors were brought low for their slaying of God himself. Now, if we ally ourselves with God, the God who brought low the men who ruled the world, who knows what we might be able to accomplish?"

Guthlaf grinned. "Well, we'd better make sure the council goes to plan then."

He winked at the two princes. "Maybe speak to a few more men tonight – let them know which way the waves are breaking."

"There are some I have spoken to who will never agree," said Osfrith. "They say that if we should part from the ways of our fathers, then their curses will follow us to the grave."

"Well, we shall see what they say tomorrow," said Edwin. "But remember: your persuasion must be gentle; I do not want any man to stand up in council to say that he has been asked at sword point to abandon the ways of his fathers. This decision must be made by all, and freely. Do you understand?" And the king looked from Guthlaf to Osfrith to Eadfrith. "Good. Now, I will sleep while you speak, for I fear that my voice shall be hard called upon tomorrow."

# *Chapter 23*

*"Hwæt!"*

Acca's voice, trained to cut through drinking songs and boastings and dogs fighting, cut easily through the low murmur of conversation. The great hall was full, each bench jammed with men sitting elbow to elbow, but there was as yet no food upon the tables and only small beer to drink. The hour was nearing noon, and the great council was about to begin. It would deliberate better, Edwin had decided, on empty stomachs and clear heads.

"Be silent, for the king speaks!"

Edwin rose. The hall quietened further, until the only sounds came from the furtive movements of slaves attempting to go about their tasks without drawing any attention to themselves, and the grumbles and rumbles of the dogs, questioning why so many men were gathered with so little food.

From his place at the high table, Edwin looked around the hall, seeking to make eye contact with as many of his thegns and counsellors as he could. Most returned his gaze frankly, although in many he saw questions and doubts, and in others the blankness of outright hostility. Few indeed appeared ready to accept what he was proposing, although some might be persuaded. But would it be enough to carry the council with him?

"Despite what Acca just said, I have not summoned you to York to hear me speak. No, I have asked you to come together in council so that I may hear you, and learn your hearts and minds on a great subject: the new teaching that has come to us from over the grey sea, and whether we should leave the ways of our fathers and accept this new teaching, as the men of Kent have done, and the Franks and the Goths and many other peoples. So now I propose to hear your words and learn your hearts on this matter, that I may better decide for my people which path we should follow. Fear not, but speak boldly and freely." Edwin scanned the great hall, feeling the mood in it shift; the council was settling, adjusting to its role. Even those faces that had been hostile were opening, preparing to make their case. For many men had come to council gripping anger in their bowels, convinced that the decision was already made and the council called for show. But the king's words had reassured them: this was to be a council as in the days of their fathers, when the weight of a king's thegns and counsellors could overbalance even the expressed wishes of a king.

"Bassus, I call on you to speak."

Edwin sat down, satisfied with the ripple that passed through the hall as he called on Bassus. All knew that the thegn of Anglesey was adamant that they should retain the ways of their fathers, his opposition strengthened by the difficulties he had had over the years in extracting annual tribute from the men, particularly the churchmen, of the island.

Bassus exchanged glances with the men either side of him, then slowly rose. The hall settled into silence.

The thegn, a man in the full strength of his years, with experience enough to leaven his early rashness, acknowledged his king across the hall, making the courtesy. He stood tall, his arms thick with rings of gold and garnet, inlaid buckles sparkling at his shoulders and a heavy gold brooch holding his cloak about his chest. Anglesey was rich and reluctant: the ideal province for the enrichment of an energetic thegn.

"You ask well, lord," he said. "As your father would have done." Murmurs of agreement spread from him, although few of the men in the hall were old enough to have served Edwin's father.

"But before I speak on the matter of this council, I must tell you of another matter. There has been no tribute from Anglesey this year. My men returned with tales of abandoned farms and missing animals, a land laid waste. Even their churches were empty. No one came to the summons and my men returned with the bare gleanings of what is our due."

"Was there sign of Cadwallon? I have heard that he yet lives."

"No, there was no sign of anyone. It was as if all the people of the island had left."

Edwin nodded. "We will speak of this later, Bassus, but I thank you for telling me. For now, let us confine ourselves to the topic of this council."

Bassus thrust out his chest. "I say no. No, no and again no." His gaze swept the hall. "From the times of our fathers' fathers' fathers, from the time when our ancestors took the whale road and came to this land, we have received the favour of the gods. When our forefathers came to this land, did the Britons give them land to farm and bread to eat? Oh no, our forefathers had to take land for their own, that they might hand it down to us, their sons and grandsons. They fought for this land, they bought it in blood. This land is blood land, their battles our weregild, and you would ask us to give that up, to forsake the ways of our fathers? I say again, no, a thousand times no!"

Spreading out from Bassus came a ripple of agreement: men nodding and agreeing under their breath, while others looked thoughtful and many appeared troubled. At the other side of the hall an old thegn, his hair now more white than blond, rose to his feet.

"I am Cenhelm of Cundall, and if Bassus has finished speaking, I call on this council to hear me."

Edwin looked to Bassus, who sat down to many congratulatory whispers, then signed for Cenhelm to continue.

"I have a question to put to the council. When our fathers crossed the grey seas, what religion did they follow?"

The answer spread from Cenhelm around the hall. "The religion of their fathers."

"And when our fathers arrived here and fought the lords of Deira for this land, and took it, which religion did they follow then?"

The murmur was louder this time. "The religion of their fathers."

Cenhelm nodded as he looked around the hall. "But the lords of Deira our fathers fought and defeated, what religion did they follow?"

The murmur grew louder, and men exchanged glances and nodded to each other. "The new religion."

"Then, O council, I ask you in all earnestness: are we mad that we should think of giving up the ways of our fathers to follow the religion of the men our fathers defeated?"

The murmurs grew louder. But Edwin sat with his chin resting upon his hand and made no answer, his face remaining as blank and unreadable as stone. Finally, the king spoke. "We will eat now. I would that when we return to council you will all continue to speak as truthfully as Cenhelm and Bassus have spoken. I earnestly want to hear your true views."

Harassed looking slaves began scuttling back and forth to the kitchen where teams of even more harassed cooks stoked the cooking fires. The steward sent out relays of slaves and servants with jugs of wine, ale, beer and mead; anything to fill the time as loaves were pulled from ovens and pigs spun faster over the flames.

The thegns and counsellors drank hard, and the hall filled with conversation and laughter, but there was a brittle edge to the talk and a harshness to the glee that suggested the tension underlying all.

Edwin himself barely sipped from his cup and when the bread finally arrived he dipped it in the wine and chewed at it in preference to the roast fowl set on the table before him.

When the food had been served, the council reconvened. Outside, the sun was drawing down in a pale, washed-out sky. Tatters of the morning cloud trailed into the east, and in the west a dark front advanced upon the lowering sun, but for the moment the sky above York was clear.

"*Hwæt!*"

The familiar call sounded out and the council lapsed into what passed for silence following a drink-fuelled feast. There were those, of course, who insisted upon passing wind and finding it amusing, but when the king turned a chilly gaze upon them they hid behind their cups.

"We heard earlier why we should not turn from the ways of our forefathers," said Edwin, "and much that we heard was true. It has given us much to think upon. Who now will speak?"

Through the silence came the dry rattle of bone. From his place by the fire, Coifi arose, arms spread, bone rattle shaking out a staccato, snake-hiss rhythm. Whispers rose around him, then spread through to the ends of the hall.

Edwin turned to look at the priest.

"Coifi," he said.

But the priest gave no indication that he had heard the king. He shook his rattle out, passing it through the flames, and spurts of violent, violet smoke puffed upwards, spitting and crackling, to the roof, accompanied by gasps from many of the watching men.

Coifi shuffled around in front of the fire, snuffling the air like a questing hound. His head snapped around, and he stared, eyes white, at Bassus. As quickly, his hand thrust out, and fingers that seemed little more than bone fingered the heavy gold brooch at Bassus's throat.

"The king gave you Anglesey, Bassus, and you have sucked the gold from it."

Bassus grasped the priest's wrist. "Are you suggesting I have not given the king his due?"

Coifi's eyes rolled white, and he laughed. For the thegn it was as if a corpse laughed into his face, and he pushed the priest's wrist away from him as if it was that of a dead man.

The priest's eyes rolled down again, and he spun round upon the assembly.

"Bassus asks if he has given the king his due. I have a question for you – for all of you." He slowly circled, taking all the hall into his query. "Have I given the gods their due?" Coifi flung out his bone rattle, rapping it upon a table. "Have I?" Those closest mumbled assurances, but Coifi was not satisfied.

"Have I not served the gods, sacrificed to them, searched amid smoke and blood and leaf fall for the weaving of wyrd, that I might know the will of the gods and the workings of the fate singers?" Coifi drew himself high and straight. "I have. I know I have. You know I have. There is no one here who has served the gods more diligently and for longer than I. I have served them since I was a babbling babe and my father offered me to the gods; I have served them well and faithfully."

Coifi rounded upon the assembly once again. "And what do I have to show for my years of service? A cloak and a rattle, and a bench in my lord's hall. That is all. All." He looked around, breathing heavily, face flushed. "Do you begin to understand? Look." He pointed at Bassus. "Look at him. So heavy laden with gold he can scarce stand under its weight, yet I tell you, for all his fine words about following the ways of our forefathers, Bassus, from his riches, begrudged even a goat in sacrifice to the gods – he gave me a salmon! I wouldn't even give a salmon to a slave, but that's what he offered in sacrifice to the gods, and what did they do? The gods showered him with gold. But to me, who has laboured in their service all the days of my life, they gave nothing! Nothing at all. So I say, let us hear what this new religion promises, for if the gods had power to reward those who labour in their service, then I would be standing here before you in gold and silver and crimson, as fat as a pig, not wearing the remains of birds long dead and with less flesh on me than a wraith. That is what I, Coifi, all my life priest to the ungrateful gods, say."

The priest slowly circled the assembly. Every face was turned to him and in most of them eyes were wide with shock. Guthlaf, however, gave the priest the tiniest of nods in acknowledgement. As Coifi sat down, a babble of voices rose up around him, excited and amazed voices, for never had such words been spoken before, and certainly never by a priest. Bassus sat gaping, his mouth opening and closing like a fish brought out from water, until Coifi, seeing him, shouted over the noise, "It was a small salmon too!" This brought a gale of laughter crashing down around Bassus, and many slopping-over cups of ale and wine were laid down in front of Coifi. He looked at them wide-eyed, then began to steadily work his way through them, smiling his thanks to his benefactors.

As the hubbub slowly subsided, Guthlaf rose. The warmaster spoke seldom in council, but when he did, men listened.

"You know me. I am a warrior. What I know is battle and death and killing, and I know these things well. I have given my due to the gods, I have looked for the weavings of wyrd, but all I have seen is a life rounded out, at start and end, by darkness and death.

For it seems to me that what we know of our time is like the flight of a sparrow that swoops into this hall on a winter's day, when we are seated, gathered together, around the fire. Inside the hall there is comfort and warmth and fellowship, but outside, the storms of winter, the snow and the hail, rage. The sparrow flies in through one door and then swiftly flies out again. Now, for that minute when the sparrow is in the hall it is safe from the storm, but after that minute of comfort the bird flies out again into the winter and the night. In such a way is our life on this middle-earth, for we walk its green fields for such a short while, but of what comes before or after this life we know nothing. Now if this new religion brings knowledge of what our fate is to be after our time here, then it seems to me right that we should follow it. For surely our forefathers, if they had had access to this knowledge, they would have accepted it too. So while we do well to follow the ways of our forefathers, there is no sense in following in a man's footsteps if that man has no idea of where he is going." Guthlaf looked around the hall. "That is what I say." Many of the men watching nodded, others tugged their beards or ran their fingers through moustaches thoughtfully.

"Very well." The king gestured to where Paulinus was sitting, at the end of the high table. "Let the priest of the new god tell us of his god. Then we shall decide."

As every eye in the hall turned to him, Paulinus bowed his head, his lips moving in silent prayer, before standing. Then, in full view of every man in the hall, he signed the cross upon his body.

"You ask for knowledge." Paulinus scanned the watching faces. They were leaning forward, ready to hear what he had to say. Not yet convinced, but open to his words in a way that he had not seen before. The priest offered up a wordless prayer for words. "This is right, for all men seek after knowledge. I have seen your seeking, in the prayers and sacrifices you offer to your gods in their sacred groves in the woods. Oh yes, I have watched from afar the blood spilled and the flesh burnt and the chants made. But to what? To idols of wood no more sensible of your words than the tree is of the axe that fells it. Ask your own priest: have these gods heard his prayers or granted him favour for his service? No, and nor can they, for they are no more than creations of your own mind fashioned into images and fed with dreams. But my God, my God walked among us, a man among men, though he fashioned the earth beneath our feet and the stars in heaven. My God came among us, for we lived in bondage, hostages taken by the evil one, death the weregild for the treason of our forefather. But God came among us and offered himself for our freedom, his blood for our blood, his life for our lives, as a king among you stands in the centre of the shieldwall, taking every blow the enemy hurls upon him."

Paulinus paused and looked around the hall. Men were leaning towards him, eyes wide with wonder, their faces as open as when they heard Acca tell one of the stories of old.

"Yes, I have sat in this hall and listened as Acca has told the stories of your gods – and I have laughed, for they are good stories. But listen well: stories are all they are. My God walked among us, and I can tell you when, and I can tell you where. The evil one thought he could kill him, but not even death could hold him, for he burst the gates of hell and rescued from eternal torment all those men who had lived before and died, hostage to the evil one. My God gives life, in this life and in the next, and he gives life to all who believe in him and call on his name.

"You ask what befalls a man when he leaves the light and safety of his lord's hall and goes into the dark. Those who reject the summons of my God, the rightful king and ruler of all, go down into the dark and there remain, in torment, prey to the evil one and his thegns. But those who accept his summons ascend to eternal life, however they die, whether it be in battle or illness or age, for while your gods care only how you die, my God cares how we live."

Paulinus fell silent. The hall was still. Even the slaves had stopped to listen to his words. The priest looked around. "Any questions?" he asked.

Bassus, near the end of the hall, stood, hitching his belt up over his broad belly. "You say you know when this god of yours lived, and where. Very well, tell us."

"He was born in the reign of the emperor Tiberius, and died and rose again in the reign of the emperor Augustus. As a man he lived in a land called Palestine, which lies on the south-eastern shores of the Middle Sea."

"Never heard of them, nor that place – what do you call it? Plestine?"

"How many emperors can you name?"

Bassus stuck out his lower lip, but no names came from it initially. "Well, there was him – what's his name? – the one who started off here as emperor. Con – Con something..."

"Constantine."

"Yes, him and...and...it will come to me..."

"In short, you know the name of one emperor, and him imperfectly. But let me assure you, the names of all the emperors are known, and preserved, in Rome, where the pope now has his seat, the spiritual successor to their earthly power. For where men once claimed dominion over the whole earth as emperor, and were thrown down in their pride, now the bishop of Rome, their spiritual successor, has been given authority as you yourself were given authority over the men and land of Anglesey by our king, Edwin, to exercise on his behalf. Therefore I, the representative of the pope to whom God has entrusted the care and salvation of this world, call upon you and everyone here today to accept eternal life, and salvation, through professing your belief in this man, this God." Paulinus looked around the hall, seeking to engage all the watching men. "Even your own priest admits your gods brought him no benefit, but my God gives life, life eternal. Is the decision so difficult?"

But the men Paulinus looked at avoided his eyes, staring down into their cups or up into the rafters rather than meeting his gaze. It seemed no one was prepared to say publicly what was in their hearts.

That was when Coifi began to laugh. It was a laugh tinged with madness and grief, the sound men made in battle when the blood madness took them. The priest unwound himself from where he squatted by the fire, shaking out his raven-feather cloak.

"You are all cowards," Coifi said, his tongue flecking foam over his chin. "Cowards! Hiding behind one another, hoping someone else will speak first and attract the eye of the fate singers. But if you who are warriors are too scared to speak lest the gods hear you, then this old priest will do it for you! You asked for knowledge and truth and life, and here it is! All my life I have sought these things in the old ways, pouring out blood and prayers to the gods. But the more blood I offered them and the more prayers I uttered, the less I understood, until everywhere I looked was confusion and despair. Pah!" Coifi spat in the fire and a plume of orange smoke billowed up into the rafters. Then he took up his bone rattle, the symbol of his office and the rod by which he divined the will of the gods and the workings of wyrd, and broke it, sending dry, white knobs of bone scuttering across table and floor.

"I abjure the gods! Let them strike me down if they have power, for if they do not I swear to cast down their idols and burn their sacred groves."

"Wait, Coifi, wait." Edwin held up his hand and the priest fell silent. "It is the part of the great council to decide what we shall do. Does anyone else wish to speak?" The king looked around the gathering. "Very well. Then I call upon all those who wish to follow the new god to stand. Those who wish to retain the gods of old shall remain seated." Edwin paused, then continued. "The time has come to make our decision. May it be the right one."

Beside him at the high table, Guthlaf rose to his feet, shortly followed by Osfrith and Eadfrith. Around the hall, one by one and then in groups, men slowly stood, then smiled in encouragement and offered words of cheer to those who followed. Soon, all but a handful were standing. Then finally Edwin too rose to his feet.

There was no cheering. Normally a decision of the great council was met by shouts and acclamation, but this was too grave a matter. The decision was received in murmuring silence, the whispers revealing the underlying dread at the temerity of their decision. But Coifi strode from his place by the fire, moving with a certainty of purpose and smoothness of motion no one had seen in him for many years. Standing before the high table, Coifi struck his chest.

"Lord, give me spear and stallion, and I will prove to the fainthearts and fearers here that there is nothing to fear from gods of wood and stone."

"But it is against law and custom for priests to bear weapons or ride stallions," said Edwin.

"I am a priest of the old gods no more," said Coifi. "Show me the favour the gods denied me: give me a fine horse and rich weapons, and I will ride from here and strike down the idols and fire the sacred groves. Let the gods stop me if they have the power. If they do not, if I return here unharmed and with wealth beyond anything the gods provided for me when I served them, then I will have proved that there is nothing to fear from them and this council has chosen rightly."

"Very well." Edwin turned to Guthlaf. "Give Coifi a stallion and weapons, and let him do as he intends. We will wait upon his return."

*

Evening was drawing down as the priest walked into a hall making the most of the second half of the feast. But as Coifi advanced towards the king, men elbowed each other into silence. Guthlaf followed in the priest's wake, for he had accompanied him on the ride to Goodmanham, where the greatest of the sacred groves in the district around York was to be found.

Coifi made the courtesy to the king.

"I see that you are not dead," said Edwin.

"Lord, I pierced the idols with my spear and hacked them with my sword, and yet I stand before you, untouched and unharmed. The rooks rose up into the air, calling to the gods, but the gods made no answer to their calls. They have no power, lord!"

Edwin turned to Guthlaf. "Is this true?"

The warmaster stepped up alongside the priest. "It is true, lord. Mayhap the gods once had power, for when we approached the grove, there came a darkness over the land, and a cold and bitter wind blew out of the north, and in truth my blood ran thin. But Coifi did not hesitate, although the peasants of that area called curses upon him and screamed insults. He struck the idols through, and fired them, and the gods did not cast him down with lightning or storm. Therefore, it seems to me that the gods of old have no strength left to them, and if we would have the blessing of a god with the strength to give victory to his votaries, then we must adopt the god who brought us victory against Cwichelm."

As the warmaster spoke, Coifi puffed up beside him, his face flushing with pleasure. Then, when Guthlaf stopped, the priest pointed to his chest.

"If I, a priest, have courage enough for this, then what of you, warriors and thegns? Will you be shamed by an old priest?"

One by one, then in groups and then all together, the men of the great council acclaimed Coifi, and the priest turned, arms outspread, to receive their praise, his face bright and his eyes gleaming.

# *Chapter 24*

Edwin looked down at his arm. The flesh showed goosebumps. He was not sure if it was the chill of the wind blowing in across the moors from the north-east, or nerves at what was to come. He rubbed some warmth into his arm and looked around. Behind him, Osfrith and Eadfrith stood waiting. They, like him, were clad in simple, unadorned wool shifts. Their arms were bare of rings and their feet were bare. Edwin pushed his toes into the rushes strewn beneath his feet and nodded to his sons.

"Are you ready?"

Osfrith, his mouth dry, nodded. Eadfrith attempted a smile, but it was weak and watery. "This is worse than waiting for battle," he said.

Although in truth Edwin felt the same, he attempted to smile encouragement to his sons.

"Ah, you too, father," said Eadfrith.

Edwin smiled ruefully. They were waiting outside the newly built church of St Peter. It was so new that some of the timbers still oozed sap, leaving glistening trails down the freshly whitewashed exterior. The posts on either side of the door had been painted in interlaced gold figures of animals and plants, but the other timbers remained bare – there had not been time to adorn them. Behind the royal party, stretching in a long line towards the great hall, was a column of men and women, all dressed in similar woollen robes to those worn by the king and princes. Indeed, for maybe the first time since birth, there was no way for someone watching to tell, from clothing or jewellery, the rank of the men standing in line, nor who was king and who thegn. Watching with frank if puzzled interest, boatmen and farmers and servants and slaves lined the route from great hall to simple church. Many a maid stifled a grin at the sight of the great of the land shuffling along in woollen shifts and bare feet, skin mottling under the wind's lash. But at least the people following left a respectful distance between themselves and the king, which meant Edwin could speak without being overheard. Even so, he looked around before leaning closer to his sons.

"This is worse than my first battle," he whispered.

Osfrith snorted. "If you really want nerves, try being left at Rædwald's court when you went off to fight Æthelfrith: that's real nerves."

Edwin nodded. "How old were you then?"

"Twelve. Old enough to know what was happening, but not old enough to go with you. You were only eight" Osfrith added for his brother's sake. "You did not know what was going on."

"I had to wait at other times," said Eadfrith.

"None like that."

"True enough – but this isn't like waiting for a battle either. It's different; more dangerous somehow."

Edwin nodded. He felt it too. Battle was familiar territory for them all: they had been born into it; war was the business of kings. But this was new. He was leaving behind the familiar, the tried and trusted ways of doing things, and striking out upon paths unknown by his forefathers. Edwin felt in his blood and his bowels that everything would be different.

The wooden door of the church swung open and Paulinus emerged, wreathed in clouds of smoke, followed by James and other men, chanting in a strange, flowing tongue. From its sound, the king recognized the chant as Latin, the language of the emperors of old and the church of now. The watching crowd gasped at the strange sights and sounds and smells, gossip passing from lip to lip, and strange, mutated versions of the new religion were passed around in explanation of what was happening. Paulinus led the procession to the king and his sons.

Speaking in Latin, and then in English, the priest asked them, "Are you ready to enter into eternal life?"

"I am," said Edwin, his voice pitched so that all around could hear.

"I am."

"I am."

The princes echoed the declaration of the king.

Paulinus pointed. "The door to eternal life stands open. Let us enter."

Following at a slow, steady pace, Edwin, Osfrith and Eadfrith processed into the small baptistery. First of all Edwin saw the queen, sitting to one side, her face turned to him and bright with joy. Upon her lap Æthelburh held their daughter, and the baby gurgled with pleasure at seeing her father. Edwin acknowledged the queen but he did not smile. This was too solemn an occasion. Instead, as he waited for Paulinus and James to make all ready, Edwin looked around, for he had not seen the inside of the building before. There was a small stone altar at the western end of the church, but the largest feature in the building was a font, large enough for two or even three men to stand in. It was filled with water enough to reach a man's chest.

Paulinus turned to Edwin and raised his hands in prayer. As he chanted, the sonorous Latin phrases washed around the king and he felt the sound pass through him, as if he were water shot through with sunlight. Although the language was unknown to him and the meaning of the words opaque, yet their music conveyed a keen beauty, as sharp as sorrow. Although the wind did not blow within the church, the king trembled, for he was in the presence of profound mystery.

Then Paulinus, standing in front of the king, anointed him with oil, marking out a cross upon his brow and his breast. The oil trickled down the side of Edwin's face and he blinked it from his eyes. Then, putting the oil aside, the priest addressed the king.

"Do you reject Satan?"

Edwin, his throat suddenly dry, tried to answer, but no sound emerged from his throat. Paulinus waited, staring at him, eyes fierce and concentrated.

"Do you reject Satan?"

Edwin struggled, his throat working, but all he could produce were small choking noises.

"Do you reject Satan?" Paulinus repeated. But this time he leaned closer to the king. "Make a sign if you cannot speak."

Edwin forced himself to lower his head. And as he did so, the power to speak returned to him.

"I do renounce him," he whispered.

"And all his works?"

"I do renounce them."

"And all his attractions?"

Edwin slowly raised his head so that he was staring directly into Paulinus's face. "I do renounce them." His voice came clearer now, and louder, so that it was possible for his sons to hear him speak.

"Do you believe in God, the Father Almighty, creator of heaven and earth?"

"I do believe."

"Do you believe in Jesus Christ, his only Son, our Lord, who was born into this world and suffered for us?"

"I do believe." Edwin's voice grew stronger with each affirmation.

"Do you believe in the Holy Spirit, the holy Catholic Church, the communion of saints, the forgiveness of sins, the resurrection of the body, and life everlasting?"

Edwin stared into Paulinus's face.

"I do believe," he said.

Paulinus placed his hands upon the king's shoulder and blew softly onto his brow.

"Depart from him, unclean spirit, and give place to the Holy Spirit."

And although the priest's breath was no more than a sigh, Edwin felt as if a spring wind, clean and wholesome and rich with the promise of summer, had blown up from the south as the first portent of the ending of winter.

Then James stepped forward and lifted the vestments from Paulinus's shoulders until he stood in front of the king in a simple tunic. Taking the king by the hand, Paulinus climbed the few steps to the lip of the font and then lowered himself into the water, the tightening of his face the only signal of its chill.

Edwin stood upon the edge of the font and looked down into the water. The ripples of the priest's entry died away and he saw himself reflected, as if from far away. The king stepped down into the water. The cold shocked him, but he made no sound.

Paulinus placed one hand in the small of Edwin's back and the other upon his brow. Water dripped from his hand and trickled down Edwin's face.

"*Ego te baptizo…*"

Paulinus pulled Edwin's head back and pushed at the base of his spine, and the king fell backwards and the water closed over his head.

"*… in nomine Patris…*"

Paulinus pushed the king, gasping, up into the air. Edwin took a breath and then felt the pull back beneath the water. There, his eyes open and staring upwards, he heard the words as if they came from far away and yet were being uttered by the very water which covered him.

"*… et Filii…*"

For the second time Edwin broke the surface, his gasps like the rattle of a man dying. But breath taken, the king let himself freely fall back beneath the water. He watched it close over him, the light catching upon the bubbles made by his submersion. As happened in battle, time itself seemed to slow and every moment became clear and precise. Sound, physical and intimate, surrounded and enfolded him.

"*…et Spiritus Sancti.*"

Edwin lay beneath the water, unmoving, the breath still in him, his eyes and ears open. Then Paulinus pulled him forth and the water streamed from his face and his hair and his beard. James leaned over the side of the font and held out his hand. Wiping his eyes, Edwin took the hand and climbed from the font. James removed the sodden woollen shift and, in its place, covered the king with a pure white cloak.

Edwin shivered. Paulinus, emerging from the font, turned to the two young men who stood nervously behind the king. Edwin pulled the cloak tight around his shoulders, and James led him to the further part of the church, where the queen awaited him. Æthelburh smiled at him. Edwin nodded his acknowledgement, but did not return the smile. Standing there dripping, the king began to tremble, but it was not the cold that made him shiver. There, beneath the water, he had felt as if he were suddenly able to breathe again; as if a tight metal band that had been slowly constricting his chest as he grew older, tightening so slowly that he never even realized it was there, had been released. He had been a slave and he had never even known it.

# Chapter 25

"What is going on?"

The stevedore, up to his thighs in water still cold from snow melt, paused for a moment in his unloading of the cargo from the flat-bottomed river boat half pulled up on the strand while he decided where to tell his questioner to put his question.

"I will pay," added the questioner. Silver flashed, catching the low angle of the April sun and scattering it into the stevedore's eyes.

"You should have said so first." The stevedore held out his hand, and was helped over the side into the boat. Most of the cargo of dried pulses shipped from places over the grey sea had already been unshipped. The stevedore looked the questioner up and down while he ran his hands down his tunic to dry them.

The question had been asked in a lilting accent, suggesting a native language that moved easily over the tongue and palate, rather than the explosive sounds of English. The questioner was a dark-haired man with the pale skin typical of a Briton, although whether he came from north, west or south the stevedore could not tell. "Right, what do you want to know?"

The boatmaster pointed up the muddy slope towards the remains of York. People were processing through the normally empty streets, while a crowd gathered around a newly built building. "I have never seen so many men here before. What is happening?"

"Why do you think all the merchants in these parts and beyond are here? It's 'cause the king called a great council, so all the nobles and warriors and thegns turned up, and they need feeding and watering. Keeps me busy."

"But what is happening now? That is no council meeting – all those people gathered there." And the boatmaster pointed to the crowds waiting outside the little wood and wattle church.

The stevedore wiped his mouth. "That'll be a longer story there." The boatmaster silently handed him an aleskin and the stevedore took a long and appreciative draw. "Good ale here, master. All this humping sacks around is hard, thirsty work."

"So is waiting for an answer from you."

The stevedore laughed, but he took another draw from the skin before handing it back. "That was good," he said, with some regret.

The boatmaster took the skin but held it loosely, in such a way as to suggest that it might be returned. The stevedore, taking the hint, pointed up the slope.

"That there is new. I don't rightly know what they call it – I heard someone say a 'curk' or something like that, but it's got to do with the new religion. You know how the queen is from Kent? Well, she came here with a priest and he came all the way from someplace called Rome, which I hear tell is where the emperors of old were from, and they both follow this new religion. Don't know much about it myself, though I've heard tell it's got something to do with eating flesh and drinking blood. I'm as keen on meat as the next man when I can get it, but blood should be made into a pudding, not drunk, don't you think? Anyway, it turns out this big council here was all about whether the king and the rest of them, the nobles and thegns, the ones with swords, should follow this new religion. Personally, I can't see why they should want to change; after all, the old gods have been good to us and you don't want to start getting the gods cross, do you? But the king don't listen to me, and from what I heard, the council decided they should follow this new religion."

"What – everyone?" asked the boatmaster.

"No, of course not," said the stevedore. "But the king and his family, they're all going to follow the new religion. I mean, did you hear what Coifi did?"

"Who is Coifi?"

"The priest. I couldn't believe it when I heard, but my cousin lives near Goodmanham and he swears it's true. Apparently, Coifi rode up to Woden's grove and put a spear straight into the god's eye (and he's only got one eye, so that must have hurt), before setting fire to everything else there. It was like he'd gone mad. Mind, from what I hear the gods haven't punished him for it; he's strutting around in these rich new clothes, waving swords around and showing off his horse like he's the only man who's ever ridden one."

"What is going on now?"

The stevedore scratched his cheek, the nails parting the thick beard. "I don't rightly know what they call it, but from what I hear tell, the king and his sons are joining the new religion. I saw them, walking from the great hall, dressed just in woollen shifts like they were ordinary people and not kings and princes, and they went into the 'curch' or whatever it is. Apparently, they're going to come out all new after they've been dipped in water." The stevedore gazed over the side of the boat at the turbid water of the Ouse. "It don't seem to work for me. I even heard someone say that they will live forever." The stevedore shook his head. "I don't get it myself. My dad got wet every day, and he's been dead since three years past, but that's what people have been saying. Make of that what you will." The stevedore looked down at the boatmaster. "Anything else you want to know?"

The boatmaster looked up at where the stevedore had been pointing, his eyes narrowing. The crowd was still waiting outside the building, but through the conversations there came the sound of chant and the trickle of tiny bells ringing. Then, cutting through everything else, a chant, exultant and piercing and enveloping all at once. Even the men unloading boats stopped their work to see what was going on.

The stevedore looked at the boatmaster. "What's that all about, master?"

"From the sound of it, your king has been received into the church."

"Does that mean the king will live forever, master?"

The boatmaster turned to the stevedore. His lips were pressed tight together and his eyes, the narrow eyes of a man used to staring into sea distances, were cold. "No man lives forever," he said.

"True enough, master. Is there anything else you want to know?"

"Not for now," the boatmaster said. "But if you hear more, do tell me." He twizzled a small piece of hack silver between his knuckles, then dropped it into the stevedore's creased hand.

The stevedore tested the silver with his teeth, then secreted it in the leather pouch on his belt. "Your ale and your silver are good, master, and so's my word." He stuck out his hand and the boatmaster grasped it. "My name is Hutha, master."

The boatmaster squeezed the hand in return. The stevedore's eyes widened in surprise; for a slight man, the boatmaster's grip was strong.

"I will remember you well. What you have told me is of great interest."

"Who should I ask for, master, if I have more to tell?"

The boatmaster pursed his lips.

"My name is Dial," he said.

PART 3

# Imperium

# Chapter 1

"This is Ad Gefrin." Edwin pointed to the great hall standing in the valley between smooth-bowed hills. "Although my heart lies in Deira, this is the place I love best in Bernicia." He turned to Paulinus, sitting uncomfortably upon the horse that the king had insisted he ride out upon, ahead of the royal caravan, to see the palace. "I built this place. Is it not magnificent?"

Paulinus, grateful for the chance to stop riding and ease his aching legs, agreed. The hall was magnificent.

"How does it compare to the great halls in Rome?" asked Edwin

"Well… well," muttered Paulinus, trying to massage some feeling back into his thighs.

"Really?" said Edwin, a broad smile breaking across his face. "In what way? Is it as large as the buildings in Rome, as beautiful, as rich?"

"Ah, well." Paulinus peered across the expanse of grassland peppered with sheep and small highland cattle, at the gleaming pillars of the palace. It was certainly big, although of course nothing on this island matched St Peter's Basilica in Rome, or the Pantheon and Circus of the emperors. "It's very good," he said.

Edwin looked at the priest, his eyes narrowing. "How is it good?" he asked.

"The – the decorations," said Paulinus. "We have nothing like it in Rome."

"You mean they're barbarian," said Edwin.

"Yes – no! I just mean they are different."

"You told me that a barbarian is a man who is not Roman. These decorations are not Roman. Therefore they are barbarian."

"Well, yes, I suppose they are. But that does not mean they are bad."

"You also told me that barbarians bring only death and destruction."

"I did? When did I say that?"

"Five days past, when we took ship from York to Bamburgh, and I asked you to tell me the history of the emperors."

"Those were different barbarians – German barbarians."

"My forefathers were Germans."

"Ah, those must have been the good German barbarians. I was talking about the bad German barbarians."

"What is the difference?"

"Oh, that is easy," said Paulinus. "The good German barbarians fought for the empire; the bad ones fought against it."

"My forefathers came to this country to fight for the emperors."

"There. I knew you were from good barbarian stock."

"But then the emperors left, and my forefathers took the rule of the country for themselves."

"Ah, but your ancestors never fought against the empire itself, did they?"

Edwin smiled. "Only because the emperors had gone. My forefathers fought anything and anyone."

Paulinus shrugged. "So did the emperors. That was how they became emperors and it was how they stayed emperors. But St Augustine says that the empire was providential, for it provided a world where the word of God could be preached. I believe the coming of the Angles and the Saxons to these islands at the end of the world was also providential."

Edwin nodded. "That is what I have come to believe. Follow me – I want to show you something." The king urged his horse on and, suppressing a groan, Paulinus followed. Edwin rode his horse up to the foot of the twin-peaked hill that overlooked his palace. Its flanks were studded with grazing sheep, and from the sheepfolds the boys who had been assigned to guard the animals during the daytime peeked out in awe at the two men. Edwin gestured the nearest boy over and dismounted.

"Here," he said, handing the shepherd boy the reins. "Look after him until I return."

The boy stared at Edwin in gap-toothed wonder.

"You don't understand, do you?" said Edwin.

The boy's expression did not change.

"Bring your horse here," Edwin said to Paulinus. "There is something I wish to show you."

A grateful priest dismounted while Edwin made his wishes clear to the boy through a mixture of gestures and phrases. When at last the boy had understood, signifying so by such vigorous nodding that Paulinus feared for his well-being, Edwin started up the hill, and the priest followed.

"Why did the boy not understand what you were saying?" asked Paulinus, panting to keep up with the king.

"He is of the hill people. The men of the mountain passes speak a strange tongue; it is like unto the language of the Britons, but many words are different, and I am not familiar with it. They come down from the hills in winter, but mix little with the people of the coast."

"Yet you are his king."

"In truth, I think these people little care who rules over them. They bring their tribute each year to my palace, then retire to the hills. They were here before the emperors came from over the sea. They were here when my forefathers came from over the sea. I have heard that their own tales say they walked, dryshod, to this land."

"Like the Israelites passing through the Red Sea?"

"I do not know. I think no, for I believe the hill men say that in those days there was no sea, but land only, rich in game and lakes. Then came the flood, and covered all."

Paulinus paused to draw breath. They had already climbed a long way up the hill and he could feel the sweat running down his back. At the bottom of the valley, beyond the palace, the priest saw the silver thread of the River Glen glittering between the silver green of willow trees. He looked ahead and saw the king steadily climbing. Sighing, the priest followed, the blood singing in his head.

At last, Edwin stopped. Paulinus laboured up the final slope, then stopped beside the king.

"What... what did you... bring me here... for?" The priest panted.

"This place is called Yeavering Bell," said Edwin. He pointed along the slope of the hill. "Of old, this was the stronghold of a king."

And following the king's gesture, Paulinus looked and saw that what he had taken to be a fall of rocks was, in fact, laid out around the crown of the hill as a defence, now tumbledown but in places still rising to the height of a man. The rocks were rough and uneven, but where the palisade survived most intact it was clear that the exterior had once been filled to make it as smooth as possible.

"Before my forefathers, before the emperors, there were kings in this land and they made their palace here. I have walked upon the heights of this hill and seen where their houses were. They have left their mark upon this hill and many others, for if you look, it is possible to see that many hilltops are ringed with rocks, the remains of ramparts that once surrounded them." Edwin pointed to the nearby, lower hill. Its summit too was ringed with stone. "But the kings are gone and their names are forgotten, though their works remain. Not even the hill men remember them now." The king pointed down into the valley. "Ad Gefrin is made of wood. When I am dead and others rule, it will decay and one day there will be nothing in this valley but grass, and my palace will be as lost as the names of the kings of old." He turned to the priest. "But you can keep my name alive. Write of me to the pope, make writing of my works and deeds, and though my palace disappears beneath the waving grass, my name will live."

Paulinus turned to Edwin. "I will do that, lord," he said.

"Good." The king breathed out. "Thank you." From the north-east, the wind cut in and he drew his cloak about his shoulders.

Paulinus, the sweat drying rapidly under his tunic, shivered. "We might not know their names, but those kings of old must have been hardy men," he said.

Edwin smiled. "Yes, they must have been."

"Indeed." Paulinus pulled his cloak tightly around his shoulders. "I have a suggestion, lord. These men built in stone, and we see around us how long the works of their hands have survived, though they themselves have departed. I will see that the church keeps your name alive in writing, but why not write your name in stone as well? That way it will long survive, in glory and majesty."

"What do you mean?"

"The church you have built in York – it is a fine building, and I am grateful for it. But would it not bring greater glory, to God and to yourself, to raise up a great church in stone, such as has not been built in these lands since the days of the emperors? Then truly people would say that Edwin is like unto the emperors of old."

"But my people have not the necessary skill in stone."

"My people do have those skills. I can send for stonemasons, master builders, men who know where to quarry stone and how to dress it and build with it, and together we will make the finest church in these islands, the greatest building since the days of the emperors, and your name will be made immortal in stone and in words. What do you say, lord?"

Edwin looked down at his wooden palace, its gold-painted roof timbers catching the sunlight, and he thought of the old broken stone buildings in York and the ramparts of the kings of old that yet stood on the hills in Bernicia. And he shivered at the weight of years and the dread of time, but he turned to the priest and said, "Yes. Let us build a church of stone." Then he pointed to the palace in the valley below. "But first you must preach to my people here. Tell them the news of life. Let them know what they must do to enter into God's kingdom. Bring them in, Paulinus, bring them all in…"

*

Standing up to his waist in the River Glen, his legs numb, his body shaking, his fingers almost entirely without feeling, Paulinus remembered, in his weariness, the king's command on top of Yeavering Bell. Looking up to the hill, he could clearly see the ring of stone around the summit. Since that day, a month or more ago, he had preached and exhorted and baptized, leading the people – quiet, uncomplaining people – from the royal enclosure around Ad Gefrin down to the River Glen, and there baptizing them, in the name of the Father, and of the Son, and of the Holy Spirit, until the blood turned to water in his veins and his voice chattered against his teeth. The fever, the cold fever, finally brought his baptizing to an end, but through the week he lay sweating and turning in bed, the faces, the many, many faces he had brought up from the living waters of baptism, played through his memory, the river washing away their sins as it drained away from their faces and they emerged, gasping, laughing, new.

Paulinus woke, clear eyed and weak, the fever finally broken from his body, to see James sitting quietly by his bed. The deacon, seeing his eyes open, leaned over, and Paulinus, the memory of all those people still distinct in his fever-clear memory, whispered to him, "The kingdom of God is here, James; it is here." Then the priest closed his eyes and slipped back into deep, healing sleep.

# Chapter 2

Edwin looked at the marks scratched upon the tile and felt his head aching in the way it did after three days of feasting. The great hall at Leeds was quiet, with desultory conversation, but at the high table the king sat bent over a tile, copying out the marks on the parchment Paulinus had laid out in front of him.

"The years have dulled my wits," Edwin said to the priest. "It would take a hammer to knock this new knowledge into my head. My sons, however… How are their lessons going?"

"When I can make them sit and attend to me, well. But that is rare. Eadfrith always has some reason that requires his absence whenever he sees me approach, and Osfrith simply turns around and walks away. It would not, I think, be seemly to be seen running after a fleeing prince, waving a slate in my hand." A rare smile cracked the priest's thin face.

Edwin answered the smile in kind. "No, it would not, perhaps. But the young ones, how fare they?"

"Ah, that is a different matter," said Paulinus, his smile broadening. "Little Eanflæd is a delight, and so quick! She is already forming her letters and reading simple Latin. Your son, Ethelhun, and his twin sister Ethelthryd are just beginning, and already they show much aptitude for learning; remarkable in children so young. The baby is still a baby, but I am sure he will be as bright as all your children with the queen."

"The queen already knows her letters. I wonder why she did not tell me before?"

Paulinus coughed politely. "Need you ask, lord? Few men, let alone kings, would wish their wives wiser than they. But the queen's mother learned her letters in Francia and required that Æthelburh learn them too when she was little. It is a skill that once learned is not easily lost."

"It is a skill not easily acquired either." Edwin rubbed his forehead. "My head aches and my hand too. I will take some food and drink, and then go on."

Paulinus nodded his assent. "If you will excuse me, lord, I must try to find your older sons. They were supposed to learn the letters M and N."

Edwin peered at the parchment in front of him. "Which are those?"

Paulinus pointed.

"Oh. Where am I?"

Paulinus pointed again, further to the left.

"Ah."

"They are young."

"Are the old not supposed to be wise?"

"Wise, yes. Letter clever, no."

Edwin scratched his beard. "My children will know their letters."

"Oh, I am sure you will too, lord. It will take some time, that is all."

Edwin nodded, and gestured a slave to bring over the ale. Paulinus bowed and left in search of the truant princes, while the king called a delighted scop closer.

"What were you singing then, Acca?"

"My lord, it is something new that I have been working on: a tribute to your reign. For now it is said by one and all that it is possible for a woman with babe in arms to walk the length and breadth of your kingdom unharmed and unmolested, so great is your power and authority. Such a thing has not been known since the days of the emperors."

Edwin looked sceptical. "I would not want the queen to try walking abroad with our baby in her arms."

"Oh no, lord, of course not. But such is the awe and fear in which you are held that thieves and robbers have left this land for fear of your justice to skulk in the north and far west, away from your rule." Acca pointed at the tufa, the ceremonial standard that stood behind the high table. "The people say the peace of the emperors has returned."

"And that is the problem."

Scop and king turned to look down the table. Guthlaf sat there, twisting the point of his seax into the wood. Feeling their scrutiny, the warmaster looked up. "I spoke rashly, lord. I am sorry."

"No, I want to hear what you have to say."

Guthlaf flicked a glance at the scop. "This is not a matter to be made into gossip."

"Acca, go and finish what you were composing," said Edwin.

The scop gaped. "But I can keep a secret, lord, truly I can…"

"Acca."

The scop sighed. "Yes, lord."

Taking his lyre, the scop trailed off, back towards the fire. Guthlaf moved next to the king.

"What do you speak of?" asked Edwin.

Guthlaf indicated the great hall with his glance. "The young men are drifting away from us, lord. Now, even for a feast, there are spaces on the benches and cups left unfilled. The young men who used to come to you before, to the ring giver, the king of glory, they come no longer. For what glory is to be found in a kingdom at peace and with a king who has no enemies to fight?"

Edwin looked out over the scattered groups gathered in the hall, engaging in desultory conversation. "I thought the young men were attaching themselves to Osfrith and Eadfrith."

"Those that come to us, yes. But even they are leaving, in twos and threes, moving on to other kingdoms where there is word of battle and glory and riches."

Edwin struck his fist into the palm of his hand. "What would you have me do, Guthlaf? Make war on my allies? Slay men who have given me their bond word? What glory would there be in stripping gold from the bodies of men who have accepted me as High King?"

Guthlaf shrugged. "I do not tell the king what he must do. But I do tell the king what is happening. The young men are going to other kings, where they may get gold."

Edwin shook his head. "We have thrown down those who opposed us, or made them allies and received hostages as surety. There is no kingdom left for us to make war upon."

"But without war, and the glory and gold war brings, there will be few men coming to us with sword in hand, seeking leave to be your retainers, and many who are here now will leave. Indeed, some have already gone."

"Where are they going?"

"To the far quarters of the land and beyond. Many have taken the whale road and joined the sea kingdoms of the islands at the edge of the world. Others have gone south, to Francia, for the kings of the Franks are generous with gold. Some, though, I have heard whispered, have gone to Mercia."

"Mercia? To Cearl? Why would young men looking for glory go to Cearl? They would find more glory in an ale house than with him!"

"It is Penda they follow. Cearl's warmaster is waging war on the marches of Mercia against the kingdoms of the Britons, Powys and Gwent, and upon the East Angles and the men of Wessex too. There is much chance for glory there."

Edwin stroked his beard in thought. "When Cearl dies, do you think Penda will stand aside in favour of my sons, even though the king has anointed them his heirs?"

"No, I do not believe he will," said Guthlaf.

"Nor do I. But if, as you say, Penda has attracted many young men to his cause, then Cearl will have neither the strength nor the will to remove him."

"No, he does not," said Guthlaf. "Not any more."

"Then we will have to remove Penda," said the king.

"The question is how," said Guthlaf.

"As long as he remains Cearl's man, we cannot wage war on him, for we would be breaking our faith with Cearl. Then, even with Penda dead, when Cearl dies it will be much harder for Eadfrith to claim the loyalty of the thegns of Mercia."

Guthlaf shook his head. "That will be hard enough as things stand. Would the men of Deira or of Bernicia accept a Mercian as their lord, even if he should have Northumbrian blood?"

"They would if I had anointed him my successor."

Guthlaf thought on this. "Yes, maybe they would. So it is important for us that Cearl remains king."

"Unfortunately, it is also important for Penda that Cearl remains alive and king for as long as possible, that he might draw men to himself and expand the realm in Cearl's name, but with his own power in view." Edwin bent his head in thought. "We must draw Penda away from Cearl, that we might strike."

"Or draw Cearl away from Penda…"

# Chapter 3

"Edwin has requested I attend upon him at York in three months'
time, when the moon returns to full." King Cearl of Mercia broke the
news to his warmaster, Penda, as he broke bread upon the table, his
old hands trembling. Penda looked up. He was spooning pottage into
his mouth with bread so old and hard it barely dampened beneath the
thick soup. The ride back to the great hall at Tamworth had been long
and hard, and he was ravenous, but the king's words stayed his hunger.

"When did this message come?"

"Two days past." Cearl pointed down the hall to where a strange
man sat alone, nursing a cup of ale while he looked around the hall.
"The messenger awaits my reply."

"Why does Edwin summon you?"

"Oh, he has not summoned me. Goodness me, no." Cearl looked
at his warmaster. "I am his father-in-law; we are allies and equals.
No, this is a request. But I am not sure that I can accede to it, Penda.
My bones are old and my limbs have forgotten the strength they
once knew. The journey is long and I will suffer for it."

"As you are allies, why not ask Edwin to come here? As you say,
you are not a subject king, to be summoned at Edwin's whim."

"No, of course not. But as High King, he has summoned all his
subject kings to York to appear before him, to swear fealty anew
and to offer tribute. I, on the other hand, am requested to appear
at my pleasure, as befits his ally and his father-in-law." The old king
beamed with pleasure at the memory of the fulsome way in which
Edwin's messenger had addressed him.

"That is… fitting," said Penda. "But think on this, lord: who goes
forth and who receives? Should it not be the father, the elder, who
receives the son, the younger? Should not Edwin come to you rather
than you go to him?"

Cearl wagged a finger made crooked by the bone-wasting disease of age at Penda, but he smiled as he did so.

"Ah, I know what you are up to, Penda, and I thank you for it. It does an old man good to think one as young as you still thinks me strong and powerful, the mightiest king in this land, but you know and I know who is High King. It would indeed make my old heart glad to have Edwin come to me, and not me go to him, but such is not the way of this world, even though I be his father and his elder. Edwin has the power, and we must bow to it, as do the other kings in this land. But let us be grateful that he wields his power graciously over us, asking rather than compelling. And since he has given me the choice, I will decline his invitation; I am too old, the journey is too far and the weather too cold for my thin blood. Edwin will understand." Cearl smiled. "Besides, the High King has already come to me."

"This is a wise decision, lord," said Penda. "If you had asked for my counsel, such would it have been, but although your arm may have weakened, your wit remains sharp."

"I will send you in my place."

"Me?" Penda's face blanched for a moment before his habitual control reasserted itself.

"Of course. Who else can better represent me and Mercia than my warmaster, the man who has increased Mercia's bounds and wrung tribute from the petty kings on our borders? There is another reason for me to send you: it would be good for you and Eadfrith to meet and become friends, for he shall be king in this land when I am dead, and you his warmaster. There needs must be no gap between the shields of king and warmaster, lest the wall break and the enemy win through."

Penda nodded. "Of course. I see now, and again your wisdom, lord, is a beacon and a lesson to me. But I have an idea too: tell Edwin's messenger that you will come. Then the High King will have no reason to rebuke you, for you show by your answer that you are most willing to attend him and the other kings. But when the time comes, I shall go in your place and explain that age and ill health have made it impossible for you to travel. With all the other kings attending him, Edwin will have no choice but to accept the explanation, and I will be able to sit among kings and princes and make my peace with Eadfrith, your grandson, that I may serve him as well as I have served you."

Cearl patted Penda's hand. "You are wise for one so young. Let it be done as you have said; we shall give our reply to Edwin's messenger. But before I do so, tell me something else. Who is the companion you brought into hall? My eyes are old, I know, but I do not recognize him."

"Your eyes may be old, lord, but they are as sharp as your wits. I will call him to you." Penda gestured and the cloaked man got up from where he had been sitting among a party of retainers lower down the hall, and approached the high table.

"King Cearl, this is my friend and cousin, Dial."

# Chapter 4

Paulinus found the king standing by the sea. He was staring out at the islands that crouched low to the water. The priest stopped behind the king and waited in silence. The last light of the day was draining away in the west, but the eastern sea was already dark, and only the white of breaking waves showed where islands began and sea ended. A bird wailed, its call echoing over the water.

"This was Æthelfrith's land; I thought it had become mine, but I was wrong. I am still a stranger here." The king spoke without turning round.

"I am sorry." Paulinus stepped forward so that he was level with Edwin, but the king kept staring out to sea.

"How is the queen?"

"She – she sleeps now, lord."

"Good." Edwin nodded, but it was as if a puppeteer moved his head up and down. "That is good. Sleep will help."

"Yes. Her women are with her. They will be there when she wakes."

"Make sure Eanflæd is with her, and Wuscfrea. She will need them then."

"And you, lord, what will you need?"

Edwin stared into the dark over the sea. "I am a king. Death is familiar to me."

"I am a priest. I too know death. But it is the last enemy that shall be vanquished and until that time we live in its shadow."

"These past five years, since I found new life, I thought I had escaped death's shadow. For it has lain over me since I was a boy and Æthelfrith killed my father. Through my years of exile, death sniffed around me, as a hound on the scent, and it took Cwenburg, Osfrith's and Eadfrith's mother. Then, when I came into my

303

kingdom, death reached out for me again, but Forthred put himself in its way and took the blow meant for me. But since I emerged from the water and entered into new life, death has passed me by. I thought maybe the God who died and lives again had given his life to us. I was wrong."

"Death will only be defeated finally when Christ returns to claim his kingdom."

"When will that be?" Edwin glanced at Paulinus. His gaze was bleak and cold.

"I – I do not know, lord."

"Who does?"

"Only God."

Edwin nodded. "Counsel shared is counsel known." He looked to the sea again.

Paulinus waited beside him, but the king said no more.

"Would you prefer that I leave you alone, lord?"

Edwin made no reply and Paulinus turned to walk back to the rock of Bamburgh when the king spoke.

"It is hard to lose one child, Paulinus, but to lose the twins so close to each other… that is hard indeed for the queen."

"And for you, lord," said Paulinus, turning back to the king.

"And for me. I have been fortunate; both my sons with Cwenburg are grown and healthy. Eanflæd can ride and knows her letters; a brighter child I have not seen. Little Wuscfrea does well too. When so many children die with their milk teeth still in their mouth, I have been blessed. Until today."

The priest spread his hands. "I have no words, lord. Only prayer. And hope."

"Hope. What hope?" asked the king. "Only the shadows wait them."

"No!" Paulinus said. "No," more softly. "There you speak with the tongue of the old religion. The old gods loved warriors alone, and gathered only the battleslain to their halls. But our God gathers children around him and calls them to him. He has called them to him now and, washed white in the waters of baptism, the twins are with him; they are with him now, lord, in heaven, not lost in the shadows of the underworld."

Edwin tilted his head back and stared up at the blank sky. The clouds had closed again and no star could be seen.

"I am their father – they should be with me."

"Yes, lord, they should be. But God overfathers all, and he has called these children back to his realm. Would not a king under you come when you summoned him, in fear and trembling? Lord, I was there when they died, and Ethelhun and Ethelthryd did not go in fear, but in peace, and the joy in the face of death that I have seen only in children."

"Will I see them again, Paulinus?"

"Yes, lord, yes. You will be with them in paradise."

"I pray that may be so. But there is much blood upon my hands; so much blood that I fear even the blood Christ shed shall not be enough to wash it off."

"Christ's blood washes us all clean if we but stand before his cross."

"I don't know where his cross is."

"You stand before it now, lord."

The king fell silent. The priest stood beside him, head lowered in prayer.

"Leave me, Paulinus."

The priest bowed and withdrew, leaving the king to the silence of wind and beach and sea.

# *Chapter 5*

The stevedores at York had not seen such a flotilla in all their days – the boats lined the quay, lashed three or even four deep, while ashore restless pickets of horses needed constant minding and guarding. Kings from the length and breadth of the land had gathered in York at the High King's command, and such gold and silver, such fine weapons and gleaming helmets had not been seen in the city since the day when the new emperor was proclaimed within its walls. Men and women and children had come from the farms for miles around to see the spectacle and to marvel at the press of people; so many that in places it was necessary to turn sideways and squeeze past chattering, pointing knots of sightseers.

But most extraordinary of all, the kings had gathered on the far bank of the River Ouse, across the water from York. Tents and pavilions were set up there hastily, and provisions rowed across the river, while gossiping villagers wondered what it all might mean and harassed slaves attempted to find ground dry enough to light fires in the sodden, alder-fringed water meadows of the east bank of the river.

"Father, we cannot wait any longer for Cearl."

Eadfrith entered the tent where Edwin, Osfrith and Guthlaf sheltered from the thin, persistent rain. Water drained off his cloak and trickled between the rushes strewn on the floor, but such had been the wetness of the season that liquid squelched up over any foot that walked upon them.

The king indicated the man standing beside him. "We have word from Cearl. He has taken ill on the journey, and is recovering. He says that he will come to us as soon as he is able to travel on, but for now he is resting at Hatfield Chase." The king turned back to the messenger. "Take our answer to Cearl, king of Mercia. We ask that he remain and rest at Hatfield Chase until he is well, and only then to make the journey to us. Tell him that we earnestly desire his good health and enjoin him not to travel until he is completely well. And tell the king that he is wise to keep Penda with him at this time." Edwin stopped and looked up at the messenger, who stood with the blank face and moving lips common to all men committing words to memory. "There. Repeat."

The message accurately repeated, Edwin dismissed the messenger. Eadfrith began to speak, but Guthlaf held his finger over his mouth for silence. Rising soundlessly from his stool, the warmaster moved to the tent's entrance and peered out. Half turning, he made the sign for all clear.

"We have him," said the king. There was no satisfaction in his voice, merely a blank statement of fact.

Guthlaf, keeping an eye open for anyone close enough to overhear, agreed.

"But we cannot keep the kings waiting any longer," said Eadfrith. "They grow restless, and nervous for their realms."

"They shall perform their obeisance to me today," said Edwin. "We feast them tonight, they leave on the morrow and we ride to Hatfield Chase overnight and come upon Penda in the morning."

"I would have us take some of the retainers of our allies on that ride," said Osfrith. "We know not how many men ride with Penda and Cearl."

"No," said Edwin. "The kings must not know of this matter, for they will fear for their own crowns should they think I may turn against them. For though we seek to remove a warmaster, not a king, yet there would be rumour and fear such that alliances against me might fester and breed. No, this must be done quietly and swiftly. My hope is that Cearl may yet even thank us for clearing the path to your inheritance, Eadfrith."

"We should have sufficient men in our households to meet any army Penda is likely to field," said Eadfrith. "After all, the kings of the land are here, with their best men. We would face only Cearl's and Penda's retainers."

Edwin looked to Guthlaf. "Did you not tell me that many young men have come to Penda's banner over the last year?"

"That is the word I have heard, lord."

"Perhaps we should send a scout. Guthlaf?"

"A scout runs the risk of being discovered," said the warmaster. "Then Penda would retreat to Mercia: far harder and a much bloodier business to run him to ground there."

"How many men now follow Penda's banner?" asked Edwin.

"I know not for sure, but it cannot be more than thirty."

The king nodded. "Even that is many for a warmaster, but it is not too great a host for us to overcome with the men of our households. What do you say?" He looked to his sons.

"Men's pledges to warmasters are not as firm as those given to a king," said Eadfrith. He glanced at Guthlaf. "No offence."

The warmaster smiled. "There is no offence in the truth."

"I would expect many of Penda's men to take flight or even to join us," said Eadfrith. "We should take gold as gifts to detach those keener on riches than glory from Penda's side."

"We will," said Edwin. "Any further questions?"

Osfrith shook his head. "I do not like this," he said. "There is too much left unknown. Besides," and the prince looked uncomfortable, as if he were bringing up a taboo subject, "should we attack Penda when he has not attacked us?"

There was silence for a moment, the silence of absolute surprise such as happens on a battlefield when an ambush is sprung. It seemed none knew the answer, for no one had even considered the question. But then Edwin spoke.

"Would you have Penda take the throne of Mercia from your brother?"

"No! No, of course not. But is it just that we attack him without provocation? After all, do we know he will try to seize the throne from Eadfrith?"

The other three men looked to each other, and then back to Osfrith.

"Yes," they said in unison.

The tension between them broken, even Osfrith laughed. "It's true, I also think Penda will try to take the throne. But maybe we should wait until he acts and then attack?"

Edwin looked at his son. "Why?" he asked.

Osfrith shifted uncomfortably. "I – I do not know. It just seems like it would be right."

"It would be wrong for the extra men who would have to die to take the throne away from him when he has claimed it. At the moment he is warmaster and his authority derives from Cearl. But let him take the throne, and the men of Mercia will be sworn to him. They will fight and die and kill for him then. No, we strike now, while he is still weak."

Osfrith nodded. "Very well," he said. "I will be ready with my men."

"Good." Edwin looked to Guthlaf, who still stood guard by the entrance to the tent. "Does it yet rain?"

The warmaster looked out of the tent, then went forth and peered into the west before sticking his head back through the opening.

"Yes, but the clouds are breaking. Should we begin?"

Edwin looked to his two eldest sons. "Are you ready?"

By way of answer, Osfrith and Eadfrith stood up.

"Then let us begin," said Edwin.

# Chapter 6

It was a sight such as had never been seen before in the length or breadth of the land, nor in any of the years of its long past. Not even when the emperors reigned was any such sight seen, though the emperor himself came to Britain and put the land beneath his purple heel.

The ship crossing the River Ouse was hung with gold and crusted with jewels; it glittered in the brilliant light that burst through the rain-washed sky. Arm rings and brooches and amulets and torcs were strung over prow and rudder and mast; indeed any object that would take them. But more remarkable even than the riches that adorned the boat were the oarsmen: the kings of the land sat each upon a bench and heaved, as a plain sailor, upon the hand-smoothed wood of an oar. Sitting enthroned at the centre of the boat, the only man who did not labour, the only man who looked in the direction the boat was travelling was Edwin. He sat with the tufa behind him, the bulls' heads that formed its four prongs dressed with torcs, and above them the crowned purple globe.

The kings laboured in silence, their heads bowed before Edwin, who gazed straight ahead at the city of York, now thronged with people awaiting his arrival, when before it had been but the ghost of a city, filled with the memories of its glory. The two kings of Kent were there, bent over their oars, and the king of the East Angles, the rulers of the West Saxons, the lord of Lindsey and the master of the Rock of Dumbarton, the kings of Elmet, and Powys, and Goddodin. All the kings of Britain and the island realms rowed the High King in silence and majesty across the river to his home city, the city where Constantine had first been proclaimed and acclaimed emperor.

Following the royal boat across the river came a host of smaller craft. Foremost among them was the vessel carrying Osfrith and

Eadfrith, who like their father sat immobile in the centre of the ship, surrounded by toiling ranks of princes and lords wielding oars with unaccustomed hands. The dignity of their progress was slightly marred by the inexperience of their rowers, with oars snagging on each other and either biting too deeply into the water or flashing over the surface, sending up plumes of spray.

Paulinus awaited them on the far bank, standing at the head of a row of robed figures, James the deacon foremost among them. The Italian had spent many frustrating months trying to prepare men for the diaconate and ultimately the priesthood, but the teaching was slow: Latin did not come easily to men whose native language shared no common roots. However, James had fared better when it came to teaching men and boys how to chant: he had produced a choir whose voices and tone came close to the purity achieved in Rome. Now, as the flotilla splashed across the river, the choir began to sing, the Latin chant spreading out as mist upon the water. Clouds of sweet-smelling smoke rose in columns from the swinging censers, and the chant became mixed with the shouts and acclamations of the crowd on the York bank of the river: farmers and peasants and slaves, thegns and merchants and boatmen all sent up their cheers as the kings rowed Edwin to shore.

The landing was awkward. Oars snagged on each other and the quay, but the stevedores waded waist deep through the chill October water to secure the boat and make it steady. Then, one by one, the kings of Britain and the islands disembarked, forming a column towards Paulinus and his companions. When all the kings had left the boat and formed up, Edwin rose from his seat. Walking a little stiffly, for the seat had been uncomfortable and the sceptre he was holding was heavy with gold, Edwin stepped onto the land.

The waiting crowd, which had hushed into expectant silence, broke into shouts and cheers, while the choir sang on, their chant rolling serenely beneath the tumult.

The princes Osfrith and Eadfrith took up station behind their father and accepted the tufa. They held the standard aloft between them, and the princes and lords who had rowed them across the river formed up, a slightly chaotic group following in their wake.

Drums and whistles and lyres struck up a cacophony of sound. The choir, herded by a harassed James and still singing, turned and began to process up the incline towards the great hall. Edwin, staring up the slope at the singers, spotted a familiar face clad in unfamiliar garb burrowing into the procession: Coifi. The priest of the old gods had abandoned his raven-feather cloak in favour of something similar to the robes worn by James and Paulinus. He was singing lustily with the choir, but even from a distance Edwin could hear the crow-like note of his singing making a harsh and abrasive counterpoint to the sweetness of the melody. The king, although he felt a smile tug at his lips, kept his face still. He was on display here: to kings and warriors and all the people. He was offering himself up as their king and they were accepting his offering. It was incumbent upon him to present himself as king alone.

As the choir approached the great hall with its doors open wide, Paulinus and his acolytes, their censers swinging, followed in its wake, the afternoon sun glinting on the golden and scarlet robes, and the stole hung around the priest's neck.

The procession of kings came afterwards. The ground, usually made muddy by damp boatmen dripping their way up the slope, had been covered in a thick layer of rushes. The kings glittered in their finery; alone among the people watching, they wore their swords at their hips. All other swords had been sequestered outside the great hall, and guarded. Warriors of the king's household lined the procession route, keeping the crowd from rushing forward, and their spears were employed to good effect when people grew too enthusiastic or pushed too close: a swift blow with the shaft was enough to force most people backwards and, if that failed, the prospect of the glittering head of the spear was enough to make the most enthusiastic of sightseers retreat.

Spreading out from the narrow column of kings, and following behind it, were the princes and thegns and warmasters, the nobility of the land: lords whose rule had been won at sword point and who kept their land with the blade in one hand and the promise to their overking in the other. But at the fulcrum of kings and warriors, alone in a bubble of space, was Edwin.

The choir entered the great hall, retaining some semblance of order but making judicious use of elbows to move the more obstinate bystanders out of the way. The wooden walls of the great hall immediately smothered the sound of chanting, leaving the procession of kings to advance accompanied by cheers, and the occasional catcall as drink-emboldened spectators hurled insults at ill-favoured kingdoms.

The kings themselves achieved an entrance that was only slightly more harmonious, for coming to the doors of the great hall there arose the question of precedence. It was only Guthlaf's brooding presence at the entrance to the hall, backed by a phalanx of his best warriors, that prevented swords being drawn and the procession descending into a brawl.

"Keep in line!" he ordered, helping the occasional king on his way into the hall with the pommel of his sword. Inside, slaves rushed to seat the kings on a long table set parallel to Edwin's own high table. It had been built especially for the event, and made long enough so that all the kings present might sit facing the High King. The kings took their positions behind their long bench, but they remained standing. The choir arranged itself behind the high table, and the swinging censers soon filled the hall with a fug of sweet-smelling, if slightly choking, smoke.

Then, alone, Edwin, High King, entered his hall.

The kings of Britain and the islands, well nigh all the kings of the land, raised acclaim to their High King, and the assembled choir chanted the Te Deum. A single tall figure, bearded and crowned with a circlet of gold, robed in purple, Edwin advanced down the hall into the face of the acclaim. Behind him his sons stood at the door, the princes and lords waiting without, while their father took his place at the high table. The kings of the land, facing him, raised a final cheer, the choir sang the last line of the Te Deum, and silence came to the hall, broken only by the sound of metal on chain as the censers swung back and forth.

The High King sat. The kings of the land took their places. Then Osfrith and Eadfrith entered, and the princes and lords. The

Northumbrian princes sat to the right of the king. The queen entered from the rear of the great hall and took her place on Edwin's other hand, with Paulinus beside her. The rest of the hall swiftly filled with everyone who could fit inside it, and some who couldn't, while the slaves and servants rushed around with wine and ale and all manner of sweet, honeyed drinks.

"*Hwæt!*"

It was Guthlaf who called the great hall to silence, rising from his place at the end of the high table and sending a voice that could call orders over a battlefield resounding through the rafters.

"The High King."

Edwin rose to his feet. He was a tall man, and all the kings of the land were sitting down. He towered over them.

"Today, in this place, we have shown a unity and a power not known since the emperors sat in judgement upon the world. Today, a woman can walk the length and breadth of the land with her babe at her breast and not be molested. Today, we have sought the blessing of the God that made the gods of our fathers, the God that brought me from exile and fear to be High King of this land." Edwin looked up and down the table at the assembled kings before him, meeting the gaze of each in turn. Some he found defensive, others cautious, still others bold. But none refused his scrutiny.

"Today, I call on you to join me, and to accept my new God. I call on you to accept his blessing, to put away the fears of the past and enter into a life of knowledge and hope. I call on you to follow the God who has brought me victory, and raised me higher than any king in this land since the days of the emperors."

Edwin challenged the kings, one by one, in silent gaze. Some fell away before him now, but Odda of the Hwicce stood before the king.

"I hear your words, High King, and give them credence; credence enough to do what you yourself did on this great question: I shall call a great council of the Hwicce and we shall debate this matter and decide whether to give up the ways of our fathers and follow the new religion." Odda looked up and down the line of kings. "What say you, my brothers?"

One by one, then the rest together, the kings arose and acclaimed Odda's words. Edwin, his face blank, looked upon them and then nodded.

"Very well. Let it be as you have said. Convene the councils of your people, and present to them the good news. I shall send men, priests, to speak at your councils, that the truth and knowledge of our new religion be accurately presented to you. But now, as friends and brothers sworn together, let us eat."

At the High King's words, a stream of slaves emerged from the kitchens and from the cooking fires set up behind the hall, carrying roasted meats of mutton and beef and venison, and sweetmeats infused with fruit and honey. As the great hall settled down into rhythmic chewing, Edwin looked to his sons.

"Eat lightly, for we have work on morrow night, and hard riding."

The queen, overhearing the quiet words, leaned towards Edwin. "What work is that, my husband?"

The king, surprised, turned back to her. "Nothing," he said. "A minor matter."

Æthelburh looked askance at her husband. "You are not telling me the truth," she whispered.

"I cannot speak on this matter here," Edwin said, speaking behind his hand. "There are too many ears."

The queen looked at him. "Is it Mercia? Say simply yes or no."

"Yes," said Edwin.

"Have care, husband."

"I will."

The queen smiled at him. Amid the noise and bustle of the hall, that smile struck the king's heart. He tried to fix it in his mind and memory, that he might return to it later, but he was called upon to speak in the matter of the wisdom of breeding horses from stock brought in from foreign lands, and the image faded from his memory. When Edwin turned back to the queen, she was engaged in conversation with the king of Elmet, a king whom Edwin had placed upon the throne, and she was turned away from him. There would be other occasions when he could see her smile. For now, there was the accepting of the tributes brought to him by the kings, the riches they laid before him as a token of their status as kings subject to the High King of Britain.

As the kings, one by one, came forward and laid before Edwin their gifts of gold – torcs and rings and brooches and buckles, marvellously worked – James led the choir in chant, and the crowd massing by the doors sent up gasps of appreciation at the treasures laid before the king.

# Chapter 7

Guthlaf led the mounted men down the old north road. The night was clear, and bright with moonlight, and the men rode with the hooves of their animals wrapped in cloth. They sounded, Edwin reflected, like a legion of women pounding wet washing upon stone. But it was a sound that died away rapidly, unlike the sharp sound of metal on stone that came when iron horseshoes struck the old cobbles of the Roman road. The night was bright enough, and the road sufficiently broad, for the journey to be straightforward.

Edwin slowed his horse so that Osfrith could catch up with him. The prince, seeing this, heeled his horse forward and brought the beast alongside his father.

"You were the last to leave the hall," said Edwin. "How many men did you leave to guard the queen and the little ones?"

"There were enough."

"How many?"

"I – I did not count, but I think about twenty."

The king shook his head. "That is not enough. I dreamed last night of men hunting the queen and the little ones through mist and rain and marsh." Edwin looked around, swiftly adding up and assessing the worth of the men who rode with them. "Send another ten back to guard her."

"But father, that leaves us but forty men," said Osfrith. "Is that enough?"

"Forty is an army." Edwin smiled. "I know it is, because it says so in my law. Forty will be sufficient to finish Penda. Send the men back, Osfrith."

The prince looked at his father. "Maybe you should ask Guthlaf, father?"

The king did not look at his son. "I do not need to ask my warmaster's advice. Send the men."

Osfrith made to answer, then shook his head, and turning his horse he urged the beast to the back of the column. From his place near the front, Edwin could hear the quiet orders, then the receding thrum of hooves cantering back up the road towards York. Edwin was not the only man to hear the hooves. Guthlaf rode back to the king.

"Where are those men going?"

"Lord," said Edwin.

Guthlaf stared at him. "What?"

"You did not call me lord."

"But – but we are on campaign. I never address you as lord on campaign."

"Do so," said Edwin. "From now on."

Guthlaf blinked, then shook his head slightly. "Where are those men going? Lord."

"I sent them back to guard the queen. Osfrith left only twenty men with her."

"But she is in the hall, and there are other men guarding the stockade. Twenty men are more than enough."

"Are forty men not enough to accomplish our task?"

"Yes, yes forty are enough."

"Then the ten go back to guard the queen." Edwin leaned towards his warmaster. "Ill dreams came to me last night concerning the queen. I would see her well protected in our absence."

"Very well. Lord." Guthlaf swung his horse back to the head of the column. Edwin made to call after him, then stopped. He had spoken so many words over the last few days that this chance to ride in silence was too precious to squander. Besides, he could wait to send out scouts until they were closer and the chance of Penda being forewarned had lessened.

The king drew his cloak more tightly around his shoulders. The night grew cold and damp and he felt it penetrating into his bones. His shoulder ached now when the weather turned to autumn and its mists and fogs lay upon the land. There would be a mist by dawn, for through the night the land was breathing out and its exhalation lay low on the marshy land to either side of the road. It was no wonder the damp penetrated into his bones as it had never done before: he was getting old. He alone of the kings gathered in York had known so many summers. Edwin tried to call to mind the dim memories he had of his father, but they had worn to shadows over the years and now he could no longer see his face. He remembered being thrown, laughing, into the air and his father, laughing also, face upturned, catching him. But now his father's face lay in shadow and the laughter sounded like his own. Edwin did not know how old Ælla was when he died, but he did know that he had already outlived his father by many years, as he had outlived most of the kings of his youth and manhood: Æthelfrith and Rædwald, Æthelbert and Sæberht, they had all gone to their ancestors. Edwin grimaced and corrected himself: they had gone to face God and his judgement. He had little doubt what God's judgement would be on Æthelfrith, but as for Rædwald, he did not know. The warrior king, always so decisive in battle, could never make up his mind in matters of religion, so had kept two temples, one for the old gods and one for the new. As far as Edwin could see, however, gods were, like kings, jealous and unwilling to share worship. He feared that his old protector was paying for hedging his bets. But surely even that was better than the whispering descent into the shadow world that would have been Rædwald's fate as a man who died through accident rather than battle. The new God at least judged a man by the fullness of his life rather than by the accident of his death.

As far as Edwin knew, only Cearl among the living kings of Britain was his elder. He grimaced again. If Cearl died of old age he would be the first king to do so since… Edwin thought back over the king lists and realized that not one of the names upon the lists that had been drilled into his boyish head had died an old man. Most died in battle, a few by accident and the rest through disease. Few had ever seen their hair turn grey, as his had. The world was silver and dark, and he was king and his sons would be kings after him, their friendship sufficiently strong to ensure the kingdom would not dissolve into civil strife.

The king looked along the column of riders and saw the unmistakeable shape of Guthlaf ahead, in the vanguard. He urged his horse on, and the warmaster, hearing the approach through the night stillness, slowed his mount so Edwin could catch up.

"Lord," said Guthlaf.

"Guthlaf." The king glanced past the warmaster and saw the man on his far side. "Bassus," Edwin said, surprised. "I did not expect to see you here."

The thegn tipped back his helmet – a simple metal dome – and made the courtesy.

"I was in York for the obeisance of the kings. Now I make my own obeisance and follow you into battle."

"Do you still follow the old gods?"

"I follow my king."

"In all ways?"

Bassus paused. "In all the ways a thegn should." His teeth gleamed in the moonlight as he suddenly smiled. "Which is why I ride with you this night."

"I am glad to have you with us," said Edwin. He looked to Guthlaf. "Ride with me."

King and warmaster spurred their horses to the front of the column.

"We should rest," Guthlaf said to Edwin. "Camp here, then send out scouts and attack Penda in the afternoon."

The king shook his head. "I am restless this night, Guthlaf. I will know no rest if we stop, and besides, it were better we come upon Penda at dawn, when his men are waking, than in the noon, when they are ready."

"We must at least send scouts."

"True. But only one, maybe two men. Impress upon them that they are not to be seen; they are to find where Penda and Cearl are camped and then return, nothing else." Edwin snorted. "I know these

320

young hotheads, their heads stuffed full with songs of glory. Make sure they understand what they are to do and, more importantly, what they are not to do."

"I will." Guthlaf made to wheel his horse back, then stopped as Edwin stayed him. "Yes, lord?"

"How long have I been king for?"

Guthlaf shook his head. "I – I have not counted, lord. Many, many years."

"You are right. It has been seventeen years. None of my forefathers ruled for more than ten."

Guthlaf grinned. "None of your forefathers were High King."

"That is – true." Edwin bowed his head for a moment, then looked up to see Guthlaf still waiting upon him. "Go, send out the scouts. We ride on; this pace should bring us to Penda by dawn."

While the warmaster made his way back down the column, picking out two men sufficiently crafty and trustworthy that they would scout, and scout alone, Edwin rode on alone at its head. The peace, after the last few days, was a balm.

But there was a restlessness in Edwin's heart that would not ease. It was similar to the dryness and nerves before battle – and indeed, the morrow would bring battle – but it was not battle fear. The king had fought enough battles to know that fear. No, it was a sense that despite all he had done, despite the battles won and the kingdoms conquered, despite a renown greater than any of his forefathers had known, it was not enough. As he rode, Edwin wondered if the emperors themselves, at the height of their power when they were masters of all the world, felt not a little like this. Riches, glory, power: they were not enough.

Edwin looked up at the innumerable stars lying in the deeps of the night. Unbidden, his hand went to his chest and there found, and took out, the cross that lay upon it. The king pressed the cross to his forehead and his lips, and placed it back upon his breast, and peace fell upon his soul.

# Chapter 8

"Penda is camped on a hillock of dry ground. The land to the north, east and west is marshy and impassable without boats. The only approach is from the south, and there are sentries guarding the way."

It was the darkest watch of the night. The moon had set and the stars, cold and intense, glittered from a sky so black the promise of new light seemed surely vain. Guthlaf whispered the scouts' report to Edwin as the column rode south.

"He believes himself secure," said Edwin, "but all he has done is place himself in our jaws."

"The scouts could not get close enough to see how many men ride with Penda. But the size of the camp suggests there cannot be more than thirty; they say twenty is more likely."

"What we would expect. Did they see anything else?"

"Too dark."

"The dawn will show us what we need to see."

They rode on, muffled hoofs thudding on stone until, at last, they turned off the old road. Penda and his men had taken the tracks into the marshes and meres that spread for leagues along the Humber, making a shifting, silent landscape, as much water as land. By turning off the road, Penda had made his band harder to trace, but he had also made it easier to trap. Edwin and his men knew this land; they knew it well. Penda had unwittingly placed himself into a trap. All Edwin had to do was spring it upon him.

The warband picked its way along the narrow paths that snaked through the marshes. Blackwater glittered with starlight. The path revealed itself more by its absence than anything else, a ribbon of absolute darkness through the star-speckled rushes and reeds that lined it. The men rode in single file, with Guthlaf leading, Edwin at the centre of the column, and his sons in the rearguard. They rode silently now and the bound hooves of the horses made barely a sound on the soft ground.

Guthlaf looked to the east. He saw the first hint of dawn, for the darkness there was drawing back towards grey. He had already passed the first marker the scouts had left for the men following: the branch broken across the way indicated that they were now within three miles of the enemy camp. Time to dismount.

The warmaster gently brought his horse to a stop, and one by one the column drew up behind. Then, as he dismounted, the men behind followed suit, each stepping carefully to the ground, for jumping could all too easily cause a sword hilt to rap against armour, sending warning towards the enemy. The men were experienced and well rehearsed; Guthlaf had no need to issue orders, they simply followed his lead. So now he took his horse's bridle and led the animal on along the path, searching for the second marker, as the eastern sky slowly lightened. He saw the twisted skein of rushes just as the first hint of colour washed the horizon. The rest of the world was still a place of silver and shadow, but the colours that announced the sun's rising were gathering beyond the curve of sky. Guthlaf ran his thumb over the bundled rushes, checking the weave; yes, it was the scout sign. One mile from the enemy camp. Time to tether the horses and assign a guard before walking on to battle.

The orders were passed by sign and touch. The scouts had left the marker by a glade lined with alder and willow; a good place to hide the horses. Guthlaf marked the two men who were to stand guard upon the animals, then made his way swiftly down the line, checking that each man had tightened all straps and buckles, muffled their sword pommels and shields, and knew the importance of silence. The preparations complete and the warmaster happy, Edwin made his way up the line to join Guthlaf at the front of the column.

"You know the paths, Guthlaf. Lead on."

The warmaster led the warband on in silence, as shadows pooled in the dark places beneath tree and sedge, leaving the flats of water and grass to slowly grow into colour. Edwin saw the breath mist before his face, and by that knew that light was reaching over the edge of the world. He sniffed the air, and through the smells of marsh and earth, rich and rotten in turn, he caught smoke, the first hint of cooking fires. They were close.

Guthlaf stopped and gestured Edwin up alongside him. He pointed, and the king saw fire bloom through a thin screen of willow and rush. Two further smoke trails ran up, thin and long, into the sky.

Edwin pointed ahead to the willow screen, then to Guthlaf, and then to his eye. The warmaster nodded. They knew each other and their battle tactics well enough for Edwin's instructions to need no words. Guthlaf was to lead the men, in silence, up to the trees and lay them in cover there. Then he and Edwin would see how many men Penda had with him.

Keeping low, Guthlaf led the warband towards the line of trees. Using hand signals, he pointed the men into hiding, then with Edwin, Osfrith and Eadfrith following he crept onwards, towards the campfires.

Lying up behind a screen of rushes, the four men observed the slowly waking camp. Edwin counted five tents. Pairs of men sat around the three fires, poking the logs. A tent flap folded back and a man emerged, stretching out his arms, then lifted his tunic and urinated into a patch of reeds. It was too far to see if Penda was abroad this morning, but he could see the Mercian pennant, limp in the dawn calm, hanging from the largest tent. Edwin had emerged in similar fashion a thousand times or more. It was exactly as he would have expected.

The king signed Guthlaf and his sons to pull back. It was only when they were back among the willow trees, and it was possible to speak, that he asked them, "Did you see anything wrong?"

The princes checked with each other, then both shook their heads. Guthlaf likewise said no.

Edwin grimaced. "It was… too normal. They are expecting us."

Slowly, one after another, the warmaster and the princes nodded.

"There will be more men hidden in the tents, but we should still be able to take the field; it will be hard, though – much harder than I thought."

"We should bring the horses in closer," said Guthlaf. "We may need them to hand."

"Yes," said Edwin. "Bring them right up to us."

Guthlaf gestured a man closer, whispered briefly to him, then sent him on his way. "The horses will be here," he said.

"Should we still make a surprise attack?" asked Osfrith.

"The only ones who will be surprised will be us," said Edwin. "No, Penda will have prepared some nasty tricks for us if we come charging down upon him. Instead, we will draw him to us. Guthlaf, form the shieldwall in loose formation. We march there – you see where the land narrows, and well before it rises up to his camp – and then call him forth. There we cannot be outflanked, and it will be shieldwall against shieldwall, a battle we will win." Edwin looked to Guthlaf, Osfrith and Eadfrith in turn. "Any questions?"

There were none.

"Very well. Form up the men, Guthlaf. Osfrith, you make the challenge. Eadfrith, take the left, Osfrith with me in the centre, Guthlaf on the right. Ready?"

The answers were grim-faced nods and the lowering of helmets upon heads. The men were experienced and well trained. A few words from Guthlaf was enough to bring them from the tree cover, out upon the level muddy ground beyond and into a loose shieldwall. The warmaster swiftly dressed the line, checking swords and shield placement, while Edwin at its centre concentrated upon the enemy camp. Even now, with a shieldwall forming up in plain sight in the dawn light – the sun was not yet risen but colour had returned to the world to herald his arrival – Penda's camp remained calm. It should have been boiling with activity: men tumbling from the tents and scrambling into armour, while orders were shouted and fires put out. But instead it remained exactly as he had seen it: three fires burning and men calmly warming themselves.

The more he saw, the less Edwin liked what he was seeing.

But he could not turn back now. Even with men as well trained and loyal as his, the word would get out: the High King ran without even taking the field. Even the most loyal man might seek a new hall and a new lord if such rumours spread, and every king in the land would start calculating new odds on defying him. No, he had to offer battle, but at least with the horses brought up close, they could retreat swiftly if battle turned sour.

Edwin turned round to check. Still no sign of the horses, but they should be arriving at any moment, and he could not afford to wait any longer. He looked to Guthlaf, who was awaiting his sign, and nodded.

"Forward!" shouted the warmaster.

The shieldwall began to advance.

It was only when it was moving that Edwin realized he had forgotten to ask God's blessing. He almost ordered a stop, but Penda's camp, up to now so still, suddenly boiled into frantic activity, with men spilling out of tents and struggling into armour. Mayhap his fears had been misplaced; in which case this was no time to stop, but rather time to attack.

"On!" shouted Edwin.

The fires in the camp were extinguished, save one, and that suddenly began to produce thick black smoke. Eyes drawn by the smoke column, Edwin saw a man loading layers of damp rushes upon the fire. His gaze followed the smoke column back up into the sky. Penda was sending a signal.

Who to?

Keeping his station in the centre of the shieldwall, Edwin looked around, but he could see nothing but dreary marshland to left and right, and he could not turn and look behind without stopping the line.

They were closing the distance. It was down to one hundred and fifty yards.

"Spears!" shouted Guthlaf, and the men hefted their short throwing spears onto their shoulders, ready to throw.

Penda's camp still appeared to be in confusion, men rushing around as if mad with fear, with not even the semblance of a shieldwall forming to face their charge. The only obstacle left was a ditch, fifty yards from the camp, that looked narrow enough to jump and was surely sufficiently shallow to wade through. Then launch the spears at men still too panicked to raise their shields, and follow up with swords. Penda was making it easy for him. Too easy.

"Halt!" Edwin's command cut through the cries and war screams. Only one or two men on the Northumbrian line kept advancing and, realizing they were alone, they backed up, looking around in the same manner as a sheep separated from its flock.

Guthlaf ran across the front of the line to Edwin, as did Osfrith and Eadfrith.

"Why did you order the stop?" asked Guthlaf.

By way of answer, Edwin pointed.

Rising up out of the ditch, plaited with rushes and reeds, was a shieldwall. Spears – long, stabbing spears – bristled from between the interlocked shields. Edwin cast his eye along the line: there were twenty-five shields in the wall. Almost as many as his entire warband. He looked beyond the shieldwall to Penda's camp. The confusion had disappeared in an instant, replaced by men calmly forming into a second line and advancing towards the shieldwall. Another twenty-five or so. How had Penda acquired so many men? Edwin looked along his own line. They were outnumbered, but not too badly. He would have to anchor the flanks of his line, so they could not be turned by Penda's superior numbers, but that done he should still be able to prevail. Looking at the armour and movement of the Mercians, Edwin was sure his men were the better warriors.

Guthlaf pushed back his helmet and scratched his forehead. "This is going to be bloody," he said.

"Anchor the right to the watercourse," said Edwin, pointing to the weed-choked river. "Guthlaf, take the left flank; ensure they don't envelop us. Osfrith in the centre with me, Eadfrith on the right."

"Father," said Osfrith, pointing. Edwin looked around and saw two men advancing from the shieldwall. One was Penda. The other... Edwin squinted. His eyes were not as sharp as they had once been, but there was something about the way the second man moved that seemed familiar. But his helmet covered almost all his face, and where the eyes should have been, there were only shadows.

"Come," Edwin said to Guthlaf. "Osfrith, Eadfrith, shape the line."

King and warmaster advanced until they were some fifty yards from their own line. Penda and his companion stopped a similar distance from their line. Edwin raised the brow of his helmet a little, planted the haft of his spear in the soft earth and waited.

"Edwin."

The king made no answer.

"You spotted my welcome then," said Penda.

Edwin stared at the Mercian but still did not reply.

Penda glanced at the silent man beside him. Edwin's eyes narrowed. From the way Penda held himself, he seemed nervous of his companion.

"As you left the shieldwall, I assumed you wanted to speak," said Penda. "I must have been mistaken."

"I am High King. I will speak to Cearl."

"King Cearl has not been well. Really, he should not have tried to come at your calling, but he insisted. Unfortunately, his sickness overcame him, and his spirit went down into the shadows."

Edwin stared at Penda. "You killed him."

The warmaster shook his head. "You would like to believe that, but I did not. The king was old. Old men die. He died. That was all there was to it."

"Very well," said Edwin. "You know Cearl's command. Your new king stands yonder. Make obeisance to him."

"I kept the kingdom for him for the last decade of his life, you know. If it had not been for me, the wolves would have descended and torn Mercia apart. But I kept it together. He knew I did so too. And in the end, as he gasped out his last breaths, he gave it to me, Edwin. He gave it to me."

Edwin laughed. "So you say, you bastard, half-born son of a slave. Do you think even the witan of your own people would believe you?" Edwin shook his head. "I have spoken enough with you, warmaster. You are no king, and I will not grant you words any longer."

"Then speak to my cousin," said Penda, "for he is a king." And the man to his right slowly raised his helmet.

Edwin stiffened; the breath hissed through Guthlaf's teeth.

"Cadwallon."

The man removed his helmet and the new-risen sun gleamed upon his black hair and white skin.

"When I came among your people in York and, later, when I took feast in the great hall in Tamworth, I was named Dial. Your people have no gift for language, Edwin, but you know well enough what that means, do you not?"

"Vengeance." Edwin's answer was quiet. He had thrown off the shock of Cadwallon's appearance almost at once and now, cold and clear, his mind worked through the battle chances. His gaze moved beyond Cadwallon to the men forming into a shieldwall. No more had appeared, and he could see nowhere to hide reserves. That left them still outnumbered, but not disastrously so.

"Vengeance!" Cadwallon shouted the word across the field, so that all might hear it. "That is my name, and today I claim it. Vengeance for your betrayal, vengeance for your pledge-breaking, vengeance for your taking my God." Cadwallon spat. "Not that God will accept you into his kingdom."

Edwin smiled thinly. "You do know my priest comes from the pope?"

Cadwallon stared at Edwin, his face bleak with cold rage.

"When I have killed you and your sons, I will descend on York and wipe out the rest of your family. Not a single child of your blood will I leave alive."

"You will have to defeat me before you kill me, Cadwallon. Bring your men against mine, and we shall see who walks from the slaughter field." Edwin paused. "But then I do not see any of your men before me, old friend. No wonder. Why would men follow a defeated, beaten king?"

"Why would they follow me? For the same reason I stand here: for vengeance."

While he had been speaking with Penda and Cadwallon, Edwin

had been attending to the sights and sounds around him: men shifting and adjusting armour, the unnatural brittleness of the laugh at a whispered joke, the soft thudding rhythm of hooves on damp earth. He had sensed as much as heard his horses being brought up from their picket line, and at first he settled back into that knowledge as he spoke to Penda and Cadwallon. But then, at first under his notice but now insistent, came the realization that the rhythm, the sound, was wrong. It was too loud, too wide, too near.

As Cadwallon spoke, Edwin turned and saw emerging from the line of willows one hundred, one hundred and fifty, two hundred riders, mounted on the shaggy, sturdy ponies the Britons favoured for moving through their mountain kingdoms. The beasts drew up in a rough line and the men riding them hefted short throwing spears onto their shoulders.

"My men have followed me," said Cadwallon. "They are here."

The earth, the so-solid earth, lurched and turned beneath Edwin's feet. Blackness clawed at his vision, the dark despair of knowing that he had led his men and his sons into a trap. Edwin looked at the men arrayed against him and knew that this day he was going to die. The acceptance settled in his heart; he had seen death through all his life and now, these last few years, death came with a hope unknown to his youth. He did not fear dying. But his sons, his boys…

Edwin turned to Guthlaf, his warmaster, and saw there the same knowledge and the same acceptance. The warmaster made the courtesy to his king, his teeth bared in a fierce, cold smile.

"I am warmaster. Let me make ready for war."

Edwin gave him leave, then turned back to Cadwallon and Penda.

"If vengeance you seek, I offer it to you now, here. I alone to the death, and passage to the men of the defeated."

Cadwallon laughed. "So might a hare bargain when caught in the snare. Yes, I will fight you now, but when you are dead I will turn upon your men and your sons and kill them too."

Edwin glanced at Penda. "You, you claim the kingship of Mercia but remain dumb? Ha, your people will know of this."

"My people will know that together with Cadwallon I brought down Edwin and brought back great treasure and glory." Penda smiled. "I think my people will be pleased to know that."

"Very well." Edwin nodded sharply to Cadwallon and Penda. "War." Then he turned and walked back to his men. And through that long walk his back crawled in anticipation of the hurled spear. But none came.

As he walked, Edwin searched for a stratagem that might bring them from the field alive. But they were outnumbered, six to one, caught between a shieldwall and riders, backed up against the watercourse that was to have secured his right flank but now precluded any escape.

Edwin stopped in front of his men. They waited upon his word, and he saw fear and desperate hope in their eyes, for always he, Edwin, had been able to lead them to victory. But not this day.

Edwin knelt before his men and his sons.

Warriors gasped, and shouted aloud. Osfrith cried, "No, father, no." But Edwin bowed his head and the men fell into silence. Then, when all was quiet, the king raised his head, and tears streaked his face.

"I have led you to death. I ask your pardon."

No man breathed a word, but one, the youngest there, a man barely out of boyhood, with tears likewise streaking his face, stepped forward and took Edwin's hand and raised him from the ground.

Guthlaf came and stood before Edwin.

"Hearth lord, heart master, I shared your life; I will share your death." The warmaster turned to the men he had drilled in war. "Ring lord, law giver, our king calls for our blood now. Will you give it for him?"

"Yea! We will give it for him."

"Will you give it for him?"

"Yea!"

"Will you give it for him?"

"Yea!"

Guthlaf grinned at the men, a bare, death's-head grin. "You all saw Cearl, dribbling and useless. You know what? You're lucky. None of you are going to get like that." The grin was lupine now, the smile of a hunter sighting prey. Guthlaf knew he was going to die, but he knew many men would die to bring him down. "Now, form up tight, no gaps."

Edwin left Guthlaf to dress the line and walked towards his sons. Cadwallon's horsemen still sat, line abreast, in front of the trees. Cadwallon himself had gone to join them, but Penda had returned to his line, where he prepared the Mercians for battle.

Edwin stopped before his sons. He looked into their faces, and saw again a face he had held on to for so many years, but had lost: that of Cwenburg, their mother, his wife.

"This is something I never thought I would have to say." Eadfrith looked from brother to father, his face a mask of grim solemnity. "Osfrith was right." And the mask cracked into the broadest of smiles.

Osfrith, grinning too, punched his brother's shoulder. "Other men would admit it a bit sooner."

"For something so remarkable, remarkable proof is needed," said Eadfrith.

"Yes, like us all dying!" said Osfrith.

"Yes, something like that," said Eadfrith. He looked to his father, Edwin, High King, veteran of a thousand battles and a hundred wars. "Can't see it myself, but is there a chance, father?"

Edwin, dry mouthed, shook his head. Overlaying the young man standing before him, he saw the boy, the baby he had dandled, gurgling and laughing, in the air.

Eadfrith nodded. "I thought not." He looked towards the enemy lines. "But there will be less of them too."

"Less, but still too many." Edwin put his hands on his sons' shoulders. "When he is done here, Cadwallon will ride on York and kill Æthelburh and your little brother and sister. But there is a hope, a faint hope, that one or two men may make it through the battle line and bring word to the queen in time for her to escape, for Cadwallon's hatred is directed at me. He will not leave the field until I am brought down. The longer I fight, the more chance of a message getting through to the queen."

"Old Bassus is the best man I have seen on a horse," said Osfrith, "and he is wily with it. Let him get a ride, and he will most likely make it to York before any of Cadwallon's men can catch him."

"I would that you two attempt to take word to the queen. Save her, and avenge me."

Osfrith shook his head. "If Cadwallon saw us attempting to flee, he would send half his men after us to kill us, and no word would the queen receive. Only a man unknown to him might be let go."

"Besides," said Eadfrith, "you are our father. We will not leave you to fight alone."

"A father who led you astray." Edwin's voice was thin, broken.

"No," said Eadfrith. "A father who gave us life, glory, honour. We repay him now, right gladly, do we not, brother?"

Osfrith put his hand on Edwin's shoulder. "A father who brought us the hope of life in the next world, in God's halls, as well as this. Soon we will see what lies beyond the walls of this world; we left the ways of our fathers and entered into the new religion for the hope it gave. Do we grow faint of heart at the test? Soon we will know, and if our faith be true I will sit beside you, father, in God's great hall."

Then Edwin took his sons, each in turn, and kissed them, and afterwards they made the courtesy to their king and father.

Edwin checked the disposition of the enemy. Penda's line was dressed, finally, and beginning to advance. Cadwallon's horsemen remained unmoving, but from the restiveness of men and beasts, Edwin judged that it would not be long before they rode.

"We will not wait upon a time of our enemies' choosing. We will meet them, and give such an account that Acca will sing of us all the days of his life. Bassus!" Edwin called the old retainer from his place in the line and explained what he wanted him to do.

Bassus shook his head. "Lord, no! I cannot flee when you fight."

Edwin grasped his arm. "If you do not get word to the queen, she will die and my children with her. You are not fleeing. I ask you, I beg you to do this for me."

Bassus stared into the shadowed, haunted face of his lord. "I stood against you in the great council of our people. I will not stand against you now. If it be possible, I will get word to the queen, or rather die."

Edwin squeezed his arm. "Don't die. Live! Live."

"If the fate singers spell and wyrd weaves, I will."

Edwin nodded. "You have kept to the ways of our fathers? We will take our new road, and fight and endure as long as we may, that you may get away. God keep you, Bassus."

"And the gods fight with you, lord."

Edwin smiled. "I hope they will, Bassus. I hope they will." He turned back to face the battle line. "It would even out the odds a little."

While Bassus selected a companion to help him catch and mount a horse, Edwin made his final checks along the shieldwall. In the cold October light, mist swirled around the men's heads as they breathed out, some puffing like runners, others breathing so lightly that they barely seemed alive. The air itself tasted suddenly fresh and damp, wakened into life by the sun's touch.

Moving in front of the shieldwall, Edwin gave his final orders.

"We advance towards the riders and the tree cover, keeping the watercourse to our left. When the riders swing out, the shieldwall will push back against the watercourse to stop the riders getting behind us. We will make Penda chase us with his line, and then, when it is close, turn and attack him. Do you understand?"

By way of answer, the men clashed the hafts of their spears against their shields.

Edwin, High King of Britain, unsheathed his sword and the watching men put up a yell that must have reached the clouds.

"We stand together, we fight together, we prevail or we fall together, and this night I will feast you in my hall in York or stand beside you before God. Are you with me?"

The answer might have pierced the very heavens.

"Then, through fate and fear, follow me!"

Edwin turned and, standing slightly in front of the line, started towards the waiting, watching line of horsemen. The men, in line abreast but still in loose formation so they could jog forward together, came after him, shields still slung over shoulders to allow greater speed. As he picked their pace up, from a fast walk to a slow trot, Edwin checked back over his shoulder: Penda had been caught by surprise by Edwin's move towards the horsemen, and was struggling to form his line into loose order and send it after him. A fierce hope blazed in the king's heart. If they could hit the line of horsemen hard and fast enough, they might break through into the line of trees. From there, men could form skirmish bands and fight their way onwards, but a successful retreat would depend on finding horses. There was little – or rather no – chance that Cadwallon would have missed the tethered horses and the men he had left to guard them. The best hope was to dismount some of Cadwallon's riders and take their animals. First, a mount for Bassus and a defence to allow him time to get clear, then anyone else he could manage.

The horsemen wheeled left and began to arc around the Northumbrians. Edwin urged the men on faster, picking the pace up to as near a flat-out run as he dared – any faster and the line would splinter, leaving the individual men easy pickings for pursuing horsemen. He looked ahead to the line of trees; only a hundred yards to go, but the horsemen were sweeping in now, aiming to get behind the line.

"Shieldwall!"

Edwin brought the charge to a shuddering halt, and Osfrith and Eadfrith began pushing their wing back towards the watercourse. The riders urged their mounts on, aiming to get in behind the shieldwall, arms raised and ready to hurl throwing spears.

"Back, back, back!" Edwin pushed the men around him to the rear, dressing the line to left and right to keep its formation, while at the wing Osfrith and Eadfrith locked shields as the riders hurtled closer.

The shieldwall stumbled backwards, tripping over rush and sedge, scrambling towards the water's edge. Edwin checked to his left. Guthlaf had the left wing firm against the water. Any horseman charging in behind the line would be trapped.

The king pushed through the line, looking towards the closing gap and saw there the leading horseman, leaning low beside his horse, urging the beast into the space.

With a scream, the Briton threw his short spear. The haft sprouted from a man's back and he went down. The rider screamed his triumph but as swiftly cut off his shout, for he saw the gap closing in front of him. Hauling back his horse's head, he tried to bring the beast to a stop, but it slid on over the wet ground, almost sitting on its hindquarters as it tried to halt.

Edwin saw it coming. The rider was a youth, barely out of childhood, light and easily carried – no wonder the horse had outdistanced all the others. The youth was pulling back on the bridle with both hands, his face a frenzied mask of fear and excitement. It was almost with regret that Edwin stepped forward and drove his sword through the boy's throat. For a moment, his gaze locked with the boy's; as always, surprise came before fear and pain. The young never expected to die.

Edwin twitched his sword, pitching the rattling, dying boy from the horse, and grabbed the bridle, pulling with all his strength and forcing the horse's head down so that it could not take flight.

"Bassus!" Edwin yelled, searching around for the thegn. "Bassus."

The thegn ran along the rear of the line and took the reins from Edwin, gentling the horse and speaking soft words to it as he made ready to mount.

"Wait," said Edwin. "Wait for my signal, then mount and ride. Ride with God's speed."

The king pushed his way back into the centre of the shieldwall, his shield men parting to make way for him, but covering him with their shields as he took measure of the field.

To left and right the shieldwall bristled with spears as Cadwallon's men rode across the length of the wall, aiming and throwing their spears. After unleashing their spears, the riders swirled around in a loose circle, collecting a fresh javelin from the bundles that stood upended near the line of trees. Penda had formed his men into line and they were advancing now, in rough order, although they were still a few hundred yards distant. Once they were in place, it would be a pushing match, man against man, and anyone peeling off would be finished by the riders. He had to get Bassus free before then.

"Move left, in line, towards the trees."

Shieldwalls moved forwards or backwards. They did not shuffle sideways. But that is what Edwin asked his men to do, with Guthlaf on the left pulling them along while trying to keep the line firm. The horsemen streamed past in another sweep and the shields sprouted a fresh crop of spears, but there was nothing the riders could do to stop the slow, steady shuffle of the line.

Penda urged his men on, but they were too far away; they would not engage before the Northumbrians reached the trees.

"Dismount. Form line." Cadwallon's order cut across the battlefield. Riders slid from their beasts, leaving the animals to be collected by the youngest, and ran towards Cadwallon's pennant. The dragon whipped backwards and forwards as Cadwallon's standard bearer waved the flag, calling the running men towards him. Cadwallon, screaming with frustration at the prospect of Edwin slipping away, pushed the men into a rough shieldwall and sent them stumbling towards the watercourse, aiming to block the Northumbrians' retreat to the trees by sheer weight of bodies.

Edwin turned to Bassus.

"Go!" he yelled.

The thegn mounted the horse in one smooth movement and in an instant had the horse galloping towards the trees. There was hardly a man left on horseback among the Britons, and those who were were rounding up riderless horses.

"Stop him!" yelled Cadwallon. He pointed at the two nearest riders, who drove their animals after Bassus, but already he was halfway to the trees. Edwin measured the distance. They would not catch him before he got to cover; then it would be a contest of Bassus's horsemanship and animal against his pursuers.

All he could do to help was to drive on to the shelter of the trees, stopping Cadwallon sending any more men after Bassus.

Edwin checked behind. Penda's line was still far off and Cadwallon's men had dismounted; he could no longer be outflanked by riders.

"Right, come round." The men of Gwynedd outnumbered them many times over, but their line was loose and still forming, their armour and their weapons lighter.

"Push them back to the trees!"

The shieldwalls closed, the Northumbrians raising their pace from walk to jog, the men of Gwynedd standing fast, still pulling in reinforcements on the flanks and to the rear. Edwin searched along the line for Cadwallon, but he could not see him, and then he focused ahead, on the man behind the shield that faced him, face red, eyes squinting against the sweat trickling into them but unable to wipe his sight clear, spear pricking out from behind shield but his leading shin and foot exposed.

Screaming his battle cry, but not even hearing it, nor those of the men pressed up against him, Edwin shoved his shield against the man's spearhead, pushing it up, then rammed the heavy metal boss with all his weight against the Briton's shield, while with his non-pushing shoulder he drove his sword into the man's shin and knee.

Face to face, more intimate than lovers, Edwin stared into the Briton's eyes and pushed him backwards, against the press of the men behind him, saw the pain and helplessness in his eyes, then drove his sword into the gap.

"On, push on, push on!"

Such was the crush that, even dead, the man did not fall, but shielded the men behind him with his body. To either side, Edwin's shield companions pushed their shields forward, using them as weapons and as rams, and the shieldwall of the Britons trembled, like a tree before the final axe stroke.

"They're breaking." To his right, Edwin's shield companion shouted in triumph. "They're break…" His words were choked off. Edwin looked to him and saw a spear point emerge from his throat. The warrior clutched at it, as surprised as any man, then pitched forward.

Edwin twisted and as he did so, a spear point slid past his shoulder and buried itself in the corpse of the dead Briton. His right hand free, Edwin stabbed out at the spear man, who was struggling to pull his spear free. The man went down, screaming, clutching his guts, and Edwin saw that Penda had broken his shieldwall and sent the men running pell mell into the rear of the Northumbrians. Already, five, six men were down, and the men of Gwynedd, who had been about to break, were rallying, pushing forward again. For a moment, behind the Britons, Edwin saw the treeline, less than ten yards away, then he was pulling the men around him back, forming a rough circle, facing out to the calling, gesticulating, screaming ring of enemies.

The battle fell into lull, men gasping, while the injured groaned and screamed and crawled, and the battle birds, crows and ravens, assembled about the field.

Edwin checked his men. His sons still stood, but both bled from cuts, while Guthlaf grinned at him wolfishly, although one arm hung all but useless at his side. They were down to some twenty men all told. Edwin counted up the enemy. They had been done great hurt, but between them Cadwallon and Penda still mustered more than one hundred and fifty men. The shelter of the trees was so close, but Cadwallon and Penda had mustered their best men there. With the warriors he had left, there was no breaking through. Looking around, Edwin knew there was no breaking through anywhere. But there was no sign of the men who had pursued Bassus returning in triumph, and the longer they fought here, the greater chance Bassus had of escaping.

"Ten to one, and we still fight!" Edwin yelled, stepping a little forward from his line. "Find nine men willing to fight alongside you, Cadwallon, and I will fight you on my own."

The prince of Gwynedd pushed his way through his own lines and faced Edwin. "A pig has more honour than you, hearth thief. So know this: I do not fight pigs; I butcher them. I will butcher you." He turned to his men. "Bring the spears."

Edwin, seeing the first bundle already approaching, backed in among his men. He looked around, saw the men licking lips, others speaking prayers beneath their breath, and he nodded to each and every one in turn and smiled. Many returned his smile, others his acknowledgement, for Edwin stood among them now as one warrior among others, and king no longer. They stood together. They would fall together.

As the spear bundles were laid out in front of Cadwallon and Penda, the Northumbrians backed up against each other, forming a two-sided shieldwall. Without words, Osfrith and Eadfrith placed themselves beside their father, and Guthlaf stood back to back with him.

Then the spears began to fly. Like hail they came thudding into shields, so many at once that to move to stop one spear was to leave a gap for another to fly through. Shields prickled with shafts, the weight of wood slowly pulling arms down and exposing heads and helmets.

One by one, men began to stagger and fall, pierced by spears, clutching at shoulders or throats or clawing at their backs. From behind the shelter of his shield, Edwin could glimpse the harvest of bodies reaped by the spear fall.

Guthlaf, standing behind him, suddenly fell away and Edwin saw the warmaster on his knees, trying to pull a spear from his shoulder.

In his ears, humming between the screams and yells of battle, Edwin heard the blood music and he saw the gore that covered his sword vibrate with the music of death, but he knew that the death it sang this day was its wielder's.

They were like animals being slaughtered, and rage rose up in him, red and blind, as it had never done before.

"Death," he cried, and his sons and his men took up the cry.

"Death," they shouted, and as the spear fall slackened they ran forward, line breaking, swinging sword, thrusting spear, throwing shield.

"Death," they cried and death they brought, crashing into the enemy who had thought them broken and bowed. But death they suffered too, pulled down beneath the weight of the enemy as a hunted bear is brought down by many dogs.

Eadfrith fell, his body limp from the clubbing blow that struck him, but the man who brought him down, a huge Mercian, snarled the battlefield despoilers away from the prince and dragged him to the edge of the field. Edwin saw no blood – it was possible Eadfrith still lived.

Edwin saw the spear pierce Osfrith, saw his son turn his face to him, saw the life light leave his eyes as the spear was pulled from his body and men like jackals began to fall on him, tugging at arm rings and tearing ear rings, and he leapt at them, sweeping the ground clear around his son, turning this way and that to keep the pack at bay. No longer human, the pack howled at him, leaping and snapping, but his sword pushed them back. Edwin reached down and closed his son's eyes.

"Wait for me," he said.

Then he looked down, surprised, at the spear shaft that had sprouted from his chest.

Edwin, king of Deira, lord of Bernicia, High King of Britain, sat down in the mud beside his son, and there he died.

There was little silence on the battlefield when the battle was over. The weapon noise had gone, the battle cries had fallen silent, but the wounded cried out, and the battle birds, knowing their time was near, sent up their victory calls.

Cadwallon and Penda, victorious, stalked forward through the ranks of their men, the living and the dead, and stood in front of Edwin.

Cadwallon toed up Edwin's sword and took it in his hand. His eyes widened as he held it, and he put the blade up to his ear. "It sings," he said.

Penda knelt down and pulled at one of Edwin's arm rings.

"What are you doing?" asked Cadwallon.

"I said, when the time was right, I would take the king's rings and take them right gladly." Penda held up the thick, golden arm ring. "The time is right."

"Take his rings, if you want them. I shall take his sword. And his head." Cadwallon turned away and signalled his men. "Gather our wounded, strip the dead; we ride for York."

# Chapter 9

"The night was filled with bad dreams." The queen turned to Paulinus and James as they walked back to the great hall from the church where priest and deacon had just said Mass. "Do you know what that portends?"

Paulinus had been loath to leave his church, now all but complete, but he thought it best to escort Æthelburh and her children – Eanflæd and Wuscfrea – back to the great hall. The princess was six now, and a fine, healthy little girl, while her younger brother had fought off the distemper that had taken the twins, and was now running off to play whenever he could slip from his sister's grasp.

"I have no great skill at telling dreams, my lady," said Paulinus. "But we are doing God's work here, spreading his word; he will surely bless you and your kin all the days of your life."

"I hope so," said Æthelburh. "But I fear for my husband."

"He is a great warrior and a great king," said Paulinus, "and he has God's favour. No harm will come to him."

James coughed, and coughed again.

"Excuse me, my lady," said Paulinus, turning to a doubled-over deacon. "What's the matter?" he asked.

"Can we promise the king will be all right?" James whispered in between further coughs.

"Of course," said Paulinus. "He must be. He is bringing God's word to this land – the Lord would not allow anyone to stand in the way of his purpose."

"But think about what happened when Sæberht of the East Saxons died – his successor reverted to paganism. The same happened with the East Angles."

"Enough," hissed Paulinus. "That will not happen here. Edwin is High King; he will bring all this land to the Lord."

"Is James well, Paulinus?" asked Æthelburh.

"Oh yes, very well." Paulinus slapped the deacon on the back, causing a genuine coughing fit, and returned to the queen's side.

"Mamma, Mamma, Mamma!" The young princess pulled the queen's hand, pointing to an approaching rider. "Why is that man coming so quick?"

Æthelburh saw the horse approaching and suddenly she felt ice water in her veins. "Eanflæd, take your brother to the hall," she said, her eyes not leaving the rider.

"But Mummy…"

"Take him now! James, go with them, please."

James was a favourite of the princess, so she protested only a little when, after swinging Wuscfrea up onto his hip, he took her hand and began leading her to the royal enclosure.

The rider, beating his horse to a final lung-bursting effort, raced towards them. Æthelburh stared at him as he approached, willing the rider to be unknown to her, but as he neared she realized she knew the man: Bassus. Beside her, she heard Paulinus reciting a psalm, but her mind had frozen and she could not decipher the words.

Everybody – the slaves about their errands, the men working on the jetty, the children playing – stopped what they were doing and tracked the rider as he approached the queen. Only at the last moment did he rein his beast in, pulling its head up and back until it all but slid on its rear to a panting, heaving halt. Bassus half jumped, half fell from the saddle and stood swaying in front of the queen and Paulinus.

Æthelburh said nothing. She could not say anything. To speak was to bring on the news the man standing in front of her had come to deliver.

But he spoke, gasping out his message, and the words drove like nails into the queen.

"You – you must flee. The king's command. G-go to your brother."

"The – the king?"

"He sent me, my lady."

"He is not dead?"

"Not when I left." But seeing the hope spring in the queen's face, Bassus stepped forward. "He was surrounded by two hundred or more warriors, my lady. Cadwallon and Penda. I have never seen such an army."

"He is a great warrior." Æthelburh looked at Paulinus, standing pale beside her. "He has God's favour. You said he has God's favour. He will come back. I will see him again."

"My lady, there is no time. You must take your children and go. Cadwallon and Penda know where you are."

Æthelburh gripped Paulinus's shoulder. The strength had drained from her legs and she feared that if she let go she would fall and never stand again, but a cold clarity filled her mind. At her husband's command, she would take her children to safety at her brother's court. Edwin knew where she would be. He would come and find them. But now she had to take thought for the children.

"A boat." She turned to Paulinus. "Get us a boat; with children I cannot travel fast enough to escape them on land, but we can escape by sea. I will bring the children." She turned to Bassus. "Come with us. I would know more."

*

In the confusion of the next hours, much was lost but much was saved. The children, excited at the adventure and too young to know what was happening, were put onto a long-prowed boat, arrived from Francia, that was waiting to be loaded with goods for the return journey. The ship's master found himself carrying a queen and her children rather than the cargo of furs he had expected.

Paulinus and James, with Bassus helping, loaded as much of the royal gold, silver and jewels as they could find into the boat, with James making dashes to the church to bring from it the Gospel book and breviary, the crucifix and chalice, which were its greatest treasures. Then, when there was still much to do, there came word from the sentries on the road that riders were approaching.

The queen, with her women, ran to the boat. Æthelburh's heart jolted. She could not see her children.

"Mamma!" Eanflæd popped up from her hiding place in the prow. "We're playing hide and seek."

"Good, good." Æthelburh looked around. "Where's Wuscfrea?"

"Hiding, Mamma."

"Hiding where?"

Eanflæd looked puzzled. "If I knew that, I'd have found him Mamma."

Æthelburh looked around wildly. "Wuscfrea! Wuscfrea, where are you? Come out. Wuscfrea!"

"Here he is."

Æthelburh spun around to see James running down towards the river, a wriggling child tucked under his arm, with Paulinus and Bassus running beside him. He passed the boy to his mother as the queen's maids scrambled into the boat.

"He wanted to hide in the church," James said.

"Thank you," said Æthelburh, hugging the squirming boy to her.

"Come, my lady," said Bassus, reaching a hand up to her. "We must go."

"What about you?" The queen turned to Paulinus and James, both of whom still stood upon the riverbank.

"Get in the boat," said Paulinus.

"My lady!" Bassus looked to the outskirts of the old city. The column of riders was approaching.

The queen half stepped, half stumbled into the boat, but Bassus caught her. The crew were already casting off, unshipping oars and raising the sail.

Paulinus and James looked at each other, then at the gap opening between the boat and the bank.

"I love these people," said James. "I will stay."

Paulinus made to answer, but James shouted, "Go!" And the priest leaped for the boat. He almost made it too, but his feet slipped on the wet cordage around the boat and he slipped back into the river. Just as he was going under, Bassus and a crewman grabbed the priest and hauled him, wet and gasping, on board.

"Row!" ordered the ship's master, and the men put their backs into it, and some of the queen's women took up oars as well, pulling the boat into the safety of midstream. Paulinus picked himself up, dripping, from the gunnels of the boat in time to see James running towards the old city while the troop of riders swept towards them.

The lead rider pushed his horse into the shallows, but the boat was already well beyond his reach. Cadwallon reined his horse in and pushed his helmet back. On the boat, Æthelburh faced him.

"I am almost glad you have escaped me," Cadwallon shouted. "I would have taken no pleasure in killing you."

"Killing women and children – is that your mark, Cadwallon of Gwynedd?"

Cadwallon laughed, a fierce and brutal exaltation. "Oh no, lady, I only kill Edwin's whelps."

"You have not killed these," said Æthelburh, holding her children about her.

"Not yet, lady, not yet."

The current and the oars were taking the boat further and further from the rider, but Cadwallon spurred his horse on, riding along the bank.

"You are a beautiful woman, and a brave one, and Christian too. Marry me, and I will spare your children if you give them to the church."

"I am the wife of Edwin."

"You are the widow of Edwin."

Æthelburh shook her head. "I will not believe that."

"You want proof?" Cadwallon reached for the sack hanging from his saddle, then paused. "Cover your children's eyes," he said.

"Don't look!" said Paulinus, but although Æthelburh folded her children to her so they could see nothing, she could not look away. She remained there, standing rigidly in the stern of the boat until the river carried her out of sight, then, trembling, her women helped her into the belly of the boat and gave her a draught of wine in an attempt to bring warmth to her pale, cold lips. She did not speak again until the boat sailed out of the Humber and took course on the whale road to the south and her brother's kingdom. As the sun westered, the queen returned to herself and she hugged her children to herself, and kissed them, then gave them over to her ladies that they might get them to sleep, although their sleep be uneasy. Paulinus came to the queen and she looked to him, and he saw in her eyes the tears of acceptance.

"Cadwallon thought to torment me," said Æthelburh, "but in years to come I will be glad to have seen him for that last time."

Paulinus took the queen's hand. It was cold. Æthelburh gripped his fingers, although she did not turn her eyes to the priest.

"Why did God let this happen?" she said. "Edwin was doing God's will, performing God's work. Why didn't God protect him?"

"I don't know," said Paulinus. He looked from the boat at the shadowing land that he had come to all those years ago, full of the fire of faith and the certainty that he would bring that faith to the pagan peoples there. "I do not know."

The queen squeezed his hand and they sat in silence as the sun set and the night fell.

# Epilogue

The young man was working in the monastery's gardens, digging earth, when the ship arrived on Iona. It was not the sort of work a prince normally did, but since his exile he had turned his hand to many tasks that princes did not normally do, and digging the earth for the monastery that had been his home for the past few years was far from the worst of his labours. It took a while for the messenger to find him, but when he did, he approached the young man with such noise that, instinctively, he drew his seax and held it out in front of him. But then, seeing who it was, he sheathed the knife.

"Oh, it's you, Brother Aidan," he said. "You know the abbot is always telling you off for running around like that. What brings you running to me?"

The monk, panting, stared at the young man as if he were seeing an entirely new man.

"What's wrong?"

"He's dead," said Brother Aidan.

"Who's dead?"

"Edwin. Edwin is dead and his sons with him."

Oswald, prince of Bernicia, son of King Æthelfrith, wiped the dirt from his hands.

"It's time I went home," he said.

# *Historical Note*

This is a true story. Well, it's as true a story as is possible to write of events that took place some 1,400 years ago, when Britain was only just beginning to emerge from the silence of the post-Roman centuries. The last legion left Britain in AD 410, and although contact between Britain and the rest of Europe did not cease overnight, it slowly lessened as the monetary economy gave way to barter and plunder, and trade shifted its focus from the Mediterranean to the North Sea. For this was when the Angles, the Saxons, the Jutes, the northern European peoples named by Bede, arrived in Britain and set up kingdoms of their own. Even after all this time, whether this change was brought about by mass movements of people – boatloads of ruddy, blond farmer types stepping off the boat and displacing the local dark-haired Britons – or whether it was more the case of incoming warrior elites displacing – that is killing – ruling families and then taking local women to found new dynasties is still open to scholarly dispute. But what is without doubt is that Britain changed. New kingdoms arose, some so fleeting they left no whisper in the historical record, others more enduring. Town life, which was well established in the southern half of Britain, all but ceased. Life became overwhelmingly rural; ties became familial and tribal.

Religion too changed. The native Britons were largely Christian, a Christianity that owed much of its vitality to monasticism. Indeed, one of the great heretics of early Christian history, Pelagius (c.360–c.420), was a Briton, and Patrick, in the fifth century, was the man who initiated a critical turn in Christian history, when he set out to evangelize a people who had never been part of the Roman Empire – the Irish (who were close cousins to the Britons). But the Anglo-Saxons were pagans, and they seem to have almost completely extinguished Christianity in the parts of Britain they conquered. Historical records died with the church, and the fifth and sixth centuries in Britain are a black but fruitful hole of legend, home to Arthur – if he existed – and a myriad desperate little battles known to none now.

Only as the Anglo-Saxon kingdoms began to consolidate, the smaller ones swallowed by the larger, do we start to find a firmer historical footing, round about the start of the seventh century. Our knowledge comes from two interlinked sources: the Anglo-Saxon chronicles – a tale of years, with key events recorded – and the extraordinary people-defining work of the Venerable Bede (c.673–735), the *Ecclesiastical History of the English People*. For the English people became Christian, and Bede, a monk of Northumbria, set out to tell that story, and in doing so he defined the English and made them into a people.

Without Bede, we would know precious little of this time. As a historian, he lays his sources carefully before the reader, telling us where and from whom he learned the information he passes on. And while there are weaknesses and biases in his history – Bede, a true Northumbrian, disliked the Mercians and gave short shrift to their kings, and he gave little credit to the Christianity of the Britons in bringing about the conversion of the Anglo-Saxons – yet he remains the father of English history and, reading him (and I heartily recommend you do), one is overwhelmingly struck by the essential kindness of the man.

It is from Bede that we learn of Edwin's conversion, and the twistings back and forth made by the king. We hear of his mysterious conversation with a stranger outside the hall of King Rædwald, in the dark and in despair. From Bede we know of his marriage to Æthelburh, of the assassin sent by Cwichelm, of his great council and Coifi's strange reaction to the abandonment of the old gods. It is Bede who tells us that Edwin was *bretwalda* – High King of Britain – and from him we learn that an alliance between Cadwallon, king of Gwynedd, and Penda of Mercia, brings Edwin down. Without Bede, we would have little more than a list of regnal dates for this period, and the odd battle year. With his history, there is enough, when allied to the recent advances in archaeology, to tell the story of this extraordinary man and his times in a way that is both compelling and, I hope, truthful.

The only change I've made is to alter the name of Forthred. In the *Ecclesiastical History*, the thegn who sacrifices himself to save Edwin is named Lilla, but to modern ears Lilla sounds so unmistakeably feminine as to wrench readers from the story. So I renamed him. Bede also tells us that Edwin conquered Anglesey. Later sources, unreliable in my judgement, relate that Edwin besieged Cadwallon on Puffin Island, a little islet to the west of Anglesey. I chose to ignore this, but a careful reading does suggest an unusual animus between Edwin and Cadwallon. I hope my explanation does neither of them a disservice. The homage rendered to Edwin by the other kings, by rowing him across the River Ouse, is recorded as being done to a later king, Athelstan. I have borrowed it for the purposes of this story.

The riddles quoted in the story, and the short extract from a poem recited by Edwin, are among the few examples of Anglo-Saxon literature to have survived the turbulence, and burnings, of the Viking incursions. They all appear in the Exeter Book, a manuscript kept at Exeter Cathedral, and one of four manuscripts that contain pretty well all that is left to us of Anglo-Saxon literature.

Finally, if you would like to learn more about this extraordinary kingdom, I recommend *Northumbria: the Lost Kingdom* (published by The History Press), which I co-wrote with archaeologist Paul Gething. It contains much of the recent advances in understanding brought about by the work of the Bamburgh Research Project, which Paul directs, and other archaeologists and historians working on this fascinating period in history.